ECHOES OF ME

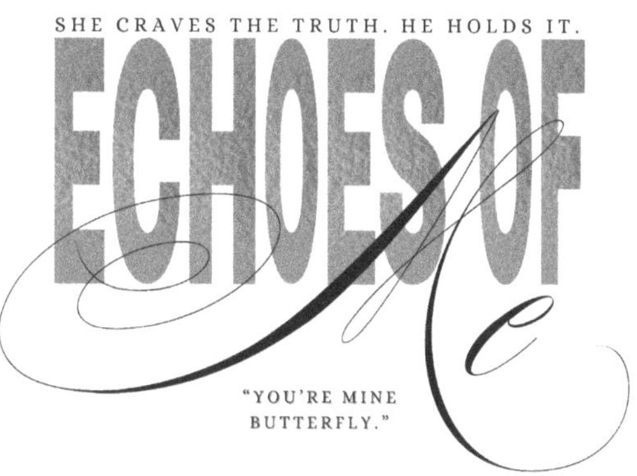

Echoes Of Me

Book Cover Design Bekki Vowles

First Edition 2025

Website: www.author.bekkivowles.co.uk

ISBN: 9781068695131

Editor: Sarah Baker @wordemporiumeditor

Alpha/Beta: Nikki, Sarah, Becky, Kerry

For those of you who like a man with a grey side, this is for you.

Content Warnings

Your wellbeing and mental health mean a great deal to me; they are precious, and we need to look after them. I want nothing more than for you to enjoy this book with all the ups, downs, and shit that goes on in between these pages. So, please take a look at the triggers and warning below:

Violence, Sexual/explicit content,

Mental Health, Trauma, Car Crash, Amnesia, Guns, Death, Choking, Fire.

And if you are good with all of the above, read on and enjoy.

Acknowledgements

This book took me eight weeks to write from start to finish, and I could not have done it without your loving and continued support.

Jenny, Anita, Holly, my closest friends, I would most likely never leave the house if it weren't for you. I never expected to make friends like you all, but I'm so fucking glad I did. I don't know what I would do without you.

Aaron, my silent supporter, best friend, and husband, you are with me through it all, the late nights, the stress, the tears of sadness, and the tears of joy. The endless snacks you know make me happy. You are the one person I will always want by next to me, even if you are asleep. (Have you read this one yet?)

Ruth, my #bookwife, when I need advice, you give it to me honestly and thoughtfully. I just wish you lived closer. It's like I have known you a lifetime. Our weekly catch ups mean the world to me.

Nikki, **Sarah, Kerry, Becky**, the best Beta team I have ever had. This manuscript came to you all unpolished and unfinished. Your comments and commitment to this book and me astound me. I'm proud to have you on my team and on my journey.

Sarah Baker, Queen Editor, your love of this book made me smile all the way through reading your edits, your hearts and comments inspire me to be a better writer, and I'm learning, because you have taught me so much. One day, I'll stop the danglers.

My boys, George and Harry, you are way too young to read my books, but one day you will. Watching you grow is the hardest and best thing I have ever seen. I want to keep you little, but I want to see you shine and be the men I know will make me prouder than I already am one day. I love that you want to know what I do, and even write your own little stories. My desk is full of sticky notes from you. Everything I do is for you.

Save the best till last. My Street team, Arc readers and followers, I have no words... Yeah, I do. I freaking love you all. Thank you, thank you, thank you. You make the struggle worth it. I'm forever grateful.

Bekki xx

A little note from me...

Women supporting women is one of the finest things you could have in your life; treasure it, keep it close to your heart always.

– Bekki Vowles x x

Family is the anchor that holds through life storms

Contents

Chapter One

I Don't Know

Sophie

Eight years old

I look down at my hands; they're shaking. I can't stop them. The older lady in the room with me keeps asking questions, but I don't know who she is.

Why aren't the lights on? I can't make out much of her face, but she looks kind; she's dressed better than I am. My clothes are covered in mud. Why am I so dirty? Wiping my hands over my pyjama bottoms, *huh,* butterflies. All over them. I try to clean my hands; they're muddy too.

The pinks, blues, and greens all smudged by the dirt.

I don't know where I am.

Something's wrong. The lady looks worried. I glance down at the key-shaped pendant around my neck, frowning because I've never seen it before, but holding it tightly in the palm of my hand feels nice, and I don't know why.

I'm scared. I... I... there's nothing.

She keeps asking me the same things.

What's your name?

Do you have anyone I can call?

Where do you live?

"I don't remember." I don't remember anything.

Chapter Two

Demands

Ethan

21 Years later

"Ethan, it's so good to see you," Dom says, walking towards me as I enter his temporary campsite—he runs our overseas operations at Cerberus Security.

"You too, Dom. It's been a while," I add, stepping up to the table he's set up. I sit on a crate box, my suit withstanding the long journey from the UK to Australia, then taking a flight to New Zealand, but my body is tired from the multiple flights.

"We have everything into place. Thanks for doing this," he says, his tone anxious as he settles himself in a chair opposite me. He points to the bunker in front of us, where I'll be heading shortly to interrogate.

"Good, we can let him stew for a while." I nod, rubbing the back of my neck, the ache in my shoulders worsening the more the day goes on.

"Ethan," he pleads. "We need answers." His hand hits the table with a thwack. I get it, I do. From the short call we had when I landed in Australia this morning, he's frustrated by the lack of answers he's been getting. That's why I'm here. To do my thing. We need to find the kid this prick took before anything serious happens. Leaning forward, resting my elbows on my thighs, I try to reassure him.

"And you'll get them, Dom, trust me," I say in my most encouraging tone. But it doesn't work; I still sound annoyed.

I always sound like this.

"We do, but the kid needs help now." Clenching his teeth together, he stands, then sits again, clearly at his limit. "If I go in there now, he'll lock up tighter than a nun's habit. He's had all of you in there since the moment you brought him back. Let him think he's got the better of us. Let him think he's off the hook. He'll let his guard down, then I'll go in. I know what we need." Dom's restless leg bounces below the table. They've had this guy in the bunker for three days, and he's not given Dom or the other members of his team a single ounce of information about the kid he snatched off the street over a week ago.

That's why they flew me over here. It just so happened I was already in Australia, acquiring something for my Gran.

I'm the best at extracting information. No one knows how I do it; I'm not sure even I do, to be honest. I just get this sense, a gut feeling, when I mention a specific word in their ear. I watch them sweat, growing more and more uncomfortable with each word I say. I listen. I was an army medic; it gave me an edge. I can pick up on the smallest sign of distress and use it to my advantage. I don't like getting physical, with these arseholes, if I don't have to. Not that I haven't, but there are other ways to… *persuade* people to get what I want.

I don't make them wait too long. An hour while I catch up with Dom's team. When I walk into the bunker, it smells like dirt and sweat, the warmth in the air amplifying the stench. Closing the door behind me, I slide the deadbolt across. I don't want anyone accidentally coming in.

The guy sits on an old chair, his hands cuffed to the legs, keeping them by his side. He's in his mid-thirties, scraggy looking, like he's lived a hard life. And I know exactly why he's in this position. Life has not been kind to him, but he's made some very bad decisions. People forget they always have a choice.

His face is red and blotchy from the heat of being in a metal room in the midday New Zealand sun. Sweat drips from his chin and temple. There's water in front of him, but he can't reach it with his hands cuffed.

That must be torture in itself. I'd laugh, but that's not something I do often.

The sound of the bolt filters through the room as I lock us in. His eyes shoot to mine as I turn to face him, frowning when he takes in my appearance.

"You don't look like the others? Who are you?" he asks, his voice scratchy. I don't answer, standing by the door observing him, waiting for a reaction. He's fidgeting, growing uneasy the more I stare at him. "I've got nothing to say to you," he spits, tiredness coating his voice as he shifts in his seat again. Good, I like to make them feel uncomfortable.

I stay silent as I walk over to him; the expensive leather of my brogues gaining a layer of dirt. I act like he's not there, watching as the hairs on the back of his neck raise, the slight shake of his shoulders the closer I get.

He feels it; he knows I mean business.

He lets out a shaky huff as I lean over him from behind, my hands reaching for the chains on his cuffs, tugging them slightly, making him jolt backwards in the hard seat with a wince.

"Arlo," I grit into his ear. He tries to lean away, but I yank on the cuffs again, keeping him in place. His shaking grows when I mention his real name. He'd managed to keep his identity hidden until Dom called. Cole found out who he really is, and a whole heap of shit on him: past indiscretions, associates, family, why he's kidnapped a kid he has no link to.

"Shit," he breathes out. "How?" His chest rises and falls as his breathing picks up.

"Family," I state. Sweat breaks out over his skin as he turns a ghostly shade of white.

"My... my... family?" he stammers, unsure of what I'm getting at, trying to look back to see me as I stand behind him. I watch his neck move as he visibly swallows his anxiety.

I like this bit.

"The ones you've left behind." I know they're safe. I've checked. They were happy with the delivery I sent them. Food and a few other items to help see them through. He left them high and dry to do this because he owed a favour to a nasty piece of shit he won't need to worry about anymore. Since he's just been arrested for drug trafficking.

"Your daughter?" His hands flex and I know I've hit a nerve.

"How... no... it's not possible," he splutters.

"Small and vulnerable." Reaching into my pocket, I take out a photo of the kid he took and place it in front of him. It's from the day he took him, right from the school gates. "No food, no water." He looks down just as I place a picture of his daughter on the table, next to the kid he took.

"Fuck, no... you can't." He's jumping to conclusions. I'd never put a kid at risk.

"What if?" I say, keeping my tone low, with an edge that makes him question my morals.

"No..."

"Yes," I grit right into his ear. His body shudders, like he's going to be sick.

"Fine." He whimpers, like the sorry piece of shit he is.

"Fine?" I mimic, still standing behind him.

"I'll tell you where he is... just tell me they're okay. Please... don't hurt them." He rattles off the address where he's been keeping the kid, and I know that Dom and his team will already be heading out.

"Time to have some fun," I murmur, the images of the kids floating to the floor as I move to sit on the table in front of him, hitching the leg of my trousers to get comfortable.

Unfortunately, he does all the wrong things for the right reasons. Kidnapping this kid was the last straw. He won't be doing it again. His family has been compensated; they don't need to suffer for his mistakes.

We made sure of that—me and my team.

Walking out an hour later, satisfied that he will never be able to do this again, I nod to the guards that I'm finished. Happy with the outcome, I like what I do, I like taking what they value, their beliefs, and twisting it, using everything against them. I chuckle as I move away and hear the guards groaning as they walk into the bunker.

The guy pissed himself.

The bunker will stink for days.

"Mr Ford," the receptionist at the desk says as I approach the front desk of the hotel. I booked it on the way out here. "You have some messages from Lady Celeste." Taking the slips of paper from his outstretched hand, I flick through, all of them from my gran. I nod and walk towards the lift. Reading through them, they all say the same things. *Call me.* I've not been gone forty-eight hours, and she can't wait to get her hands on the new painting I acquired yesterday.

After some serious negotiations, I'll be coming home with a small, unseen sketch of the *Edger Dagas, Green Dancer*. I have it in a locked case, ready to hand over to her: Lady Celeste Ford. Slipping my phone from my pocket, I dial her number. I know she's waiting by the phone for me to call, even with the time difference; she always does. I smile as she answers before the first ring is done.

"Ethan. Do you have it?" The excitement in her tone makes me want to chuckle. She is the biggest kid when it comes to finding a new piece.

"Yes, safe and sound." For an eighty-five-year-old woman, she sure can squeal when she's excited.

"All that hard work paid off. The moment they authenticated it, I was there to pick it up. It's all yours."

"Ours," she corrects me. "I knew you were my favourite grandchild for a reason." Rolling my eyes, I scoff.

"I'm your only grandchild. I have to be your favourite." She ignores me.

"When are you back?" I shake my head, knowing she'll be on tenterhooks until it's in her hands.

"Where's this one going?" I ask. The family estate is full of her collection, one she considers to be ours, as I've been the one travelling the world to collect it.

"Don't you think it will look magnificent in the orangery?" My family has had the estate in Livington for generations. But it's only Gran that lives there now.

"It will. My flight leaves later tonight. I should be back tomorrow."

"I'll send a car to pick you up." She hangs up as I walk into the lift, heading for my suite.

Chapter Three

Waste

Aggie

"Jasper, we don't need to be there yet," I groan. I want to yell, but won't. Instead, I pinch my lips together in frustration, turning my back to him.

"It'll be better if we wait there, *together*," Jasper states adamantly, shutting the door behind him as we step out from the motel we checked into over a week ago. It's nothing fancy, just enough to sleep and get clean. I was ready to sneak out this morning and leave him behind. Unfortunately, he had his beady little eyes on me as soon as I rolled out of bed.

For reasons I can't understand, he doesn't want me to be out of his sight. I can't even express how fucking annoying that is.

We had this very argument last night, and he ended up having yet another tantrum, like a bratty three-year-old throwing his toys out of the pram. He stormed off, slamming the door behind him, because he didn't get his way. He didn't go far, just sat outside the room. It was pointless. I've not changed my mind; I'm still not going with him.

Why do people change so much?

Is it too much to want a relationship where we're on the same level, or they listen to what the other one wants without... *this,* and the guilt that follows when you see that look in their eye, when you don't do things their way.

Internally groaning, I think about how he'll spin it around to be all my fault and make me feel guilty in the process.

Not this time. I'll take whatever he throws at me later. I'm not wasting my time in a freaking airport.

Jasper has that hot surfer dude look, maybe a little bit preppy, like he's trying to be something he's not. There's always been an edge to the way he speaks, but he was so much fun that first month or so. The sex was good, I've had better, but he made up for that with his charm. We got on, then he got clingy when I wanted to do some stuff on my own. Told me it wasn't safe, that a woman like me should never be on her own. He tried to tell me all the bad things that could happen to someone like me. *Like me?* What's that supposed to mean?

He tried to scare me into staying by his side. He even went into graphic detail about how someone could kidnap, murder, and dismember my body, and no one would ever know. I shudder at the memory and the vivid dream it placed in my mind that night.

Well, buddy, I've been alone and travelled alone most of my life, and I've been okay so far. Ever since then, I've seen little changes as to who he really is. Things you don't see at first, then sneak up on you, like the tantrums. The way we only do what he wants, how he wants my opinion—jaw clenched as he asks—but never takes it. It's really getting tiring to be around him, but we have our flight home together today. Thank goodness he's not coming back with me. He'll be getting the train back to… hm, I can't remember where. Or if he said, for that matter.

You won't be seeing him again anyway, not after the flight.

"I don't want to waste the time we have here just… sitting around inside," I almost shout, trying to keep my cool. New Zealand is breathtaking, and I don't want to spend my last few hours in the airport, watching the planes leave the tarmac in a cold, air-conditioned box.

"We need to be there four hours before the flight leaves," he states, pinning me with a furious glare. He adjusts the backpack on his shoulder, speaking to me like I've never travelled before in my life. It's all I've ever done, on and off, only this will be my last for a while.

I have a more pressing matter to deal with. One I've put off for too long.

"Yes, Jasper, I know. That still leaves us with three hours to spare." I gesture, holding up three fingers in his face, and shaking them for emphasis.

"No, we're going to the airport," he counters, swatting my hand away. He tries to grab my arm, but I shove him away. I've been out here for the last three months. I met Jasper on my second day while waiting to get the bus from Auckland to Milford Sound. We hit it off, and we've been touring this beautiful country since.

His incessant need to be with me, and becoming increasingly needy, has started to darken my light. I've let it go; I think it's just the travelling getting to him, and knowing we'll part ways when we're back in the UK.

"Then you go to the airport. I'll meet you there in a few hours." I turn to walk down the road. There's a beautiful beach where I can spend some time before getting on the long flight back.

"Aggie, what the fuck? You're just going to leave me?" I spin back around to face him, clutching my backpack.

"I'm not leaving you; I'm going to the beach. We're just not going to be in each other's company for a while." Separating for a short space of time is sounding better by the second. I can feel my shoulders relaxing already. It's going to be one long flight sitting next to him in this mood.

"Fine, suit yourself. You're terrible at being anywhere on time. Don't blame me if you miss our flight." At this point, I may just miss it to annoy him and have a quiet flight home tomorrow. I won't. I used the last of my money to get our flights. I can't afford another.

"I won't be late. We have a full seven hours before it leaves," I mumble, rolling my eyes as I turn back to the path that leads to the beach.

"What am I meant to do?" Oh, for fuck's sake. *Fuck off.* It's on the tip of my tongue.

"Go to the airport, like you want to. I don't care. You're a grown man. Figure it out." I don't look back as I say it; I can tell he wants to drag me back and make me go with him.

Not happening, sunshine.

Walking down the path, I feel the tension drain from my muscles the further I get away from him. The path opens up to a small street before the beach comes into view. I pass a small bakery on my way and grab a coffee and a bagel. The beach is beautiful, so open and freeing. It reminds me of home, only not as warm. The breeze from the sea cools my skin as I walk over to a large boulder that sits on the sand. It's got a flat top, perfect to sit on. There's a bank of sand behind it, making it easy to climb with my hands full. I reach the top easily and only have to balance my drink for the last few feet to the top. Placing my coffee and food to one side, I take off my backpack, opening one of the many side pockets in search of my sketch pad and pencils.

God, I miss my paints, but I can't travel with them. Not only are they heavy to lug around, but I can't choose a colour at the best of times, let alone pack a few basics to see me through.

Looking over the view of the sea in front of me, I sip my coffee and start to sketch. I've been selling my sketches for years. I don't make much, then again, I don't need much. No house, no car, nothing to tie me down.

I can't wait to get back into the small studio space I rent when I'm home. It's full of my creations, past paintings, good and bad, blank canvases ready to be used with the fresh ideas I've had from this trip.

The freedom of movement is what fascinates me, capturing the living moment in a drawing, full of colour; it brings life to any two-dimensional canvas. It's so satisfying when it's finished. God, I've missed my studio. It's the only thing I've kept up payments for. I gave up my place when I decided to head out here. I'll be crashing on my friend's sofa when I get back until I can find a job and secure a place to live.

I want something different this time around. My flat was nice, but it wasn't me.

Jasper was right about one thing: I'm crap at keeping time for myself, and by the time I look at my phone, I've been drawing for over three hours.

Sighing heavily, because I really don't want to leave, I pack my things up and lie down with the backpack under my head, delaying the inevitable a little longer. I know I need to get going in a bit. It'll take me a good half an hour to walk to the airport. Closing my eyes, I let the sun warm my skin. I'm heading home for a reason: it's time for me to find out the truth. I can't put it off any longer. The more time that passes, the more I think about it. This time I won't give up.

It's time.

Chapter Four

Some People

Ethan

I've opted to fly back first class. I was offered the family jet, but it would have meant spending another day or so here, and I need to get back to work. Always work; it seems to be my life lately.

We seem to have hit an all-time high in the number of new clients we've gained over the last few months. Now the pressure is on to keep it there. Alongside the pressure from my parents to be more available to them and the family business—the one I have no interest in—and then, of course, there is the life that being the grandson of a Lady brings. She's the very reason I flew to Australia in the first place.

I don't have a spare minute.

I can't even remember the last time I took a few hours off, let alone a whole day.

On the way out here, I was going over applications for new guys to bring in ready for training, a day and a half's work in the space of one flight. Only, the more work I do, the more it seems to triple.

It's never-ending.

Fuck, I need help. I'm drowning in it all, barely keeping my head above water. I work late, I'm always in early, and I don't take holidays.

This trip would be the closest thing I have had to a holiday in years. But even as I've walked, driven, and flown, I've worked: taken calls, arranged meetings, typed reports, tasked teams with new projects and assignments, organised training, refurbs, projections for the next three years.

My head's full of it.

I need an assistant. *Desperately*. My diary's rammed full; I'm trying to juggle everything. Sleep evades me most nights, as my head flips through the things I've done, could have done better, and shit I need to do. When I do drift off, it's restless.

I need someone who can keep up with me and not flake when it comes to working odd hours or the workload. Jill, our office manager, has been doing what she can, but it's time to branch out. It's not her job to run my family life along with the business at Cerberus.

I've asked Jill to look for an assistant for me, for personal and work. I need someone by my side whenever I need them.

Stepping into the cool, air-conditioned terminal building, my body relaxes from the intense heat outside. I make my way through to the crowd of people queuing to check in, ready to find mine.

"Where the hell have you been?" a guy shouts behind me as I move. "I can't believe you left *me* here to wait for *you*," he says as I get in line to check in. "You've been gone for almost four hours," he adds. I already want to take him down a peg for talking to anyone like that, then I hear a soft huff of frustration, I can only assume it's from the person he's talking to, but I don't turn around.

I just listen.

"I went to the beach." Her voice is soft, calming almost, as she speaks, "It was beaut—" He cuts her off. *Arsehole*. I don't want to hear him talk.

"I had to hang around here and wait by myself when you were off doing God knows what." There is a thump of a bag being thrown to the ground. "Aren't you going to apologise for making me wait?" he shouts, and all I can attribute it to is a child's tantrum.

"*What?* No. Why do I need to apologise? Jasper... I..." I think she's lost for words or exasperated at how immature he's being.

Shit, what a dickhead.

"Where are you going?" the woman huffs. I peek over my shoulder to see he's moved to the other line of people, away from her, leaving his bag at her slender flip-flop-covered feet. *Huh.* Multi-colour painted toenails, and a gold toe ring. *I like it.* Internally, I groan at myself.

Fuck, I'm looking at a woman's foot and liking it? It's been too long.

"If you're going to be a *child*," she retorts, and I'm glad we're on the same wavelength, "take your bag and check in on your own." Does she have to sit next to him the entire flight back? We're in the same queue, so we're obviously heading to the same destination.

A flick of an idea forms, but I dismiss it as I carry on listening.

"Why don't you want to spend your time with me?" he says. *I could tell you at least three reasons right now.* "We won't be together when we get back. I don't know when I'll see you next," he whines, but there's something in his tone I don't like. He's trying to win her back, but there's no heart to it. My flick of an idea really starts to take shape. I'm all for a good argument, but this is just manipulative.

"Fuck this," she groans, but it sounds more like a sigh. "Jasper, carry your own bag. I'm not doing this again." *Again?* The woman mutters. This guy's a prick. I wonder if they're dating or married? Whatever their relationship is, I doubt it will last long at this rate.

From where I'm standing, I can't see her, but her voice does something to me. It's like smooth caramel wrapping itself around my ears.

I could listen to her for hours.

The fact that he's annoying her irritates me. I smirk, knowing how I can make her day a little better.

"I've had enough of waiting around for you," the guy says, his tone condescending. "Selfish bitch," he mumbles, loud enough for everyone to hear.

"Oh, my god," the woman grits out, like she's ready to blow. "I went to the beach," she states again, emphasising each word. "I don't have to do as you tell me, Jasper." Yeah, I'm doing it. A low buzz hums through my skin, like I can feel her anger flowing over me. I think she needs a break from this arsehole.

"It's about time you *did* do as you were told," he adds. Pressing my lips together to keep my mouth shut, it takes everything not to turn around and give him what he deserves.

My fist in his face. Fuck, it would be satisfying.

"Are you serious?" the female bristles, sounding fed up. "Like I've said a hundred times, last night and today, you had the opportunity to come with me to the beach, to spend our last few hours soaking in the vibrancy of this amazing country." I like how she described this place. "But you decided to come here and spend seven hours inside a concrete box." I can't help but peek as I reach for my case to move forward. The guy's eyes flick to mine as I straighten to my full height. Case in hand. I get the smallest glimpse of her tanned, toned legs, the gold anklet, with a butterfly pendant that sits loosely around her slender ankle. I flex my finger around the handle, suppressing the urge to reach out and glide my fingers over the chain, over her soft skin.

"If you could step forward, sir." I hear another voice as I imagine what her legs would feel like beneath my fingers. Like the most expensive silk you could buy. *Delicate, soft, supple.*

Drawing my eyes to the male at the desk, I step forward. Unable to hear the rest of the argument behind me. I'm confused at how easily I went from zero to turned on just at the sight of her ankle and legs when I don't even know her, or what she looks like.

"Passport and ticket, please." I hand them over. "Can I ask a favour?" I ask, ready to give the woman behind me at least a little light at the end of her day.

"Of course, Mr Ford," he says, as the smirk on my face grows.

Chapter Five

Grateful

Aggie

I'm staring at Jasper in disbelief. I can't believe he just called me a selfish bitch. Who the hell does he think he is? Leaving his bag where it is on the floor, I step over it, showing him that he can go fuck himself. I move forward, watching the guy in front of me as I walk up to the check in desk. I have no doubt he heard everything. I'm grateful he was gentlemanly enough not to say anything, or pass judgement, unlike some of the other people around us, side eyeing us, ready to make their opinions. That, or he didn't give a shit. I can't blame him if it's the latter.

I can't wait to get out of here and away from Jasper. Then, like a sinking ship, I remember we pre-booked our seats to sit together. It was a great idea at the time. Now I'm severely regretting it. Groaning out loud in frustration, I watch while Jasper marches over and snatches his bag from the floor, giving me a warning look. I huff out a laugh at him. What was I thinking?

Seriously? What happened to the guy I met three months ago? I have to sit next to his whining arse for the next three hundred hours. That's exactly what it's going to feel like.

I know he won't let it go. He'll follow me around like an angry, lost puppy, making excuses as to why he's been reacting that way and still blaming me. I'll have to suck it up and deal with it for the next... I look down to check my watch. My shoulders slump as I sigh. *Shit,* the next twenty-five to twenty-six hours. Now I feel like I want to throw a tantrum. I laugh at myself a little, trying my best to remember it's only a fraction of time.

The tall, bulky guy in the suit walks away from the check in desk, and I can't help but check out his arse as he places his hand into the pocket of his trousers, pulling the fabric tighter around a backside you could only describe as steel; perfect. Hands down, a better arse than Jasper. There's actually no comparison, still watching that fine arse walk away. Jasper's bum is almost flat. This guy's arse you could really dig your fingers into.

My whole body rolls with a delightful shiver at the thought.

If that's not a sure sign you need to finish things with Jasper, what is? Oh yeah, the fact that he's a douchebag.

Stepping up to the check in desk, Jasper is right next to me, before he shoves me to the side and hands over his passport and ticket before I can hand over mine. The guy at the desk takes it from his hand, giving us both a kind smile as he checks the details and we check in our bags.

"Your flight is still scheduled on time, sir. Enjoy your flight." He holds out his hand, gesturing for my ticket and passport. "Miss Hope, I have some excellent news for you," he says as he checks my ticket. "You've been upgraded to first class. It comes with all the benefits of the first-class lounge, free drinks, and a buffet." He smiles.

"What do you mean?" I'm confused. First class?

"You're flying home first class tonight," he says, glancing at Jasper, who's standing with his mouth wide open, his cheeks flushed in disbelief.

"Oh." I don't know what to say as I let it sink in. "Just me?" I ask in question, hoping to fuck it is.

"Just you," he states in a firm tone, his eyes never leaving mine.

"You... you mean, *she* gets to go first class, and I have to sit on my own in coach?" Jasper exclaims, exhaling loudly as he leans forward.

"You won't be on your own, sir," the guy says. I can't help but laugh. I've just struck lucky.

Stepping into first class, after spending a few hours or so in the first-class lounge, and having a glass or two of white wine, along with some delicious treats, I'm happy to be by myself for the entire flight home.

I could dance around at how much this has changed the tone of my night.

Jasper, on the other hand, has been blowing up my phone with messages telling me just how ungrateful I am. That I should have given *him* the ticket. And that I must have planned this all along. I've not messaged him back, nor do I plan to, which I'm sure has only annoyed him more.

Seems like a 'him' problem.

I've been welcomed onto the flight and led to my seat, my hand luggage taken off me and placed in a locker just under the TV screen in front of me.

I'm in the middle aisle; there are two seats facing each other, with a small partition between them. The attendant told me it can be removed if I were sitting next to anyone I know. I'm not, but I'm sure I'll make some sort of conversation with whoever sits there; we'll be facing each other after all.

Taking a seat, I lie back and close my eyes, feeling the soft, warm leather as I run my fingers over the chair/bed beneath me. Stretching my legs out. I notice a few others filling the spaces, but no one is in the seat next to me. It would have been nice to make a friend.

Ethan

I prefer to walk around the terminal rather than sit in the lounge before a long flight. I hate waiting, preferring to be the last to board. I found my time in the terminal more amusing than I thought I would, but then I flickered into disgust. In between emails and calls, I watched the guy from the queue, pacing, swearing into his phone, almost frantic, his eyes wandering to every other female, while he called and texted who I can only assume is the woman that was with him earlier. She was nowhere to be seen. *Good for her.* After a while, he seemed to calm down, but only after a blonde gave him the eye. I watched as his focus honed in on her, seemingly forgetting about the woman he turned up with. I despise men like him. They are the reasons women can get so guarded when it comes to meeting men.

Arsehole.

Climbing the steps to the plane, I'm guided to my seat by the attendant. I stop where I am, at the edge of the aisle, when I see some brightly coloured toenails wiggling ahead of me, propped up on the cupboard, as she's handed a drink while we wait to take off.

I knew we were on the same flight, but what are the chances we'd be placed next to each other in the unofficial couple's seat? I think the check-in guy got the wrong impression of my good deed.

Not that I mind, because when she stands, I get a spectacular view of her lengthy, smooth as silk, bare legs.

Perfect. She's wearing an oversized tie-dye hoodie that swamps her, so bright I have to squint my eyes. It makes it seem like she's not wearing anything underneath, and for all I know, she's not. It finishes just below an arse I desperately want to see. My cock thickens. Jesus-fuck, I need to calm down.

"Sir, your seat," the air attendant whispers. Watching as 'butterfly' ruffles her short honey blonde hair, making the jumper ride up her thighs, I get a glimpse of her arse cheeks, as they peek out the bottom of her denim shorts. *Fuck.* Her creamy skin looks ready to be devoured. I have to tear my eyes away before I make things uncomfortable for everyone.

Walking to my seat, I get comfy in the chair right next to hers, as she settles back, glancing in my direction with the most encouraging smile, on peachy plump lips, but not saying a word. Even from my quick glance, she's stunning. I quickly lower my eyes to my laptop bag.

Am I really craving for this woman to speak?

Yes, yes, I am.

I nod my thanks to the air attendant as I glance at my bag. For the first time in my life, I'm actually nervous to look over the retractable partition to see her again. I've been in—had been in— a relationship a few years ago, for three years. A match my mother still thinks was made in heaven. She's as delusional as the woman I was with.

I've not told her the truth about our split. I was all in, ring on her finger, ready to plan the wedding. Things changed; she wasn't who I thought she was. Was I in love? I don't believe I was. But I was devastated, three years down the drain, when I found out she'd cheated on me with an associate from my parents' business. A guy I introduced her to at a party two Christmases ago. As much as I'm done with her, she doesn't feel the same way. I've heard all the excuses, but it won't do her any good. I'll never go back after what she did. That doesn't stop the fact that she and my mother want us to get back together.

It's never going to happen.

Nerves are not something I ever deal with, but this woman, the one next to me, with her long legs and easy freedom, makes my heart dip in an unsteady beat.

Shake it off.

Standing, I take off my suit jacket, leaving me in my waistcoat, and I place it on the hook next to my seat, and rest my laptop bag on the small table in front of me. Only then do I get my first proper look at the woman sitting next to me.

Holy shit.

She's stunning. My heart hammers in my chest as I take in her features.

Skin like tinted porcelain, highlighted with a sun-kissed glow, rosy lips, and eyes so bright, it takes me a moment to take in the colours of sea-green, almost emerald.

"Hi," she chimes over the partition, and I recall how much I liked how she spoke; when her soft, calming voice fills my ears.

"Hello." I nod, my voice deeper than normal. Trying to get my senses back together so I can form a coherent sentence, I watch her lips stretch into a grin.

"I'm Aggie." There it is again, smooth like velvet.

"Ethan," I state, then remember my manners. "It's nice to meet you, Aggie." I like the sound of her name on my tongue. *Aggie.* I say again in my head, just to keep it there a while longer.

"It definitely is, Ethan." Fuck. The way she licks her bottom lip when she says my name, I'm going to be sporting a hard on for the duration of the flight. "I'm a talker, Ethan." Jesus, I have to bite my tongue to stop my mouth from falling open. I get a visual image in my mind of what she'd say if I were between her perfect legs. "If you're not into it, then just tell me, and I'll keep to myself," she says, her eyes locking on my face, as she sits up in her seat, resting her bright toes on the locker again.

I'm into it. Her. Aggie.

"You can talk, Aggie." My voice comes out like a purr, my dick agreeing with my response. "I may not say much back, but I'm listening." Her lips part as she takes a breath in. I want to watch her chest rise and fall with each one, but I'm a gentleman. So, I watch it in my peripheral, like the perv I seem to have become in the last few minutes.

"I'll let you get settled," she says as she starts to turn away from me. I want to reach out and tell her no, that she can stay where she is, and keep talking, because I want to hear everything she has to say. But I don't. Instead, I nod in response and loosen my tie. Pulling out my laptop, I power it up and settle in like she suggested. I'll do a few hours, then get some sleep. It's already 8 pm.

I've been working away for the last hour and a half, only putting it to one side when we took off. But I can't concentrate; she's distracting. Not that she's doing anything, she's not spoken a word, or looked in my direction. I can see she's doing something, but I can't see what.

I want to know.

Her soft hair's fallen over her face as she's leant forward like me, headphones on, lost in what she's doing. I want to know what could hold her attention for so long.

I could watch her do nothing. *Fuck, what's wrong with me?*

There's Wi-Fi on the plane, so I've been able to go through my emails. I've sorted through the shortlist of applicants to the security side of things, and I should be receiving the full list of applicants for the personal assistant's job from Jill when she gets into work. The time difference is frustrating when I've been a day ahead. I feel like I backtrack when I arrive home.

Shutting my laptop, I remove the table and call for assistance. I want to lie down. I don't want to sleep yet, but they'll make the bed up for me. I stand up when the attendant comes over and gets to work. The entire time I watch Aggie drawing. I snap my eyes away when she moves, looking at what's going on around her. She slips off her earphones, placing them on the table over her sketch pad.

"What's the time?" I think she's asking herself, but I answer anyway.

"Just after nine-thirty," I tell her, glancing at my watch.

She leans over the partition and taps the guy on the shoulder to get his attention. "Could you do mine for me, please?" she asks with a soft smile.

"Of course, Miss Hope." The guy says, his eyes lingering a fraction too long on her. I don't like it, my fist clenching at my side. I try to reason with myself that I can't hit him. She's not mine. Aggie grins wider and thanks him. *Aggie Hope.* "Would you like me to remove the partition, so you and Mr Ford can talk more freely?" he says, gesturing between us. She bites her *fucking* lip, her teeth sinking into her perfect, plump flesh, as she looks at me. My cock's rock hard in seconds. I want to drag it from between her teeth and replace it with mine. I'll happily sit with my hard on.

"What do you say... Ethan Ford. Would you like to speak with me more freely?" I didn't think it would be possible for my cock to get harder. But it does, painfully so. I want to adjust myself, but I can't. I'm all for it—the pain, taking the partition away, being closer to her, the way I'll fuck my own hand when I'm alone. *Fuck yes.* I nod my answer, and she releases her lip from its confines, licking over where her teeth have left a faint mark.

Jesus-fuck.

Chapter Six

Shifting

Aggie

Ethan Ford. He's as fine as his name sounds. And I have to remember that I have *a* Jasper somewhere on this flight. I'm pushing all thoughts of him away as I talk to Ethan. Like he said, he doesn't talk much. He just sat and listened. We're facing each other, legs stretched out on our little beds. The gap between us seems like too much, but as we speak, the gap grows smaller.

"What were you drawing?" he asks, his eyes roaming over my hands bundled in my hoodie, then my sketch book.

"Um..." I don't normally tell anyone, not when they are just sketches.

"You don't have to tell me. I know artists like to keep them close to their chests until they're ready." That's the most he's said. And a shiver coats my skin at the finality of his words, like he's expecting me not to answer.

"Yes, but I want to show you." I do. Running my fingers over the black sketch book, I don't feel nervous to show him like I have everyone else. In the months I've been with Jasper, I've never shown him anything. He tried to steal my sketch book once, and I lost my shit. He then told me I was hiding something, telling me I was pathetic, that it's just drawings. I didn't speak to him for a day, then somehow, we were back to normal. I didn't get it out in front of him again. Maybe he snuck a peek when I was asleep, and he realised I have nothing to hide.

"I'd be honoured to see anything you draw." Why are his words so... powerful? Gulping down the rise of my arousal, as the low pulse between my legs hammers gently, I take a quick breath. With my sketchbook in my hand, I sit cross legged in front of him, closer than we have been. Ethan sits up as I pass him my work. My skin turns to fire the moment our fingers brush, and it hits straight between my thighs, almost taking my breath away.

Ethan's eyes roam over my fingers, trailing up my arm to my neck, and when they settle on my lips, I instantly want him to kiss me. I want his lips on mine. I want the scrape of his stubble against my soft skin. I watch his eyes darken as he flares his nose, then pulls his hand away, leaving me disappointed. And so turned on. The need to be alone is overwhelming.

He pulls the book gently from my hand, and I watch it slide through my fingers; my breathing picks up as he opens to the first page. I want him to like them. I'm not nervous, just... giddy he wants to look. He doesn't smile; barely moves a muscle of his suave face. Ethan just looks—his eyes thirsty to absorb every detail as his fingers brush over the pages. I can't read his expression, but it's warmed, as his eyes flick from drawing to drawing. We sit like this for a while: me watching him go through the drawings I feel are my personal thoughts, my own take on the world, and the way it moves. I don't even realise I'm smiling until he frowns. I flinch, my smile disappearing. Then I see the drawing he's come across. The one I don't know why I drew. It's dark compared to the others; there's no movement, only dark shadows cast over a wooded area, scary almost.

"Explain this one to me." He almost sounds angry, like it's offended him, which is ridiculous.

"It was from a dream I had," I say, honesty flowing through me. "Not a good one," I add.

"Then why put it on paper?"

"I felt like I needed to. It happens sometimes." It was the dream that night when I knew I needed to head back and find the truth about myself. I felt like it was part of something bigger.

"Have you had the dream since?" He looks concerned. Why, I'm not sure. I've not thought about it since I drew it.

"No," I admit, my shoulders relaxing. Why did I tense up?

"Good," he says, his voice gruff, and he flicks to the next page. I grin at the startling contrast of the two drawings. "Beautiful, Aggie," he murmurs, the pads of his fingers tracing the lines of the butterfly.

"I have that as a tattoo." His eyes move to mine, like he needs something from me.

"Where?" I'm startled by the question, biting my lip as a small laugh escapes me.

"The very top of my inner thigh." His eyes dart down to my crossed legs, then snap back up like he didn't mean to look. As short as my shorts are, you can't see it. "It's actually more of a trail," I add when his eyes meet mine again.

"What do you mean?" he asks, rubbing his chin in confusion. I doubt this man has any tattoos. He looks like the perfect English gentleman in his high-priced tailored suit, that stretches with every move of his toned body. Shifting my legs so I'm kneeling, I lift my hoodie to reveal my stomach. His eyes widen, then darken from a pale silver to a deep grey, when he sees my stomach.

"It starts here," I say as I point to the fine line of flowers just underneath my left breast. "They trail down." My skin tingles from my touch, but more so, from his gaze on my flesh. My finger follows the lines over my stomach to the top of my shorts, where I part my legs. The tip of my pointed finger traces the line beneath them and comes to a stop, high on my inner thigh. "It stops right here," I add, tapping the spot slightly. Ethan groans. It's only then I look up and find his hooded eyes transfixed on where my tattoo ends. His breathing is laboured. "I'd show it to you..." He growls this time, his fingers inching forwards, like he needs to touch it, me. Fuck I want him to. Swallowing the air as it gets trapped in my throat, I softly say, "But I don't think it would be appropriate. Not on a plane full of people." *What's happening?* I feel so many things: heart racing, palms sweating, body on fire. I'm alive with the need for him to touch me. *Anywhere* the fuck he wants.

"Definitely not something I want to do in front of others." He groans, his hand flexing as he pulls it away.

"We'll be dimming the light in five minutes, Miss Hope." Huh? Lights? Snapping out of our haze, we both look to the attendant as Ethan mumbles a thank you. "Anything I can get you beforehand?" he says.

"No, yes, a water, please." I struggle to form a sentence.

"You have a stocked mini fridge beside you. There should be a few in there for you."

"Oh, thank you." I open the little drawer, taking out the bottle, completely breaking the connection Ethan and I had, as the attendant moves away.

"Good night, Miss Hope," Ethan says before handing my sketchbook back and settling back, closing his eyes. I watch like a weirdo for a few moments before I realise what I'm doing and do the same. Falling into an easy sleep, with Ethan only centimetres away.

I'm woken by a loud voice and muffled sounds in the not so far away distance. I ignore them and focus on the feeling of warmth like I've never felt before, a warmth that spreads over my stomach. I relish it and the tingles it elicits in my lower abs.

Stretching as I try and wake my tired body, the warmth on my stomach shifts to the top of my thigh. I freeze. Sucking in a shaky breath, I dare myself to look down. Peeling my eyes open, my heart skips as I internally squeal. A large hand and thick fingers caress my thigh. Fuck, it sends my core wild as I watch them tentatively playing with my sensitive skin just below the hemline of my shorts. *Ethan.*

He's touching me in his sleep.

The noise behind grows louder, but I don't look away, too transfixed on how we got into this position. We're both halfway down the small beds, our bodies level and touching. I can just see the underside of Ethan's face as he lies on his side, facing the partition, his shirt-covered arm reaching through the gap in between us, his hand wrapped around my upper thigh like he owns me.

I don't hate it, very far from hate it, actually.

I'm not going to move until he does. I'm going to enjoy being touched like this. It makes me feel good. Closing my eyes, I will his hand to move up just a fraction, not giving two shits where we are, or who could be watching.

He groans, and the caresses stop. I'm internally pouting when he slips his hand away, leaving me wanting more. He sits up just as the noise in the background gets louder, my own groan matching his. He gives me a gruff, sleepy chuckle as his eyes flick to where the noise is coming from. I sit up.

"Morning, Miss Hope," he says, his voice gravelly from sleep. God, my eyes almost roll to the back of my head with how good he sounds; like every woman's dream. "My apologies," he continues, glancing between my legs, appearing anything but sorry for where we've found ourselves.

"The only thing you should apologise for is taking your hand away, Mr Ford." I half smile, like I'm joking, but I'm not. I want the feeling back. He doesn't smile, just sucks in a lungful of air.

"Unfortunately, Aggie, you have something to deal with," he says on his long exhale. I'm confused for a second, not understanding what he's talking about. When I hear Jasper's raised voice.

"What the hell?" I'm flying out of my bed before I finish. I make my way towards the commotion Jasper seems to be making, only to find him arguing with someone at the top of the stairs that leads to our section of first class. I shake my head in disbelief.

"What are you doing?" I whisper shout, not wanting to disturb any of the other passengers.

"I want my seat," he shouts, drawing looks as other passengers start to wake from the noise.

"Sir, you don't have a seat up here. You need to go back downstairs," One of the staff members says, holding him back from stepping a foot onto our floor. I'm lost for words at the immaturity of the man I've travelled with for the last few months. My temper flares, my eyes hone in on him, ready to give him shit. I almost run towards him, when I'm pulled back and placed behind an enormous body of a man. Ethan. My eyes flare before drifting closed for the briefest moment as his scent washes over me, calming the fight in me instantly. Stepping to his side, I look up at him.

At full height, he towers over me, and not only does he make me weak at the knees, but he's also making me fear for Jasper's life. The way Ethan stares at him, like he's nothing, makes the breath leave my body. Every cell eviscerates at the protectiveness of a man I hardly know. The plane goes silent the moment Ethan makes his presence known. Eyes darting between the two men. Jasper, in all his stupidity, eyes him like a challenge. Taking a step towards us, Jasper pushes the attendant away from him. I move as quickly as I can to make sure she doesn't fall, catching her as she stumbles back.

I focus on Jasper, ready to run at him, but Ethan's hold stops me. His heavy hands firm on my waist as I come to a complete stop mid-stride. Jasper and I face to face, as Ethan pulls me back to his side. Arm still gripping my waist in what? A warning not to move? When Ethan steps up to him, his intimidating presence flowing, the whole area of the plane goes tense. Waiting.

Fuck.

"Sir," Ethan says with a voice that could chill you to the bone. My hand comes up to rest on Ethan's back, as his tense muscles flex beneath my fingers. "You need to make your way back downstairs." I gulp. "Or I'll have you arrested for disturbance of the peace." I fully believe he would, and I wouldn't stop him.

"Aggie, tell them you know me. That you're my girlfriend," Jasper shouts in frustration, pointing his finger at me. Ethan tenses further. "We agreed to swap seats, tell them. It should have been mine in the first place." Ethan shifts closer. He doesn't move, just stands stoic, his breathing even and calm, as he watches Jasper, but I feel his muscles flex under my touch, like he's preparing to pounce.

"Are you serious?" I ask Jasper, embarrassment flashing over my skin. "Unfortunately, I do know this man," I say, stepping from beside Ethan, but he doesn't let me go forward, and Jasper's eyes catch the way Ethan's arm wraps protectively around my waist.

"What the fuck?" he shouts. "Are you cheating on me?"

"We're no longer together, Jasper." I try to move from Ethan's grasp but fail.

Jasper's nostrils flare as he goes to step into me, and I don't flinch when he reaches for my arm. I'm not scared of him. Only Ethan's faster; he drops his hold on me, somehow moving me away before grabbing Jasper and spinning him around away from me, cuffing his hands behind his back, as he does.

Where did he get the handcuffs?

"This isn't over, Aggie," Jasper spits out before Ethan moves him down the stairs with so much ease it's like he does this for a living. I realise just how much I liked Ethan fighting my battles.

I've never experienced that before.

I must have apologised to everyone a thousand times on the way back to my seat. Ethan doesn't reappear, and weirdly, I miss him as I settle back on my bed. When the attendant brings breakfast and a drink, she looks at me, leaning a little closer.

"Mr Ford has asked me to pass on a message," she says, handing me a folded piece of paper.

"Thank you," I add as she walks away, leaving me to read in privacy. Unfolding the cream textured paper, I read it over and over again.

Miss Hope, he's been dealt with. He won't be bothering you again. Enjoy the rest of your flight.

Ethan

I don't see him again for the remainder of the flight or in the airport. And I don't give Jasper a fleeting thought.

Chapter Seven

Jet Lag

Aggie

"You're back," Layla shouts when she swings open the door. "I've missed you so much. Why didn't you tell me you'd landed? I would have picked you up." Her arms come around me in a cuddle I've needed since I entered the airport back in New Zealand. "What's the matter? Has jet lag got you? Are you hungry?" she asks, wrestling the bag from my back and taking it into the small living room, and resting it against the sofa. She turns to me again, hugging me harder this time.

"It's good to be back, and thank you for letting me stay. I promise I won't be here long," I add, hugging her back this time. I look over the cosy home she's made for herself. Layla's been like a sister to me ever since we found each other in a bar three years ago. We've been inseparable since, apart from when I go on my little trips. But we talk almost every day without fail.

"The sofa is yours for however long you need it. It's new. I got a pull-out one." I give her a smile as I step back. "I was about to call the police when I didn't hear from you after they upgraded your ticket. What happened? How was first class? Was it just as good as I think it would be?" I chuckle at all her questions.

"Better," I say, my lips pulling into a smile. The feel of Ethan's hand still lingers on my skin.

"Before you start, I need to let you know. I've filled out a few applications for you, when you said you'd need a job when you came back." I laugh. This is Layla through and through: always making sure everyone is okay. "I hope you don't mind. They were all office jobs, some part-time, some full, one with hours you could pick." She's also full of life and never stops talking. "I'll show them to you." She heads for her laptop, and I have to stop her.

"In a bit, okay? I need to sleep. My body feels messed up." I move my hands in a circle around in front of me for emphasis.

"No, you can't sleep. I read up on jet lag, and you have to ride it out. Sleep when we sleep, or you'll be out of sync for longer," she pleads, holding my shoulder to get her point across. "I'll just lie down for a few hours," I tell her, stepping back to hit the sofa.

"Nope, we have plans." She cheers, hands on her curvy hips.

"Plans?" My body is too tired for this; I need sleep, and I need it now. Sitting on the sofa, I lean my head back onto the soft cushions that will be my bed for the next few weeks and close my eyes.

"No, nope, get up, *Chica*." She holds my hand, pulling me. "You need a shower, a gigantic coffee, and a full-on day."

"Oh my god, what have you planned?" I sigh, already fighting the fatigue that's invading my muscles.

"I've not seen you for months. The least you can do is spend the day with me before we both get stuck with work, and then we won't see each other as much."

"I'm going to be living with you," I state, trying my best to sit back down. But she walks me towards the shower, plopping an energy drink into my hand as we go.

"Drink up. We have things to do." I love her enthusiasm normally, but I want to crash out.

"Please, just an hour's sleep?" I whine, needing something.

"It's for your own good. I've seen you sleep after a trip. There's no way I'd be able to wake you from the dead." My eyes flutter closed as I remember how

I woke up this morning, last night? I don't know. *Ethan.* I press my thighs together at the thought of his hot hands on my skin. My eyes pop back open when I'm moved forward again, and a towel is placed in my hands, along with my favourite candy cane bodywash.

"You went shopping for me?" she frowns, like it's a stupid question.

"Of course I did. You sold or threw away all your stuff before you left. I wanted you to feel at home." She shrugs.

"I do feel at home, but that's because you're here," I say, leaning in to rest my head on her shoulder. I also know she can't afford it. "What else did you buy?" I ask, knowing it won't just be the bodywash.

"Oh... not much." She waves her hand dismissively while ushering me into the bathroom.

"I know what 'not much' is to you. What did you do?" I fake scowl at her.

"I drove to your studio and picked up the things you stored there. It's all in the small closet I made you under the stairs."

"You didn't need to do that, but I appreciate you did." My heart swells knowing my things are close by, and that she was kind enough to fetch them for me.

I can barely keep my eyes open. I think I've been awake forever. Looking at the time, my eyes blur, making it difficult to see my watch. Maybe... twenty-eight hours? I have no idea at this point, but I know I'm going to sleep blissfully wherever I land.

Layla, true to her word, has kept me busy. She cooked the most amazing breakfast, packed us a picnic, and we headed out. After grabbing an enormous coffee from Bruno's, the local café, we headed over to my studio to say hi to everyone who's been checking on it for me.

I'm planning on spending tomorrow in there, going over my drawings from my trip to see what inspires me to paint the next piece for my fluidity collection.

"One last stop, then you can go home and sleep, I promise," she says as she steers me into the bar at the Brasserie. "We're getting one cocktail to celebrate that you're home."

"Why just one?" She looks me over as I sway a little.

"Because I think you could fall asleep standing up right now, and I'm not carrying your arse home." I burst out laughing, like I'm already drunk. She's right. If I have more than one, I'll be a goner. "Plus, you don't drink while you're travelling, so it's been months. One will be more than enough for you," she adds, as we take our place at the end of the bar. She's full of good points today. I don't drink alcohol when I travel; it's too dangerous.

"Thank you," I spout, side hugging her.

Ordering our drinks with the barman, we wait and watch while he makes them. Layla looks over my shoulder and stiffens, darting her eyes down and away from whatever she's just seen.

"Are you okay?" I ask, resting my hand on her knee next to mine. I go to turn around, but she puts her hand out, stopping me. She seems to be doing that a lot today.

"I'm fine. It's just that Leon and his friends have just walked in. For whatever reason, I just can't be around them. They make me nervous." It's a strange reaction to have, considering she works for the wife of one of them and must see him, or them, a lot. I don't know much about any of them, other than what Layla's told me—they all work together, or own a business together. Hell, if I can remember, but I think Layla finds them intimidating.

"Okay?" I question, and she nods in response. Maybe she needs some help to see them a little differently. "Let's have some fun. How about we order them a fancy cocktail each, my treat?" She scrunches her nose, then nods again. She's had a crush on Leon for some time—not that she'd admit it. My chatty friend becomes silent whenever he's about and I have no idea why.

"Can you imagine them with a cocktail in their hands?" she says, chuckling. I've seen Leon briefly, but I've never met the others.

"No, because you won't let me turn around to look," I say teasingly. "Who are they all, anyway?"

"Fine, take a look. There's Leon." I give her an eye roll, because *duh*. "Owen, Charlie's husband, Cole, Ari's husband." This is Layla's new friend, who she's been doing work for on the side of the things she does for Charlie in the flower shop. "And Ethan." *Ethan?* The name brings back of rush of feelings for what Mr Ethan Ford did for me on the plane. Turning my head slowly to get a look and see what type of men they are, my anticipation rises at the hope of seeing him again. I know it won't be him. There's *no way*.

I was wrong.

It's him.

There he is. *My Ethan.* Sucking in a quick breath, I whip my head back around so fast I almost fall off the stool I'm sitting on. I'm not sure I want him to see me. The embarrassment I felt on the plane after what happened with Jasper floods my cheeks

The bartender places my raspberry daiquiri in front of me, and it has a cute little paper butterfly clip attached to the straw, along with Layla's spicy mimosa, with a flower umbrella.

"Can we grab a few more to be delivered to that table over there, please?" I ask the barman as he takes my payment.

"Sure, they'll have mocktail. They're not drinking tonight," he says like he knows them well. "Do you need the menu?" I nod and he hands it over. Flicking through the pages, we giggle looking at the flamboyancy of some of them, and settle on the ones we think will work best in their big, burly hands.

"Oh, and please don't say who they are from." He looks puzzled but carries on. After placing our order, adding who each one is for, I sit back and enjoy my drink.

"They're about to take it over," Layla quietly giggles, even though they can't hear us through the crowd of people.

"They look so confused." She smiles as she takes the final sip of her drink. "Leon's looks too small in his hands." She laughs, her cheeks flushing as she watches him. "Cole's smiling, and Owen is just frowning at it like it's going to cause him harm." *What about Ethan,* I want to say, but she has no idea that I know him, and I don't know why I haven't told her. "Ethan's… still the same, unsmiling. I've never seen him smile. He's always serious." My own smile pulls at my lips as I take a sip of my drink. My mind wanders back to the plane. Did he smile? *No,* not really. I wonder why? Maybe I could make him smile. I can't help but think what it would look like stretched across his lips.

"Time to go before I pass out," I say, jumping from my seat. "I need to sleep." Leaving our empty glasses on the bar, we slip out unnoticed.

Chapter Eight

Butterfly

Ethan

Owen's been trying to ask who bought us the drinks, like he thinks someone is trying to kill us with mocktails. Mike, the manager of the Brasserie, just laughed and walked back behind the bar. Cole and Leon are laughing at their chosen drinks. Leon's is some sort of mimosa with a slice of chilli floating on top, and a pink flower umbrella on the side. Cole's is a pink cosmopolitan, with a small twist of orange hanging from the glass. Owen pushes his bright blue drink into the middle of the table, uninterested in taking a sip.

I, on the other hand, can't take my eyes away from the tall glass in front of me, rimmed with sweet sugar. I don't drink cocktails, never have done, but this one, my mouth waters in anticipation of just how sweet it will taste. I want to savour every mouthful; I want to gaze at its vibrancy, inhale the deep fruity sweetness. *Goddamn*, this drink is so much like her, *Miss Hope;* the bold colours, the sweetness. It's the butterfly that sits so perfectly on the straw, and the memory of the lifelike butterfly tattoo I never got to see, or touch, that keeps me from drinking it.

When I woke on the plane, I smiled to myself, knowing exactly who I'd been touching in my sleep. And who I continued to touch when I woke. It may have been wrong, but, fuck, she felt good. My hands flex at the recollection of her supple, smooth skin under my fingers. It took me longer than it should have to remove my hand and apologise. Not that I was sorry for any of it. Far from it.

It only makes me wonder how far she would have let me go if her boyfriend hadn't disrupted us. It's wrong to touch anyone without consent, but fuck, I was asleep when I did it, and she didn't push me away. I knew she was awake and enjoying it; the tiny moans escaping her lips turned my semi-hard cock to steel.

Twisting the cool glass on the table, I know this drink is from her. I can't tell you how I know, I just do. Taking my phone out of my pocket, I slide open the camera app, and discreetly take a photo of it, and slide it back into my trouser pocket.

"Why'd you take a photo?" Leon asks beside me. *Damn*, I didn't think anyone was watching.

"Gran," I say simply, not wanting to admit the truth.

"Yeah, Lady Celeste sure does get a kick out of these things. Here, take another of them all; she'll love it." She would. She'd laugh and ask me what it tasted like. Although I won't show her this one, this is for me.

"Ethan, we have the applicants for the PA position ready if you want to go through them. Sorry, I didn't get them to you yesterday." Jill, our office manager, says, walking into my office.

"Sure," I say, finishing an email to my father before I turn my attention to her. She takes a seat opposite my desk and sets her notepad on her lap.

"They are on the common drive. I uploaded the candidates an hour ago. I've been through them. We just need to discuss details."

"Like what?" I ask, sounding a bit short. I don't really have the time for this, but I need to be the one to choose.

"Availability. Some need to give a month's notice, some already have holidays booked and can't start until after that. Some are less qualified than others, but their references stand out."

"Okay," I murmur, reading through the twelve applications. "Remove anyone who needs to give more than a week's notice. I need someone now." She nods, scratching names off her list.

"Okay, that leaves us four, Ali, Hannah, Meghan, and Aggie." My breath catches at the name. *Aggie?* There's no fucking way it's the same Aggie. But, fuck... *what if it was?*

To have her working beside me every day? *Heaven.*

I don't listen as Jill tells me about the others. I'm sure they're all good enough, but I want to know if it's *my* Aggie. Clicking the file open, I wait for it to load.

"The last, Aggie Hope," Jill says, and my body heats hearing her full name. *Fuck, it's her.* My attention is fully on what she has to say now. "She can start immediately, some great references from the gallery, and a handful of other jobs." My face is as blank as ever, but my heart pounds in my chest like a jackhammer. Could I hire her? We don't have any rules about dating in the workplace. *Shit, I'm getting ahead of myself.* For all I know, she could still be with that dickhead I escorted to the back of the plane the other day.

"Is she the only one who can start immediately?"

"No, there are two others. Shall I organise interviews?" I nod, disappointed that we have to go through the process when I already know who's getting the job. I open up the diary to see when I'll be free to sit in on the interviews. *Shit.*

"I don't have time to sit in with you." Jill frowns and I realise my mistake. I never interview. That's always down to her. I don't say anything. I don't need to explain myself. Jill knows me.

"Okay. I'll interview like *normal*, then give you a rundown."

"Arrange it for tomorrow. The sooner they start, the better."

"Consider it done," she says as she stands and leaves.

"Aggie," I murmur to myself. *She applied for the PA position?* I can't keep the frown and small smirk off my face as my mind reels with questions. Did she know it was to work for me? If not, will she like that it is? What will she think when she walks in on her first day?

Yeah, I'm definitely hiring her. I shoot a message to Raff, my housekeeper, with a list of things to organise for Aggie, things she'll need when we're not here. I've not been able to get her out of my head since I walked away from her on the plane. I had to sit and listen to that arsehole of a boyfriend tell me just how selfish she is for not giving him the seat; that she knew it was meant to be his, and took it anyway. If only he knew it was me who upgraded her seat just so she could have some peace from him.

I look over Aggie's application again. She's twenty-nine—fuck, almost ten years younger than me. She worked at the gallery on the seafront before she quit and went travelling. How have I never seen her around? She's been gone for months; I wonder if New Zealand was her only destination? I have so many questions. Where else has she been. There are so many gaps in her history; are they all from travelling?

She's so free.

Unrestricted.

An ache settles in my chest; it's almost uncomfortable. The more I think about it, the more I think I envy the freedom she has. Would that mean she wouldn't stay as my assistant? How long would she wait before she leaves again?

Clicking out of the file, I backtrack to find the original email she sent with it. I'm not sure how I feel about her applying for the job after we met. My name's all over the form. Finding what I want, I scroll to find the date: three days before we met. I'm oddly relieved, but then why didn't she bring it up when we talked?

An hour later, Jill emails me to confirm the interviews for tomorrow. Aggies' is at eleven-thirty. I just wish I could be here to do the interview. Unfortunately, I have another, more pressing matter to deal with, in the form of my parents.

Chapter Nine

Colour

Aggie

Sliding the wooden door of my studio open, it squeaks in protest as I push it along the wall, and back closed again after I step inside. The smell of paint hits me, and I immediately feel at home. *I've missed this.* Travelling has my heart, but painting has my soul singing with excitement.

The small space I rent doesn't look any different from when I left it, although I expect that Layla cleaned the dust away before I returned. This is what I needed: to be here, if only for an hour or so.

My eyes sweep around the room, familiarising myself with what I have again, and how I left things. My finished canvases are stacked against the far-right wall, under the frosted stained-glass windows. The drying rack just to the left sits full of finished and half-finished paintings from before I left. In the opposite corner awaits my coffee machine. It's seen better days, and only just manages to make a coffee, without spurting too much water everywhere else but the mug.

My collection of paints, in every colour imaginable, are placed next to the machine, in a tall self-built cabinet with a pegboard to hang them, so I can see them easily.

Leaving the large open space in the centre of the room, where my easel leans with a blank canvas already placed and secured, ready for me to apply what my mind conjures.

I squeal excitedly, doing a little spin on my toes in the centre of the room, sparking to life an idea. I practically skip over to my rest area, grabbing a sketch pad and pencil on my way. Filling up the water on the coffee machine, I flick it on, placing my mug under it before I pop the pod in the top. Waiting for it to come to life, I drop myself into the pile of extra-large soft cushions, all different textures and colours. I sink into them, my still-tired body relaxing the moment my arse hits them, my imagination running wild with the idea like I can already see the finished painting hanging on the wall of an enormous house.

My toes point in eagerness. I've not danced ballet in years, but it would fit in perfectly with my new collection.

I start to draw, my pencil flying across the paper as the idea unfolds before I forget because I have to leave soon for this job interview... the first of three I have lined up. I thought I would have more time for this before I had to look for a job, but fate has other ideas. And I'll go wherever she sends me. Life's more fun when you go with the flow.

I had to restrain myself in the studio. I had the overwhelming urge to strip and get messy with my paints; it was hard not to get stuck in and put some colour to the collection of drawings I've created on my travels, but I'll be back there tonight.

My first interview was a no from me. On paper, it was perfect. Good hours, decent pay, but I didn't fit. The dress code would have cost me a week's wage, and it was implied I'd need to smarten up for the job. *No, thank you.* Go fuck yourself. I didn't say that, obviously. Just left with a smile.

This one sounds just as good though. A personal assistant for Cerberus Security. I didn't see the details as Layla did the application for me. I read over the description; it sounds interesting, plus it has flexible hours. I don't know what that means. But if it gives me time to paint, I'll be happy.

Smoothing my hands down my skinny jeans, I step into the foyer, looking over the sleek, modern black interior as I walk towards the reception desk. After giving my details, I'm asked to sit in the small waiting area until my name is called. I watch men and women come and go. Most of the people who walk past are in suits or combat-style gear. Some in gym wear. It's confusing, but I watch with eager eyes, taking in the way it works around here.

The lady at the reception desk seems to run it all. She knows everyone's names, along with what they are supposed to be doing. She's on the phone giving orders, with eyes glued to the screen as she works.

"Miss Hope, I'm ready for you now," she says as she stands and moves around the desk towards me. Standing as she approaches, I pull my bag to my shoulder and yank down my jacket that's got caught in the back of my jeans.

I'm led to a small office, where she sits on the other side of the table.

"I'm Jill," she says, introducing herself and gesturing for me to sit. After making me a cup of coffee, she asks the normal questions: why I want this job, what will I bring to the position, and if I'm willing to work late or odd hours. I give my answers as best I can. I like her, and we seem to get on, because in between each question, we get off track and chat easily about other things.

"Well, Aggie, I like you. I have to put it past the boss first, but I'd like to offer you the job. You seem like a good fit for Cerberus, and the personal assistant position would be perfect with your experience."

"Thank you. I'm excited to start."

"I'll call you later once it's all finalised. And get the paperwork started. Are you able to start tomorrow?" That's sooner than I was expecting, and my hope of getting some more time to paint deflates a little.

"Sure," I say with false confidence, not wanting to admit I still have no idea who I'm going to be a PA for. "What time?"

"Meet me downstairs at eight, and I'll get your access cards registered."

"Perfect."

I hit the ground running. I walked in this morning, and Jill gave me the papers to fill in, an NDA to sign, a laptop, and work phone and told me *he's* gone away on business, and I didn't need to be in the office. I could work from anywhere. I knew I should have looked at the application last night, but I was so happy, and too deep into painting an explosion of colour to worry about the finer details.

Now, I feel bad for not knowing who I work for. I guess I'll find out sooner or later. Someone will say his name eventually, right?

He left me instructions to get to know his diary and organise... well, everything. Looking at it, it's a mess. But I'll get to that later. I also don't have an office or a desk to work from. Jill said she'll have that sorted in a few days. I laughed as my imagination ran away with me, seeing myself sitting in a small cupboard under the stairs, while my new boss sat in luxury.

After handing me everything, Jill gave me my first job: to deliver a painting to his house. So, I stash my things behind her desk, only taking my small bag with me. I don't have a car yet, so I order a taxi.

Two minutes away. Perfect. My fingers run over the large, wrapped frame, wondering what sort of art he likes. I don't like to judge people, and I have no idea who my boss is yet, to even get a read on the type of person he is, let alone to speculate on the sort of artwork he would hang on his walls.

People always surprise me with their tastes.

When I arrive at the front gates, they open like they're expecting me. When the driver pulls up to the door of a massive, modern McMansion, I can't help but stare at just how beautiful it is. Enormous window walls, looking out on to the stunning grounds.

"You must be Miss Hope, his personal assistant," a man, who I can only describe as butler, says as he walks down the stairs towards me and the painting I have securely in my arms. "I'm Raff. I look after the house and grounds." He holds out his hand for me to shake. He didn't say my employer's name either. Damn.

"Aggie," I greet him, shaking his hand.

"Jill told me you were heading this way. I'll show you where your office is here, for when you need it."

"My what?" I say, and he frowns.

"He didn't tell you, did he?" He shakes his head, rolling his eyes.

"I've not met him yet, for him to say anything." *Him, he, his.* It's *definitely* a man. I need to brush up on my detective skills. Not that I have any to start with

"From the way he spoke this morning, it was like he'd already met you," he says, tapping his chin. "Anyway, this way." Taking the painting from my hands, he leads the way into the house, and my eyes bulge at the luxury of the place.

As he leads me towards the back of the house, room after room, he points out what they are as we pass, like I'll remember. Stopping at a giant kitchen, he tells me I can help myself when I'm here. This all feels weird. Not in an impending doom sort of way, but in a 'why am I being allowed into his house' kind of way, given access to his home and food, when I only started today. Like two hours ago?

"This is your pass key for the house. It will allow you access to all the main areas. You've been emailed the security information, event schedule that his parents sent over this morning, tailor information, along with his mother's contact details for correspondence."

Holy fuck. I may be in way over my head here.

"I'm sorry, what?"

He spins around, pinning with a look. "It's everything you will need to make his life a little more stress-free."

"Okay," I say, accepting my fate.

"A word of warning. His mother can be a little full on. You're best to stay on her good side." *Noted.* Avoid as much as possible.

"What will happen if I get on her bad side?"

"Not much. Her bark is worse than her bite. She has a plan for him, one that he has no intention of seeing through, but she's... determined."

"How long have you worked for the family?" It's obvious he knows them all well.

"A long time." He smiles. I'm somehow glad *he,* whoever my boss is, has Raff on his side. We walk for a few more minutes in silence before we come to a door filled with coloured glass windows.

"This will be your office when you're here, Aggie," he says softly, as he opens the door and steps into the most beautiful space I have ever seen.

"No," I say.

"Yes, Miss Hope." He laughs. "All yours." I feel like I've just been given the keys to a new flat, one that's bigger than any flat I've had before. The room is bigger than Layla's entire downstairs. Bigger than my last studio flat before I left. It's warm and bright, and everything looks so expensive that I'm too afraid to move. The desk sits in the middle of the room, full of everything I would need. "He asked to give you this," he says, handing me a leather wallet. I open it to see a bank card and a small piece of paper, with the information written on it to set up the banking app.

"What's that for?" I flip the wallet closed and try to hand it back.

"Expenses. He doesn't expect you to pay for anything. This will cover whatever you need. *His* words, not mine." He smiles again while I wonder if any of this is normal for a PA. I have no idea. It seems a lot.

"I'll leave you to get settled in." He turns, but I can't stay here. Not in a house I don't know, working for a man I don't know.

"No, I won't be working here today, but thank you," I say, moving to catch up with him.

I slip the leather wallet with the bank card into the back pocket of my jeans and pull out my phone, ordering an Uber to take me back to the offices.

"Miss Hope." He frowns. "He wants you to be comfortable."

"Why? I've never met him." When he doesn't answer, I blurt, "I'm sure I'll use it, but I have some things to take care of back at Cerberus."

"It was good to meet you, Miss Hope. I'm looking forward to working with you."

Chapter Ten

Bogus

Ethan

Three days; that's how long it's been since Aggie started the position as my PA, and I've not seen her beautiful face, not once, and it pisses me off. The day Jill hired her, I got called away with the guys to our northern branch to oversee some of the tactical training and medical refurbishments we've been putting in place.

I put everyone on edge because I knew Aggie had been to my home, and I was fucking hundreds of miles away. Every question they asked was met with a grunt or a glare.

I was never like this with my ex. Never this obsessed with seeing her, or wanting to speak to her. What's got into me?

When I walked back into my house last night, I could smell her; the lingering scent of sweet peppermint, and wondered if she was here working late. I wandered down the halls in the vain hope of catching a glimpse. But Raff informed me she'd not taken to the office I'd fitted out for her. She'd not even sat in the leather chair, or used the coffee machine.

I know she's been working remotely, but where? Jill said she had no clue, but her workload had decreased, so she didn't care, as long as she had less to do.

I shouldn't care either, but I do.

I want her to be comfortable while she's working.

Where has she been working if not at my house or Cerberus? *Home?* Where does she live? I open the laptop, ready to find out, but slam it shut again. *Okay, stop, that's taking it a little too far. You've met her once, you had a few conversations on the plane, then you touched her up in your sleep. Let's gain some distance and think before you act.*

Today's the first day back in the office. It's early, with only me and Leon in today.

All the correspondence between me and Aggie has been through Jill. If Aggie knows it's me, she hasn't said anything. And if she doesn't, she'll be in for a surprise when we have our first meeting today.

There's a fizzing anticipation under my skin.

I'll see her today.

Over the last three days, she's reorganised my entire calendar; she's managing my time more efficiently already, and we've not even spoken. Even down to where my meetings are held—making people come to me, instead of me going to them—that alone has saved me over two hours a day.

There are a few questions I have about some blank meetings she's scheduled. I don't know what that's about. I'm sure it's just a mistake on her part.

Opening the computer back up, and clicking on the calendar, I add in a meeting of my own, and hit send. Within seconds, it's accepted that she'll attend, and my anticipation soars at the fact that Aggie Hope will be sitting in my office within the next hour. It's going to be torture waiting for her to walk in.

Fifty-eight minutes later, I smell her before I hear the faint knock at my door. Her scent relaxes my shoulders as it weaves through the gaps in the door, permeating the air in my office.

"Come in," I murmur. I gulp, eager to see her. The handle moves down, and I lean forward, resting my elbows on the dark wooden desk in front of me. I see rainbow fingernails as she pushes the door open. Too fucking slowly. My eyes travel up her arm, and over to her face as she comes into view.

I'm holding my breath.

"Morning, Mr…" The words die on her tongue as she looks up from the pad she has in her hand. "Ethan?" she chokes, her tone subtly shocked, her entire frame changing from professional to something more personal. "What? No way?" she stammers, her voice higher than I remember.

God, she's beautiful.

She backs away before taking a few steps closer. I stand, righting my already perfect tie, to keep my hands occupied, and come around the desk, forcing my lungs to take a steady breath.

"Aggie," I say, my voice deepening with how good she fucking looks in tight-fitting jeans and a bright green loose shirt that dips low at the front.

"What are you doing here?" she asks, confirming she had no idea it was me she was working for, and I relax a little more.

"This is my office." She's just staring at me, like she can't get her head around what she's seeing. I walk right up to her. The smell of her perfume, or shower gel, gets stronger the closer I get, making my mouth water. *Does her skin taste like it?* "You're my personal assistant." She's so close I could touch her. "Will this be a problem?" I ask, as she rakes her eyes over me from my dress shoes to my clean-shaven face. A pleased grin graces her face. The corner of her beautiful lips tipping up to show the glint of her teeth underneath. We're only a foot apart now, but I want to be closer.

"No, it kind of makes it better, actually." She smirks, and my cock agrees, growing thicker in my briefs. "I didn't know."

"I know," I say, her body language gave her away. My hand moves of its own accord, reaching for the sleeve of her shirt that's rolled up to her elbow, feeling its softness between my fingers. My mind clears of anything but her. Her breath hitches as her eyes flick to mine, tracking the way I'm watching her lips, and the soft exhales that escape.

"Mr Ford," she breathes, stepping back a fraction, "we have things to discuss, *work* things." She clears her throat, like she's trying her best to be professional. It snaps me out of whatever that was she held me in.

Fuck, she's intoxicating.

I grunt, walking away from her, hating our distance already. My mind starts to buzz from too much going on and not enough time, like it does every time I work. It leaves me exhausted. I perch on the edge of my desk, my eyes still fixed on Aggie as she walks over to the chair and sits down.

"I have some questions," I say, attempting to get back to work.

"So do I, but I bet they're not the same ones." She giggles, lifting her eyebrows.

"What did you want to know?" I ask, and she falters, shaking her head.

"No, you first, then we'll see about mine." Taking the scribe from where she placed it on the chair, she clicks it on, sliding the pen out slowly, I've never seen anything so provocative, as it slips from its holder. *It's a fucking pen.*

"I appreciate what you've done over the last few days while I've not been here. I'm sorry I couldn't be here sooner." She crosses her legs, and it makes them look even more tempting. Longer somehow.

"There's no need to apologise, Mr Ford." Goddamn, I like the way she calls me that. "You were called away. I've seen the notes and actioned what was needed. I've placed the orders, and Jill's been informed of the changes you wanted to make to the staffing positions at the York base." I'm taken aback for a second, processing what she's done since I made those notes last night.

"Next time, you'll come with me." I don't know why I said it—it was never my intention to have her travel with me—but now I have, I can't say I'd change it.

"I'm sorry?" Her eyebrows rise again, and I like getting this reaction from her. Like that she's challenging me.

"I said, next time you'll come with me," I repeat, widening my legs as I fold my arms over my chest.

"Yeah, I heard what you said. Maybe you should ask if I would come with you next time?" A gruff laugh escapes my lips. She freezes at my reaction, staring at me like I've lost my mind. I don't remember the last time I was pulled up on my behaviour.

"I'll ask," I say after a second.

"You know, Ethan, I've been told you don't laugh often. Or smile, for that matter. And in the two minutes since I've been in your office, you've done both."

"I hadn't realised I'd smiled. I'll rein it in." This time it's her who laughs. It's like a balm to my soul. I fucking love the sound.

"You have a sense of humour too," she mocks.

"No, just a reputation to keep. Our little secret?" I nod towards her.

"You'll have to try harder, Mr Ford." The way she calls me Mr Ford should be kept for the bedroom only. I'm going to enjoy working with Aggie. She's the calm my mind needs.

"Down to business. You had some questions," I say, grumbling, trying my best to remain impassive. She takes one last look at my lips, her fingers drifting across her own, like she's thinking about kissing me, before her eyes lower to the pad in front of her.

"Why do I have an office in your house?" she questions, diving right in. I'll be honest-ish.

"I need you close. You're my personal assistant. If I'm working from home, you'll need to be there too, so having your own space seemed like the right thing to do." I also want her in my home as often as I can. I want her smell in every room, in my bed, on my pillow. I don't say that though. Instead, I watch her contemplate my words.

"It's bigger than my old apartment." *Really? Fuck?* How big is her new one? It must be bigger, or she would have said.

"There's not much I can do about that," I add dryly, and her eyes sparkle.

"You've also given me a bank card and full access to your house. Is that normal for a personal assistant to have?" She's tapping the pen on the edge of the pad. Is she nervous to ask me these things?

"I don't know, but it's what you'll need going forward, and I expect you to use the card for anything you need."

"Okay," she tells me, but I have a feeling she won't use it for herself like I want her to.

"Where have you been working from? Jill said you've not been here, and you've not been at my house, so where?" My question surprises me as well as her; she blanches, only a fraction, but I catch it.

"I hadn't realised you were keeping tabs on me. I've been working from... *home*." She's hesitant at the last word. "Is that a problem?" *Yes.* I want to say. I want to know where she is, always. Is that unreasonable for someone I've met twice? *Yes.* But no fucks given.

"No, not when I'm away, and you can't make it."

"Good. Jill and I are sorting my space out this afternoon, for when I'm here."

"Great, I'll need you with me more often than not." She is my assistant, after all. "I have some blank meetings in the diary. Is that a mistake?"

"No." She shows me the calendar. "This is time I've carved out for you to do whatever you need." I draw a blank, having no idea what she's on about.

"Whatever I need?" It's a foreign concept to me.

"Yeah. Going through your diary for the last year, I noticed you don't really do anything for yourself. So, I've scheduled you in some time."

"That's..." I don't know how to finish that. "Thank you. You went through the past year's diary and everything we have coming up?" I'm not questioning her; it just shocks me that she's done it.

"Yes." She's not apologetic. Why would she be? "If that's all, I need to sort out my new office, and I've got some things to collect for you for your next meeting."

"Where did you learn all this?" I want to dig deep into how she works, what she knows. *Everything.*

"I did an online university business degree while I was travelling a few years ago."

"Impressive," I say, raking my knuckles on the desk. I'm not ready for her to leave yet. Even if she'll still be in the building, I want my eyes on her.

"So, is that all?" she asks again.

"Fine," I grunt. "I'll need you here for the meeting to take notes for me, and I have a dinner reservation tomorrow. I'll need you to be there too. You'll need to call the restaurant and add yourself to the table. Familiarise yourself with Mr Deakin's business." He's an arsehole, but a key client.

"I will," she says, backing out of the office and leaving me with a hard on the size of Everest, as I watch the sway of her hips in those tight jeans.

Chapter Eleven

Tricks

Aggie

I got to the restaurant early and am waiting outside for Ethan, my Hot Boss, and Mr Deakin to arrive. On the way over in the taxi, I wanted to go over everything I've learned about Mr Deakin, and from what I've heard from Jill, he's a bit of a prick, but brings Cerberus a lot a business. But I got distracted by my search for solutions for why I came home, forgetting all about the notes completely.

It's been playing on my mind, the reason why I'm back. I need to do more to help myself. I just don't know how, so I googled it. *Memory loss,* not for the first time, but this time I kept looking. Hence, the distraction on the way here. The article I read led to another and another, and the hour's ride took no time at all.

The articles made me realise I need to try more things. I've never shied away from anything other than this, but this is something more. Something I'm almost scared of. I'm scared to find out about where I came from, but I need to, or it will drive me crazy not knowing. I've never shared this detail of my life with anyone. Too afraid to admit and come to terms with my own reality. Because I know I can't answer the questions that will follow, so until I can, it will remain a closely guarded secret.

I've skirted over what happened to me as a child, brushed it under the rug, not wanting to admit or deal with it. I know I need to; that's why this article caught my attention.

Triggering, it's called. A full, scientifically proven study, *I think,* or a strategy on how inducing endorphins can trigger emotions, so that the mind can be tricked into experiencing a memory.

Simple, right?

I don't have the memories, but maybe it… something, will force my memories to come forward. I don't know what I experienced before that day, so I have to try everything. Something has to work, right?

It's a good place to start. I've been to therapy, but all it did was remind me I was on my own and I quit.

Looking down at my phone again, it says to start with something light like eating chocolate. Fuck that, if I'm doing this, I might as well make it a little more daring.

My heart thumps, wondering if it will work, and what, if any, memories it will bring. The side effect of not remembering is, you don't know if they'll be good or bad, if they eventually come back.

I can only hope they are good.

My mind wanders with all the things I could do to kick start the process.

Diving, climbing, high wires… there are too many of them scrolling through my mind.

Clicking the scribe open, I make my own notes on things I'd like to do. Starting with rock climbing. Getting my phone back out, I search and there are some places close by, a few are indoors, but I prefer to be outside. If I'm to do this properly, I may as well do it how I like.

Booking the appointment for the following day, I block out my time as unavailable in the diary and send Ethan a note that I'll be away from my desk for a few hours, but I'll make it up the same day.

I'm so distracted, I don't hear my new hot boss approach until his hand lands on my lower back. I flinch until I realise it's him, then my body turns molten. My eyes close at the contact, as his fingers press gently into my soft skin through my jacket. Standing at my side, Ethan hums, like he likes the way my body feels against his hand.

"Mr Deakin, this is my assistant, Miss Hope," Ethan says softly, bringing my attention back to the man in front of me. I plant a smile on my face, hiding the embarrassment of being too distracted to see them approach, and then by Ethan's touch.

"It's lovely to meet you, Mr Deakin," I say, extending my hand. My cheeks heat as I step forward to shake his hand. Only he leans into me, kissing my cheek, too close to my mouth. I cringe, twisting as far away as I can, but then he lingers a little longer than acceptable. I frown, shocked by his forwardness, and start to pull away as soon as I can.

When I look over Mr Deakin's shoulder, I find Ethan glaring at the man holding me, his face rigid, those grey eyes stormy, focused on where his client just kissed me.

I gesture towards the door and urge them through, doing my best to ignore the tick in Ethan's jaw as we step into the warmth of the foyer. The maître d' greets Ethan like an old friend, eye-fucking him like she knows what's underneath the suit. But even she gets a grunt from him in response. I give her an apologetic smile after handing her my coat. Even if what she was doing was inappropriate, she didn't deserve that. What's crawled up his backside?

Ethan's face remains like stone, his whole body radiating tension, like he's ready to explode. Why is angry so hot on him? I want his hands on me; I want to feel that tension up close. I want to feel it over my skin. I gulp down the urge to make him madder, and bite my lip instead, grinning to myself, as he silently ushers me in front of him.

"What was that?" Ethan growls, causing my skin to shudder at his deep tone. He steps close behind me, his hand once again on my back, only this time it feels like a claim, his fingers sliding around my waist possessively as we enter the restaurant.

"What?" I murmur, confused, turning to see him over my shoulder.

"You let him *kiss* you," he hisses through a clenched jaw, and I spin around, my hand landing on his warm chest, and I momentarily forget what I'm going to say as his heat radiates over my palm. I gulp again, this time for a very different reason as the heat between my thighs intensifies from just a touch.

"What was I supposed to do? Move away and ask him not to touch me?" *I was caught off guard, for fuck's sake.*

"Yes," he states, before he moves around me, so he's turned away from our table. His face is so close to mine, I can taste his breath: rich dark chocolate and mint. My eyes dart to his mouth. I want to lick his lips, relish the richness on his tongue. His hands on my waist creep up, his thumbs brushing tenderly just underneath my boobs. My vision blurs slightly at his touch. Then it's gone. Leaving me standing there, dazed, like nothing and everything just happened.

I watch him as he strides to the table, standing behind his chair. I clear my throat, not sure what's just happened between us. My hand drops back to my side as I stand there, contemplating his reaction.

"Are you joining us, Miss Hope," Ethan exclaims, pulling out a seat for me next to him, and away from his client.

"Yes, sorry," I apologise, doing my best to walk the last few steps to the table as normally as possible, a strange energy flowing between us. This best not last long, If Ethan's going to be in a mood the entire meal, then I'm off as soon as I can break free. I plan on ending my evening well. Not stuck between grumpy and slimy.

Underneath grumpy would be satisfyingly satisfying.

I squash the images playing through my mind of Ethan, hovering over me, trying to focus on why we're here.

Why are we here?

As I sit, Ethan slides my chair a fraction closer to his. I frown at him while our guest looks over the wine list. Ethan gives me nothing other than his stern, hard jawline as he picks up the menus and hands one to me.

Ethan doesn't say much while we order. In fact, he leaves the conversation to me and Mr Deakin. I ask him everything I can think of: work, family, friends. And he's happy to answer them all. I have no idea why I'm here. There's been no talk of business, and he could have done this meeting on his own.

Ethan nods and murmurs the odd word of agreement when our drinks order arrives, keeping his opinions of Mr Deakin's family affairs to himself as he tells me of his *'current'* wife and how they spend most of their time apart. A not-so-subtle way of telling me he's willing to see other people, and his wife won't even know.

Taking an enormous sip of fruity wine, I jump when Ethan's knee knocks into mine, almost spilling my drink. The zap of electricity that shoots up my leg from his touch makes me shudder. I expect him to move it back or give me some sort of silent apology, but he doesn't. In fact, he presses closer, widening his legs to keep touching mine.

My breath catches, but I cover it behind my wine glass. I have no idea what's happening. I like it; I want the touches, big or small. I sneak glances at the grump when the waiter arrives and pours more wine for us.

There's an ease to his features as I press my hand to Ethan's thick thigh, as I twist around to reach for my bag on the back of my chair to check my phone, testing what's happening between us. Ethan shifts his leg closer, causing my hand to slip a fraction further up, and I hear a strangled groan from his throat. I smirk, knowing I caused that reaction.

When I move my hand away from his leg, Ethan hooks his foot around my ankle, my entire leg from knee to ankle now resting on his, beneath the table, out of sight for everyone but us. I watch as his face relaxes, like he's satisfied we're touching.

We listen to Mr Deakin as our food arrives, and we eat, Ethan's solid, warm thigh against mine. It may look like I'm listening, but my mind is on the rigid man next to me. The way his hand holds his drink, his long, thick fingers wrapping around the glass as he lifts it to his mouth, sipping the amber nectar in a way that makes my body ache, and I feel that familiar itch to capture him in a drawing. The raw masculinity as his throat bobs with each swallow. I'm a hazy, wet mess.

My mind's eye flits back to the moment I woke on the plane, the way his hands felt on my skin. The need I felt to have more of him, to keep him touching me. Will it happen now that I'm working for him? With the soft material of his trousers pressing into my bare leg, my head is a mess, along with my knickers. I'm only given a brief interval when his phone rings, and he steps away from the table. I'm lust drunk, leaving my leg with goosebumps.

"You'll have to come to my new place on the coast, Aggie. It's stunning. You could pack for a weekend. I'd love to show you around," Mr Deakin says from across the table, and it's like a bucket of cold water has been thrown over me, bringing me back to reality.

"That's very kind of you, Mr Deakin..." I say, trying my best to think of the best way to turn him down without being disrespectful.

"Please, call me David." He leans slightly forward.

"David," I say tentatively, "unfortunately, I won't be able to. You're a client, and it would be inappropriate of me to accept your offer." I watch as Ethan makes his way back to our table. I'll make my excuses in a minute and leave; they don't need me here. I don't want to catch any more unwanted attention from David.

"If you ever change your mind, you have my number." I do have his number, but you can be sure I will not be calling him.

"If *what* changes?" Ethan almost sneers, sitting back in his seat, looking between us.

"I've been trying to get your sweet assistant to come and stay at my new property on the coast," David says, swirling his wine around the glass before taking a sip. Ethan's eyebrows raise a small fraction as his eyes crinkle at the corners. You can barely notice his eyes darken on the man opposite me, but he remains as stoic as ever. Only I can feel the sheer disdain rippling from him. I wonder what would make him snap? If I'll ever see the true Ethan, the one he keeps under wraps. I don't believe for a second that this is the only version.

It can't be.

"And what did *my* sweet assistant say?" Ethan's cool tone sends a chill down my spine as he rests his fisted hands on the table, his knee coming back to rest next to mine.

"She turned me down," David admits, and there's a slight twitch to the corner of Ethan's mouth, and I want to smile at him in return.

What did he think I'd say? *Yes, sure, I'll come and spend the weekend with you.*

"Perhaps the boyfriend wouldn't approve?" David asks, his eyes drifting to my left hand. No ring there, sunshine. Subtle way of asking if there's anyone in my life.

This is one of those situations where you know you can't tell the truth, because if you do, you'll need to sit through more of the one-sided flirting. And batting them off is exhausting.

"I'm not sure he'd take to me spending the weekend with another man, David," I say, my voice small. Ethan coughs as he takes a sip of his drink, and to my disappointment, he moves his knee away. "As a matter of fact, I'm meeting him shortly." I don't look, but I can feel Ethan's eyes on me the moment the words leave my lips. He has to know I'm not telling the truth; he saw me break up with Jasper. He cuffed him and led him away. He can't think I'm still with him, or that I've got myself a new one in the space of a week.

Pressing my hand to Ethan's leg once more, my fingers skim the fabric, but again, he pulls away from my touch. It leaves me feeling rattled as I take out my phone. Tapping on the screen, I book a ride home. "If you don't mind, gentlemen, I need to leave you to it." There's an Uber eight minutes away.

Both men stand as I do, David wishing me a good evening, and Ethan moving with me when I step away from the table. He ushers the server to get my coat, like he can't get me out of here fast enough.

"I'll just make sure she gets to her car safely," Ethan says, looking down at my empty glass of wine, then nodding towards Mr Deakin as the waitress pours him another glass. He just smiles as we leave the table.

Taking my coat from the server, Ethan helps me put it on, holding it for me, his hand skimming the back of my neck, when he slides the coat up my arms. Butterflies erupt down my spine, dancing their way to my stomach. He frees my hair from the back as I tighten the belt around my middle. "Are you driving?" he asks, his tone clipped. I've only had two small glasses of wine. I'd never put myself at risk like that.

"I got an Uber."

"An Uber?" he says, sounding confused, and I smile. He opens the restaurant door for me. Thanking him as I pass into the cold evening air.

"Yes, the car company that picks you up and takes you where you need to go," I add sarcastically, shoving a hand in my jacket pocket, while I check the app with the other, showing him it's only a few minutes away.

"I know what it is, Miss Hope," he says as I move down the path, away from the window of the restaurant. "What I don't understand is why?" I shrug.

Leaning against the wall, I place my phone in my pocket. Ethan stands in front of me, looking at me before he moves closer, too close really. His hand comes to rest above my head as he leans dangerously into me. *Fuck.* I'm not sure. I feel like I'm going to burst. He's so close I can feel his warmth through my jacket as he leans down. There's nothing but him, all around me; it's breathtaking. Just like him.

"Tell me, Aggie. Are you still with him?" His lip curls upwards as a snarl escapes. My core instantly wants to feel him inside me. The sound alone is enough to make me whimper. By some magical force, I manage not to.

"Who?" I murmur, my breathing picking up as a fire spreads to my entire body. His eyes hold mine, a turbulent grey like a storm rolling in.

"Jasper-fucking-Isaac."

"No," I blurt.

"Then who?" His eyes smoulder, and his forearm rests above my head. There's barely a breath between us. I swallow down any air I can, only I can *taste* him; the drink he sipped before we came out, sweet and spicy. I lick my lips, hoping to get another fuller taste of him.

"No one, I lied," I admit. It's breathy but I can't help it.

"Thank fuck," he breathes as his mouth crashes to mine, his free hand coming to the nape of my neck, holding me closer as he takes my mouth with his, teasing, tasting, and nipping at me like he can't get enough. His fingers slip into my hair as I open for him, my entire body moving from the wall to press into his. My nipples hard, brushing against the soft fabric of my bra, causing me to moan into his mouth. I need to touch him; I never got the chance before on the plane. But before I can get my hands out of my damn pockets and on him, he pulls away, leaving us both breathless. Kissing the corner of my mouth, his thumb trails my lips, swiping along my skin, before he lets go. My tongue darts out on instinct to taste where he touched me. Leaning into me, his nose nudges my ear, his hot breath making me shiver.

"Never wait outside again, not by yourself. You either ride with me, or wait inside," he rumbles into my ear. My pulse races. "It's not safe, Aggie." And no matter how hard I try, I can't seem to settle my heart from beating out of my chest.

Is he... watching out for me?

"Ethan, I..." I have no idea what I want to say, but my heart grows in my chest, liking the idea that he wants to care for me. My mouth and brain catch up pretty quick. "I'm a grown woman, Ethan. I've taken care of myself all my life. I don't need you stepping in now." Yep, I said it. My mouth ran away with me when he's only trying to be nice.

Damn it.

"All your life?" he questions, and I blink it away, not willing to answer, because I can't. I don't know if it's been my entire life or not. I watch his hands move to my waist. I'm lost in thought. The hole in my chest that's always been there grows a little deeper, and I turn away.

"Answer me, Aggie." I shake my head. Ethan steps away, giving me the space I need, his hand pressing firmly into my waist for a paused moment. "I'll get my answer one day," he says, removing his hand as he turns away, leaving me standing there.

"Have a good evening, Miss Hope." His deep, almost baritone voice rumbles through me, making me quiver as he walks back into the restaurant.

It takes me a moment to realise my ride is here. As I step towards the waiting car, I feel his eyes on me.

Chapter Twelve

Stolen Kisses

Ethan

I have every intention of kissing Aggie again. Fuck, she felt amazing as I backed her into the wall last night. I hardly touched her, and she didn't even touch me, but it was like my body ignited as soon as my lips brushed hers. I'm hellbent on doing it again, capturing her delectable mouth.

I want to discover… everything about her.

Not just how she feels, and how she tastes, but I want to know her favourite food, her preferred coffee, how she takes it, everything… every fine detail of her life I want to learn from her lips.

But I can't find her, I know she's here, I saw her ride pull up half an hour ago, I've just checked her office, and she's not there again. I've walked around the house and nothing. Where the fuck has she gone? She let slip something I know she had no intention of telling me yesterday. Has *my* Aggie really had no one to care for her all her life? She closed up so quickly after that, I knew to step back; to give her space, I could see the flash of panic in her beautiful eyes. I'll get my answers when she's ready. But in the meantime, she'll have me. Any way she needs me.

Knowing she's near is wreaking havoc on me. I'm hyperaware of her. I know she's close, but I can't see her. I'm wishing I had a smaller house right now. Fewer rooms to search through.

It took everything I had to move away from her last night, to take my lips from hers. The second she said she'd lied about the boyfriend, the relief I felt was inexplicable. I didn't want to wait. I couldn't.

Fuck, she felt like magic on my tongue when she parted her lips for me. The hint of wine on her tongue making her taste so much sweeter.

I'm on the phone with my mother and have been since she arrived. She's been arguing about the arrangements for the charity gala we're holding next weekend. I walk back to my office to check the security feeds to see if she's left and I hadn't realised. I also haven't seen Raff, which isn't unusual, but he usually hovers just in case I need anything. Taking the phone in my hand, while my father drones on about placements and appetisers, I click on the screen and scan the inside cameras first.

Nothing.

No Aggie, No Raff.

Switching to the cameras that cover the outside. I'd have no idea if she left in her car because she got a ride again today. *Where's her car?* She ignored my question last night about why she was getting a taxi. Scanning the seating areas, I spot her and Raff sitting outside. Laptop open, phone to ear, one hand making notes.

Shit, she looks good.

Why is she outside?

I watch as Raff tries to make them both a hot drink, from the pot, cups, and selection of teas he's arranged on a tray, but she drops her pen and swats his hand away, saying something I can't hear before Aggie pours them both a drink. Raff laughs as he stands and heads towards the back door, sipping from the cup in his hand.

Why isn't she working in the office?

I hang up on my mother, fed up with listening to her wanting to change everything I've already put into place. I head out of my office, passing Raff on my way.

"She smiles more than you," he says with a smug look on his face.

"Arsehole," I mutter as I make a beeline for the kitchen.

Opening the back doors, I step onto the large terrace, trying to remember the last time I came out here. I head towards the wisteria-covered seating area, currently being occupied by Miss Hope.

She makes everything look brighter, more inviting.

"You have an office, Miss Hope," I say as I approach where she's sitting crossed legged at the table, cushion in her lap, looking comfortable. She flicks her gaze to me before settling it back on her laptop.

"I like to be outside, Mr Ford." The corner of her mouth raises, almost smiling.

"Please call me Ethan," I almost beg, but my voice thankfully stays its natural tone. The way 'Mr Ford' rolls off her lips, I imagine what I can do to them.

"But you have an office." I don't know why I'm arguing with her. Aggie shifts, unfolding her leg, letting it dangle off the edge of the seat. She's wearing a short black skirt over tights.

"I know, it's very… beautiful." Why does that feel like an insult? I look back at the office I had fitted out for her, confused. It's got everything, art on the walls, sculptures, everything, a lavish desk, and coffee machine. No expense spared.

"Meaning?" I ask, moving forward, eager to be closer.

"It means that today the sun is shining, and I'll be working from this very spot until I finish at two." Huh.

"Why not the office?"

"Is my work getting done?" She's making a point. And I think I'm going to lose.

"Yes, I just…"

"Then I see no need for me to be tied to an office desk," *Jesus-fuck*, she said it, not me. I have to force my eyes to stay open as I conjure images of her tied to my desk, me taking care of her every fucking need, while she comes so hard she passes out. I edge closer until I'm standing by her side. She looks up at me, her eyes daring me to challenge her. "When I can, I will sit outside and enjoy this amazing garden you have." The sun has already made her cheeks a little rosy, even if it's October. It suits her. *I wonder if her whole body would flush as she comes undone?*

I'm getting way ahead of myself.

"Then I'll join you." My eyes wander over the hard seating; it looks like it's going to bite my arse.

"You don't sound so sure, Ethan." I'm not, but I like being wherever she is, and I want to kiss her again, and I can't do that if we're in separate offices.

"I'm sure." Shooting a quick message to Raff to bring my things outside. I sit next to her at the large outdoor table, sending a few emails from my phone as I wait for Raff. Leaning back, I watch her work, her fingers flying over the keyboard. The skirt she's wearing slips higher on her thigh as she hitches one foot under her arse. Showing me a glimpse of her creamy thighs. *Stockings* she's fucking wearing stockings.

"You're staring," she says, her gaze landing on where my eyes have been trained on her thighs for the last few minutes.

"I am." I can't help it.

"Why?" she asks, turning to face me.

"You're finishing at two? Why?" It's my turn to leave a question unanswered.

"You're avoiding the question, but I have an appointment I need to keep." She smiles. "I'll make up my hours later today. I should be back by four at the latest."

"There's no need to make it up." She's already done everything I needed today.

"I will. Oh, and about last night." Shit, she's going to tell me she hated it. Does she think it was a mistake? I don't say anything, I just let her continue. "You kissed me."

"I did." Best god-damn kiss of my life.

She slowly stands, and I watch with fascinated eyes as Aggie stretches her arms over her head, elongating her body. Her chair scrapes, moving back as she does. My dick's throbbing at the sight of the black lace circling her thigh. I get up, moving the chair to stand behind her as she lowers her arms.

She doesn't flinch at my closeness, but the gooseflesh that scatters over her skin has my hand rising to trace her neck.

"Did you enjoy it?" I whisper into her ear, my hands coming to the hem of her skirt. My cock hardens with each touch. My fingers skim the silky cream skin just beneath the fabric, and she shudders as she inhales a breath.

"Best kiss I've had in a long time," she says as her hand joins mine at her thigh. Her delicate fingers trace my knuckles, giving me goosebumps of my own.

"You're my boss, Ethan," she states, like she's trying to deter me from what's about to happen.

"That I am, Aggie." My fingers trace circles on her thigh. Her breathing picks up a notch. Fuck so does mine.

"This would be a bad idea," she whimpers as my hand creeps up under her skirt. Her hand drops from mine.

"Not a bad idea. It's a fucking excellent one," I murmur, sweeping my tongue along her neck.

"Ethan," she rasps. My lips trace the column of her throat. My free hand comes around her neck, cupping her jaw as I turn her head and capture her lips with mine. Softly this time.

I'm in no fucking rush to end this.

My hand stills on her thigh, pressing her back into me, her arse fitting against my hard on. I groan into her mouth as she licks my lips, parting them.

"Do you want this, Aggie?" I mumble, parting us briefly, "Do you want my hands on you?" I palm her soft flesh slowly, getting dangerously close to the apex of her warm thighs. "Touching you." My lips seal over the pulse in her neck. "Do you want me to please you," I say, smirking into her softness as she groans, "in every way I can?" I need to get my answer. I have to ask. I won't do anything more without her consent.

"Yes." It's so quiet, I barely hear it.

"Yes, what, Aggie?" I tease, my tongue lapping at the skin on her neck, like it's the sweetest treat; my taste buds salivating for more.

"Yes, Ethan, touch me. I want your hands on me. I have since you felt me up on the plane." She smirks breathlessly.

"I knew you enjoyed it." I smash my lips to hers again as my hands fist the material on her skirt, she grinds her arse into me. My dick's ready to break through my trousers as her soft arse settles into me, like it belongs. We kiss like we need each other to survive.

"Ethan." She turns her body to mine without breaking our connection, cupping the back of my head like I am hers. Gripping her thighs, I lift her up, sitting her on the edge of the table, her legs wrap around mine.

"Are you wet for me, Aggie?" She nods, her heat grinding into my groin. "Show me."

"Here?" she says, her hooded eyes flicking to mine, unsure.

"Right fucking here," I growl, bending to nip her lip with my teeth. "Show me, Aggie. Show me what I do to you." I gulp in anticipation.

I can barely breathe when she reaches between her legs and slips her finger into her underwear. Her legs fall from around my waist when I widen them so I can see her perfectly. She moans the sweetest fucking sound I've ever heard. Aggie guides her hot pink knickers to the side, she slides her finger through her folds. I watch the movement like I've never seen anything like it before.

She's captivating.

I catch the smallest glimpse of the butterfly tattoo, which rests against her inner thigh, and I'm jealous of its permanent position. When she brings her glistening fingers out, I almost sink to my knees and take a taste for myself. I don't have to think twice as I hold her hand steady, dragging her fingers over my lips and onto my tongue. Sucking them into my mouth, her eyes roll to the back of her head.

Flawless.

She tastes as sweet as she smells.

"Incoming," Raff shouts through the back door. It's our code for my parents. *Fuck.* Why now? Of all the moments to turn up.

"My parents are here," I grunt as I kiss her lips, letting her taste herself.

"Your parents?" She looks confused for a second until it registers. "Shit." She jumps off the table as I step back. Aggie pulls her skirt back down, before she takes her seat like nothing happened. Only the slight flush on her peach cheeks giving her away.

Fuck, this is going to be fun.

Chapter Thirteen

That Mouth

Aggie

Oh my god, I'm a mess on the inside as Ethan's parents walk through into the garden. Ethan's heated eyes are shining as he smirks, darting his tongue out, and running it along his lip, where he rubbed my wetness a few seconds ago. His eyes close, like he's savouring the taste, before he schools his features. Back to… indifferent?

My heart races as his words play over and over again in my mind. *Do you want me to please you in every way I can?* I don't know how it happened. I was sitting next to him one moment, and the next, his hand was making delicious waves over my skin. Then, he kissed me again. In all my twenty-nine years on this planet, I have never gone from zero to a million on the horny scale from just one touch. God, it was good. I felt him on my lips and under my skin the entire way home.

One touch and I was soaked.

I'm never going to stop him from kissing me. I like the way it makes me feel. Like I'm alive for the first time in years.

His parents walk over to us, and his mother's eyes land on me as Raff trails behind them carrying Ethan's laptop, as his father aims for the man who just rocked my core.

The stoic man that is Ethan, who just tasted my... arousal, licks his lips again. His eyes heavy for a moment, he stands like nothing happened. I'm doing the same thing, burying myself in emails and reports, but smiling, I can't stop smiling.

But damn him, my insides are twisted.

My eyes rake over him, immaculate suit, hand in pocket, and there it is, the evidence... the very big bulge in his trousers. Obvious, if you look, and I'm looking. It's straining against his zipper. Big, thick, and it pleases me that he's just as affected as I am.

His mother leans into Ethan. Just as he runs a hand over his mouth. Slow motion pictures move faster than what I'm seeing now.

Shock rakes my system.

Ethan smirks, like he knows he's unable to do anything. His grey eyes on me, instantly making my core flutter. He rolls his lips, tasting them with his tongue as his mother presents her cheek for him to kiss... *he wouldn't?*

He's going to kiss his mother with my wetness on his lips.

His eyes stay on mine. I want to look away, but I can't. He's watching my every reaction. Ethan sucks his bottom lip into his mouth just before he presses his cheek to his mother's in greeting. *He didn't.* A small sigh of relief leaves my lips; no one hears it but me. I'm mortified at how close he came to *doing that.* But weirdly, and worryingly, so turned on that he's tasting me on his lips, I press my thighs together.

I want to finish what we started.

My eyes are on Ethan. The rush I feel is like nothing I've experienced, and my mind flashes with colours and music. But just as quickly as it came, it's gone. Faltering for a second. I try to regain the sliver of a memory that just ran through my mind, before I regain myself.

What the hell was that?

I absentmindedly shake his dad's hand as he introduces himself with an easy smile.

"You must be the assistant?" His mother's tone is tart, like she already dislikes me. I nod, doing my best to focus.

"She has a name, mother. Aggie, this is my mother, Florian Ford, and my father, Charles Ford."

"It's a pleasure to meet you both," I say, extending my hand to meet his mother's. She ignores it, gracefully pressing her lips together as she turns to her son. Ethan shakes his head at her but says nothing as they all walk away together.

I sit back down, busying myself with my work for a while, as they talk about next weekend's gala, in full earshot just a few meters away on the other side of the terrace. I catch all the changes they want to make. I shouldn't be listening, but I can't help it. I'm also making notes of all the things I'll be expected to do as a result of their conversation.

Finishing the analysis Ethan asked for this morning before I arrived, I email it to all the owners of Cerberus. Looking over my laptop, I see Florian take something from her bag as she walks up to me.

"You'll need this," she says, handing me a little black book.

"Thank you. It looks like one of those books people used to have full of women's names." I laugh, but she's not laughing with me. Okay, not the joke type of person. Ethan's out of earshot as him and his dad walk the garden.

"It is," she scolds. "*His* little black book." She grins, looking over to Ethan before dropping it into my lap. What? She can't be serious, who even has one of those? And why would his mother have it?

"There are names in here of all the women he... *should* be seen with at the galas, balls, charity events, and even casually. We have a reputation to maintain." Wow, she really means business. There's a small pinch in my chest.

"Great, do I pick them out, or is that left for you?" I pause for a second, "Does Ethan get a say?" I shoot off the questions my brain thinks are most important, only to get a glare in reply.

"These women are important and influential. With you as his assistant, you'll need to make sure he's with one of these women every time he's photographed."

She's serious. Poor Ethan, but I get it. It's his life, not mine. If this is what happens, this is what happens.

"I'll make sure of it," I say, flicking through the book, seeing dozens of names, with details of who they are, their relationship status, work position. There are a few other numbers and symbols written down—things that don't make sense. Is it people he's... dated? Slept with? Wined and dined? I'm not sure I want them to make sense.

"Good. They'll help raise his profile." I look over at the man in question. I'd say his profile is pretty good. A gentleman, kind, protective, a little scary, successful, and so good looking it could actually hurt your eyes. There's a lot hidden beneath the surface that I want to discover and hold as mine. *Hold as mine?* He's almost ten years older than me. The fleck of grey hair at the sides of his short army cut hair just makes him more distinguished.

"I'll make sure it happens," I add, remembering what his short hair felt like beneath my fingers. I have no idea if this black book is something Ethan would want or not.

"I'll let you know who will be joining you this time. I have your details."

With that, she stalks back towards the house, and I pack up my things.

I wave at Raff as I pass him in the hallway. I need to change my clothes before I head to my first rock climbing lesson.

"Ouch," I cry. That hurt. Shaking my hand out of the rope after it pulled on the skin of my hand. I'm on a fake, but hazardously high, climbing wall in the middle of a field. It's over thirty metres tall, and I've just climbed to the top. The thrill that ran through my veins was bliss, but no memories came to mind. Nothing, it just leaves me disappointed, even if I'm glad I tried.

Standing at the top of the wall, my lungs heaving, my muscles burning from the climb. I take in the view. Grey clouds, that's all I see. It should be sweeping meadows, a vast landscape of trees and greenery from the farmland below, but the weather turned just as I made it to the top; now it's just grey skies and raindrops. The ropes securing me to the wall are so tight against my skin, I'm sure I'll have marks tomorrow.

"Careful on the way down. It'll be slippery," the guy next to me says, before he makes sure my rope is secured.

"Miss, if you're doing this, you need to make it quick or take the covered stairs down. We need to be gone before the wind gets any stronger and starts to blow you around." That has me sold.

"Okay," I lean back, not wanting to waste any more time here. I like to finish what I start. And it'll take a hell of a lot less time to get down than it took me to get up here. I make the first jump. The rope tightens, and I fall the first few feet securely. My feet land on the wall as the rope and harness hold me tight.

As I push again, releasing the rope to send me down, my foot slips, and I yelp as I'm propelled and spun sideways into one of the fake rocks attached to the wall, my arm slamming into the rounded edge. Tears well as I bite the inside of my cheek. The pain doesn't last long; the discomfort ebbing away as quickly as it came, leaving a dull throb behind.

Fifteen minutes later, I sigh as I settle into the car, flicking my wet hair back. I never regret anything I do. It all leads me on the path I know I'm meant to be on, but right now, I want to eat junk food and cry into my pillow.

It was supposed to work. I was meant to have... I don't know, *something*. What else can I do if this doesn't work? How else can I bring my memories back? I need this void inside me to come alive and tell me what I need to know about myself.

It's all missing.

I open my notes app to find my list and tick off rock climbing, adding a sad face emoji after the tick.

No one has ever told me the truth about how I became a foster kid. All I know is that I have no family, none. It's always been just me.

I remember the day I met my foster family. It was late, really dark outside when they took me in. I remember it vividly, every detail, every thought I had, every emotion that ran through my body as I cried.

What I don't remember is anything before that. Nothing. It's blank. Blackness.

Nothing but a hollow void in my mind and deep emptiness in my heart.

Chapter Fourteen

Too Far

Ethan

Me: Cerberus office today.

Aggie: I know.

Aggie never came back to my house yesterday. She said she would make up her hours, even when I told her not to. But she never came.

To my annoyance, I kept watching out for her.

I know she knows where we are today, it's all in the shared diary, but I wanted to make sure she knew I'd be here.

Is she avoiding me after yesterday? *Maybe.*

Did I take it too far?

Fuck. I took it too far, didn't I? I crossed the line. She's my assistant. *She let you. She said yes. She wanted you to touch her.* I watched her walk away yesterday. I watched her arse sway from side to side as she left my home without even a backwards glance in my direction.

My annoyance grew the further away she got, not at her, but that my parents interrupted us. Fuck, I was ready to have her on that table, spread out wide, my tongue inside her pretty hole. I would have made her come repeatedly. She has no idea just how much I'd get off seeing her come over and over again. *In my hands, by* my hands.

I'm in a foul mood today because of it. Because I never got to hear her moan from my touch, and she never came back when I desperately wanted her to.

I did some digging last night to check that the ex-boyfriend is nowhere near her. It's safe to say that he's back living with his parents, over two hours from where we are. He's an arsehole I never want to see again.

It's only seven. I'm here early, but I see her walking into the office just as I take a seat and fire up the laptop.

"Aggie?"

"Morning," she says, as she walks up to my door, dropping her bulky bag to the floor as she comes towards me. She places a large takeaway coffee on my desk and walks back out again. She looks even more beautiful today with her legs covered in a pair of black wide-leg trousers that fit perfectly snug over her backside.

"Aggie?" I shout before she can disappear. She stops, turning with a smile; the way it highlights her eyes floors me. "You're in early?"

"I'm your assistant, Ethan. You're here, I'm here." I frown.

"How did you know I was here?" I ask.

"I have my ways." She smirks. "You like to get an hour's work in before any calls, and your first one's starting in just over an hour."

I don't answer, just watch as she walks away again. I pick up my coffee, taking the first hot sip. Perfect. Black, with a hint of vanilla. I've never told her how I like my drink. How does she like her coffee in the morning? Walking out the office, I'm greeted by Leon's smiling face, which annoys me as he's blocked my view.

"Who got you a coffee?" Leon asks.

"Aggie," I state.

"Oh, your new assistant. She seems nice, best friends with Layla." I'm not surprised he knows this. This guy has been obsessed with Layla for well over a year now, but apparently, she wants nothing to do with him.

"We have a meeting at eight. Some of the newer recruits are being signed off from training, and we need to assign their first jobs." I ignore him. I know what the meeting is about, as I had Aggie set it up for me.

"Did you see where she went?" My eyes scan the area, not seeing anything.

"Aggie?" His eyes light up when I nod my answer. "Yeah, the small cupboard on the opposite side of the offices. I think that's where Jill set her up. Not ideal, but it's better than nothing." Bristling at his words, I step into him without thinking.

"The cupboard?" I growl. My blood simmers at the thought of her shut away, especially when she said she likes to be outdoors. The fucker's grinning face smiles wider at my reaction.

That won't do. I'm not having her in a room with only a small window.

"Yeah, it looks good for a small space. Jill and Aggie did a great job," he says, rubbing his hands together like he wants to say something else.

I storm past him. It's unacceptable. I mean, I can't have my assistant on the other side of the building. I round the corner of the small corridor, seeing the door shut. I don't bother knocking, swinging the door open, making her jump as I step in.

"Ethan, what are you doing?" she says, standing from the small desk in the corner. Closing the door behind me, I place my nearly empty cup in the bin.

"Come here," I say. To my surprise, she rounds the desk, coming to stand in front of me. "You won't be working in here." My frustration shows as I clench my jaw.

"This is where Jill set me up, Ethan. There's no other space for me to have an office."

"You'll work from mine," I tell her, my tone final. I have no idea how it will work, but it's the best idea I've ever had.

"Ethan, be serious. I can't do that." She crosses her arms over her chest, but all it does is highlight her perfect breasts in that shirt.

"I'm serious, Aggie." There's a beat of silence, and I move forward, crowding her. "Grab your things," I growl, watching her eyes heat at my words.

"Mr Ford." Her voice is low, almost unrecognisable, as she places her hand on my chest. It's my undoing. My eyes dip to her throat, watching as she swallows.

"Miss Hope." The air is tense around us, and when she bites her fucking lip, I lose it. Taking her in my arms, the need to feel her overwhelms me. I pull her into me, spinning us around and backing her against the wall. She's tall, but I'm taller. Thoughts of her under me make my pulse race. Before I can make another move, she's tugging my head down and crashing her lips into mine.

Fuck, yes. She's kissing me; not holding back. I grab her thigh, hitching it, fisting the material before I slide my hand up to palm her arse. I've never felt this feral for a woman in my life. Not even my ex-fiancée.

I'm hard in seconds as she grinds into me. My hips piston of their own accord, creating the friction we're both seeking. Aggie moans into my mouth. My aching cock begs me to go faster, harder. Our kiss turns messy, my tongue searching her mouth for more.

"Ethan, this could get complicated," she pants, breaking the kiss.

"Only if we let it," I murmur, taking her mouth again as my hand reaches the curve of her breast, tracing the outline with my knuckles as she arches her back from the wall. My thumb rides the hardened peak of her nipple through her blouse and she gasps, her warm breath on my cheek.

"Fuck... Ethan," she stammers, as I descend my mouth over the soft, flushed skin of her neck, trailing wet, open-mouthed kisses to the hardened peaks through her top. The electric blue material darkens as my tongue swipes the sensitive bud before I take it into my mouth and pull.

The sound that leaves her lips makes me do it again. Garbled words, followed by a cursed, "Yes." I unbutton her shirt while she works my belt free from my trousers.

"Can I touch you?" I ask. She pulls away, her flushed grin teasing me. I want to see how far that flush goes over her body.

"I think we're past that, Ethan." She looks down at my mouth hovering over her nipples. "But, fuck yes, touch me, take me, give it to me." I do just that, tugging the cup of her bra down to reveal the soft pink bud waiting for my attention. I take it between my teeth, flicking the end with the tip of my tongue. She tastes sweeter than I could have ever imagined. She slides the zip on my trousers down, palming my dick, the pre-cum already leaking through my boxers. Fuck, that feels good. The base of my spine sparks to life as she wraps her hand around my length, through the thin fabric of my boxers. I grit my teeth together at just how fucking good it feels to have her hand on me.

"You're massive," she murmurs. My dick thrusts into her hand.

She slides her hand from my neck to unbutton her trousers, slipping them to reveal a tiny triangle of bright blue material covering her mound. I trail my fingers from her breast to her stomach as my mouth continues its assault on her perfect nipples.

"I can smell your arousal already." I trace the line of her underwear, my fingers hovering over the tattoo I've yet to see in full. I'm a goner, my mouth salivating with the need to taste her again. It won't be here; the first time I take her with my mouth, I want to hear her scream my name.

For my ears only.

My mouth moves to hers again, as I move her underwear to the side, feeling her for the first time.

My heart almost stops. She feels like silk, undeniably irresistible.

"Ethan." She shudders, and I play with her core, teasing her slick folds.

"So wet," I murmur into her neck. My finger glides through her arousal as she grinds onto my hand. I know what she needs, and she'll get it.

"Eth..." she moans as I skim her clit, her own hand leaving my cock, as she slips it into my boxers to take my bare length into her soft warm palm.

"Fuck, Aggie," I hiss as she pumps my length. *Jesus-fuck.* My head drops to her shoulder as I try not to come in three seconds flat. I slide my middle finger into her warm, wet channel, holding it there as she gasps from the intrusion, her walls fluttering.

She twists her hand slightly, adding a gentle pressure where I need it. I need her to come quickly. If she carries this on, I'm not lasting any longer than a horny bull. I add another finger, stretching her before I pump them in and out, slow at first, but the more feral I feel, the faster I go. Her arousal drips onto my hand as I suck on her neck, wanting to leave my mark.

"Harder," she mumbles as her head tilts back. I set a punishing speed, fucking her with my fingers, and she takes everything I give her.

I want to bring her to her knees, where I've been since the day we met.

Our breathing intensifies, and our kisses grow frantic. Her legs start to quake as I curl my fingers, searching for the spot that will have her screaming out in pleasure. The tips of my fingers graze the bundle, and she clamps down, holding me tighter as she comes undone all over my hand, my mouth covering hers to capture the sounds of her pleasure.

I want them as my own.

My release fires out as she continues to pump me through her orgasm. My balls draw up as I come in my underwear with such force, I can barely breathe. Roaring into her mouth as she sags against me, spent, exhausted, beautiful.

"Fuck, Ethan." She winces as I remove my fingers, still holding me as she comes down.

"Are you okay?" I ask, trying to catch my breath. She nods, then gives me a weak but breathy, "Yes."

"How am I meant to work with you when I know what your hands are capable of?" I smirk, lifting my fingers to my lips as I taste her release. Her eyes flutter closed when I suck them clean. Aggie's hand is still around my semi hard cock, her fingers smearing my release over my dick.

"If you keep your hand there, we'll be doing that again very soon." She grins, looking even more beautiful with her flushed cheeks, chest, and stomach. "I will fuck you against this wall."

"You could, but you have a video call in…" She pauses, glancing at the watch on my wrist. "Twenty minutes, and apparently, you're making me move offices." She shifts and starts to redress herself. She takes a small pack of wipes from her bag, offering me one to clean myself up.

"Damn, I was looking forward to having you in the cupboard." I groan as I kiss her swollen lips.

"Ethan Ford, we're going to get in so much trouble." Chuckling, she buttons up her shirt. The wet marks from earlier are still there. She sighs, and I shrug in response. I'm not sorry.

"I co-own the company, Aggie Hope. I can cause as much trouble as I want." I'm never getting over this; I never want to.

Chapter Fifteen

Fancy

Aggie

Yesterday, Ethan had my desk set up in his office. I tried to help, but he called in everyone else and made me sit at his desk while they set me up on the opposite side of the room. To be honest, Ethan's office is big enough for another four desks, with extra space to spare.

I was only worried about this setup for a few minutes, but after I got myself a coffee and him his afternoon cup of tea, we just slipped into a flow. It was still tension filled, and distracting every time he walked past, or moved or grunted, and when he removed his jacket, rolling up his sleeves, I had to force my eyes away from the veined thickness of his forearms.

But we work well together.

Every now and then, I'll catch him staring, but then he'll catch me too. It's foreplay at its best. I want more of what we did yesterday so badly, it's all I've been able to think about between calls, and meetings.

It's different today; we're busy and people have been coming in and out of the office all day. I feel like the phone is currently glued to my ear, with the number of requests for Ethan to join meetings from Cerberus to his parents' business.

I've declined them all.

There is no way he can do all of this by himself. It's too much for two people, let alone one, however good he is. He needs to say something to his mum and dad. Ethan told me he wants nothing to do with their business, but it seems his parents have other ideas.

I can see why he needed me; just doing this alone would take up so much of his precious time. At least I can politely refuse them. I think Ethan just blocks out their constant nagging. I have no idea how he does it—they are just relentless. I'm currently sitting with my head in my hands, silently groaning as I watch his mum call yet again—this one I send to voicemail with no guilt.

I have the joy of his mum coming in later, something to do with the gala next weekend. I have his suit ready to be collected and hung at his home, and a spare one to hang here if he works too late to go home.

I've spoken to her more times than I can count today already. She's rude, obnoxious, refuses to let me deal with anything, and only wants to speak with Ethan. What have I done to piss her off?

Exist maybe?

That seems about right from the way she speaks to me; her husband, on the other hand, I like him.

The phone starts again. Peeking through my fingers, I see it and groan. She huffs when she hears my voice.

"Is my son incapable of answering the phone to his own mother?" she shouts.

"No, Mrs Ford, he's in a meeting. And can't get to the phone right now," I say for the hundredth time today.

"I need to speak with him. Now. It's urgent." I take a deep breath, which I hold for a few seconds, before I answer. She should know the drill by now.

"May I ask what it's regarding?" I cringe, palming my head in frustration.

"No, you can't. It's none of your business." I can hear her husband in the background, but I don't catch what he says. "But if I have to talk to you and not my *only* son, then please inform him that I need him to check the seating

plans for next Saturday. I need to confirm the name of his date for the gala."
Interesting.

"If you'll hold for just a second, I can check that information for you," I say, not letting her speak before I press the button to let her listen to awful hold music. I know she hates it, since she told me last time I did it. I look over to Ethan, who's deep in conversation with Leon in the central area. I stand and poke my head out of the door.

"Mr Ford, I have your mum on hold. Again." He turns to face me, making Leon pause whatever he was saying.

"*Ethan*." Ethan torts back to me, frustrated at calling him Mr Ford, and I roll my eyes. "Hang up on her," he says, and I stifle a laugh with my hand. "She'll be here in an hour anyway."

"I can't hang up on her, *Ethan*. Why does she keep calling. It's a tiny bit frustrating." I add, and excessive. I stand from my seat, and lean against the door frame. So I can hear them better.

"I know why," Leon says, looking at me, as I step out of the office, phone in my hand. I frown, confused. But he doesn't explain, just offers me a drink and makes his way to the kitchen to get them. Ethan says nothing about his mother, but stands from his chair and walks over to Cole's office, where he taps on the door.

"You got a spare minute?" he asks, his eyes bouncing between me and Ethan.

"Sure, what do you and your lovely woman need?" Ethan just shakes his head.

"I need you to block my mother for a few days."

"Again?" Cole says, and I hold back a laugh, knowing it's not the first time.

"Please," Ethan murmurs.

"I'll wait till her calls cleared."

"Thanks," he says with a nod.

"Anything for an easy life," Cole shouts as Ethan walks back into his office, his jaw tight as he passes me.

And I want to take it away. The time I scheduled for him to take for himself, he used to do more work. Maybe I need to rethink how I can get him to relax. I'll have to get creative.

"I have something for you," Ethan says, passing me. I hold up my finger for him to wait as I bring the phone back to my ear so I can get rid of his mother. When I take the phone off hold, a message pops up on my screen.

Mr Ford: *You'll pay for shushing me later.*

My cheeks warm as I read it. In my silence, his mother starts yapping while I send him back a message of my own.

Aggie: *I hope so, Mr Ford.*

He reads my message, his reaction making me sweat in anticipation. He curses under his breath, then moves like a tiger stalking his prey. He sits at the edge of my desk, eyes on me. I swallow, looking up at him, unable to look away. My teeth sink into my lip as his thigh brushes my arm as he shifts closer. Is this what edging feels like? Because what he's doing right now is torture.

I've never been a thigh person, not until I saw Ethan in his expensive suit; the way the material moulds to his skin, like he was born to wear it. Each one cut exquisitely, enhancing what he hides underneath, the power and elegance of the English gentleman that he is.

I want to strip him bare, slowly, so very slowly... run my hands over the muscled ridges that bulge through his shirt and trousers. My arm jerks as Ethan nudges me to hurry up, snapping me out of my lust haze. His mother's still on the other end of the phone and has no idea I'm daydreaming about doing very unladylike things to her son.

I focus back on the phone call, hoping my voice comes out normal and not like I'm in heat, ready to hump his leg.

"Sorry," I stammer slightly. "Mrs Ford, Ethan's in a meeting with Leon at the moment, but he'll see you in an hour." I hang up and put the phone down on my desk.

"Hang up next time," he growls, standing from my desk, and I get an impeccable view of his backside. He shuts his office door, turning the lock, before walking over to the far side of the room, opening a door I thought was a cupboard, and steps inside.

Huh.

I scurry to his side to take a peek. It's an en-suite bathroom bigger than Layla's kitchen.

"I had no idea this was here," I say, gazing around the hidden room.

It's all black marble tiles, highlighted by gold finishes; masculine, but it has a comfort to it. It's so inviting, I can see myself taking a sneaky shower here. When he takes a garment bag from the hidden door beside the walk-in shower, I step closer.

"This is for you to wear," he says, turning to find me close to him. There's a slight lift to the corner of his mouth, like he's pleased. "What's wrong with what I'm wearing?" I say, looking down at my leopard print pencil skirt and oversized jacket. His eyes roam from my heels, up my legs to my jacket, which has nothing underneath. He doesn't know that bit. I wanted to surprise him if anything happened again.

"What you're wearing now wouldn't look right at a gala."

"A gala?" I ask.

"Yes, next Saturday's gala." I want to ask if I'll be there as his assistant. I know we've messed around, but I'm not sure I'm date material. And after what his mother said, I assumed he already had someone from his little black book escorting him, and he'd just not confirmed it with her.

"With me," he states, like he can read the question on my face. "Try it on."

"Now?" I ask, a little shock in my voice.

"Yes," he demands. I love it when his voice gets low like that.

"Has anyone ever told you how demanding you are, Ethan? And no, if I'm going with you, it'll be a better surprise when you see me there. I'll try it on later." I'm desperate to take a look though.

"I won't be meeting you there. I'll be picking you up." Oh. I like that. "A date," he clarifies.

"A date, to a gala?" I ask, cautiously, I've been on plenty of dates, but none quite so formal. He doesn't say anything else. Just continues to stare at me, a slight frown to his perfect brow.

Ethan lifts his chin towards the bag, encouraging me to look. Taking it from his hands, I hook it up on the shower screen and unzip it. Why am I nervous about it? *Because the hot billionaire just bought you something to wear for a date at a gala.*

Yeah, that would do it.

My hands shake a little as I separate the sides of the bag, revealing the most stunning white-gold dress I have ever seen. It's dusky pink lining gives the whole dress a soft glow, and under the shimmering white gold beading, it clusters into stars, which are woven into every inch of it.

It is subtle, understated, and yet completely extravagant at the same time.

I'm speechless.

"Ethan," I whisper, more to myself than to him, as I continue my perusal. Daring myself to touch it, but too afraid to.

I run my fingers over the inch-wide straps before turning it to see the back, but it's backless. A cluster of beaded stars at the base of where the dress will sit on my back.

My breath hitches at just how beautiful it is. "Ethan, I can't accept this," I say softly, stepping away from it. I want to run my hands over the material, I want to see how soft it would be against my skin. "It's too much. I have dresses I can wear." Sort of, I could wing it, but there's nothing compared to this. I feel him behind me before he speaks, his tone low against my ear, as his hands encompass my waist, pulling me to him.

"You'll wear the dress, Aggie. And you'll look even more beautiful in it than you do in your jacket and skirt." He kisses my neck, making my skin erupt once again in goosebumps.

I have no idea what is happening between us, but I like it. And if I had to guess, he does too, from the way he kisses me, to the endless touches he ghosts over my skin, when I walk past him, hand him a file, or even pass him his morning coffee. There's something there.

"First, we need to talk."

"What about?" I ask, leaning back into him.

"Tell me you'll wear the dress." His warm breath races over my skin.

"I'll wear the dress." I moan as he lightly bites my neck. I whimper when his hands start to edge up my stomach, where he proceeds to pop open the buttons on my jacket. I'm naked underneath, and I think he's just noticed. My insides coil in anticipation as I wait for his response. His breath hitches as his hand squeezes my breast.

"You've been naked under here all day," he growls, as his teeth scrape the curve of my neck. My entire body almost convulses from the pleasure he's raking over my skin. "And you didn't tell me."

"It would have ruined the surprise." My voice isn't mine.

"You did this for me?" I can feel him smiling against my skin. His hand covers my breast, lightly tugging my nipple, and I almost fall to the floor.

"Yes." I've never dressed for a man before, but this morning I wanted to do something that would make him smile.

"I need to take you on a date before next week. I'm not sure I can hold on much longer, Aggie."

"Why wait?" I tease, needing him just as much.

"I like to do things… my way, Aggie." What does that mean?

"Ethan, your hand is on my god-damn tit," I purr, not willing to give up the moment when I know just how skilled he is with his hands.

"Tonight, Aggie, I'm taking you out." He groans, buttoning up my jacket. He spins me to face him. "When I take you for the first time, Aggie, it won't be in a bathroom like some seedy fling. It'll be in my house, in my bed." His large hand cups my cheeks, swiping his thumb over my lips, before he places a soft, chaste kiss there. When he steps back, I get my smile. It's not much, but I'll take it.

"Like I said, we have a few things to discuss first."

I can't focus; I'm having some sort of out-of-body experience. My misfiring mind, unable to catch up with just how quickly Ethan could stop himself.

"Okay," I manage to say, as he zips the dress bag back up and leads me back to his office. I sit back at my desk going through the motions until it's time to leave. I gather my things, but before I can leave, Ethan stops me.

"How are you getting home?"

"Uber," I say.

"No, not safe."

"It's fine."

"Where the fuck's your car?"

"I don't have one. There wasn't much need for one while travelling, so I sold it before I left."

"Right." He doesn't seem happy with the answer.

"My driver will take you home tonight, and you'll use him to go wherever you need to go from now on."

"Ethan, there's really no need." I try, but the look on his handsome face tells me I'll be doing whatever he says.

"There's every need, Aggie. You work for me now."

Ethan's driver dropped me off about an hour ago, and I've been raiding my limited wardrobe for something to wear to our date tonight. Only, I have no idea where we're going or what we're doing.

Is it right to be dating my boss?

It just makes it harder to choose what to wear.

Layla walked in just after me and has been less than helpful since I told her I was going on a date with Ethan. I swear, her jaw hung open in shock.

"I still can't believe it, Ethan Ford. *The* Ethan Ford, the man who can scare the demons out of you with just one look, is taking you on a date?" I frown.

"I didn't mean it like that. He just never talks, hasn't dated anyone since..." She lowers her head as she stops talking.

"Since..." I mimic, trying to get her to finish what she started to say.

"Since he broke off his engagement."

"Engagement?" I mumble. I mean, I hardly know the man, but I can't see him being engaged to anyone. It actually gives me an odd feeling in my chest.

"Yeah, I can't remember when it was, but no one knows why he put an end to it. I remember reading about their separation in the news."

"Wow."

"Ethan Ford," she says again, and I throw a shoe at her.

"Help me decide what to wear, Layla," I beg as she throws it back at me, just missing my leg.

"Where is he taking you?" That's the million-pound question.

"I don't know," I say honestly, looking through my small collection of tops I have.

"He didn't tell you? Not even a hint." I pull out a red blouse.

"Nope."

"Message him. Tell him you need to know." Bringing up Hot Boss on my phone; yes, I changed it, this seemed more appropriate, I type out my message.

> **Me**: I'm having a wardrobe crisis.

I hesitate before pressing send, wondering what he'll say. I burst out laughing when I get a quick response.

Hot Boss: I can send a stylist over, give me thirty minutes.

Then I panic.

Me: No.

Me: Don't be ridiculous.

Hot Boss: If you need the help, Aggie, it's there.

Me: All I need is a hint to where we might be going or what we might be doing tonight.

Hot Boss: I could tell you in a message, but I'd prefer to have you naked before I tell you what I plan to do to you tonight.

I beam at his response, my skin flush with hot ideas of just what he might do to me.

Me: I need to know what to wear, ready for you to take off.

Hot Boss: Anything will be good on you.

Me: You're not helping.

Hot Boss: Casual. We won't be going far.

Me: Thank you.

Hot Boss: *winking emoji face*

I burst out laughing. I think messaging Ethan has just become my favourite thing to do.

Chapter Sixteen

Casual

Aggie

If this is what Ethan calls casual, we may have a problem moving forward. I'm in jeans, boots, a camisole top, and an oversized, thick cardie. I've done my hair in soft curls and added a little makeup. But Ethan... *goddamn him,* is still in a suit. All be it a different one, but still an expensive three-piece suit.

That he looks divine in.

As always.

It's annoying, but I think I can live with it. I mean, he's great eye candy every single day. Nobody, and I mean *nobody,* would pass up seeing his fine arse in suit trousers every day.

"I thought you said casual?" I scowl, looking him over as he drives us to wherever we're going. His brow furrows for a second, looking down on himself. "This is one of my more casual suits. What's wrong with it?"

"Absolutely nothing, it looks... good on you. But my version of casual is... well, this." I gesture to myself. "Next time you tell me casual, tell me smart, then we'll be on an equal footing when we go out together." *Next time.* I said it; it's out there. I want there to be a next time, and we've not even been on a first date yet. We're quiet for a while as he drives. If he notices, he doesn't say anything. "Do you even own jeans?"

"No." A simple answer, but my mouth hangs open anyway.

"No? You can't be serious." I'd spit my drink out if I had one.

"Of course, I own jeans. I just prefer a suit." His lip twitches.

"Thank god, I was about to take you shopping." I turn, facing him as the car slows down. "You made another joke. I was beginning to think the first one you made was a fluke." There's that slight lift of a twitch of his cheek again. And my heart does a strange bump thing. His hands grip the steering wheel as he turns into the car park. "Where are we?"

"Livington." Fucking hell, he's frustrating.

"I got that, Joker. Since it took us all of three minutes to get here."

"We're about to have a private dining experience from one of the top chefs in the area." Of course, it wouldn't be a movie and snacks.

"And I'm in jeans," I add sarcastically. To which I get a shake of the head as he gets out of the car.

Opening my door, I push it open, but I freeze as Ethan glares at me. He opens the car door the rest of the way, offering me his hand. When our hands touch, a spark runs the entire length of my arm. Is it just me? I don't think so, but I doubt he would ever admit to anything like that.

When I'm standing in front of him, he draws me in, our bodies touching, and the sparks continue to fly across my skin. Ethan tucks my hair behind my ear. "From now on, I'll be the one to open your door," he murmurs against my lips before he kisses me.

"I'm perfectly capable of opening a door, Ethan."

"I never said you weren't capable," he adds, kissing me again. "Just because you can, doesn't mean you should." He eases back to look me in the eye, that damn brow raised again.

"Ever the gentleman," I tease.

"You have no idea just how un-gentlemanly I can be, butterfly." *Butterfly?*

"Jesus, Ethan. You can't say shit like that out loud." I smile. "It does things to a woman."

"Does it do things to you?" he grumbles in my ear. I flush as heat crosses over my body, my head slowly nodding my answer. I can already feel his erection hardening against my stomach. If we carry on like this, we'll never leave the car park.

"Just how I like it." He nuzzles my neck, his teeth dragging over my skin, before he steps away, leaving me wanting. "Let's go." He takes my hand in his and leads me towards a small backstreet building. My lust fog simmers away as we get closer to the almost derelict building.

"What is this place?" It looks like a warehouse, the outside boarded up, with minimal street lighting. A fraction creepy. We reach an arched entrance, where the door opens like they knew we were here.

"After you," Ethan says, and we pass through, his hand on my lower back, guiding me forward. I love the way he's always touching me. It makes me feel something that I've never experienced. Safe. Wanted.

My eyes go wide, trying to take everything in as my breath stutters in my chest. It's a sensory overload for all the right reasons; it's... extravagant, and tranquil in equal measures. The smell of clean forest air hugs me, making me feel grounded. It's spacious and open. Even with the running water cascading down the walls. Living walls full of vibrant plants bring your eyes up to the ceiling, focusing on the chandelier that sits elegantly in the centre, sparkling like the brightest star.

It's beautiful.

Dotted around the floor are pods, varying in size. It's like we've stepped into our own luxury getaway. I can't see inside them as they are covered in greenery, and I won't allow my imagination to run away with me. I want to experience it without any expectations.

"Welcome to the forest," someone says as we come through the door.

"Mr Ford, your area has been prepared. Please, follow me." Ethan ushers me forward, his hand never leaving mine, as he walks just behind me. All it does is send tingles down my spine.

"If you're trying to impress me, it's working," I hum, turning to him, as she leads us towards the back of the building.

"I'm not trying to impress you, Aggie. I want to see you smile." My knickers might as well just fall right off, because, fuck me, if we weren't in the company of other people, I'd mount him like the tree he is. My smile widens as I squeeze his hand.

"I'm smiling, Ethan, from the inside out."

"Fuck." he murmurs.

"Your server will be with you shortly," the woman says as we step up to a wooden door.

"Tell them to bring it all. We don't want to be disturbed," Ethan says, his voice stern.

"Of course, sir, we have your order and drinks ready." The woman turns and leaves.

"I'm nervous," I admit.

"There's no need to be anything but you when I'm next to you," Ethan says, dropping my hand and placing his on the door, urging me to go first.

I'm lost for words. I thought the outside was breathtaking, but this is out of this world. There's no dining table like I expected, just a wooden, decked area in the centre, with a low table in the middle. Every surface is covered in greenery, and the night sky glitters across the ceiling. I know it's not real, but holy shit, it feels like I'm outside, looking at a million stars.

"Ethan?" I spin around and launch myself at him. Too overwhelmed to be anything but damn excited. He catches me as my arms fly around his neck. "Where the fuck did you find this place?" He chuckles, grabbing my arse, bringing my legs around his waist.

"I wanted our first date to be memorable," he says quietly, as he kisses me; his tongue sweeping my lips, seeking entry. A low rumble emanates from his throat.

"Best date I've ever fucking had." My words come out breathless as we part.

"We're far from finished, butterfly. The night is only just getting started." Oh god, he's ruining me for other men, and I don't mind.

"What else do you have planned for us? Because I'm not sure you can top this."

Unwrapping my legs from his toned waist, I slide down the front of him, and he works to unfasten the belt on my coat before slipping it off my shoulders and placing it on the rack. Then he takes off his dark grey suit jacket, hanging it next to mine.

"If I told you that, baby, there'd be no stopping me from stripping you bare."

"In that case, how about some foreplay?" His eyes widen at my words. I can see his gaze flick around the room like he's checking for something. But I step away.

His breath catches as I crouch down in front of him, and undo my boots, sliding them off, my bare feet brushing against the cool grass covering the floor.

It's the first time I hear him laugh. Like a full-blown deep belly laugh. Fuck my life; my ovaries flutter before they burst as wetness floods my knickers.

"Fuck, keep laughing like that, *Joker,* and there'd be no stopping me from stripping *you* bare," I mock, and he laughs harder. He proceeds to grab me and haul me over his shoulder before he drops me on the cushioned deck, crawling over me. My legs part, welcoming him in between them.

He fits so snugly between them, I don't want him to leave.

He's so hard. I can feel him through my jeans, as he presses his length against my core. My eyes flutter closed, as he lowers his forehead to mine.

"As much as I need to be inside you, to feel you wrapped around me," he groans the words, "you will eat first. I pre-ordered the food. I want you to taste it all before I taste you for myself." And there go my knickers running off, like they know they won't be needed ever again.

I'll just wear a skirt and go commando from now on.

Easier for everyone all round.

He leans back, pulling us up to sit, settling into the plush floor seating like he owns the place. "What sort of food does this place do?" I ask, feeling so content, I close my eyes for a second, and I see it, a flash of a scene playing in my mind of laughter and warmth. But it's not us. And just like before, it's gone again.

"I selected the Italian and the Spanish platters. It's like tapas, only bigger and better."

"I do hope you're right. Not just because I'm hungry, I also love my food. It's one of the best parts of travelling. You get to experience all the different kinds of foods, each country has to offer." Ethan lets me talk just like he did on the plane, and I know he's listening, as he nods and hums and squeezes me tighter, the more I say.

"Have you travelled much?" I ask as the server comes in carrying a jug of... something pink, with two tall glasses.

"Work mostly, or in the army, sometimes for my Gran when she needs me to go and escort a new painting home for her." He pauses while the server places the drink on the table, before leaving us again. I open my mouth to ask why, but he answers my unspoken question. "She has a deep distrust of delivery companies, especially when it's something valuable, so she sends me. I've been doing it since I was eighteen, I think." There's a fondness in his voice when he talks about her. Removing his arm from my shoulder, he sits forward, taking the large jug in his hand and pours the pink mix into the tall frosted glasses.

"Your drink, Miss Hope," he says, passing the first glass to me. I take a sip and my favourite cocktail bursts to life on my tongue. "To repay you for the one you bought me last week.

I almost choke. There's no way he could know it was me. I give him a fake scowl.

"It was the way it smelt of you, the butterfly was just a happy reminder of what I've yet to fully see." His finger drags over the spot of my butterfly tattoo, sending a wave of pleasure to my core.

"My butterfly?" There's a double entendre if ever I heard one. He nods, his eyes lowering to my covered thighs. I smile, unable to stop myself.

"Your butterfly," he says. "I've dreamt of seeing it up close since the moment you mentioned it on the plane.

"You can touch my butterfly anytime you want, Joker." I add with a wiggle of my eyebrows.

"Tell me about your travels," he adds, changing the subject, but keeping his hand between my thighs.

"I have so much left to see, of a hundred and ninety-three countries, I've only seen thirty-four. Did you ever get to see the places you visited?"

"No," he says, and I think I hear a hint of regret in his tone. I'm learning pretty quickly that Ethan gives almost nothing away, but if you look closely, you can see the faint changes in his expression, and it tells you so much.

I can't imagine a life like his, where work always comes first. For me, work is a means to an end. I make the money so I can travel and replenish my art supplies.

"I've never had the time," he says.

"I took off on my own when I was eighteen," He stiffens at that, but doesn't say anything. "Since then, I've been all over the world."

"Was there someone who looked out for you?" I can see it's been playing on his mind.

"No, no family." He frowns like he wants to rectify it, but knows he can't.

"I'm sorry to hear that," he says, pulling me closer to his side. I sink in.

"I've never known any different, Ethan." It's the truth. "You can't miss what you've never had."

"You have me now." His voice is softer as he tells me.

"It's our first date, Ethan."

"I know, but you can count on me." My heart swells to double its size, vanquishing some of the walls I've built around it because I believe him.

"Thank you." I don't know the right words to say; it seems like too much to spill my shit and spoil this moment. His hold tightens as he kisses the top of my head.

This man.

The door knocks again, and we're saved from any more deep conversations as the food is brought in on large trays by three servers. I sit up, smelling the aromas that waft my way.

"Ladies first," Ethan says. I take two plates and fill both with matching food.

"Together," I say, handing him one. We eat in relative silence, only comparing what we like best.

It's comfortable. Easy.

Over two hours, three strawberry daiquiris, and pudding later, Ethan stands, indicating it's time for us to leave. He walks to the door, fetching my boots from where I left them.

This has to have been one of the best nights of my life. Holding my hand out to take them, he shakes his head and crouches down in front of me, sliding each boot on like I'm his Cinderella, before he takes my hand, helping me stand.

"You like this, don't you?" I ask tentatively.

"Like what, Aggie?" he asks, pulling his jacket on.

"Taking care of people."

"Not people, Aggie." His cautious grey eyes meet mine as the blip in my chest intensifies. "You."

There's no saving me now.

Chapter Seventeen

Stale

Ethan

Our fingers are still linked as we walk from my car up the front steps to my house. I've not stopped touching her. I can't help myself. Aggie's almost bouncing; the few drinks she's had have done nothing to dull the energy she exudes; she's a breath of fresh air in my stale life.

"Are you ready to tell me what you have planned for us next?" She gets a spark in her eyes when she teases me. It makes me want to wrap her up and not let anyone near her.

Stalling my step, I spin her around, pressing her up against my front door. Raff's not here, so I don't need to worry about prying eyes.

"I'm not the talking type," I murmur as my hand sinks between us, cupping her sweet core, growling when I feel just how warm she is. She gasps, tipping her head back, and I take full advantage, swiping my tongue along the column of her throat, tasting her peppermint perfume. "You're addictive, Aggie," I grumble.

I have every intention of showing her just what I want to do to her, but I need to get her inside before I fuck her. I'm desperate to take my time, but I'm not sure I can. I've been painfully hard all night. We've had foreplay for a week, and my cock's been in my hand every night, just thinking of the things I want to do to that sweet pussy of hers.

"Open the door, Ethan," she begs, her voice soft and husky. I do, and we stumble.

"Bed." I groan, urging her toward the stairs.

"Anywhere," she says. "It's been a long... week, waiting for this... Ethan." She gasps for breath as I continue my torment on her mouth. I'm not sure I'm going to make it up the stairs. My rock-hard dick's begging to have her, pushing against my zipper, pre-cum already leaking from my tip. It has been since she got into my car three fucking hours ago. In those tight as fuck jeans that leave nothing to the imagination.

Lifting my hand from her core, I flick the button on her jeans, lowering the zip. She pulls her coat off, then her cardigan, throwing them somewhere behind me. Her hands tug my jacket in desperate need to get it off. I devour her mouth again as my hand dives into her jeans, while my other hand peels them down, exposing her lace-clad sex. She undoes my tie, almost ripping the buttons off my shirt as she tries to get contact with my skin. Aggie moans when my fingers slip into her knickers, tracing the soft lines beneath as I find her. I drag my thick finger through her already soaked folds, and she gasps when I tease her entrance.

My shirt's hanging open, Aggie's hands are everywhere as she feels every hard muscle of my chest, abs, and shoulders. She kisses my neck and moans as I sink my finger inside her, not stopping until it's all the way in. Fuck, she feels incredible. I can't wait a minute longer.

"Ethan." She's moaning my name, and it will only ever be *mine*. My hand frees her from her jeans as I lay her down on the stairs. Her hand grips the rails as I pump my finger in and out of her. Her wetness makes the most delectable sounds I have ever heard, making my cock strain against my zipper.

Her top comes off next, leaving her in just a small band of material that covers her perfect breasts. Her nipples so hard, I can see the rosy peaks through the lace, begging to be taken. I lick my lips, bending down to take one in my mouth.

"Fuck, Aggie," I rasp against her nipple. "I'm not going to make it upstairs," I suck on the hardened bud, making her writhe beneath me. "Take my cock out, baby." My body hovers over hers, as her hands move down my heaving chest and abs.

Curling my fingers, I stroke against her G-spot, watching her mouth part as she whimpers, more arousal coating my palm. *Fuck, yes.* I add another finger as she fumbles with my belt. I need her wet and stretched for me. I'm feral for her. There will be more time to please her the way I want to later, but right now I need to fill her.

Her fingers undo my belt and then my trousers before she pulls down my boxers. When she reaches for my cock, I groan, watching her hand wrap around my steel length. I rock my hips into her hold, my cock growing heavy as she strokes me up and down. My skin ignites in fire when she applies the smallest amount of pressure, sweeping her thumb over my sensitive head. I almost lose it.

My fingers pick up their pace as I watch us, touching each other; it's the most erotic thing I have ever seen. She lowers my trousers and boxers over my arse, giving her and me more room. She's watching too as her core grips my fingers.

"I want to fuck you, Aggie," I say through gritted teeth, trying to keep control of my need for this woman in check.

"Then fuck me, Ethan." She moans, I growl. A second passes. Fisting her knickers, I tear them from her, making her gasp, before I remove her hand from my cock. "Please," she whines, and it's all I can do not to come over her beautiful tits.

"Condom," I groan, not wanting to move.

"Fuck a condom, I want to feel your heat inside me. I'm clean," she rasps. *Fuck, yes.* I've never gone bare with anyone.

"I'm clean too." I got myself checked after my ex.

"Then fuck me, Ethan."

"Are you sure?"

"Yes." I fist my cock in my hand, dragging it through her wetness as her legs part wider.

"Ethan, please," she begs, "I can't take much more."

"You'll take it all, butterfly," I growl, as I press the tip of my cock to her entrance and hold it there. I slide my cock in an inch. Her eyes fly open as I slowly push inside her.

"Fuck." She gasps again. "Breathe, baby. I know you can take it," I groan as I nip her lips, my tongue soothing any sting I may have caused there. She breathes out, and I push in a few inches more, feeling her warmth around me. My muscles tense as I wait. Jesus-fuck, she feels unbelievable. So tight.

I sink in further, her core pulling me in like she needs me. My lips crash to hers, tongues tangling with need as I push all the way in until I'm balls deep into my perfect woman. I swallow her moans and groans as I start to move, feeling every blissful inch of her coating my dick.

"Fuck." I'm fucking Aggie on the stairs. This was not how I planned it, but hell, if I'm able to resist her anymore. My arm winds around her back as I take more control, holding her to me as she spasms around my cock, telling me she's close. My movements turn feral as my hips rut, fucking her harder. Holding her tighter.

"Ethan…" She doesn't finish as her walls clamp down, and my vision blurs. I slow, needing a second before I blow my load.

Losing control or my resolve, my hips move, fucking her into the stairs as she meets my every move with equal abandon. Sweat drips down my back as she digs her nails into my heated muscles.

"E… I …more." I do as she asks, my cock burying so deep inside her, hitting where she needs it most. A smile creeps over my lips, knowing she'll feel me for days after this. Her feet slip from the stairs as her core tightens around me. I hold us together, too caught up in the moment to let go.

"Fuck, Aggie, you're strangling my cock. I can't hold on." I push forward, her heels digging into me, bringing her flush to my groin. My body aches for release, the fire in my spine spreading as I rut into my butterfly, and she takes everything

I'm giving her. My balls draw up, a flash of heat, shooting through me, as she comes around me, soaking my thighs, my name falling from her lips.

I force my eyes to stay open as hers roll back in her head. I find my own release right alongside her, shooting everything I have inside my woman's warm, soaked core. Claiming her. Warmth floods my body, and my heart pounds like a shot of adrenaline to the chest. *Fuck*. I keep going, thrusting harder, deeper, when I feel her rise again. Her beautiful, sweat soaked body, breath, and core clutching onto me, as another orgasm rolls through my butterfly. My orgasm lasting longer than ever before. I see stars as I bury myself in her with one last thrust, as she tips her head back, her body sagging. I hold her to my heaving chest, unable and unwilling to move, never wanting to let go of this amazing woman.

"Ethan," she says breathlessly as I rest my head against hers.

"Aggie." She takes my sweat-soaked cheeks in the palm of her hands and kisses me so tenderly, it's my undoing. I kiss her back, hoping it's enough.

When we finally untangle, I carry her upstairs to my bedroom where I place her on my bed and start the shower in my en-suite. My need to take care of her after what she's just given me, the soul-shattering sex, is almost overwhelming. She watches my every move, propped up on her elbows. Her eyes wander over me as I get everything I need. When I'm ready, I lift her off the bed and peel off her clothes before I carry her to the bathroom and place her under the warm water.

My eyes linger on the tattoo that trails from her breasts to between her thighs. She draws in a deep breath as I trail my fingers over the vines of her tattoo, until my fingers nestle in between her thighs, where she keeps the design hidden.

"Spread your legs, baby. Show me what I've been craving to see." I get down on one knee, the water from the shower cascading over my back. Taking hold of her ankle, I lift her leg, resting her foot on my thigh, opening her wide for me.

"God-damn, you're beautiful, Aggie." I groan as I take in the view in front of me. Her pink lips swollen from our fucking, my cum leaking out of her, and the most stunning butterfly tattoo I have ever seen, snuggly resting on a leaf on the crease of her groin. I trail my finger over the life-like design, and she shivers. "Perfect," I murmur as I start to wash her between her legs. Her breath hitches as I wash the evidence of us away. Her hands drift down my body as I stand; her eyes darkening as they reach my cock. She bites her lip the way that drives me crazy.

"Do you like what you see, Aggie?" She nods, like she's too shy to admit it. "Words," I tease.

"Ethan, you're magnificent. Every inch of you." Her lust-laden eyes linger on my already hardening cock. I take it in my hand, stroking myself as she watches.

"Don't move," I tell her. I reach behind her, grabbing the bodywash I bought just for her, squeezing it over her shoulders. I take my time cleaning her soft skin, memorising every inch of her. My gut sinks when I see her arm.

"What's this?" I growl as I take in the enormous purple bruise on her arm. She doesn't say anything, just looks at me confused. "The bruise on your arm, Aggie." She looks at it and slowly smiles.

"Oh, that's nothing. I banged myself against a wall the other day." Her fingers come to trace over mine. "It's okay."

"If you're sure."

"I'm sure, Joker."

Chapter Eighteen

Snap

Aggie

"Have you seen it?" Layla shouts in my ear when I answer the phone to her on my lunch break. I love her to bits, but I'm tired, having spent all weekend at Ethan's and hardly sleeping. Functioning for work is definitely seeming more difficult today.

"Seen what?" I ask as I pop my ready meal in the microwave and set it for three minutes. Looking at my reflection in the mirrored glass front, I see a blush creep over my cheeks. Ethan took every opportunity to be inside me. Fuck, I even woke up with his dick in me. He was still asleep, so, I woke him up by cupping his balls. Lazy bed sex is the best, especially with Ethan.

I'm sore as hell now though, my body aching in ways I have never felt before. Each twinge brings a new memory of Ethan's hands on me, I thought the spark would fizzle out after the first few times, but it seems to have turned into a firework, an uncontrollable one. With one look, I'd be a puddle, almost begging him to fuck me again. Hot, sweaty, and so god damn sexy, I had to pinch myself to believe it was all real. I'm fucking my boss, but it seems so much more.

Every time he touches me, it's mine to take. His possessive touch was *mine*. Even as he made us breakfast, lunch and dinner, his hands were on me. Teasing

"

me, like he needed the contact, just as much as I did. He took care of me in every way I needed, without asking. He just knew.

Even with my sore muscles, I have a feeling that if he told me to drop my knickers in his office today, I would, and would willingly bend over the desk for him.

"The article," Layla screams, bringing me back to reality.

"What article?" I ask, and she groans at me, like I should know what she is talking about.

"I'll send it to you." My phone pings with a message and a link. "Read it and call me back." She hangs up and I open the message I freeze.

There, right in front of my eyes, is a picture of me and Ethan leaving 'The Forest' hand in hand, looking happy. I smile, remembering the way it felt to be his sole focus. When I glance at the image again, my heart sinks. It would be a good picture if it weren't for the headline. *'Lady Celeste's grandson, Ethan Ford, caught sneaking around with a nobody, Aggie Hope.'* I can't say we were sneaking around. I guess I am a nobody compared to Ethan's status, but it doesn't make me any less than him. *Fucking tabloids.* As I read, it only gets worse, casting assumptions about working for him, and how a workplace romance never works in the long run.

That I must be after either a promotion, money, or I am sleeping my way to the top, seeing I've managed to get my hands on one of the most eligible bachelors in the UK. It even pins me for the reason he broke it off with his fiancée. A sarcastic laugh leaves my throat. Wow. That's low. I sit in the chair, lean back, and read it all again.

I wonder if Ethan's seen it. He's not come to me about it, so I'm going to guess he doesn't know. Or he's not bothered by it. I shouldn't be bothered by it, but I am.

The more I think about it, the tenser I get, my teeth grinding, as anger fills my veins. My food is forgotten as it pings that it's done in the background. I lean forward, the chair screeching across the floor as I shove it back, and stand. I storm out of the kitchen, ready to tell Ethan about it, when I get a notification saying my next adventure awaits.

I stop.

There's a zip-lining experience with a space for today. I don't want to run into Ethan's office, all guns blazing; that's not how I do things. I need time to think. This will hopefully give me the escape I need, and the jolt my malfunctioning brain needs to remember.

When I get to our office, I'm lucky he's not there. He'd want to know what's wrong, because he'd know. He'd see it on my face how angry I am, and I don't want to take it out on him.

Clicking on the link, I book the slot they have for this afternoon, block out the diary using my mobile, and grab my bag, leaving before Ethan can ask me where I'm going.

This place is well over an hour away, and after a quick run back to Layla's, I change into a pair of leggings and a hoodie.

I feel guilty sending Ethan's calls to voicemail. But I need this slice of freedom; he just needs to give me this afternoon to calm down. I'm sure I will. But right now, it makes my blood boil that they can write horrible things about me, while Ethan comes off like the golden boy. I mean, he is; he's done nothing wrong either. And with that, my anger seems to fade a fraction. I know he'll talk me through what's happening. Maybe I was wrong to do this so quickly. Running out and not giving myself time to talk to him first. The weather is not the best today, even I can see that. I'll be soaked by the time I'm finished, but it's booked now, so it's too late, and I'm not one to back down from a challenge. There's a ding on my phone after I send another one of Ethan's calls to voicemail. Turning the screen over in my hand, I see a message from him, and my eyes dart away as guilt churns my stomach. After a second, I look.

There's nothing else, no more messages, no guilt trip, no anger, nothing. I think I expected him to act like Jasper: get all prissy with me for doing something on my own. But there he is, proving me wrong. I tip my head back on the car's headrest, feeling worse than ever for just leaving. He'd never stop me from doing something I wanted. He's never said so, but I have a ball of hope in my chest that says I'm right.

There's an unanswered question in his message. He's concerned but won't voice it. After our weekend together, I want to be more open with him, so I send him the link to the article along with a message.

And I will be. I like what's starting between us, and I like him a lot.

By the time I pull up to Ethan's and get out of the Uber, I'm exhausted and cold. The wind and rain while I rode the zip wire were like ice cutting into my skin. I've not been able to get warm since. No matter how hard I try. When Ethan swings the door open, a shiver wracks my body, but it's not from the effect he has on me; not this time. It's the cold seeping into my bones. Catching me in his arms as I almost fall forward, he wraps them around me; the warmth of his chest, even through his shirt, has me sinking into him.

"What's wrong? You're freezing?" He holds me closer, kissing the top of my head, pulling me inside.

"I'm fine, honestly," I say, my teeth chattering as another shiver takes hold. Maybe I'm not okay. I should have gone home.

"I'm sorry. I shouldn't have come. I think I'm getting a cold." My muscles feel drained.

"You came to the right place," he says, tightening his arms around me. "Aggie, where have you been?" His tone is low, like he's been worried.

Hiding my face in his chest, I don't answer him. I take in his warmth, like a hot water bottle to my cold skin. I'm not ready to tell him. I could make up a lie, but my gut tells me he'd see straight through it.

"I can't seem to get warm, although you're helping," I say, holding him firmly around the waist.

It should be alarming how comfortable I feel around him. How I want to be with him anyway I can. I'd compare it to when I met Layla. I knew we would be firm friends as soon as we spoke. I wasn't prepared to let that ray of sun slip through my fingers. This feels like that, but more... I don't know, life-affirming.

"Let's run you a bath." *Then we'll talk,* that's what goes unsaid.

"That would be amazing, thank you." My shoulders relax. Layla only has a shower, although it's perfect, I've missed sinking into the water.

We walk up the stairs, Ethan keeping me close as he rubs his hands over my arms to get me warm. He leads us through to a much larger, more elegant bathroom than his en-suite. Sitting in the centre, larger than life, is a rolltop tub big enough for three people. He sets the water running, adding some bubbles. *Fuck this man.* Ethan is watching my shaky movements as I try to take off my clothes with a concerned eye before he helps tug my hoodie over my head. He bends down to take off my leggings and socks.

"I'm sorry about today," he says, standing back up as I take my underwear off. "I should have taken the time to warn you about what dating me would mean." His hands cup my face, stroking my cheek tenderly with his thumb.

"We're dating?" I frown, rolling my lips together. Yes, that's the only thing I took from that sentence. It makes me a little giddy that I could be dating Ethan Ford.

"Yes," he says on a growl, like there would be any other answer than the one he's just given me.

"We've been on one date," I state, popping a shaky hand on my hip for emphasis.

"It may have been one date, Aggie," he says, brushing his lips over mine, "but I've spent the weekend between your beautiful fucking legs," his hands drop to my sides, tugging my naked shivering body to his, "and I don't plan on changing that, be it one or one-thousand dates, the outcome will still be the same." His hands grab the fleshy parts of my arse, kneading them, and my breath hitches when I feel his cock growing hard against me.

"Sweet talker." He grunts out a laugh as he leans in to kiss me, firmly this time, and I groan in acceptance. *I'm dating Mr Ethan Ford.* I can't wait to tell Layla.

"I've sorted everything," he says, pulling away from my lips, "with the article," he adds when he sees me frowning. I'd already forgotten everything about it, with his body so close to mine. "You don't need to worry."

"I wasn't worried, just angry they could write those things when they don't know me."

"Well, your feelings were valid. I can't promise it won't happen again, but if it does, I'll do exactly what I did today."

"And what was that?" My hands come to his sculpted waist. God, I love the feel of him under my hands. The way his shirt glides over his skin.

"I got them to retract the article, with an apology going out in an hour on your behalf." I almost choke.

"How?" I ask, looking up into his mischievous grey eyes.

"Slander." The way he makes it sound is deadly, but his eyes now sparkle, like he won the lottery or something.

"Slander?" I repeat, then it dawns on me. "You threatened them with slander?"

"Yes." His tone is so serious, I don't really want to argue with him... but it's not really in my nature to be quiet.

"Why? It wasn't even that bad. I could have lived with it." Okay, I'm not really arguing. I like that he did it, makes me feel... cared for again.

"I told you, I'm here to take care of you, Aggie, in any way it comes and in any way you need." I *really* like this side of him: deadly but caring. Is that a thing?

"Right." I shiver again, even though his bathroom feels like a sauna. "This caring thing I could get used to. It just catches me off guard every time you do it," I mumble as his lips brush mine.

"I don't want to push you on anything, Aggie. But I want to know everything about you." That was a one-eighty. I swallow the thickness in my throat. I want to tell him, but the words have never left my lips before. "When you're ready."

"I'll tell you if you tell me everything about you." Especially about this fiancée of his he's never mentioned.

"I'll bare my soul for you, butterfly." Tears prick in my eyes at his words. They're so genuine. I wrap them around my fragile heart like a soothing balm, as it cares and protects, just like the man whose arms are wrapped around me.

"But right now, you're getting sick. Get in." Never in my life have I liked taking orders from a man, but the way Ethan orders me to get in that bath, I'd submit every time.

"Are you going to join me?" I say, licking my lips when he turns me to walk over to the already full bath.

"Always." Helping me in, I sink my aching body into the water, watching it swirl around me. The bubbles part and cover my skin. Relaxing back into the heat, I close my eyes, enjoying the moment. When I feel the water shift, I open my now tired eyes to see Ethan's jaw-dropping frame sinking into the water in front of me. His muscles flex and shift as he reaches for me, pulling my back to his front.

"Don't get any ideas," he adds, as I rub my hands over his thighs.

"I have a lot of dirty ideas." I tuck my chin to my chest, hiding my grin from him.

"Later," he says, sinking us both lower until my lusting body is covered. "I need you to be well, Aggie." My head rests back against his chest as he strokes my hair from my face.

"As long as I'm with you, I know I'll be fine." Tilting my head, I look up at him, and he lowers his mouth to mine.

"Do you mean that, Aggie?"

"I've been in relationships, I've dated, had one-night stands." That gets a growl, and I relish in the rumble across my back. "I've done it all. But this right here. This feels so much more than anything they were. Yeah, I do. I mean it."

"Fuck, I don't think I could let you go, even if you wanted me to."

Chapter Nineteen

Unexpected

Ethan

After the shit show yesterday, with the article, I couldn't have asked for a better ending to my day. To hold her in my arms and not have her angry with me, it was more of a relief than I expected. I had message after message from the guys over the weekend asking if I was alive, and to send them an SOS if I needed rescuing. I told them all to go fuck themselves.

It's not their fault. If you could count on anyone to work a weekend, a late night, and be on call, it would be me. Well, would have been me. I can't say I even thought about it, *if at all.* If I can spend all my weekends with Aggie, uninterrupted, then I'll be taking weekends off for the foreseeable.

I'll employ someone to take the shit shifts. I'll restructure our company if it means I can get more time with her.

When I walked into the office this morning, they were all sitting around the table waiting for me, and I could tell from their looks, they had questions. Leon's shit eating grin told me all I needed to know. They're happy for me and want to talk about it. I'm not a talker, so I turned around and walked back out, returning to my home office and avoiding them.

I've not been with anyone since my ex, and they know it. I love them like brothers, but god-damn, they don't half like to gossip. My phone is still blowing up from our group chat. I've silenced the notifications. I'll speak to them when I'm ready.

I should be wary about being with someone else; the shit that my ex, Scarlett, put me through should have been enough to put me off for life. But for whatever reason, I'm not. I don't know Aggie well enough yet to say she'd never hurt me, but I have a feeling that she lives by a set of rules that would always make her and those around her happy. Treat people how you want to be treated. Maybe Scarlett could learn a lesson or two from Aggie.

Fuck, no, I never want the two of them to meet. I'd like to keep that smile on Aggie's face for as long as humanly possible, and as soon as my ex gets even a hint that I'm dating someone, she'll become the devious witch I know she is.

I've avoided being with anyone for so long, I was beginning to think there was no hope. My mother pushed Scarlett and me together, a match made in heaven, she said. In hell, more like. On paper, she was perfect: ran in the same circles, similar background to mine, beautiful on the outside. She didn't really care about what I did; it was all superficial. She hated every second I spent with my Gran and the guys and didn't mind telling me what a waste of time it was.

Never again.

I missed having my eyes on Aggie this morning. When we woke, she wanted to head back to her place to change, but I'd already sent Raff to buy her some new outfits to keep at mine.

She laughed at me, called me foolish for wasting my money on her, but smiled anyway as she tried them all on, before settling on a fitted dress that zips all the way up her back. She looked so good. I tried to unzip her to take her back to bed, only she ran in the opposite direction and made us both a coffee with Raff.

I checked her over again this morning, no signs of a temperature. I think she got to me just in time last night.

She was chilled to the bone when she came through my door. Why was she out in that weather? She uses an Uber to go everywhere. That's something else I need to deal with. I gave her the card to use; I want to make sure she's using it.

I said we had things to talk about, and the card is only the start. She definitely needs a car.

Aggie's at the gala venue this morning, talking with the staff, running through the agenda, but she'll be back here after lunch. While she's gone, I need to take a look into a few things, mainly where she's disappearing to.

I open the bank account linked to the business I set up for her, and the balance is still the same, no transactions. It's untouched. That's impossible. She's using that car company at least twice a day, she buys me and the guys' coffee every other morning. Fuck, she even told me she'd booked in to have her hair done for the gala this weekend, along with buying shoes to go with the dress. I should be seeing transactions from over the last few weeks. Aggie has to be using her own money, but she's not been paid yet. And won't be for another few weeks as we pay monthly.

There's only one way to sort this out.

"Mr Ford, your grandmother is here," Raff says, interrupting me as he appears at my door just as I pick up the phone.

"Where is she?" I sigh as I put the phone back down and stand. I love my Gran, but she never tells me when she's coming.

"In the formal living room, sir."

"Thanks. Can you bring in some tea and cakes? You know what she likes."

Raff nods, moving towards the kitchen. Leaving everything behind in my office, I head for the living room to see my Gran and show her the new painting I had Aggie bring to the house on her first day.

"Tell Raff, I don't want tea," she says when I walk into the room. I glance at the misplaced items around the room, like she's been peeking to find my hidden secrets, unbothered if I find out what she's been doing. She's pouring herself a gin. "I'd much prefer some of that nice, flavoured tonic. Do you have any?" I huff a laugh.

"No, and it's only ten-thirty in the morning. You should have tea." I'd take it off her, but she'd fight me. I move to kiss her on the cheek as I pass. Standing at the back of the sofa, I lean on it, waiting for her to take a seat.

"Always such a stiff, dear. It's five o'clock somewhere." My grandmother, Lady Celeste Ford, never plays by the rules, and has a perfectly imaginative set of her own which she follows, and some she makes up along the way.

"I'm just thinking of your health, Gran," I add, shoving my hands in my pockets.

"Tosh, my health is fine. I've not gotten to eighty," *eighty-five,* "by being careful, and I don't plan to change now." I can only try, and have been trying since she got me and the guys wasted the night we all returned from the Army. It was such a good night, exactly what we needed, and she knew it. We lost six of our friends in our last tour. I couldn't save them. It lives with me every day, but not as much as the betrayal of one of our own, even if he suffered the same fate as the others, I'll never forgive him for that. He led us into that ambush, for his own gain. He let his friends suffer the worst fate.

Then, when we arrived home, Gran took all our numbers. It was also a way for her to check if we were there for each other. She saw my grandad suffer when he returned from the war, and didn't want us to go through what he did. But in true Gran-style, she started sending us funny videos, messaging us inappropriate jokes, letting us see the lighter side of life, after the hell we went through.

She's the complete opposite to me.

"Fine," I relent, knowing it's a lost cause.

"You're just jealous, you can't join me."

"Sure, whatever makes you happy." She grins, the wrinkles in the corners of her eyes creasing further as she smiles wider.

"You make me happy, dear," she adds.

"Have you hung the painting I bought back from Australia yet?"

"First thing I did. It looks spectacular, just like I knew it would. I stand and stare at it every time I pass." She sighs contentedly.

"I'm glad it all worked out," I say, and she smiles.

"I see you have a new painting wrapped in the corner. Are you going to show me?"

"How long have you been here?" I ask.

"Not long." Which means over half an hour. Raff needs to quit letting her in without me knowing. What if I'd been with Aggie? "Before you start, don't blame Raff. I like to have a walk around before we talk." I hum, knowing there's no way I can stop her.

Raff walks in with a tray of tea and cakes, looks at my grandmother's choice of drink, and shakes his head. "I'll grab the flavoured tonic for you."

"She has you twisted round her little finger," I murmur under my breath. But he hears me loud and clear.

"No, Lady Celeste asked me to restock your bar when she was here last week." The bastard pauses, and I know he's going to say something else. "We also have the ingredients for Aggie's favourite drink, sir." He smirks, knowing exactly what he's done.

Prick.

"Aggie? Who's Aggie?" My grandmother turns from her spot at the bar, pinning her eyes on me as she scrutinises my reaction. And damn, she's good at reading me. "You really like her," she adds as her eyes sparkle.

"Aggie is my new assistant," I answer, my tone low, hating myself for labelling her like that when she's... more.

"Oh." She looks disappointed. "Why do you have her drink order then? If I remember correctly, you never kept Scarlett's wine in the store cellar." Her grey eyebrow arches at me, knowingly. Raff laughs. He's always been a better friend to my grandmother than me.

"They're dating, Lady Celeste," Raff says over his shoulder as he leaves the room. *For fuck's sake.* My head dips, and I can't help how my heart thuds against my ribs, hearing someone say we're dating out loud. I knew she'd have no idea, just like my parents don't. If they knew, I would have heard about it. We tend to stay away from the tabloids, especially online ones, which is why I had no idea about the article until Aggie sent it to me.

"You're fired, Raff," I shout after him.

"No, he's not," Gran chastises. She's right, he's not, but I will get him back for this. Somehow.

"Dating? Ethan, is that right? I want to meet her. Where is she?" She looks around the room like I've been hiding her behind the sofa.

"She's at the venue for the gala. You'll meet her. She'll be there with me this weekend." I walk over to the bar and pour myself a finger of scotch. I think I'm going to need it.

"Does your mother know yet?" she asks tentatively. The sparkle in her eye dims for a moment. My mother may be her daughter, but they've never seen eye to eye on anything. Very different views on what a Lady should be doing with her life, instead of living like my gran does, and also how Grandad did while he was alive.

"No," I say with a grimace. "If she knew, you'd know about it."

"You're right, I would. Ethan, you know she has high expectations for any woman you date." I shake my head and pour myself a little more. Taking a sip, I look back at her.

"And look how the last one turned out." Gran's the only one I've told about my ex cheating on me. "Aggie's... different."

"Good. I'd hate for you to have someone like Scarlett again. Gosh, she was vile. Thinking she could sleep with that man and still be engaged to you. Moron, utter flipping moron, that's what she is." Gran finishes her drink, so I make her a new one, handing it to her as we each take a seat on the couch.

"You'll love her, Gran. My mother, maybe not so much, but I really like her," I admit.

"That's all that matters, dear. I want you to be happy with whomever you choose." She shuffles on the couch, her eyes swinging towards the painting.

"Now show me this painting. You kept it quiet. Where did you get it?" she asks, placing her drink on the coffee table in front of us.

"The small gallery on the beach. I noticed it while I was there with a few friends. Bought it the following day."

"It must be good. What caught your eye?" she asks, rubbing her dainty hands together. Placing my glass down, I stand and walk over to the painting still wrapped behind the couch.

"It's not something I would normally go for. For a start, the colours are vivid, but the way it's painted is beautiful. Graceful, almost." I unwrap it; the brown paper and bubble wrap falling to the side. "See." I stand it up in front of her and she gasps as her fingers brush over the ballet dancer.

"Who's the artist? I don't have my glasses to read the signature."

"Luna Solace. Never heard of her before, but she's good. Look at the way the brush strokes—" I'm interrupted, Grans repeating the name.

"Luna Solace? No, it can't be, it has to be a coincidence. *Luna Solace*." She gulps down the words like they hurt. Setting the painting to one side, I sit on the coffee table in front of her, taking her hand in mine when I notice how deadly pale she's gone.

"Gran, what happened? Are you okay?" I check her pulse to find it's racing, and her hands feel clammy. *Shit.* Could she be having a heart attack?

"Raff," I shout. "Call an ambulance." He comes running in, phone to his ear, already giving instructions on our address when he has no idea what's happening. He hands over the phone, taking over my position on the table while I tell them everything I know. My eyes are on Gran's greying complexion as she runs a hand over her chest. Handing the phone back to Raff, I lay her back on the sofa, propping her feet up to get circulation flowing where she needs it most.

"Gran, you need to focus on me, breathe with me, in for four, out for four. Tell me where it hurts." Her eyes fill with tears, but she says nothing except the name on the painting.

We were rushed through A&E and taken to a private room where they did test after test, each one checked over by me, for my own reassurance. But they found nothing. She had a panic attack, the on-call doctor told me, and I can't say he's wrong. One of the worst ones I have ever seen, and I've seen some bad ones, during my time as a medic in the army. Shit, I thought she was going to die.

"I've asked them to keep you overnight. I want to make sure it doesn't happen again."

"I think you're overreacting, Ethan," Gran says, looking shaken, but otherwise okay.

"You're still staying. I'll make sure you have everything, I'll ask Raff to bring you some things, and I'll keep you company." I'm not leaving her side.

"You don't need to stay, dear."

"What happened, Gran?" I'm so confused. "One minute you were drinking gin, the next... a panic attack. Have you ever had one before?" She doesn't answer, but looks me dead in the eye.

"Oh, Ethan, I've kept this to myself for so many years. I never thought I would see her name again, and I don't know what it means."

"Gran?"

"There's a story behind that name, Ethan. One I didn't think would resurface," she says, her voice shaky.

"Tell me?" My heart's in my throat, thinking she could be in trouble.

"Take a seat, but you have to promise me, whatever I tell you, it won't go any further than you. Not even the guys."

"You're worrying me," my tone subdued, as I take a seat on the chair next to her bed.

"It's not a nice story. I've never told a soul, not even your grandfather. He was away when it happened."

"How long ago was this?" I hold her frail hand, and she clutches me tightly.

"Twenty-one years ago, almost to the day actually." I help Gran sit up when she tries to do it herself. "Your grandfather was in China, your parents and you had gone with him."

"I remember. I was sixteen." It had been a great trip.

"I remember your excitement when you came back. That's when I knew I would send you across the world to get my paintings." She smiles, taking my hand. "A few nights after you all left. I decided to take the dogs and go for a night walk in the woods. I was just about to head back when I heard a loud crash. God, it was awful, Ethan. The noise. I still hear it. The screaming. I ran in the direction until it all went silent, and all I could hear was someone crying." She wipes a tear from her cheek with the back of her hand. "The dogs found her first, curled up in a ball."

"What the fuck, Gran?" She shakes her head, and I know I need to keep my mouth shut.

"It was a young girl. She was covered in dirt. I checked her over. She had a few scrapes, but nothing serious. The overpowering smell of smoke lingered in the air. The poor girl didn't say a word, just looked towards the road. She was shaking so badly. I told her to stay where she was while I went to look to see if there was anything or anyone hurt. I don't know, I went on autopilot, knowing she couldn't be there alone, or her family could be trapped. I mean, she was in her pyjamas. I found a car upside down, flames starting to take hold. Oh, god," she sucks in a deep breath, calming herself. "When I looked inside, there was a woman trapped. I still remember her eyes. So vivid. The poor thing was bleeding heavily. I couldn't stop it. I knew she didn't have long, but I couldn't leave her. I just couldn't. So, I took her hand and held on tightly. Even with the flames getting closer, I wasn't going to let her be there alone, Ethan. I couldn't. When she realised I was there, she looked relieved." She gulps down a breath. I guess the next bit is going to be hard.

"She told me over and over again that she'd made her daughter run into the woods to hide. Her words were slurred; she was almost frantic to tell me."

"Hide from what?" I ask.

"There were people after her, bad people, she said. She made me promise to find her and keep her safe. To hide her away if I could. When I told her she was already safe, she burst into tears, thanking me." Gran closes her eyes. "When she saw light in the distance, she tensed, wincing in pain, and told me to run. To leave her and go to her daughter. I didn't want to leave her. I knew she'd never make it to the hospital; there was too much blood. She asked me to grab a bag from the back and leave. That it was everything I needed to know." Gran swallows, obviously reliving the moment she left her in the car.

"I left her, Ethan. I left her alone to die. I ran back to her daughter and hid with her when I heard a car screeching. Then shots were fired. I feared the worst. I just prayed she passed before they found her. I knew then I'd do anything to keep this girl safe. I had no idea who she was or what had happened. After it all went silent, we heard them searching the woods and ran to the house, the dogs silently leading us back. I turned off all the lights, trying to ask her questions about who she was, what her name was, who her mother was, but she kept saying she didn't remember."

"Gran," I sigh.

"I know, dear, I've kept her secret, and I kept her safe." She sighs, sinking into the pillow.

"So, the name?"

"That was her mother, the woman who died in the car. I called the police after I hid the girl, telling them I'd heard a car crash on the road. They ruled it as an accident. It was never spoken of again. No mention of a daughter, just a woman driver's life taken in a tragic accident."

"How is that possible? Surely someone was missing her?"

"I have no idea, Ethan, but she's remained hidden. I lost track of her when she was eighteen. I've not heard anything since." I have so many unanswered questions right now. I don't even know where to start.

"How did you hide the girl?"

"Those are things that will die alongside me, Ethan. You don't need to know anymore, but I will ask you one thing."

"Anything, just name it."

"Find the person who painted it. Find Luna Solace."

"I can, it should be easy, but you said the woman died?" I say, stating the obvious. If she's already dead, then there's nothing to find.

"She did. I lay flowers on her grave every year." I'm confused as fuck.

"Why do you need to find who it is?"

"I want it to be a simple coincidence. Clarification."

"I don't see how it could be anything else. But I'll find them for you." She closes her eyes and drifts off to sleep after a few minutes. I'll do my best, even if I have no idea what I'm looking for.

Chapter Twenty

Old Friend

Aggie

Ethan said I could take the day off, since he's with his gran at the hospital today. I've been asking how she is since he messaged me yesterday, and he told me she'll be going home later today. That was the only message I received.

He must be so relieved.

I've never had anyone to worry about like that, so I can't imagine what it feels like to think you might lose someone right in front of your eyes.

Since I got the call from Raff yesterday about Ethan's gran, I've had everything handled. Between me and the others at Cerberus, we've covered everything he needed to do, giving him the time to be with her. When I told Owen, Leon and Cole about Lady Celeste, they all seemed as worried as Ethan. It warmed my heart to know he has so many people who will help and support him. Having the day off was wishful thinking on my part since I've diverted all his calls to my phone.

Pressing the phone to my ear again as I answer yet another call, I walk into my studio building, waving to everyone I see. I've not been here since the day I got the job at Cerberus. And I want some time to focus on my painting, but the way today is panning out, I may just be sitting, answering calls and not painting at all.

I make my way to the top floor, climbing the concrete stairs as I listen to Mr Oldbrook drone on about not being able to speak with Ethan.

I can't wait to sink into my own little piece of heaven. Taking my keys from my bag, I lean against the wall, repeating that Mr Ford will be back tomorrow.

"Mr Oldbrook, I will pass on the messages regarding the cover for your daughter. It is important to us." I mean what I say. Placing the key in the door does nothing and that's when I realise it's unlocked. I cringe, rolling my eyes at myself. It's not the first time I've left the door unlocked.

Sliding it open, I step in and pull it closed. Closing my eyes, I let out a sigh of relief as the guy on the phone admits defeat that he won't be talking to Ethan today. "Thank you, Mr Oldbrook," I say as I hang up the phone before he can start the same story again. "Thank fuck," I groan, feeling the tension ease in my shoulders; only my entire body tenses again when there is a rustling sound to my side.

Turning my head, I open my eyes, "Oh my god," I scream when I see a man, dressed head to toe in dark grey, browsing through the stack of finished paintings in my rack, like he owns the place. I freeze on the spot, my heart beating frantically in my chest.

"Who are you? You can't be in here," I yell, as he chuckles. *Chuckles?* He makes his way to another stack, unfazed by my entrance. He's tall, well built, older. I note. His gloved fingers tracing the edges of the frames. The action sends a chill down my spine. "Please leave." He eyes me, a sadistic smile on his face, my stomach sinks, with unease as he steps closer, the heavy thud of his boots echoing eerily around the room. "How did you get in?" I ask, as he continues to stare at me, his long coat stiff, and unmoving as he steps towards me.

There's something about him that screams, *you should be scared.*

And I am. But I won't show it. This is my space.

"I'm an old friend," he sneers, tilting his head in my direction. I have no idea who he is; there's nothing familiar about him. Sliding the door back open behind me, I move to the side so he can get past and leave.

"You're no friend of mine, please leave or I'll call security." He's not in any rush, walking over to the brushes I keep by the small sink and inspecting them.

"I'll leave," he says, his tone dark and disconcerting, "but we both know there's no security here." He saunters towards me, his dark eyes set on me. I'd squirm, but I seem to be unable to move.

"Leave and don't come back," I manage to say, stronger than I expected.

"I can't promise anything, Sophie." With that last statement, he walks away closing the door quickly behind him, I lock it, relief washing through every fibre of my body as I take a step back.

He's gone.

"What the hell was that?" Grabbing my phone from my pocket, I call Max on the ground floor unit.

"Hey, you," Max greets me. He's a photographer and uses the space to develop his film.

"Max, there's a guy just about to leave. Can you get a photo of him for me?" I ask in a rush.

"Sure, doing it now."

"Thanks, has he gone?" I ask, my voice shaky.

"He's just got into a very expensive-looking car. I got all the plates and great pic of his face." He's quiet for a moment. "Is everything okay, Aggie?"

"I don't know. I just found him in my studio. I'll look through, make sure nothing is missing."

"I'll be up in a minute to help," he exclaims.

"Thanks, Max," I say, ending the call.

"There's nothing missing," I announce after we looked around. Max checked the windows to find them all still locked and intact. "What was he doing here?"

He must have come through the door, but no one saw him come up. And you have to pass four other units to get to the stairs.

"Maybe he just wanted to look around. We get someone at least once a month poking their nose in, thinking they can treat the place like a shopping mall."

"Yeah, maybe you're right." Although it feels far from it. The whole thing feels off, and it's left me a little scared. Why call me Sophie? I guess he has me mixed up with someone else. My hand comes to rest over the key necklace I have, soothing me like a friend as I hold it in my hand. It's the only thing that's always been with me, a part of me and I have no idea why.

"You okay if I go back downstairs?"

"Yeah, I'm good." I think. I'm not sure. Everything in me is telling me to tell Ethan, but he's got too much on his plate right now. Nothing's missing or broken, Max was more than likely right; it was just someone looking around.

An hour later, I'm back on Layla's sofa with my eyes closed as Layla gets ready for her date. She's been showing me dress after dress, and I keep telling her she looks amazing in them all, but she won't believe me.

"If you can't settle on a dress, then why wear one. You have a great jumpsuit in that wardrobe, why not wear that?" I sigh, almost reaching my limit.

"I'd forgotten all about it. I'll go and try it on." I wait again for her to come back down the stairs, sipping my cocktail from a can. I have the house to myself. I've been spending most nights at Ethan's, but with his gran poorly, I've hardly heard from him all day.

I miss him.

Layla asked if I wanted to meet up after her date—I get the feeling she's not holding out hope for this one—but I'm too tired to be going out. I want to watch a movie and have an early night. A few minutes later, Layla comes back, changed and with shoes in hand.

"You were right, this is perfect." I beam at her. *Thank god.* I don't think I could have lasted another outfit change.

Layla left an hour ago, and I've been looking at my phone like I'm waiting for it to dance in front of me. Layla has been messaging me, about how bad and boring her date is. She knows she can send me an SOS, and I'll rescue her, it won't be the first time. But I'm getting nothing from Ethan. It's been almost twenty-four hours since I've spoken to him. I want to make sure he's okay, but I don't want to intrude.

A message doesn't feel right, too impersonal, and can be misconstrued as something entirely different than its original intent.

Picking up my phone again, I record a voice note and send it over, hoping he listens and knows I'm thinking of him.

Layla: Save me from snoring into my gravy.

Me: On my way, lover.

Layla's gone to bed. We had quick drink after the SOS message, but she needs to be at the flower market at five in the morning, so she called it a night. Pulling out my phone as I sit on the sofa in the dark. I still see nothing from Ethan.

Lying back, I tell myself it's okay, that he's with family, I know his gran is important to him, and that alone makes him a good man. He talks about her more than he does his parents. But there's a niggle I always feel when I like someone. That little bitch inside me that tells me I'm not good enough and that he deserves better. His family goes back centuries, and he knows it all. Mine, I have no idea, I can't remember. I don't even know if Aggie is my real name. I can only assume, I have or had family, but they never came for me, so I guess I don't

I'm slowly running out of ways to jumpstart my memory. It all feels like too much at times. Just like right now alone on a sofa-bed, nothing to my name, massively overdrawn on my bank account, and the man I seem to be growing attached to, ghosting me. Sort of.

Okay, he's not. He has a very good reason. But I still want to know he's okay.

Not feeling tired in the slightest, I open up the photos of the guy Max took today, on my phone, and scroll through them. Why was he in my studio? There was something about him. Even though I'm sure I've never seen him before. Opening my phone, I type in the licence plate of the car into the search bar to see what comes up.

Nothing, other than the full details of the car. I don't know what I'm trying to find, but it's a dead end. Locking my phone, I lie back, staring into the darkness.

The longer I lie here, the more active my brain becomes, thinking of all the things I need to sort out for myself. A place to live. I'll start looking tomorrow. A car. That will have to wait. I may need to walk more to save a few pennies on the taxis I've been having. Then there's the big one, the one I can't stop thinking about. I need to find out who I really am. I'll keep trying until it happens.

Chapter Twenty-One

Contract

Ethan

The moment she walks through the front door to my house, my shoulders instantly relax. I've missed her. Fuck, I wanted her with me yesterday.

I half expected to get a million messages from her asking questions, but I had nothing. For a while yesterday, I was irrationally angry that she'd not even bothered to ask how I was. I lost my shit, when my parents went back to work after a quick visit to my gran. How could they? I ripped up the magazines I'd bought gran in frustration. Unable to take me anger out on my parents, and Aggie, but needing a release, it didn't help.

Then Owen called at the end of my tantrum, and told me that Aggie had forwarded all my calls to her phone, and divided two days' work between them all. I was speechless. *Still am.* She did that for me; no hesitation, no complaints, and I felt like shit for thinking she didn't care. For a split second, I placed her in the same mould as Scarlett—that woman never put me first—and yet Aggie did it without question. My chest tightens when I think of what she did for me.

She's still not switched the calls back to my phone like I expected, so, my early morning has been quiet, allowing me to focus on what I started before my gran came to the house. I've pulled up Aggie's contract and amended a few things to be beneficial to her. They will also ease my worry about her safety, the money she's using on my behalf, and my guilt for being a judgmental piece of shit yesterday. I know she has no idea about any of the thoughts that went through my head, but this feels right.

I like that she's proving me wrong about dating again.

Listening to the voice note she sent me late last night did something to unravel my heart. I've listened to it almost on repeat since.

Her sweet words were full of concern; she spoke nothing of work or anything else, just how she'd missed me, wishing my gran well, and that she would be there for me when I needed her.

I needed her, and I realise that now.

I don't want to be without her again. And I'll make sure I'm not.

"Morning," Aggie says quietly as she walks into my home office with a small paper bag in her hand. There's a slight awkwardness there that I know is my fault, and I need to fix it. I should have reached out to her, even in a message, but it just didn't feel right.

"I got these for you. I don't know if you managed to eat much yesterday." I huff a laugh. *Fuck.* She's perfect.

"What's so funny?" There's a slight scowl on her perfect face as she steps away from me.

"You... you're taking care of me, just like you did yesterday." Taking a quick glance at my screen, I hit print and listen for the printer to start. On autopilot, Aggie walks over to it, collecting the documents, and coming back, handing them to me.

"I didn't do anything yesterday. I had the day off, remember?" She says, matter-of-factly.

"I remember not receiving a single call or email."

"Ah, yeah, um." Her cheeks turn a beautiful shade of deep rose.

"I know what you did, Owen rang and told me."

"It was nothing," she says with a small shrug, and I believe she means that.

"No, Aggie, it was everything," I say, handing her back the papers. She doesn't even glance at them. "And I'm sorry you had to take on that responsibility. You didn't need to do that. I know you're my assistant, but…" I can't form the words.

"I did need to do that. You had family stuff you needed to deal with, and while I can't relate, I understand, they come first." There's a flicker of dark across her eyes.

"What do you mean?" She doesn't answer, sweeping it under the carpet like the last time when she said she'd been *taking care of herself all her life.*

"I was worried yesterday," she says, "you always take care of everyone else. I wanted to take care of you." She glides the paper bag towards me before she sits on the chair opposite. I open the bag, my mouth instantly watering from the smell of cinnamon pastry.

"Come here," I say pushing my seat back from my desk. Aggie stands and comes around the desk. She goes to sit on it, but before her arse can land on the shiny polished wood, I grab her hips, placing her on my lap. "Thank you," I rumble, taking her chin to turn her face to mine, my lips dusting hers. "And I'm sorry," I murmur, delicately kissing her lips. I love how sweet she tastes. She leans away from me, shifting slightly in my lap like she's trying to get a better look at my face.

"Why are you sorry?" She frowns.

"I should have at the very least spoken with you yesterday."

"Ethan—"

"No, I don't have a valid excuse, I'm just sorry. It won't happen again. I won't leave you out." Cupping her face, I bring my forehead to hers, soaking in everything about her.

"I'm your assistant, Ethan." She states, There's flash of melancholy across her face before she hides it away. I growl, my insides twisting that she thinks that's all she is. I lean back slightly to get a better look at her.

"You're so much fucking more than that and you know it." She grins, her eyes coming to life at my words.

"Am I?" she murmurs, her warm breath fanning over my lips.

"I've already told you this. You're *mine*, butterfly. In any way you are willing to let me have you." My heart thuds in my chest.

"I like the sound of being yours, Ethan." She kisses me, it's light, but the intention behind it is everything. The binding around my heart loosens some more with every touch and every bit of kindness she passes my way.

"Fuck, I missed having you by my side last night. I hardly slept," I rasp, breaking the kiss. She sighs like she knows exactly how I feel.

"Tonight then?" she says, already thinking ahead.

"Tonight, will you let me make it up to you?" I ask, taking her plump lip between my teeth, pulling lightly as she whimpers. My cock was hard the moment she sat on my lap. Just feeling her warmth through my trousers gets my blood rushing south.

"There's nothing to make up for, Ethan."

"I missed a night with you in my arms, baby. There's plenty to make up for. If you'll let me." My hands grab her thighs, the skirt she's wearing already riding high on her legs, showing her delicate skin.

"I'll let you." That's my girl, I think. Fuck, there's nothing better than this. Having her forgiveness, having her in my arms, here with me.

"Thank fuck," I groan, taking her mouth greedily with mine. My tongue sweeps her lips, begging for entry, but I pull away. "Reach forward and read that paperwork." She looks confused until I spread her legs apart. "Get it," I demand.

She pulls the printed pages towards us. "What is it?" She gasps as my hand glides up her inner thigh. "Ethan, I can't concentrate while you do that," she moans, but she doesn't shove me away. Instead, my girl leans back against my chest, the paperwork forgotten. Moving my hand, I brush my fingers up her back until I reach the nape of her neck, tugging her hair until she arches her back.

"You will read every word while I make you come." My words are like fire, lighting something inside me, I never want to put out.

I let go of her hair, urging her forward with the palm of my hand on her back. The slow journey makes her arse rock on my cock, my fingers digging into her soft skin as she moves. My free hand drifts towards her parted legs, inching her skirt higher, until I feel the lace of her knickers. Aggie sucks in a sharp breath as I press firmly on her clit.

"Oh-my-god." She tries to move her hips, but my hold is too firm.

"If you don't read, you don't come," I demand in a low tone which makes her whimper. Grazing my teeth over the soft skin of her neck, I add, "Now be a good girl, and read your new contract to me."

"New contract?" she says, with a shaky voice, barely above a whisper.

"You'll see." I have no idea how she'll react to it even if it's all in her favour.

She starts reading, as I spread her legs wider. "Louder, baby." She does as she's told, reading the first paragraph word for word as I edge her knickers to the side, my middle finger playing with her entrance. "Read your new benefits."

"I... Ethan..." Her fist clenches on the desk.

"Now," I growl, sinking my fingers deep inside her in one easy thrust. Her head falls forward, and she groans out a noise that make my cock pulse, and grow. My fingers scissor inside her warm wet core, as she starts to read, groaning out each word.

"Fuck... early... payment... of... salary..." she moans, her head rising and settling on my chest, as I curl my finger inside her.

"You stop, I stop." Her walls tighten around my already drenched fingers. She lets out a frustrated groan and carries on.

"Company vehicle provided..." I add another finger, hooking them this time, grazing them over her G-spot. Her legs shake. "oh... mmm... or the... Ford family... car service. Fuel allowance." She shudders as I pump my fingers in with more force.

"Good girl." And fuck me, the way her body almost convulses at my words. Fuck, it makes me harder, and happy to see she has a praise kink. "That's it, butterfly." She mumbles the next few words while her core flutters around my fingers. But I don't hear them. I know what it says, but all I can focus on is the way her body's writhing against mine.

"I can't... accept this, Ethan... oh, fuck." I push my palm against her clit, and she bucks her hips.

"You will," I grunt as her perfect arse grinds on my cock, clouding my vision. I know she's close so I bite down on the curve of her neck, and she comes all over my hand with a moan so fucking loud, I'm glad I don't have neighbours.

Those are for my ears only.

"Fuck, baby, I need to be inside you. Get yourself over my desk and bend over." She positions herself on my desk, her skirt up round her waist and her arse in the air. Waiting, I take a moment to savour the view of her peachy, flushed skin. I peel down her knickers, letting them fall to her knees. Parting her legs with my feet, I brush my fingers through her wetness, listening as she groans my name, repeatedly, her head tilting to the side to look at me.

And I'm a goner.

I work quickly to undo my belt and trousers, shoving them and my boxers down. I fist my dick, groaning loudly as it's already leaking with pre-cum. I slide the head of my cock through her folds before I push myself all the way in. Her back arches, and she's almost screaming as I fill her. Her hands grip the edge of the desk as I push as deep as I can.

"Perfect, you're so perfect, baby," I mutter as I lean over her, angling myself deeper than I thought possible.

"Ethan, oh god." she moans as I pull out halfway, gripping her hips with my hands. I trust back in, setting a punishing pace, fucking her until she grips me like a vice.

"Fuck, baby, that's it." Bringing her hips back to me, I slow my movements, guiding myself in and out, enjoying the view of filling her perfect body. "Take me, baby. Show me what a good girl you are and come all over my cock." I grunt through clenched teeth, holding back my own release as the lightning sparks my flesh, waiting for her to fall. The carnal need I have to watch her come makes me shift, almost ripping her from the desk. Turning her to face me, I watch her eyes roll to the back of her head.

"Yes, baby. Soak me." The deep guttural moan she makes before shouting my name makes my balls draw up, pleasure bursting along my spine. I'm unable to hold back, spilling inside her, holding her tight to me as my mouth captures hers in a sloppy, all-consuming kiss.

"Butterfly," I groan, my body sated and exhausted, as we slump back into my chair, my dick still throbbing in her. "Ethan, god-damn, it gets better every time."

"Sure-fucking-does. I never want us to stop." My dick agrees by remaining hard, even though I've just come. "I'm ready for round two if you are." I can feel our combined pleasure dripping down my thighs.

The laugh she gives me makes my dick twitch inside her, and she gasps as she slips off me. Me and my dick groan at the sight of her. I don't give her a chance to get away from me. I pull her back and lay her on my desk before she can say another word. She doesn't even try to protest as she wraps her legs around my waist. She tugs at my tie, loosening it before unbuttoning my shirt and shoving it down my arms. My dick is waiting, painfully hard for the woman I can't get enough of. My hands bunch the cotton of her shirt, and I tear it off, sending her buttons flying once again. I suck her nipples through the lace of her bra. She even tastes sweet.

"I'm going to... fuck it, rip it all off," she mumbles through chaste kisses. Clasping her bra with both hands, I pull, watching it split down the middle as her breasts bounce from being released. Taking them in my calloused hands, I tease them, nipping at her nipples and sucking them into my mouth. I can't get enough of her softness.

I can't wait. I inch my dick in, slowly this time, taking in the glory as it disappears into her warmth.

I set a slower pace, her hips working in unison with mine. Her hands glide up my chest to hold the back of my neck, gripping onto me like her life depends on it. My thumb brushes over the hard peak of her nipple, making her suck in a gasp. I do it again, learning what she likes, and I'll keep learning, because, fuck, she's quickly becoming my every thought.

Chapter Twenty-Two
Snuggle

Aggie

We're in his bed after we moved upstairs, when we realised we weren't going to get much done today other than each other. I'm snuggled into Ethan's side in a sex haze.

Bliss.

"Why a butterfly?" Ethan asks, brushing a featherlight touch over my tattoo. I get the feeling he's been waiting to ask about it for a while. I know this one's an easy answer, but I'm dreading the questions that getting closer to him could bring. Letting out a slow breath to make sure he doesn't notice my nerves, I'll deal with them as and when they come. I won't lie if he asks me.

"Oh, um, I guess there are a few reasons." I prop myself up on my elbow. "I love the colours, how fragile but bold they are, the way they transform themselves, but there's a small part of me that likes the spiritual representation they hold," I say, shrugging my shoulder, hoping he gets it without me having to explain.

"What's that?" I smile as he wraps my hair around his fingers. I guess I'll explain. His grey eyes shine on mine, intently listening to what I have to say. I like this bubble we're in.

"They can represent someone you've lost; it means that they're watching out for you whenever they're near." Looking down. I can't hold his gaze. It feels too much.

"Have you lost someone, Aggie?" he asks, sitting up as I lie back in the rumpled covers of his bed.

How can I answer that?

"That's a hard question to answer," I tell him as honestly as I can. Sadness fills my chest for no apparent reason other than I don't know.

I can assume I have. I don't have anyone. I must have come from someone, but... there's no memory of a family, a love, or a loss.

"You don't have to answer." His tone is soft, reassuring. "I want to know you better, that's all." *How the hell did I land someone like him?* Kind, giving, passionate, affectionate. Everything Layla told me about him being angry, never talking, or smiling, seems like she was talking about an entirely different person.

"I was a foster kid," I tell him. I never went to different homes like some other kids. I stayed with the same couple I grew up with. They were good people, but kind of let me fend for myself. They didn't tell me they loved me; they took care of me financially, made sure I was healthy and fed, but there was no emotional input. No curfews, very few restrictions on what I could and couldn't do. It was great.

"I'm sorry, I had no idea," he sighs, his voice gruff like it's upset him. I'm taken aback for a moment at his empathy.

"That's okay," I force out. "I don't know my story beyond that. Maybe I was too young. I don't remember." He kisses the top of my head before moving down the bed to face me.

"Did you ever look into it?" he asks cautiously, trying to be sensitive to my past. I did look into it, and that's where it gets a little weird, confusing and harrowingly worrying. I can't share that with him yet. It's too much for anyone to deal with, let alone someone I've just started seeing.

"Yes, but there wasn't much to find." It's like a fist grips my chest. I'm not lying, but I'm also not telling the truth. There was nothing to find. He tips my chin up to meet his gaze, his brows dipping, creating a crease in the centre.

"I have resources you could use to find out more?" I'm not sure if it's a question or a statement. My pulse hammers. I know what they do, of course I do. I've seen the files and information they have on their clients. But I can't and won't use it. There's nothing to find. No family, no history, nothing.

"There's nothing to find, Ethan, but thank you." God, I wish I could say I've come to terms with it, so I don't need to look into my past.

But I haven't.

Harrowing, I mentioned that, right? And it is... I don't know how else to describe it. Because there is no fostering file on me. Yep, nothing. That's the reason I left my foster parents' house when I was eighteen. I contacted social services to request my file, I had no idea I could have done it earlier, no-one told me. They said the name wasn't on their system. Of course, being a hot-headed person I am, I went home asking what the hell it meant, only to be met with silence, questioning looks, and limited answers. They said it didn't matter, I was looked after, move on.

How could I? I'd been lied to all my life, and they didn't want to tell the truth, or didn't trust me enough to explain what happened to me.

I left that night, never went back home, or to the ballet school I'd been attending since I was fifteen, and never looked back. I moved on just like they asked me to. I miss them. We've been in contact since, but it's always been brief.

"Will you answer a question for me?" I ask, stroking his chest as he hums a yes. "How long were you engaged for?" He tenses and sucks in a breath. "Have I touched a nerve?" I ask.

"Yes and no," he grumbles. "We were engaged for less than a year, but we were together for about three. I ended things over two years ago."

"That must have been hard, all that time on one person. What happened?"

"She slept with someone behind my back, thinking I wouldn't find out. And when I did, she asked what the big deal was." *What a bitch.*

"Holy-shit, that's awful," I say, unable to imagine being betrayed like that.

"It wasn't pretty. The fallout was big." He smiles, confusing me. "I've only ever told one person about what she did."

"Who?"

"Gran." Goddamn, how can this man be sweet and dangerous at the same time?

"I would never have believed that Ethan Ford, grumpy, silent, annoying, sex god, and silent joker, would be a softie for his grandmother." I chuckle, flicking his nipple. He hisses, lifting my finger to bite the tip before sucking it into his mouth.

"Sex god?" he says, removing my finger from his mouth with a pop. I slap his chest playfully. "The guys know bits, but it was my Gran who drank me under the table, the night I found out."

"I'm sorry, what?" I really want to meet this woman. The more I hear, the more I want to meet the legend.

"I came back home so fucking angry, I threw a bottle of thirty-year-old whisky across the room. Livid with myself more than anything. For not seeing it sooner, for her reaction to it all." He sighs, then rolls his eyes like he's remembered something. "My Gran just walked in like she's always done, after Raff rang her telling her what was happening. She plonked herself next to me on the couch and handed me a new bottle of the whisky, telling me I'd better drink this one, and forget the whore ever existed, or she'd never speak to me again. I don't remember much after that." I burst out laughing, covering my mouth with my hand. *What a woman.*

"She sounds like a woman I'm definitely going to get on with." Is it presumptuous of me? Hell, I don't care at this point. He's given me so many orgasms in the last few hours, I'm as attached to him as my vagina is.

"She already likes you." I gasp this time. He's spoken to her about me? My heart does a very odd turn in my chest.

"You've told her about me?" My eyes widen.

"No, Raff did." I laugh. Of course. Stupid brain thinking otherwise.

"That man likes to stir the pot, doesn't he?" I add, trying to cover my weird reaction.

"He does." I snuggle closer, my eyes growing heavy as he draws circles on my back. He wraps his arms tighter around me, so there's no space between us, just how I like it. "I would have told her anyway," he voices, his tone low and settling as I drift off to sleep.

When I wake up, it's dark outside, and Ethan is nowhere to be seen. But the smell of food wafts through the open door of the bedroom. Grabbing a shirt, I follow my nose to the smell of roast chicken.

Finding Ethan in the kitchen, shirtless, chopping food, is one of the finest sights I have ever seen. Every muscle in my body tightens. His muscles work and flex with the slightest movement of the knife. I can't see what he's wearing below the waist; the counter in front of him is blocking my view.

"What are you cooking?" I ask from the doorway. He looks up, eyes meeting mine, and places the knife on the counter. Wiping his hands on a towel that hangs over his shoulder, the one I had no idea was there, being too distracted by his abs, arms, and... well, that's it. It's enough to floor any woman.

"Warm roast chicken salad," he says as he walks over to me. I don't seem to be able to move when I see what he's wearing. My jaw hangs open.

Fuck, who knew sport shorts did it for me? Not me. But *holy-hell*, they do. I lick my lips, my mouth going dry. I need to swallow, but can't.

He tips his head to the side, watching me clench my thighs together.

And full-on *smirks*.

I've never seen it before, and if the shorts that are hanging from his hips, showing me that divine V that leads to the best cock I've ever seen, wasn't enough to make me wetter than I have ever been, than that smirk. *God-fucking-damn him*, he's ruining me, I'm never coming back from this, him.

He's talking, leading me to sit on the stools that surround the counter where he's cutting salad. "Try this." He shreds a piece of chicken. "Open," he says, then places the chicken on my tongue. "Eat." I moan at the flavours: herbs and lemon, with a buttery, salty warmth.

"That's good."

"Just good?"

"Good enough, that if you leave the kitchen, I'll eat the whole damn thing."

"I'm not leaving you or the kitchen unattended." He steps away, and I pout. "If you want to eat, I need to cook." I pout again, but realise I get to watch. And give him a smirk of my own.

"I'd help, but I feel I'd injure myself." His eyes shoot to mine, that brow creasing again.

"Why? Can't you cook?" I steal another piece of chicken that he's placed in the bowl.

"Oh, I can cook," I say through my mouthful.

"Then why would you hurt yourself?"

"Dressed like that, Mr Ford," I love the way his eyes flare when I call him that. "You're a dangerous distraction."

Chapter Twenty-Three

Needy

Ethan

Stretching my body, I stand from the chair I've been in all day. I'm done with today. This meeting started at 9 am, and it's now five. Leon, Cole, and Owen all look ready to throw in the towel.

We don't do these sorts of meetings often. But we've been requested to participate in a… private sector job. We're joining forces with other teams from Spain, the US, and the UK, and it is always a logistical nightmare. Add in transportation, accommodation, food, border control, immigration, and customs red tape, and paperwork, we needed the day to get it all straight. But we now have a plan in place to start shipping what we need at the end of the week, ready to set up camp for when the guys arrive.

Shutting my laptop down, I nod to the guys and leave. Almost eight hours in a meeting with only glances of Aggie, when she popped in with tea and food for us, has almost killed me. But I couldn't put my hands on her. Now I'm desperate to.

And that's where I'm heading. I don't care that I'm at work, I need to feel her.

During the meeting, I noticed she blocked out another few hours in the diary for Monday afternoon. She only books them when I'm not with her. I want to know where she goes. Then again, I crave to know everything she does, and everything about her. I loved that she opened up to me yesterday. Fuck, it meant so much to me. I think that's why I told her about my ex when she asked.

Every time she comes back from wherever she goes, she has a new bruise, a red mark or a limp. Something's hurting her, and it makes me sick to my stomach that she's doing it willingly.

I've been cataloguing all her bruises since I found the bruise on her arm. I've seen a lot of bruises in my life, and I can't figure out what is causing them; there doesn't appear to be any consistency. Still, that slow, easy smile that used to creep onto her beautiful face, when she would leave to do whatever it is that she's doing, is fading each time she comes back.

"Shit," she curses when I step through the door of my office. My eyes shoot up, worry encasing my chest when I see blood.

"What happened? Are you okay?" She jumps at my sudden appearance.

"I'm fine," she says, but she winces. I hold her wrist still as reaches for a tissue.

"You're bleeding; you're not fine." She tries to tug her hand away, but I hold tight. "Sit," I almost yell.

"It's a paper cut, Ethan," she states as she takes her seat. I kneel in front of her, checking the cut on her finger.

"Let me take care of you," I plead. She cups my face and leans into me.

"Hi." She kisses my cheek. "Okay."

I open the drawer in her desk and grab what I need. She hisses when I apply the antiseptic cream.

"Sorry," I mutter as I wrap her finger in a plaster. "All done."

"My knight in a suit." She laughs as I stand back up.

"Come here." I reach for her to stand with me. "I've missed you today," I say into her hair as I hold her.

"I've missed you too." I walk her to the edge of the desk, my hands on her sweet arse. I go to lift her onto the desk when she stops me. "As much as I want this, Ethan." My hand creeps up to cup her breast. "I can't."

"Can't?" I ask, gripping the nape of her neck to get a better angle as I lean in and kiss it. "Are you sure?"

"No, I'm not sure. Fuck, Ethan," she whines, as I suck her tender skin into my mouth, I won't leave a mark, not this time.

"What would sway you?" She's already panting.

"Can you be quick? I'm heading out," I growl, not liking that she's limiting my time, but I'll take it.

"I can be quick, but I don't like it." I spread her legs. Thank god she's wearing a skirt today. "Pull your skirt up." And she does. We both groan when I pull her knickers to the side and edge my finger inside her.

"Soaked," I moan, I sliding my fingers out and through her folds. "Get my cock out," I demand as her arousal seeps from her. She makes quick work of getting me free, and when she wraps her hand around my cock, I pull back. "No time, baby." She's wet enough. If she wants quick, that's what she'll get. I'll make it up to her later. I'll edge her for hours. Lifting her onto the desk, I slip her shoes off.

"Feet on the desk." Her cheeks flush with arousal as she does what she's told.

Settling my hips between her legs, I fist my cock, dragging it through her slit, covering myself with her juices. "Hold your legs." She grasps the backs of her thighs, holding them tight as I thrust in. She bites her lip as I fill her. I know she can take me, but I give her a second. The small nod she gives me, along with the walls rippling around me, lets me know she's ready. I pull out and push back in. "Fuck," I grit out through clenched teeth. "You feel incredible."

"So. Do. You," she manages between my ruthless thrusts. I move my hand to her clit, circling it, and as I add pressure, her walls clamp down on my cock, and I groan, "Fuck." Her hand drops one of her legs. I almost protest, but she covers her mouth, her whole body quivering, hooking her legs over my arms, to keep her where I want her as I fuck her into her desk.

"Ethan, I'm...." I feel it. She never has to say because I feel her walls pulse as she comes apart as my orgasm rises through my balls. I roll my hips, my dick coaxing her sweet spot as sparks fly over my skin. I come hard and so deep inside my woman, she'll be dripping for hours. She drops the other leg, now hanging from the desk, and wraps her arms around me as I collapse on top of her, resting my weight on my arm.

"Was that quick enough for you?" I tease. She beams at me, and it's the best sight when I'm still inside her.

"Just what I needed for a night out." I shake my head and tentatively move away from her. She's quick to stand and walk to the bathroom.

"Where are you off to?" I ask, pulling my boxers and trousers back up.

"Out. I'll see you tomorrow for the gala?" she shouts through the door as I hear it flush. I sink into my chair, waiting for her to come back.

When she walks out, she still looks like she's been fucked. The whole office smells like sex. Aggie walks over to open the window to let some fresh air in. When she picks up her stuff to leave, she comes over, placing her palm flat on my desk before bending down. I kiss her when she leans in.

"You're not coming back to mine tonight?" I ask, disappointed that I won't see her.

"Not tonight, Joker. I'm off out with the guys from the studio; they head out every Friday, and I've not been since I've been back." She sits on my knee.

"Can I come?" Fuck, I sound desperate and needy.

"You want to come with me?" Her eyes sparkle, like she likes that I've asked.

"Yeah, if they're people you like, I want to get to know them," I say, rubbing her knee with the pad of my thumb.

"Okay, pick me up from the house at eight." She doesn't look annoyed that I'm crashing her night out. "What do I wear?" I ask, and she laughs as she heads out the door, not answering me.

I'm just getting out of the car when I see the front door open. Aggie steps out, and my heart pounds when I see what she's wearing. From bottom to top, my gaze takes in every inch of her black boots that reach the top of her knees, leggings that hug her thighs, and a shirt that looks to be mine. Fuck, it looks good on her. Keeping the car door open, I start walking towards the house. Layla is behind her, and they chat for a second, before she heads towards me.

Do they live together? These houses are only one bed. I meet her on the small pathway, ducking to kiss her, before I lead her to the car, holding her hand.

"Do you two live together?"

"For now," Aggie says, settling into the car and fastening her seatbelt.

"Is she moving out?" She laughs, retaking my hand in hers.

"No, I will be. I'm sleeping on her sofa while I find a place to live." I'm instantly irritated at myself for not checking sooner. Of course, she wouldn't have a place to live. She's been travelling for the last few months.

"What's stopping you from getting your own place?"

"Nope." She shakes her head and sits up to face me.

"What do you mean, nope?" I mimic, and she gives me a knowing look.

"If I tell you, you'll do exactly what you did with the car and expenses thing. My bank account is already looking healthier than it should be, given I've been working with you for two weeks, and I don't get officially paid until the end of the month. What you gave me was over three months' wages." *It should have been more.* "This is my thing, I don't need your help with it. You're already helping by letting me sleep in your bed, as well as paying me to do my job." I hold my hands up in defeat. I won't say anymore. When she finally decides to let me in and see her place when she gets one, I'll kit it out, making sure she's safe there.

"Have you used the car yet?" I bought one for her, knowing she'd hate all the big trucks and vans we use.

"No, not yet." She states.

"What about the bank cards?" She rolls her eyes, and it's cute when she gets frustrated with me.

"Again, no, I've had no need. I have used the car service though, to get home, remember? In fact, I found a great little place today. I'm going to view it over the weekend. I think it'll be perfect." She's beaming, wiggling her arse in the seat with excitement, and I can't deny, I would do anything to keep that smile there.

"Can I come and see it with you?" I ask, watching her excitement calm.

"No," she says flatly, a look of horror in her eyes. The smile on my face drops as I watch her bite her lips, hiding her initial reaction.

"Why are you hiding it from me?"

"I'm not hiding it, Ethan, it's just very... very different to what you would consider a home."

"If you like it, so will I." I couldn't care less, how small or I have a feeling... unconventional, it would be, I'd be there. "Will I ever see it?" I feel wounded by her reaction, and I think she sees it, even when my face is like stone.

"Of course," she blurts. "I want it signed on the dotted line before I show you." I'm not convinced. She actually thinks I'll hate it. Which worries me. *What sort of place is it?*

The car slows to a stop before I can make another comment, and I jump out to open Aggie's door.

"You understand, don't you?" she says as she steps out. "I've been on my own a long time, Ethan. It's going to take me a while to get used to having someone in my corner." My hands slid around her waist, pulling her to me.

"Yeah, butterfly, I understand." Walking into the bar a few minutes later, we're surrounded by people, most of which all hug and kiss Aggie on the cheek. I'm not happy about it, but I think she'd give me shit if I told them all to get their fucking hands off my woman.

Someone called Max takes us over to a corner where they've set up for the night. Everyone's watching Aggie, I can't blame them, she's stunning to watch. She turns around and takes my hand. "Everyone, this is Ethan. My..." She seems stuck on what I am to her, and I watch her, internally smirking at the battle she has in her eyes at what to call me. Boyfriend, lover… partner?

Husband.

I'd like that; to call her mine forever. But we have only been together for a few weeks. I won't finish for her. I want to see what she comes out with.

"Friend." *No*, that's not happening. I bring our joined hands to her stomach, I clutch her waist, bringing her to me, skimming my lips over her ear. The growl that leaves my throat makes her visibly shudder. I nip her ear, making sure her attention is on me and no one else. With my tone deathly low, I let her know exactly how I feel about being introduced as a *friend*.

"Naughty girl, aren't you, butterfly." I breathe in her shudder. "Introducing me as your friend." Aggie whimpers, her lashes lowering as her hand tightens in mine. "Friends don't scream my name as I fuck them," I trail a finger down the arch of her neck. Lowering my voice so only she can hear me, I say, "Friends don't whimper when I take hold of their pussy and make them come." Her breath stutters as she gulps, "You're anything but a friend, Aggie Hope. I'm giving you my word," I know all eyes are on us, and I'm claiming her as mine in front of everyone in this bar. "Ever call me a friend again, and you'll see just how um-*friendly* I can be when it comes to you."

She spins around when I loosen my grip. I have no idea how she's going to take what I've just said. I meant every word. I'll teach her a lesson.

Aggie wraps her arms around my neck, "Fuck, Joker, that was… the sexiest thing anyone has ever said to me." She places the smallest kiss on my lips before she steps away.

I'm left with blue balls, imagining every way I can tie her down and punish her. Instead, I have to watch her be her perfect self with everyone around us.

It's a good night, I keep the drinks coming for us both, as she dances and chats about her travels, I listen intently to learn as much as I can about her and her life.

I'm left at the table with some of the other guys, as Aggie and another woman I can't remember the name of sneak off to the toilet together.

"Max," the guy next to me says, introducing himself. "Not a friend then?" he jokes.

"Not a friend, but we're still new." He nods in understanding.

"I get it. I'm in the same boat with Russ over there." He waves to the guy at the bar.

"How long have you known Aggie?" I ask, eager to know anything he can give me.

"Years. We rented our studios at the same time about four years ago. We've been friends ever since," he says, lifting his drink and taking a sip.

"What do you do there?"

"I'm a nature photographer. I use it to develop and print my work. On occasion, I take pictures of people, like the other day when Aggie found that random dude in her studio."

What the fuck?

"What guy?" I say through clenched teeth, my mind reeling. Aggravating me, like a hot poker dragging over my skin. She's not mentioned anything. Was she scared? Did she think she couldn't tell me? Fuck, this is what I do for a living. And I wasn't there for her. Maybe it was nothing, but if he took a picture of the guy, Aggie couldn't have felt like it was *nothing*.

"I don't know." He looks down, as if he's unsure if he should say anything. "He was already in there when she arrived the other day."

"What day?" I demand. I'll get everything I can on him, make sure it's nothing. I ask Max some more questions, and he tells me everything he knows. Turns out, it was the day I spent with my Gran. Fuck, now I feel like an even bigger wanker for not speaking with her that day.

"Send me the photos." I grab my wallet and get him to scan the code, so my information will be saved directly to his phone. "If you see anything else, call me immediately." He looks at his phone, checking my information.

"Cerberus Security. Shit, I've heard good things about you guys." Max looks back at me, his eyes a little wider than they were before, now he knows who I am. "Is everything okay?" he asks.

"It will be. How's the security of the place?"

"Non-existent really. We have a code to get in, but most of the time it doesn't work."

"Don't tell Aggie you've told me about it. I'll sort it out," I assure him.

I bring up Leon's contact on my phone and shoot him a quick message.

> **Me:** Can you get me the floor plans for the studio building Aggie works in?

> **Leon:** Sure can, my friend. Are we raiding or surveilling?

> **Me:** I'll be setting up cameras over the weekend, so I can do some surveillance.

> **Leon:** What's going on? Is Aggie okay?

Looking up from my phone, I watch as she comes back to the table. She has a massive smile on her face, her cheeks flushed from a few drinks and dancing; she looks more than fine to me.

> **Me:** She's good. She found a guy in her studio the other day. Just want to watch out for her.

> **Leon:** Consider it done. I'll get what we need and help you fit them.

Between this potential threat to Aggie and what my Gran shared with me, I'll be glad to have Leon's help.

I've been digging into Luna Solace—the woman my gran told me about. I've come up with nothing, other than the car crash details from the night she died

Luna was an artist, other than that, a nobody really. There's no mention of a daughter, but Gran only gave me a fraction of information to go on. I'll keep looking. I've contacted the gallery I got the painting from, but they denied me any access to the personal information. If I can't find anything more, then I'm more inclined to write it off as a coincidence. We don't even know if the girl in the woods was her actual daughter. If the Solace woman had a daughter, there'd be a record of it. But there's nothing.

Maybe it's best kept in the past.

Chapter Twenty-Four
Not Me

Aggie

"Ethan, I've had a call from the venue. I need to get down there. Something about things going missing." I'm rushing to get my stuff from my desk. I'll be cutting it close to get my hair and makeup done and be ready on time. I'm already behind, but with this, I may have to cut something off from my list.

Make up, I can do that myself.

"Does my mum know? She should be around?"

"I've not heard from her since we coordinated arrival times yesterday," Ethan frowns like she should be there to sort this shit out, not me. She hates that I'm with Ethan, she's made her dislike of me very clear every time we've spoken since. She hung up on me twice, and Ethan once, after he told her I would be his date.

"Get someone else to deal with it; you're my guest tonight." He sounds annoyed. I can't blame him, I am too.

"I'm still your assistant, Ethan, and this is your family *work* thing. She asked for me, and I can't let them down." Stupid responsibilities.

"You can. I'll call them and get someone else to deal with it." He's already dialling the number as I shake my head at him.

"No, please don't." I rest my hand over the one dialling the number. He hangs up, kissing my knuckles.

"Aggie," He looks pissed, not at me, I know that. "Who did you speak to?" He swings his chair towards me. We weren't even supposed to be in the office this afternoon. I had the viewing of my new place this morning, I had a call from Ethan asking me to go in and do a few things as he'd been called to a small job. I was happy to help; the man's given me an extortionate amount of money to 'compensate' for what I've spent over the last few weeks. So, if he asks me to work more, I will. It's also the reason I got my new place as quickly as I did. The extra cash helped, along with the Cerberus job reference.

"Susan, why?" I say, after taking a moment to remember.

"You sure?" I baulk, and he smiles. "I'm just asking, not questioning you."

"Of course, I'm sure."

"Only everything was good a couple of hours ago, when I called to confirm our arrival time."

"That is odd, but it is what it is." I huff. I've confirmed a few times over the course of the day. It's just my luck that it would all go wrong when I need to get ready.

"I'll come with you." He makes to grab his jacket, but I stop him.

"No, you're already behind. You need to get ready and be there on time. Worst case, I can meet you there. In fact, I'll head home and grab my things and get ready there."

"No." The crease of his frown line grows deeper.

"No?" God, he's frustrating sometimes.

"I'm not having you getting ready in some shitty backroom." That's cute. Frustration gone.

"I don't have time for this," I tell him, my voice softer now.

"Fuck," he mutters, picking up the phone again. Before he can argue with me anymore, I take his face in one hand and place a long kiss on his cheek.

"See you there, handsome," I say as whoever's on the other side of the phone answers, and I run out the door.

I think I hear him say something about taking the car, but the elevator door is already closing behind me.

Opening the door to the gala hall, I'm in awe of how beautiful it is. They have done such an amazing job. I've had a look around, and I can't see anything out of place or missing. *Strange*. I've even checked in with the staff running the event for us, and they can't seem to find out why I was called. *Stranger still*. I've taken it upon myself to check over everything anyway. Inventory, food, deliveries, guest list, seating arrangements, flowers, the lot. My phone pings in my hand as I walk through the last section. My stomach sinks with disappointment that I won't get to my hair or my make up appointment now. I was looking forward to being pampered for a while. Letting out a heavy sigh, I look at my phone.

Hot Boss: I tried to get you a room to get ready in, but they're fully booked. I'm so sorry. Where are you?

Me: You're sweet, but it's okay.

Hot Boss: Where are you?

"Excuse me?" Turning to the voice next to me, I find a man standing too close. I step back, but he seems to follow. My phone forgotten, I put on a smile. "Yes?"

"You work here?" There's something strange in his tone, like he knows I don't but is asking anyway, questioning what I would be doing here. His arm comes out to take hold of mine, it's not sudden or threatening, but my stomach recoils.

"No, I don't," I croak, my voice somehow missing its normal spark. I stumble backwards, looking over his shoulder, like I've seen someone and need him to notice. I'm scared, but he's not giving me a real reason to be. He double checks, looking where I have my eyes trained. And thank fuck because Susan... *Susan* walks through the door.

"Aggie, I hear you've been looking for me," she says, coming closer. God, I'm grateful, and my heart slows from its previous wildness.

"Yes, thank you for finding me." I sidestep the man.

"What can I help you with?" she says, smiling at the guy still standing too close to me. The whole situation leaves me feeling a little flustered and uneasy. He gives me a weak smile, then disappears through the door. "I didn't mean to interrupt you," she says, looking between us.

"That's okay. I have no idea who he was anyway." I mentally shake off the weird interaction.

"I don't think he's a guest. Doesn't look familiar. We have the same crowd every year at the gala, maybe he's a plus one," she says, with a small shrug of her shoulder.

"Maybe." An invisible shudder travels up my spine, leaving me feeling *vulnerable*.

"One of the guys said you were looking for me. I've been out all day, an emergency at one of our sister hotels. All sorted now. What did you need?"

"Oh." She's been out all day? "You called me?"

"No, that can't have been me. Like I said, I've not been here." What the hell is happening?

"So, nothing's missing?"

"I'm lost?" *Me too.* I don't have time for this, Ethan's arrival is set for thirty minutes time, and I still need to get ready.

"Never mind, is there a staff room I can get ready in? I'm running late."

"Yes, follow me."

"Thank you." Something about all this feels wrong. My stomach flips with unease. Something's not right.

Ethan will have to wait for his message. I've got a gala to get ready for.

I practically run to the entrance in my dress, my heels clicking on the tiled floors as I go. Ready to meet Ethan at the door, once he's done his press bit. I was supposed to be by his side, but I'm a little relieved I'm not. I'd hate to see what they had to say about me this time, and I don't want Ethan managing the articles that surface every time we're together. He already has a lot on his plate. I'm nervous. This will be the first time we're seen together as a couple, something he hammered into me when we left the bar last night.

I'm not nervous about being seen with him, I never could be, but the reactions of everyone else. That makes my anxiety rise. I'll have to let his mum know that I'll be throwing her precious little black book in the bin.

Now that's cheered me up.

Catching my breath when I reach the door, I watch the cars come and go, dropping off the guests in all their finery. It's wonderful to watch.

Ethan's parents arrive first with a woman I don't know. They stand together like they know each other well, laughing and joking. I wonder who she is. When Ethan's car pulls up, my smile spreads as he steps out in, fuck me, a tux. I knew it was a tux; I got it ready for him. I'm melting at how delicious he looks. All black with an ivory tie, the same colour as my dress. My chest squeezes when he looks around. His step falters when he sees his parents, but then continues in their direction. "What did he see?" I mumble to myself. What made him do that?

I watch him intently, his left hand in his pocket, eyes still scanning around. I hope he's looking for me. I swallow when he reaches his parents, the woman with them steps up to him, placing a hand on his arm, and running it up to his shoulder.

"Who is that?" My voice is a little louder this time, the unease I felt earlier settling into my stomach again. I jump when someone answers me.

"Don't they look perfect together?" Turning to my side, Susan's eyes are locked on Ethan and the woman touching him.

"Who?" I know who she's referring to. I'm not stupid.

"Ethan and Scarlett." *Holy fuck.* That's her. His ex-fiancée. I take a step back, not knowing what to do with all this... haze of hate and turmoil, rushing my system. My heart's pounding, knowing what she did to him, and yet, he's letting her touch him.

Like nothing happened.

"Do you think they're back together," she asks, and I startle. No. He's with me. "I heard a rumour that there is going to be some sort of announcement tonight. Maybe the weddings back on." *The wedding back on? Back together.*

All rational thoughts leave my brain, wedding, engagement, she's there, I'm not. Taking the clipboard from Susan that holds the guestlist to check off when people arrive, I snap, "I'll do this. I'm sure you have plenty to do."

"Would you, thanks," she says, oblivious to my inner turmoil. "Will you bring it over before the dinner drinks?" I must be hiding it well, the mess going on in my chest and head.

"Sure." I slink back and watch everyone arrive, marking them off as they hand in their coats. Almost on autopilot.

I don't bother finding Ethan. I don't feel like being part of any of this. I know that none of it is true. He *was* looking for me when he arrived.

Why didn't I walk out there?

Finding my backbone, I head over to Susan to hand her the list, ready to find Ethan and enjoy our night, like we planned.

"Oh, Aggie, I'm glad I found you. I have something for you," Susan announces.

We exchange papers, mine much smaller than hers. Biting my lip in excitement at the folded bit of paper, imagining a secret note from Ethan telling me to meet him somewhere, I walk toward the dining hall where the drinks are being served, opening the note as I go.

Scurry back to your pathetic life. Ethan is mine and always will be.
Scarlett James, soon to be Ford.

Chapter Twenty-Five
Never You

Ethan

Where the hell is she? From the moment I stepped from my car, I've been looking for Aggie. I can't focus on anything. *She's* meant to be by my side, not fucking Scarlett. I cringed when she took my arm in front of the cameras. Wanting to keep the peace, I let her, but, fuck, it felt so wrong. Like I was cheating on Aggie. As soon as we stepped into the hall, I moved away from her, but the bitch seems to follow me, smiling like this is normal. It's not normal. This was meant to be me, showing Aggie to the world. Telling everyone she's mine.

I scan the room again, but nothing. Has something happened? Surely security or even a staff member would have alerted me if something was wrong. My shoulders tense as I grind my teeth, not knowing where she is.

I'm losing my patience. The smile on my mother's fucking face is pissing me off. I'm trying my best to keep my cool, but the way Scarlett keeps trying to hold my hand, purring into my ear about random shit that could be said out loud, I'm about to fucking blow.

Why isn't my butterfly here? I want to yell it to everyone around me.

The phone call in the office unsettled me earlier; the tension in my stomach got me thinking she was being set up to fail. And now she's not here, not answering my messages, I guess I was right.

"Darling," My mother chimes, her tone sickly sweet. "It's good to see the two of you back together again."

"We're not together," I snarl, trying again to step out of Scarlett's grasp. The cheating bitch flinches at my words. She knows what she's done, and acting like the victim is enough for me to snap.

Almost.

The words are on the tip of my tongue. I have to grind my teeth together, forcing myself to stop. I take a breath. This is not the time or the place to lose my shit.

"Ethan, can't you see Scarlett loves you?" Wow, really? Mum's going there.

"I do, Ethan." Scarlett looks up at me through too much mascara.

"Really?" I ask, sarcasm dripping from me, as I eye her with so much disdain, she should fucking run.

"Of course she does. Can't you see she's perfect?" *Fuck you, fuck you all.*

"Perfect?" That's enough. I can't do it anymore.

"Ethan, you're being nasty," my mother scolds. The vibration in my chest is a dead giveaway that I'm at my limit. My heart's pounding, fists clenched in my pockets, hiding them from view.

"Nasty? Really?" I say, anger intertwining my words.

"Is this about Aggie? I saw the way you looked at her when we came to the house." My mother cuts in before I can carry on.

"She's just an assistant, Ethan. She's no good for someone like you," Scarlett chips in. At least my dad tuts, letting his opinion be known, in his own way. I know he likes Aggie. They've talked a lot over the past few weeks.

"Someone like me?" The fucking audacity of this woman. "Where is Aggie?" I ask, the feeling in my stomach growing heavy. Scarlett looks away.

"How would I know?" she states, and the fucking bitch is lying to my face. I look to my mother, and she glances at the floor. My dad looks between the two of them.

"Flo, what did you do?" he asks, taking her arm and turning her to face him.

"Nothing, honestly."

"She doesn't deserve to be here, Ethan. It should be you and me. Not *her*." The way she says it spikes my frustration to pure anger.

"What the fuck did you do?" I seethe at Scarlett.

"What should have been done weeks ago." I want to wring her neck, but I won't touch her. Instead, I stand in front of her. "I told her to leave, that she wasn't needed." She smirks. "That we're engaged." My eyes widen. She did what? I'm at a loss for words. She thinks she's done me a favour by telling Aggie this. My stomach clenches as I replay her words in my head.

Maybe she has.

Relaxing my shoulders, I step back.

"The phone call this afternoon, that was you, wasn't it?" I spit through clenched teeth.

"Yes," Scarlett admits, her smugness makes me want to vomit.

"Why?" I know why, but I want to hear her say it.

"You were getting in too deep. I saw the article. She's a nobody, Ethan. Your family deserves someone with class." I laugh in her face. Fucking class.

"Flo, if you had any part of this, that's cruel even by your standards," my dad says, as he makes to walk away, but I grab his arm.

"You need to hear this." He frowns but stands by my side. The bustling noise around us dims as guests start to listen. Everyone is watching as I turn back to the two women. I can't hold it back anymore. Aggie means more to me than any of this shit.

"Aggie has more class, grace, and kindness than I have ever seen come from either of you." Focusing my anger on my ex, I continue, "I was prepared to never tell a soul what you did, to keep your reputation intact." I look her over, glaring. "How could I have ever thought I loved you?"

"Ethan." My mom tries to stop me when Scarlett's eyes go wide like she knows what I'm going to do. And I don't care who hears it.

"Your input tonight has only made you look a fool. I will never touch Scarlett again. It will never be you," I say to Scarlett. "Never in my lifetime, or beyond." Flicking my murderous gaze to my mother, I say, "The woman you think is so perfect for me, the woman you want me to be with so badly, had an affair. With someone I introduced her to from your company. Another reason I will never work for you or take over the business."

"No, you're wrong," she mutters, looking to Scarlett.

"Flo, don't you dare say another word." My dad's warning goes unheard. "I'm sorry, son. I had no idea." I nod, and he walks away after a firm squeeze of my shoulder, leaving me with the two women I don't want to see, or be seen with.

"That speaks volumes about you, doesn't it, believing her over me, your own son."

"Scarlett, say something. Tell me he's wrong," my mother pleads, her voice high, like she's losing hope. Scarlett shakes her head, tears welling in her eyes. She knows I'll never touch her again, and from the crowd that's gathered closer, now everyone else does.

"If you don't mind, I have my perfect woman to find. One who deserves so much more than either of you ever will." *My* Aggie.

Turning, I leave them in my wake. I don't feel angry anymore. All I want to do is track down the most beautiful woman I have ever met, inside and out.

I call my driver to meet me out front. I don't care about this shit. The gala will still happen whether I'm here or not; funds will still be raised. I've done enough.

I blow through the front door, almost running for the car as it pulls to the curb. Opening the door, I climb in, the partition already down.

"Have you seen Aggie?" I ask him.

"No, sir, she's not used the service today." Fucking woman. My shoulders sag, my head hanging low. *Think, Ethan, where would she go?*

"Did she drive?" How do I have no idea how she got here? Fisting my hand, I punch the seat beside me, my driver, Ash, seeming unfazed.

"I can find out for you, sir," Ash answers, picking up his radio.

"No, drive to her house, I'll check." Pulling my phone from my pocket, I need to be the one who does the work to find her.

I call her and get nothing. Shit, why isn't she answering? Opening up the sign out form for the company cars, there's nothing there either. Even after everything I put in the contract, she's still been stubborn and using a taxi. Does she know how unsafe they can be?

How vulnerable it makes her?

The car stops before I can think further. I climb out and jog to the front door, pounding on the green painted wood. The door opens, and I'm disappointed when I see Layla.

"Ethan?" Layla looks startled as she pulls the door open wider.

"Where's Aggie?" She rolls her eyes.

"Why?" She's being a good best friend. I get that, but I need to know where she is and now.

"I need to speak with her. Please, is she here?" I peer around her, but she shuts the door a fraction, so I can't see what, or who's, inside.

"She's not here. She was. Left about an hour ago." She could be anywhere. My hands run through my hair in frustration, clasping together at the top.

"Where did she go?" My voice is teetering on panic.

"I'm not sure I should tell you." She squints at me, her eyes scrutinising. I don't know if Aggie said anything or not.

"Please, Layla," I beg, "I'll give you anything?" She tuts at me and says something in Spanish I don't understand. "Was she okay? I fucked up. I didn't know," I plead. "I need to make it right with her." She leans against the door.

"You have one chance. If you hurt her, Ethan, I'll make Charlie kick your arse." Charlie is Layla's boss and an ex-MMA fighter. She would kick my ass.

"I won't mess this up," I promise. "Where is she?"

"At the studio. I gave her the new key you sent over when you changed the locks." I'm already turning towards the car when I shout a thank you over my shoulder.

Once I let myself in to the newly secure building, I race up the stairs to the attic space studio she has. My heart and stomach are twisting in hope that she's okay and will forgive me. I have no idea what I'll find when I open the door. Layla never answered me when I asked if she was okay.

I hear music when I reach the top, loud. It's a classical piece; the music floating through the slightly ajar door. Opening the door more, I gaze up, and freeze, all the blood rushing south, my brain, head, ears and eyes trying to capture the enormity of what I'm seeing. Rooted to the spot, just inside the door, I watch the most beautiful scene unfold in front of me.

She's completely naked, her slender, curved form in nothing but streaks of paint covering her perfect skin. A pair of ballet shoes cover her feet, the silk ribbon laced up her calves, tied in a bow at the top. *She's dancing.* Gulping down the true beauty of her freedom. I stand there motionless as she dances to the music, slow and gracious in every sweep of her arm and bow of her leg. *Ballet.* With the lights low, it's erotic to watch, and I never want to close my eyes for fear that it's all a dream. I want to hold on to this memory for the rest of my life. Slipping fully into the room, I close the door behind me, locking it tight.

Fuck, if I'm going to let anyone have eyes on *my* woman like this.

She moves her body over the stretched-out canvas on the floor, spreading paint, as her feet and arms graze its surface, in a variety of blues and greys. There are so many things I don't know about this woman. I like that she keeps me guessing.

A ballet dancer.

I grunt a laugh, recognising my favourite ballet come to life in Aggie: Swan Lake. Her movements precise and elegant, while each stroke glides the colours around the canvas, like she's planned every move, and every stroke. She's too lost in what she's doing to hear me; her eyes closed as she spins around. I'm breathless.

Smart, funny, sassy, stubborn, beautiful, she's a flash of colour in every spectrum.

I don't know how long I stand here: a minute, an hour. I don't care. I'm too hypnotised by her to do anything but fall a little more for this beautiful soul. The moment the music stops, she stands perfectly still, arms raised above her head, until they fall to her side. Her eyes slowly open, bringing her back to reality.

Aggie's breathing is heavy, echoing mine. Slowly calming herself, I think she knows I'm here; the small smile on her lips gives her away, but I stay where I am anyway.

"Ethan..." she whimpers my name on an exhale, and it sounds like she's calling me home.

I feel out of control when I'm around her. I like it, love it. She makes me think about myself, and not just about making everyone else happy. I want to make her happy, so fucking happy. More than anything on this earth, I want my Aggie to be happy. I feel weak for the first time in my life because I'll fall to my knees for her.

If that makes me a weaker man, then so be it. I'm not living without her anymore.

I want to step into her world and feel freedom with her.

I want to claim this moment as ours.

Her eyes focus on me, never wavering from my face. "Fuck, Aggie." Like a shot of adrenaline, the reason I'm standing here comes flooding back. "I'm so sorry, tonight was…"

"Stop," she says, holding her grey-blue hands out, "you don't need to explain anything, Ethan." She's calm as anything, while my body is going through a torrent of abuse from my emotions.

"I do. My mother and…" She shakes her head. "Let me explain, please," I beg. I can't not apologise for them.

"Ethan, I know none of it was you." I blanch. How can she know that?

"Then why did you leave?" I sound fucking desperate, and maybe I am.

"I watched the two of you together. I saw the way you looked for me, I saw how uncomfortable you were at her touch. I had no idea who she was at first until someone told me." Her jaw tenses. "I saw everything, Ethan; the way your mum smiled at the two of you together." There's a slight incline of her head, indicating she's uncomfortable. "That was before I was handed the note." Why is she calm when I feel frantic?

"What note?" I ask, having no idea what she talking about.

"The note Scarlett had sent to me." What the fuck?

"Let me see it? I'll fucking kill her for this, for doing this to us." My chest heaves and my hands shake with anger that my ex could be so fucking manipulative.

"Too late. I chucked it."

"What did it say?" My breath catches in my throat. It must have been bad for Aggie to leave like that and come here.

"Just how the two of you were to be engaged, that you were hers, that I was… to scurry back to my pathetic life." My jaw hangs open. I should have run her out of the event for that. She'll never be associated with us again.

"Your life is anything but pathetic. It's free, it's yours… and I will never fucking be engaged to her again, baby. Please, you have to believe me," I beg. I need her to understand she's it for me.

"Ethan—" she starts, but I cut her off. I need her to listen. I run my hand over my hair, trying to get the right words.

"What you saw was... fuck." How can I explain, I'm a dickhead. "I don't know, for the cameras..." Why didn't I leave them to it and search for her? I regret everything about this evening.

"I know." She backs away from me as I step forward, and I feel sick. She's going to leave me.

"I tried to find you. Why didn't you come to me if you saw me?" I need to know.

"Because I don't need that shit in my life."

"Aggie, please. No." My throat goes dry, but I force the words free. "You don't want me?" My words are strained, gulping down what's happening, refusing to let this go.

I've never been this man standing before her. Stoic and hard, that's me, but this man, this man is real, this man wants a technicolour life decorated by the painted woman in front of him.

I'm becoming him for her. Fuck, I hope she can see that. "I can't imagine a world where I don't want you, butterfly." I have to accept that what I feel may be worlds apart from what Aggie does.

"No, I want you, Ethan. I want all of you." She smiles, and I almost fall to my knees with relief. My head tips back, as my body relaxes as a rush of shaky laughter leaves me. Twisting my heart with disbelief and pure fucking joy, before coursing through my veins. Her smile widens, and it makes her eyes shine brighter than the forest bathed in sunlight. She means it. "I just don't need to be there for the shit she wanted to put me through. It doesn't make any difference to us." My heart stops, she still wants me. Us.

I hate that we're still standing apart, but I need to tell her everything that happened tonight.

"I told my parents and the whole venue full of people what she did to me. I don't know why I kept it secret. Fuck, I was stupid, Aggie." My hands run through my short hair. "So fucking stupid." They come to rest on the nape of my neck. "The first words out of my mouth were to defend you. You're my first and last thoughts, baby. Have been since the day we met." I step closer. "I defend what's mine, and I always will." I know I'm rambling, but fuck it. "I may have said... you have more class, grace and kindness than any one of them could only wish to have. Then I left and found you here, dance painting... naked to my favourite Swan Lake music." She laughs and shimmies, making her blue painted breasts jiggle.

Jesus-fuck.

"You're not stupid, Ethan. You try and see the best in people. I see it every day. It's a part of you I... never want you to change. I live my life the way I want to. Always have done, and I won't let anyone test me, not when I know they have no chance of winning. It's not a fair fight." She smirks. "You're all I think about too. We'll fight together."

"We're good?" I check.

"More than good, Ethan. It means Scarlett knows she's losing you to someone else. Me." She points to her heart.

"I'm yours, baby," I confirm.

"Thank fuck," she teases, her eyes sweeping over my tux, as she bites that fucking lip.

"Let me be there for you, butterfly."

I wrap her in my arms, popping her lip from between her teeth with my thumb. I bend down, taking her lip between my own and softly bite down. She moans into my mouth, but pulls away when she realises I'm plastered to her painted body.

"Ethan, your tux," she squeals, her hands pushing my shoulders, before she sees the mess she's making doing it, grey handprints littering my jacket. "Shit," she yells as I bark a laugh. I couldn't care less. I'm framing it, I bet there's a perfect one of her breasts on the front.

She's here, I have her in my arms, and she still wants me, even after what my mother and ex did to her.

She left because she didn't need to be there and put up with their shit. From now on, I think I'll be a bit more like Aggie.

"I have more." I take her lips again, slowly kissing them; it's not hurried, it's hard and slow. Bruising almost.

"I'm serious, Ethan," she says as I move us onto the wet canvas, stripping my clothes as I go.

"So, the fuck am I." I groan, working my way down her body, laying kisses on every inch of her, covering myself with colour. "Now, wrap your fucking legs around my head, and hold on tight, butterfly. I want this." I kiss her naked core, inhaling deeply. Fuck, she smells divine. She gasps as her hips jolt from the floor, "and you, more than anything." Grabbing her ankles, I place her feet on my shoulders, her ballet-toed feet crossing behind my head, holding me firmly in place. She's exactly where I want her, her core right in my face. I inhale her scent, "Fuck, baby, that smell alone is enough to make any man grovel."

"You're not any man, Ethan," she whimpers as I press the flat of my tongue against her clit, making her thighs clamp around my head.

"God-damn. That's it, baby." There's paint everywhere I look, from her face to her ankles, my own hands smearing the colours over her body, making new marks on the canvas below. The sound of her coming undone on my tongue makes me needy to hear more. I don't let up, keeping the pressure on, relentlessly pumping my fingers in and out of her. She whines as I flick it with my tongue, teasing her through her first orgasm into the second. She's drenched, her small frame trembling beneath my touch.

"Ethan, I can't..." I suck her clit, hard, and she groans so loud I'll have to delete anything from the cameras I placed here today.

"Yes, you fucking can, butterfly." I push deeper, my fingers hitting the beautiful bundle of nerves. She pants my name, swears and curses, her body trying its best to move away, but I know she can do it. Her hands grip my shoulders so tight, I can feel her nails digging into my skin.

"Fuck, yes, baby, that's it. One more." Our eyes meet, my hands on the back of her thighs, keeping her where I need her. I watch as it washes over her, her body tensing, almost violently shaking as she releases over my face, screaming my name as she comes.

"Stunning, butterfly, *fucking stunning.*" I'm struggling for breath with the way her legs almost cut off my air. "Ethan..."

"We're not done yet."

Crawling up her body, I swipe some wet paint from the canvas, and I sign my name in the paint over her stomach, grinning like an idiot at my work. I take a blue-tipped nipple in my mouth and suck hard until her back arches. I line my dick up at her entrance, wetting my length with her cum. Her hands roam my back, urging me on. I edge in, my head resting on her chest, and she gasps. Lifting her legs one at a time, I place them on my shoulders. Her core dragging me in, I groan as her heat surrounds me. I want to be so deep inside her, she'll never forget me.

Rolling my hips, I thrust all the way in, and she mewls, pushing herself against me harder. I shift, kneeling to lift her hips to meet mine, the heels of her feet digging into my skin as her hand flies above her head to hold the top of the canvas. I take slow, deep thrusts, each one building an intense buzz at the base of my spine.

"Ethan, I..."

"Fuck, yes, butterfly. I can feel you fluttering over my cock." Pumping in and out, I keep my pace, feeling every quiver, every flutter as I move inside her.

Gazing at her below me, my abs tensing from the need to fuck harder, I press her clit between my thumb and finger. She screams, "Ethan," making my cock swell. I'm already leaking inside her.

Her honey blonde hair is a mess, now sticking to the side of her face, perfect paint smeared skin, flushed, and glowing from two orgasms. I pound harder, the tip of my dick hitting where she needs it most. Her toes curl as she finally comes, and her release covers my thighs, the perfect O on her lips as she silently screams through her orgasm. I lose it, fucking her with abandon as she tightens herself around me.

"Feel me, Ethan, wrapped around your cock, making you come." *Goddamn.*

"Aggie." I can't stop. She feels too good. My balls tighten, and a shudder runs down my back, exploding down through my cock, forcing me to rut, coming deep inside her.

"Fill me, Ethan." She groans as I come. "Fuck, yes," I roar in her ear, pressing my cock into her as far as I can, just to hold us here.

"Oh god, Ethan…" She's coming again. Breathless, I force myself to move, my cock so fucking sensitive but wanting to extend her pleasure for as long as possible.

"Fuck, butterfly," I hum, still holding her tightly, her grip on me just as unforgiving. I roll us so she's on top of me, and she snuggles into my chest as I slip out of her.

"I think we made a mess of my painting," she says groggily. I can feel the smile on her lips as she kisses my neck.

"I don't think so. That's mine…" I tell her.

"Why?"

"I want a constant reminder of how you make me feel, how you make me lose control."

Chapter Twenty-Six
Wiggle

Aggie

Closing the boot of Layla's car with a thud, I walk to the passenger door of her yellow beetle and climb in. We packed my things into boxes and bags and loaded them in the backseat, with the boot filled to the brim.

It's early, like five am, but the time works for both of us. Layla needs to be at the shop early for the flower delivery, and I can start work at seven and unpack later. It won't take long to unload the boxes before I head into work. I got the keys yesterday. They were delivered to Layla's, just like I asked.

"You're going to love this place." I wiggle excitedly as Layla drives us.

"It makes me nervous how excited you are. It means it's a little extra, doesn't it?" I laugh, my cheeks heating. She's not wrong. It may even be a lot extra.

"Maybe, but it's me."

"Oh, no." She sighs, but then giggles. She's well-versed in some of my eccentricities.

"Hey, don't shame me for liking what I like," I poke her in the ribs. She flinches, groaning.

"No shaming, *Chica*, just a realisation that we need to keep an eye on what you buy."

"Sounds like shaming. And who's we?" I ask, frowning in the darkness.

"I mean you and me, but I guess we can add Ethan into the mix now." She's up to date about everything with the gala, his ex and his mum. She's solidly team Ethan when I told her what he did and what he said.

"No, I don't want to scare him off just yet," I mock, kind of knowing he's not going anywhere. I mean, the guy found me naked, ballet dancing last night, while painting with my body. Then fucked me into my own painting and bought it. My god, it was one of the best nights of my life. If he's up for it, so the fuck am I.

I left Ethan sleeping blissfully, sexed out, and took an Uber back to Layla's. We spent our Sunday ignoring the world. He even turned his phone off. I almost fell to the floor in shock, which led to a light spanking before another round of mind-blowing sex. I had the absolute pleasure of watching him cook again, a roast dinner this time.

He's a talented man.

I did message him to say I'd meet him at work, so he didn't freak out and start looking for me again.

Chuckling to myself, the joker even wrote a cheque out for over fifty grand for my painting. I pretended to pocket it, but ripped it up when his back was turned. It'll be my gift to him.

If he's sticking with me, it's the least I can do for him.

"Is it practical?" I bit my lip, because no, it's not. "I'll take your silence as a no. What's missing?"

"Um... a kitchen." She slows down to look at me and takes a breath in through her nose. She's making me nervous.

"No kitchen? What the... what kind of place has no kitchen? What will you do for food? You can't order takeout every night." She's going to have so many more questions when she sees it.

"If I tell you while you're driving, you'll turn us back around." Her hands clench the wheel.

"Oh, *Mia Dias, Chica…*" She bobs her head briefly before focusing back on the road.

"Don't Spanish me," I add, grimacing.

"I will Spanish you if you deserve it. Okay, let's go see what I'm dealing with."

We pull into a parking lot just down from the harbour. Layla's going to freak out. I climb out of the car, almost holding my breath, waiting for her to clock where we're heading. Wiping the palms of my hands on my jeans, I'm nervous. I know I shouldn't be, but Layla has always been that little voice of reason telling me not to do stupid shit. I have a feeling that this may be that stupid shit she'd tell me not to do.

"Why are we in a car park here?" she asks, stepping from the car.

"It's down here," I say, laughing nervously.

"Now I know you've done something you shouldn't. That laugh says it all, Aggie." We each grab a bag from the car and walk down the path.

"We seem to be walking away from any sort of building with foundations and land." She groans, looking around, as the only buildings in sight are the restaurants and bars on the front. All of which are closed.

"We are. It's not in a building." Her eyes flick to me, wide with questions I know she's holding back.

"We're getting closer to the harbour."

"We are." I grin.

"Please tell me you didn't." She knows, but she doesn't want to say it.

"I can't, because I did," I squeak, moving swiftly out of the way as she tries to whack me.

"Bought or rented." She's being that overprotective friend again.

"Rented. Do you know how much a boat is to buy?" Fucking astronomical, that's how much.

"You rented a boat without a kitchen to live in?" She drops the bag, both hands on her hips, as she stares at me in shock.

"Yes." I smile as we walk down the jetty to the small boat I'll now be calling my home. If the sun were out, she'd see it was painted a beautiful pale blue, with tiny flowers on the side. "She's called Purple Passion." She just stands there, staring at it.

"A rare flower. I like the name, but it also sounds like a giant purple vibrator." I was waiting for it. Every time I thought of the name, it's name made me chuckle. I am going to live in Purple Passion. "A boat," she groans, "no wonder you didn't tell me about it."

"I'll open it up, then we can grab the rest of my things." Stepping up on the back of *Purple Passion*... do I need to learn the right words? Is it bow? Portside? Stern? Maybe I should. I open the door and step inside. Fuck, it's cold. The woman who let me in yesterday showed me how to set the timer on the heating, so I do that first, while Layla brings in the bags, looking around as I start to flick the lights on.

"It's cute." And it is. It's cosy and homely. "I'll admit that. Not much room, but it's definitely you," she admits, still looking a little annoyed at me, but she knows she can't change my mind once I've done something.

The space is tiny, with a bed and sofa taking up most of the room. There's a folding table attached to the wall with a microwave and kettle on the shelf above. There's a small shower room behind the bed, with a small wardrobe built in. It's so cosy, I get a flutter in my chest. I feel like I'll be happy here.

"I'm sure Ethan will fit," I say, imagining him in the tiny space. He'd look so out of place, but I also can't wait to show him.

"I'm not sure he will. Why isn't he helping you move?" she says, placing the bags down.

"I've not told him I'm moving today," I say as guilt makes the flutter in my chest disappear. "As much as we know we want to be together, I'm not sure what his opinion of this would be. He's..." I don't know the right word for it. "Used to a different life."

"That's an understatement. His bathroom is probably bigger than this."

"About three times the size, and that's just the spare," I add, Layla's eyes going large, before she glances at the clock on the wall and sighs.

"I need to go. Let's get the rest of your things. Can you answer me one question?" Her expression is serious.

"Sure," I say, as we make our way back to the car.

"Is it safe?" There it is. I'm surprised it took her so long.

"Of course it is." I think. I never paused to ask the woman who showed me around. "The woman who lived here before is only renting it to me because she got herself a bigger one," I say, like that makes a difference.

"That helps, I guess. But please make sure you call if you feel uncomfortable in any way."

"I will, promise." We make quick work of the rest of my things, and she leaves me to it after a hug and a promise of moving in drinks at the weekend. I spend the next hour hanging my clothes in the small closet before I head to work. Only the walk there feels different, not only because I don't walk anywhere, but I'd normally get a taxi, but something's different. Something keeps me checking over my shoulder as I walk, my heart in my throat each time I look back and find nothing, not a soul, other than a few passing cars. I know it's because it's still dark, and I'm on my own, but even when I walk into Bruno's café, the door closing behind me, to collect my order, the feeling doesn't go away.

Chapter Twenty-Seven

Hurt

Ethan

I've cleared my schedule for the hours Aggie's blocked out today; I'm going to follow her. I tried to ask where she goes again last night as we ate dinner, but she shut me out again.

I only want to make sure she's safe, because I don't believe she is, not when she's coming back with bruises. Plus, she found someone in her studio and she's not told me about that either.

Fuck she got a paper cut the other day, and I wanted to set fire to it for hurting her. We're as paperless as we can be, but I'll be adding extra measures to make sure she never touches another piece again.

"Make sure you take one of the cars when you leave," I say when she tells me she's going. I know she wasn't going to, she never does, but I need her to use one today, so I can follow her.

They all have trackers.

I already feel like shit for doing it, but I can't get it off my mind until I see for myself that she's okay.

"Okay, I'll take one." She places a kiss on my lips and hums, just as I do, and I want more. "I won't be long."

"As long as you come back to me," I add, palming her arse.

"I have to show you my new place tonight, of course I'm coming back." This is news. My lungs seize for a second, knowing she'll be living on her own.

"You moved?"

"Yep, this morning before work." I groan. What the hell? I don't like that she's cutting me out; it's a big thing to get a new place and move in, and not tell your boyfriend. *Boyfriend?* I don't like that either. I'm too old to be a boyfriend.

"Aggie, I could have helped." This woman will be the death of me, I'm sure.

"Layla helped." Again, she didn't come to me, and that stings.

"Why didn't you tell me?" I stand, taking her waist in my hand and pulling her to me.

"I wanted it to be a surprise." She looks cautious. What's that about? My thumb hooks into the loop of her jeans, keeping her flush to me.

"Are we heading there after work?" I ask too eagerly.

"We can. I need to unpack, so you can help." She's teasing, but I'll make sure she has everything she needs.

"I will. We can grab some food on the way over." I'm glad she's showing me, but the look she's giving makes me think she's not telling me something. Then she bites her lip, and I know for sure something's up.

"What aren't you telling me?" I mock scowl.

"Nothing. Takeout would be good, it doesn't have a kitchen." The words rattle in my head before they register.

"What type of place doesn't have a kitchen?" Lifting her chin with my finger, I search her eyes for an answer, hoping she'll be honest with me.

"My place." She beams at me and steps away. "I should get going."

"Going to tell me where you're going?" It's a last-ditch attempt to get any sort of answer.

"No." She chuckles as she walks to the door. I feel like shit for what I'm about to do, but I need to make sure she's safe.

Making my way to the kitchen, I wait for her to step into the elevator while making a coffee to go and load the tracker on the app we have. She takes the smallest car, one I added to our fleet when she said she didn't have a car.

Leon and Owen walk into the kitchen together, just as I place the lid on my carry cup. "I'll be back later."

Of all the things I expected Aggie to be doing, this was not it. Never this.

I half expected that she was going to her studio to paint, but that wouldn't explain where the bruises are coming from.

This, on the other hand, does explain a lot. Or not enough. I don't know what I think about it.

A rage room.

Where you go to beat the shit out of stuff. I never pegged her for taking her anger out on anything, let alone violently.

I've heard of them, but never been to one until now. I place the mask over my face and put on the black coverall. She's in the room next to me. I can see her through the Perspex partition, beating the living daylights out of an old telly, then a vase that smashes into hundreds of tiny pieces. I've never seen her so aggressive.

I've not even picked up the bat they told me to use, I'm too focused on her. She rips off her mask, and my skin tingles with unease. My hands fist in my overall pockets, watching her smash more shit with no protection on her face. She should be wearing it. I want to bang on the window and tell her to put it back on. Go in there even, and put it back on her slightly sweaty face. But if I go in there, she'll know I've followed her.

And I don't want her to know.

She walked in smiling. If she's been coming here, it could explain the bruises; maybe it's her way of releasing, working out any tension she has. Maybe that's why she's so... herself all the time.

What's she holding on to that could make her need this?

I know I should wait for her to open up to me, maybe I'm not asking the right questions? I should leave her to it. That's the only thing I'm left thinking about as I walk from the untouched room. Why would she need to hide this from me? My shoulders sink. I made a big deal out of something that was nothing. But why does my gut tell me I'm not wrong, that this is something I need to know about?

I need to move. If she finds out I followed her, she'll for sure finish things between us, or at least castrate me. I should have trusted she would tell me in her own time instead of stalking her like an idiot.

Rolling my neck to release the tension building, I hear it: a loud cry after a smash, coming from her room. *Fuck, she's hurt.*

I don't think.

Still in my mask and coverall, I race to her door. Slamming it open, I scan the room and see her slumped against the wall, head in her hands, sobbing. My heart thunders against my chest. She jumps up at the sound of the door crashing against the wall. She doesn't pause, taking the bat in her hand, ready to swing at me.

Fuck, yes, butterfly.

"Who the fuck are you?" she shouts, her voice trembling.

What? Shit, she can't see my face. I still have the mask on. I can't untie it quick enough. "Aggie," I say, my voice muffled under the mask, making me sound like some creeper.

"Get away from me." Her voice is scratchy from crying. Aggie brings the bat higher, like she's aiming for my head. There's a flicker of pride in my chest.

"It's me, Aggie." She stops, her whole body rigid, and there a flash of anger in her eyes as she glares at me. "Butterfly," I groan, stepping up to her. She goes to hit me just as I get the mask off.

"Ethan?" she startles as my hand grabs the bat heading for my face. She relaxes, and then her rage is replaced by confusion. I take the bat off her and drop it to the floor.

"What happened? Are you okay? Are you hurt?" My hands roam her body as she stands stock still in front of me. "Tell me, baby. Why are you crying?" Her breath hitches as a tear falls down her cheek, making my heart shatter in my chest.

"I'm not hurt, I'm fine," she mumbles, wiping her face with the back of her hand.

"Then what happened? You were sobbing?"

"Why the fuck are you here, Ethan?" Her eyes narrow as her fists clench and her nostrils flare.

She has every right to be angry.

"I was worried. I'm sorry," I plead, holding my hands up in defence.

"Worried about what? Me?" she quizzes, her eyes bouncing from me to the bat, like she wants to use it.

"Of course, you." I'd roll my eyes, but it's not my thing. Instead, I level my eyes with hers.

"I don't understand." Her tone is threatening and confused.

"Butterfly, every time you'd come back from one of these events, you were hurt." I brush her cheek with the back of my hand, keeping a slight distance between us. It's killing me not knowing why she was so upset. "I needed to see for myself you weren't in trouble."

"In trouble?" Wrong choice of words. *How do I explain?*

"I'm sorry. I can't help where my mind went." I'm messing this up.

"You're fucking sorry. You followed me here. How did you find me?" She's not interested in why, not yet anyway.

"The car," I say, tipping my head towards the car park at the side of the building.

"It has a tracker in it?" I nod my answer.

"Because I wouldn't answer when you asked this morning, you decided that you'd fucking stalk me to see for yourself." Yep. That's it, nail on the head.

"Yes," I admit, like it's a painful lump in my throat.

"Fucking hell, Ethan, at least try and lie to me." She laughs, *laughs* at me.

"Baby, I have an issue with seeing people I love hurt. Do you know how much it pained me to see you covered in bruises?" Tilting her head to look up at me as I gaze down at her, Goddamn, even with a tear-stained face, she's stunning. "It physically hurt me to see you like that." Her soft hand covers my grated heart, easing the panic I feel on the inside.

"You really want to care for me, don't you?" Her smile warms, but it's still sad.

"More than anything." I kiss her briefly on the top of her forehead.

"Why?" *Why? Life, love, loss. So much loss*. I couldn't help them.

I step back, I... my chest feels tight. I palm it, trying to rub away the pain. Images flicker through my mind of our last tour. My friends, I couldn't help my friends. I had to watch them die, one at a time, feeling useless.

"Ethan, what's happening?" Her hands brush over my shoulder as she follows me back, not allowing me to be consumed.

She kisses me, bringing me back from wherever I was heading. I've been so busy for so long, I don't remember the last time I really thought about them, or what me, Owen, Leon, and Cole went through.

"Not here. I've said it before; I'll tell you everything, baby, but not here." Like she can sense I need to leave, Aggie holds my hand, and she leads the way.

"Okay, let's go. I'm still angry with you," she mutters, "but I want to understand you, Ethan. I want to know. I'll figure a way to get you back for this." I'm sure she will. This is not how I saw this day going.

Handing Aggie her cocktail, she grins. We're sitting in my lounge; the fancy one, she called it when we walked in. "Thank you."

Sitting opposite her, I take a sip of my own drink—a whisky on the rocks—and lean forward. Aggie's staring at me. "I know I have some explaining to do."

"Just a bit." She's angry with me; the silence on the way here told me so.

"I care, Aggie. Maybe too much sometimes. But I can't help it."

"Is it something to do with when you were in the army?" I glance at a photo on the fireplace; a group shot of all of the squad three days before our last mission, before it all went to shit.

"Yeah, I've always felt the need to care for people." From the age of five, I'd pretend to be a doctor. "I think what happened to those guys just intensified it." Standing, I take the photo and hand it to her. I gulp down the loss, seeing their smiling faces, knowing I'll never see six of them again.

"What happened?" She's quiet as she says it, her finger running over the faces of the people she recognises.

"I went into the army because it was expected of me, a family obligation. But I couldn't take the route they wanted me to. I never wanted to be a ranking officer, I wanted to help others, be on the field, not sit in a chair commanding others, so I became a medic instead. Fuck, I loved every second of it until I didn't." Sitting back down, I take a breath and start from where I feel comfortable.

"On our last tour, our last mission, we were ambushed." She doesn't need to know the morbid and horrific details. "I had to watch my friends, six of them, die. I know there was nothing I could do. They would never have survived their injuries, but I couldn't ease their pain. I had to watch them suffer while feeling helpless. We all felt it, but it was my responsibility as their friend and medic to get them the help they needed." I pause. "I failed them."

"You didn't fail them, Ethan." Her voice sounds determined to make me see.

"How do you know?" It's a cheap shot; I'm lashing out.

"Because you've told me you had no other options. If you did, you would have got them what they needed. Were you with them when they passed?" Her words are softer now.

"Yeah, every single one." I held their hands, cried with them, and pocketed their letters to their loved ones. I even said a prayer when they passed.

"I get it, Ethan. I can't understand what you went through, but I can see why you are the way you are." My muscles relax a bit hearing her say she understands.

"I like taking care of people. I'll never change that," I admit, frowning at my hands.

"I never want you too." She smiles, lifting my face to hers this time.

"I'm sorry I took it too far, baby. I..." I don't know how to apologise for what I did.

"Please don't say anything else. I should have been honest with you." Aggie comes to sit next to me, resting her head on my shoulder. "I'm sorry for making you worry when there was no need to." I wrap my arm around her and kiss the top of her head.

"Have I ever told you, you're perfect?" I say into her hair, my chest lighter already.

"No, and please don't. There's no such thing as perfection."

"Too late, you're perfect, Aggie Hope. You're perfect for me." We stay like this until her stomach rumbles.

"I want to tell you why I was there, Ethan, I just don't know how yet." Fuck, there's more to it than I thought. "I've lived with it in my head for so long that letting someone hear it seems daunting." Her voice trembles as she speaks, and I hold her tighter.

"I'm not going to push you. I never would. But don't shut me out."

"You'll be the first person I tell. Promise." She squeezes my hand, confirming her promise.

Chapter Twenty-Eight
Spot

Aggie

I didn't get takeaway with Ethan. I went home alone last night. I told him I needed a bit of space. Yesterday was a lot. For both of us.

There's a tension between us. We both know it, but until I can open up about my past, that's going to stay there.

I'm not sure the boat was a good idea. It feels lonely, too small, too claustrophobic.

I took a walk last night to clear my head. Why haven't I told him? I can't answer it; it's the feeling in my chest that stops me.

The one that makes me pause every time.

Ethan's out seeing a client today. I miss him around the office; the lonely feeling from last night on the boat has crept over into today. I don't want to be alone, so I've moved to the desk next to Jill for company as I tackle the workload for the day.

I'm sorting through all the latest emails, like I do every morning. Then I move onto clicking between the diary, meeting request emails, and scheduling the following week's meetings, when suddenly a new one pops up. I sigh; I was so close to finishing, but then I realise that this one's addressed to me, *personally*.

I get emails all the time, but that's on my personal account, which is not linked to this computer. This one is on the Cerberus email, which only the people here use. Maybe someone handed it out by mistake. The header reads, *My Dear Aggie,* and sent only a few minutes ago. Clicking to open it, I sit back, reading it through. Then, I read it again.

What the hell?

Is this real? Hope soars in my chest as I read it through again.

> *Dear Aggie,*
>
> *I hope this email finds you well.*
>
> *I don't know how to start this conversation, so I'll just get it over with. I knew your mum.*
>
> *I saw an article online a few weeks ago. I was shocked to see you. For a moment, I thought it was her, you look just like your mum. Same eyes, even the shape of your face.*

Holy fuck, I can't breathe. This can't be real. But... the article went national, so it could hold some truth.

My heart is beating so fast, I'm sweating. Clutching my pen, I read a little more.

> *I'd like to meet with you. We lost touch when you were small. Unfortunately, I don't know what happened to your mum, but I'd love the chance to get to know you and maybe get back in touch with Luna again.*

There's more, but I can't focus on it, the text on the screen blurring into one jumbled mess.

Luna, Luna.

Is that my mother's name? It has to be, I'm freaking the fuck out.

"Is everything okay, Aggie?" Jill asks beside me. *No, yes. I don't know.* Closing my laptop, I lean my head over the back of the chair. "Having one of those mornings?" she asks.

"Something like that. I need to head out again." She sighs, shaking her head, no doubt assuming I'm on another errand for Ethan.

"I hope your day gets better, sweetheart."

"I'm sure it will," I smile as best I can, grabbing my coat and putting it on. My chest's pounding, and my mind spinning with every possibility of what meeting this person could mean. With a small shake to my hand, I put my laptop in my bag and walk to the door, taking the keys for the car with me before anyone can stop me.

Placing the bag with the laptop on the seat carefully, I start the car and drive to the one place that I know I'll be able to breathe, and process this.

Luna. Fucking hell, I thought I made it up. I thought... *Luna.* That's *her* name. My mum's name. Tears well as the enormity of those two words crowd me.

My mum.

I've never known anything about her, and for such a small thing, this feels vast.

I've been using it for years, signing my work with it. How is that possible?

Getting out of the car, I pay for my entrance ticket and walk through the plastic curtain of the butterfly farm, finding the old wooden bench I've sat on so many times before, there may be an imprint of my arse on it. Placing the laptop on my crossed legs, I look around to try and ground myself. It's like a calming sea of colour as the butterflies flutter past. The butterfly farm is hot all year round, the sound of running water from the middle of the enclosure calms my racing heart. I then open the laptop.

Did I imagine it? Is my mother's name Luna?

When the screen comes to life, I reread the email over again, giving myself the space and time to feel the words and see them without any sort of emotion. I don't want to give myself space to think too deeply about it. I want to understand what this could mean for me. But I also know I need to be cautious; I'll tell Ethan. See what he thinks, but I want to meet her. I read that she's retired and grew up with my mum, and would love to meet if I felt up to it.

Before I can stop myself, I'm typing out a reply.

Hi, Connie,
Thank you for getting in touch. I'd love to meet. When would you be free?
Aggie

That's it, sent. I have so many questions, so many things running through my mind, I can't concentrate.

I can't believe this is happening. I could finally find out about my family. My email pings with a notification. When I look down, Connie's replied.

She wants to meet today.

I can't do this on my own. Picking up my phone, I dial the one person I need.

"Ethan."

Ethan

The second I see her call me, my heart leaps. I don't give a fuck that I'm in a room full of trainees, or that they're all staring at me while I watch my phone ring. She left after our talk yesterday. I hated watching her walk away from me, but she can have anything she needs. Space, time, money, my heart, and soul. Done all hers.

"Butterfly," I answer on the third ring.

"Ethan." It's quiet.

"Where are you?"

"The butterfly farm." I don't say anything, just let her talk. "It's the place I come to think." Walking out of the training centre, I head to the path that runs around it, away from prying ears.

"What do you need to think about, baby?" I rasp, thinking the worst, after yesterday.

"I received an email."

"Not that uncommon, given what you do," I joke.

"Funny," she says sarcastically. "It's from a woman who claims she knew me and my mum growing up." She let out a shaky breath, like saying out loud confirms that it's real.

"What does it say?"

"Just that she knew us, and lost touch, not much. But she wants to meet me. I don't think she knows I went into care. She asked if she could meet up with my mum too." Her voice cracks as she says *Mum*.

"And," I ask, already knowing she wants to tell me more.

"I've already emailed asking to meet her." Of course she has. "Ethan, what if it's not real?" *Fuck,* I gulp down my own anxiety about this because I can hear the worry in her voice.

"Then we'll deal with it," I reassure her, trying my best not to picture a worst-case scenario. "I'm coming with you," I state, I don't want her alone with a stranger. No fucking way.

"I think I need to do this on my own, but..." There's trepidation in her tone. I don't like this.

"But what, baby?" I quiz, my brow furrowing.

"Will you help me set up a meeting spot?" I'll do more than that *if* she asks.

"What do you have in mind?" I ask. I don't want to make suggestions; it all needs to be Aggie's choice.

"Maybe the beach?" Not ideal; there are no cameras. I'm already thinking of a backup plan, a contingency that I'll put in place. "I can tell you're already thinking of a plan. Don't go overboard." I huff a laugh and smile.

"You're getting to know how my mind works, baby. I like it."

"I like you, Ethan, so fucking much." My next inhale seems freer, like I can breathe for the first time in years.

"So, fucking much, butterfly. Meet me at mine and we'll make a plan."

She called me when she needed me; she didn't shut me out. Goddamn, that means the world to me. So, I need to be patient and not fuck it up by being an overbearing prick.

I'll hide that. I can't stop it.

Aggie

"Can I see the email?" Ethan asks as we sit ourselves at the island. We arrived at the same time, coming together with a hug on his drive.

"Sure." I'm nervous. I've never let anyone in on this side of me before. Layla knows a few things, but this is massive for me, and I think he can tell. I open up the laptop, and click on the email, turning the screen towards him so he can read. I watch his eyes flicker across the screen as he reads it, while my thumbs tap on my thighs.

"What was your first thought? It must have been a shock?" I press my lips together, then blow out a breath.

"Honestly, I didn't think this day would ever come." I lean my elbows on the granite top, and sigh. "I've been alone for so long, Ethan, I think I almost gave up on finding out anything about my parents."

"Is it something you still want?" he asks, and it shocks me, because I don't know.

"Yes and no." I wince at my own honesty.

"It's okay, you know. I know you've already decided to meet her, but the ball is in your court. You can change your mind." I smile and take his hand. God, he's what I need.

"I appreciate that, Ethan." I hesitate. "I'm scared, but if I don't meet her, I'll always be asking myself what if?"

"What are you scared of?" he asks, his tone low and sensitive. He's holding my hand between his two now.

"Everything, nothing, the unknown." I laugh, and it's a shaky one.

"It could mean you get to know your parents." He leans forwards, running a finger down my cheek. It's comforting.

"That's massive, isn't it?"

"It is, but if it's what you want, then you need to go and meet her."

"I could find out who they are, why I was placed in care. It could lead to so many unanswered questions being explained."

"It could. I'm happy for you, Aggie." He looks worried. There are moments when I'm wrapped in Ethan's arms, warm and safe, that I see echoes of me, a life I've had. But they're so far removed from my reality, I think it's my imagination playing tricks on me.

"I know that's the best case scenario, I also know it could be someone fucking with me."

"Baby, try not to think like that."

"I have to. If I place all my hope on this one email having all the answers, it could lead to a whole world of hurt. I have to be realistic." I'm not an idiot. I know people can be cruel. I'll have no idea until I meet this woman. This is the only hope I have left; the things I've been trying haven't worked. That's why I broke down in the rage room. I've lost hope.

"I know you want to do this on your own, and I won't change that." He grins. "No stalking, I promise." I grunt a laugh. "All I'm saying is I can make plans to be by your side in minutes." I like that he wants to take care of me, even if it is a bit overwhelming sometimes. I'm smiling at the thought of him stalking me. His own worry for me overpowering any common sense.

It's kind of cute.

"If it doesn't go the way I hope, I'd like that. I'd like that a lot," I say, leaning in to kiss his cheek. *Fuck,* how has this man become so much in such a short amount of time?

I have a feeling he won't be far away if I need him. We make a plan for me to call or message him after we've met. Along with a pin drop of where I'll be. He'll be waiting by the phone for me.

Chapter Twenty-Nine

Echoes

Aggie

I'm finding it hard to swallow; my mouth is so dry. Even in the cold, my palms are sweating. I clutch at my necklace for reassurance, only to remember it's still in my jewellery box on the boat. I didn't want to wear it to the rage room, and I didn't get round to putting it back on last night.

I've waited twenty-one years to find something, anything out about who I am. And now I could be minutes away from finding out my real last name, or even if Aggie, well, Agatha is even my real name.

I'm waiting at the bench at the beach, like I suggested to Ethan. I thought he'd have something to say, but he's been nothing but supportive. Letting me make all the decisions, but talking me through what he will do if it's not what I expect, just in case I need him, or it gets to much for me. His way of saying, just in case it's some prick trying to screw me over. I can't stop my hands fidgeting. I keep standing, looking around, then sitting again. I arrived early, thinking she could be as excited as I am, and she'd be here before me. But she's not here yet.

It's only five minutes past.

Calm down.

Even though it's almost winter, this stretch of the beach is still favoured for walking dogs. There are a few people walking and running by. Ethan was happy for me when we talked about what it could mean, at least finding some answers as to what reasons I could have been placed in foster care.

There's still so much to tell him. If this goes well, I'll explain everything. I didn't mention my mum's name to him. I want to know for sure before I say anything about my past. It could be a fluke—unlikely, but it is a possibility that someone could be messing with me.

Wrapping my coat closer as the wind picks up, I pull my scarf over my mouth to fight off the chill. She was supposed to be here fifteen minutes ago. *She's just running late.* I'll wait. I have a list of questions I want to ask in my head, but my hope is dwindling.

Do I stay? My fingers are turning to ice, and it's already getting dark. My good mood sinks when I think she might not be coming.

My laugh gets snatched away from my throat as I hear someone behind me. Turning to look over my shoulder to see if it's her, my eyes go wide as my heart rate peaks, then dives into my stomach. He's too quick for me to move away in time.

"No," I yell as I'm hit in the side of my head by an elbow, silencing me. My hand flies to my face and my head falls forward, as pain splinters across my cheek.

What the fuck?

A hand grabs my hair, yanking me backwards. I let out a scream at what feels like a thousand burns rage over my scalp.

"Got you," he snarls. I'm wrenched back further, my back arching over the back of the seat, my hand frantically grabbing for my hair, desperate for him to release me. An arm lodges around my throat, yanking me backwards. My legs scramble to keep up as I'm ripped from the seat by my hair. The air in my lungs snatched away from me as his arm tightens, choking me, repressing any cry for help I may have had.

I can't breathe. I don't know what to grab more of, my hair or his arm. Shooting pains cover my back as it scrapes across the wood, my legs hitting the floor painfully when they land. My choked scream is muffled by my inability to breathe. I can't get anything in with his arms rigid around my neck. *No.*

"Where is it, Sophie?" The man barks, his face close to my ear. I want to turn away, but I can't. I can't breathe as he tightens his grip. I'm fighting, my legs and arms grabbing and tearing at whatever I can get hold of. When I don't answer, his knee connects to my ribs. My eyes widen as I cry in shock, a gurgled shout passes my lips from the burn radiating up my side, and I feel sick when he does it again. He pulls at my clothes.

Oh god. No.

Ripping my pockets, tearing at my coat, then at the collar, tugging it away from my neck and chest. I kick harder, my fight coming back tenfold, trying to free myself. His hand reaches around my throat, his cold, gloved hands pressing into my skin. My pulse drops. He's going to kill me.

My body shudders with fear.

Fight, Aggie. Fucking fight.

"Tell me where the fuck it is." His patience is wearing thin as I still don't answer, but I don't know what he means.

"What?" I try and answer him but choke on my own words. He can have anything. His knee connects with my hip, this time making me drop my weight to the floor as a searing pain shoots through my lower side.

"You're a waste of space, just like she was," he grits, his arm loosening around my neck as he spins me around. His fist comes for my face, and my hand comes up to try and stop him from punching me, but I'm too slow. He hits me just below my eye. My vision blurs, spiked tendrils of pain explode over my cheek and eye, forcing me to close them. I hear him walk away. "I'll be back for it," he says, a chill takes residence over my skin.

I slump to the floor, my body exhausted from the fight, my eyes fluttering as I see the stars appear in the night sky. My head rolling to the side, I watch him walking away. Leaving me alone. Just like always.

I want to wake up from this nightmare, but my eyes are focused on the face in front of me. She looks just like me, only I see fear in her eyes as she mouths something. I hear the faint words over a crackle... *Run. Please, butterfly, run.*

Chapter Thirty

Struggle

Ethan

There's that feeling again, in the pit of my stomach. I've been waiting at the office for Aggie to send me the pin to her new place, but it's not come. I'm sitting at the central table, with a cold coffee in my hand, swirling it around. I can't focus on work. I tried to distract myself, but my mind keeps wandering to Aggie. She said she'd message me when they were done, but her last message said she'd been stood up. Maybe she needed some time to process what's happened; I know I would. But this tightness in my stomach, it's getting worse with every passing minute.

I promised not to follow her, but right now, it feels like a promise I need to break. I hate that she's gone to meet a stranger by herself. It goes against everything; every grain in my body to stay here, and wait.

It's only been twenty minutes. I want to tell Cole to search the local cameras for her, I want to trace her phone, I want to *fucking* be there. And I'm not. Because she told me not to. I don't want to break her trust, so I've stayed rooted to the spot since she stepped out of the door.

It's fucking ruining my soul not to be close to her right now.

The Cerberus building is close to the beach, a five-minute ride in the truck, that's my back up plan, if I stayed at my house, it would a fifteen minute drive.

Here I have all the resources I need to keep an eye on her. If I choose to. I won't unless I see reason to.

Leon slides the chair back next to me and takes a seat. He eyes my tapping foot and my now cold drink, that been sat there since she left.

"What's wrong?" Leon can always read the room, so it's no surprise he's asking. When I don't answer, he says, "That serious?"

"I don't know."

"What don't you know?" His tone is serious.

"If Aggie's okay."

"Talk to me. What's going on?"

I fill him in on the basics, not telling him what Aggie wouldn't want me to share.

"Where were they meeting? We can head down there." He stands, clapping his hands together.

"The beach. She sent me a pin drop." I show him the screen I've been staring at.

"Have you checked the studio cameras? Maybe she went there when she didn't show?"

I never thought of that. I shake my head, accessing the live feed for the studio. When I don't see anything. I shake my head again.

"We'll go to the beach then. Check it out." *Do it*, my inner voice demands.

"I can't. She asked me not to follow, but..."

"But what?" he asks.

"Gut feeling, something's not right."

"Get your fucking keys, we're going." They're on the table in front of me, my hands grabbing them while I stand, Leon by my side.

"What if she finds out, and I've fucked up again?" There's a question in his eyes when I say it again, but he holds back, knowing it's not the time.

"What would you rather happen? Fall out for a few days, or ignore your gut and find out she's in trouble?" Fuck, he makes a good point. We race down the stairs, and I blip the lock on my truck before we reach it. Climbing in, I'm pulling away before Leon has even closed his door.

There's no need for directions. I've been staring at the location since she sent it to me. My foot is to the floor as we race the streets, just so I can get my eyes on her. Reaching the car park, I jump out, Leon by my side in seconds, when his phone starts to ring. He pauses, glancing at the screen. "It's Layla," he says, urging me forward. Maybe she has news on where Aggie is? He hangs back, but keeps walking as I push forward, running to the beach she would have been sitting at. Trying to calm my shit before I see her.

I run the length of the path, spotting the bench, but I don't see her. I spin around in circles, my hands running over my head in desperation. Where the hell has she gone? It's dark and I can't see far, but the faint streetlights from the street are enough to show me there's no one around.

I'm frantic. Surely if she was okay, she would have answered her phone, knowing I'd be my overbearing self and worry the shit out of the situation?

Leon's talking on the phone, looking at me, with something like regret in his eyes. My gut sinks.

"What?" I ask as I approach him. He grabs me by the back of his neck, then points to the truck, mouthing, "Get in." I do, trusting him with my life as always. He climbs in beside me. I start the engine and head back onto the main road. "St Helens," he says, and my grip on the steering wheel tightens, my knuckles shining white in the dark. *The hospital.*

"Floor it, she's been admitted to A&E. Layla's with her."

"Fuck," I roar, I should never have questioned myself, I should have fucking stalked the shit out of her. I could have fucking been there.

I *should* have been there.

"Don't," Leon says next to me, bringing me out of my head. "You promised her, you kept your word. This is not your fault." That's not how I feel, and he knows it. I could have prevented this from happening. I could have kept her safe.

"Ethan." I side eye him, letting him know I'm listening, while I tear through the streets to get to the god-damn hospital.

"She's beat up pretty bad, bruising mostly. No bones broken. She was lucky."

"Fucking lucky?" My jaw's so tense I could crack my teeth.

"Wrong choice of words, she's going to be okay, Ethan."

"What happened?"

He blows out a breath. "From what Aggie told the paramedics, she was attacked."

"Who?" He shakes his head and I bite my tongue to stop myself from lashing out.

"I don't know, not yet," he adds.

"Promise me something, Leon. Help me find this fucker."

"Already on it, the guys are in the office pulling up any footage they can." I can't temper the rage building inside me.

I'll never forgive myself for this. I promise she'll never feel at risk again, not when she has me and my brothers by her side.

"Aggie's in there. They moved her to a private room, but she's sleeping," Layla says as we storm through the doors of the hospital ward she's in. My heart and mind are frantic.

"What happened?" I need to be by her side, but I want a full med rundown on her condition. I'll be the one looking after her from here on out. She'll want for nothing. I'll hunt down the doctor after I've seen and kissed her first. Fuck, I need to hold her right now.

"I told Leon. Did he not say?" She eyes Leon, her voice small as she focuses back on me. "Okay, she has injuries to her face, ribs, hips, and head." She bursts into tears and Leon wraps her in his arms. "She was beaten up, dragged by her hair..." Her voice wavers, and I can't breathe. "Kicked... in the ribs, before being punched in the face and left... Oh god," she cries into Leon's chest. "They left her there alone."

My knees buckle, my hands falling to the wall to support me. I can't take listening anymore. Leon's palm lands on my shoulder.

"Get in there. She needs you," he says.

Sucking air into my depraved lungs, I trudge to her room, feeling so heavy I can barely lift my arm to push the door open. Lifting my head when I get inside, I break, almost leaping to her side.

Aggie lays in the hospital bed, sheets covering her perfect body. She's too still. I know she's sleeping, but it kills me to see her like this. My chest caves when I take in what this prick did. Her beautiful face is swollen and red, her cheek bruised.

I should have been there.

This is my fault.

"Butterfly," I whimper, my voice cracking. "Never again," I tell her sleeping form, as I listen to her soft breathing, "I'm going to find this mother-fucker, and make sure he pays for every blemish on your beautiful body."

She doesn't stir as I speak, but her body relaxes, like she knows I'm here. That's enough. For now, that's enough.

My fingers run gently over the swollen and bruised marks on her face. Watching her breathe, knowing she's here, with me, alive. When it could have been so much worse.

When she wakes, I'll ask her some hard questions, but for now, I'll take details of each and every mark on her pale skin, I'll watch the bruises darken, and be there when they fade. I'll clean her up and make her feel safe again.

She'll know she belongs to me, because after this, I'm never letting her go.

Chapter Thirty-One
Mine

Aggie

Holy-shit, my side burns as I try to rub shampoo into my hair; it almost takes my breath away. I'm trying to shower on my own for the first time in days. Ethan's been by my side, not letting me lift a finger, but today I needed some space. I had to beg him not to come in with me, but now I'm regretting it. I let the shampoo slip through my fingers and wash down the drain. I can't do it, not yet anyway. I want him to wash my hair, or just hold me up, while I let the water do its work.

I'd sink to the floor, but it would hurt like hell; my hip twinges with every twist and turn. My ribs and face took the brunt of the attack.

I was attacked.

He called me Sophie, just like the guy before the gala did. It can't be a coincidence. *Can it?* I don't know what it means, and from his reaction, I'm not sure I want to find out. Not if this is what happens. Looking down at myself, I'm an array of colours, not pleasant ones; angry reds, purples, and blacks, that keep me from forgetting.

I think I blanked it all out the first few nights. Ignorance is bliss, right? But I can't ignore those words I remembered in my sleep last night.

Useless, just like she was.

It woke me, the dream, or memory, it was like it was happening again, I was covered in sweat and disoriented until Ethan spoke, bringing me back to reality, calming me with his words and gentle touch until I fell back to sleep.

Standing underneath the spray of water, it's hot on my sensitive skin. I've not seen myself in the mirror yet. I've not wanted to face how I look. Not yet.

Everything I do hurts actually.

Sighing, I give in, crying into my hands as I press myself to the wall. "Ethan?" I hiccup as another sob wrecks me. He'll be outside the door listening, just in case he's needed. I have needed him. I don't know how I would have done any of this without him. After a day in the hospital, I was discharged into Ethan's care. Honestly, I'm not sure they had a choice: he was like a bull in a china shop. I woke up to find him quietly arguing with a doctor. Something about a scan, and them being inadequate. He stopped when I groaned his name. The glare Ethan gave the doctors could've levelled the building. Needless to say, I was sent for a scan half an hour later.

I was fine.

God, the way he looked at me was like I'd been brought back to life. It was gut-wrenchingly beautiful. He dropped to his knees beside the bed, his grey eyes lost in mine, as he told me he'd be forever stalking me if it meant he could keep me safe.

I told him not to be an idiot. But, fuck, my heart shattered. I felt so... loved.

The man hasn't been to work in the last four days, not even taking a phone call, as far as I'm aware. Even with the pain radiating through me, I'm smiling. For the first time in days, and it's all because of Ethan.

He can do that, even when I'm crying and at my worst moments, he can make me smile without any reason.

Not even a second has passed before he's storming through the door he refused to let me lock, and stripping to his boxers. "I'm here," he says calmly, taking my hips in his hands, and slowly turning me to face him, kissing away my tears. "It hurts so much," I whimper.

"It will get better, baby, I promise." Cupping my cheeks with his hands, he kisses me softly. "A few more weeks and you'll be back to naked ballet dancing for me." I want to laugh, but I smile up at him instead. "Let's get you washed. Layla should be here for lunch soon." I nod, and Ethan takes control, washing my body with so much care and attention, I never want to have it any other way.

"I like this," I tell him as he wraps me in a towel. "You're spoiling me. I'll get used to it, and want nothing less from you," I joke.

"I'd gladly touch your naked body for the rest of my days," he reassures me in that low, sexy tone that makes me quiver. Tugging the towel lightly away from my chest, he peeks inside, like he's not just been naked with me.

"You're the only man who's ever been able to turn me on at the flick of a switch."

"You're turned on?" A devilish grin edges his lip.

"Yes, you've just washed me down and told me you'd touch me forever. How could I not be?" He growls, bending to kiss my parted lips.

"I like turning you on. Are you wet for me, butterfly?" he murmurs into my mouth before his tongue sweeps against mine.

"Soaking," I pant, my hands lifting to his firm, wet chest. He parts my towel, his hand sneaking into the opening. Kissing me deeply this time, his hand drops to my core, teasing me. I moan his name and he groans, dragging a finger through my drenched core making me whimper. "It's too soon, baby." I can feel his smirk on my lips. *The fucker*. He did that on purpose. With one more swipe of my clit, he removes his hand. I groan in annoyance, making him bark a beautiful laugh that sets off the fireworks in my chest.

"You're mean," I grumble, his forehead leaning against mine as he calms his laughter. Opening my eyes, I bite my lip when I find the warmth of his grey eyes shining back at me.

"I'm only looking out for you, but trust me, when I think you can handle it, I'm going to fuck you on every surface of this house, so god-damn hard, you'll blush when entering every room in the future, remembering each and every position I had you in as I made you mine." He's smirking as I lose all my breath.

"Please."

"Two more days."

It's going to be the longest two days of my life if he's going to torture me. *It'll be so fucking worth it.*

"Do you think he realises that paintings yours?" Layla says as she wanders around the fancy living room.

"I don't think he does. It was bought before we met. I don't get the details of the buyers unless I ask for them," I say, trying to get comfortable on the giant sofa, and failing miserably. It's a self-portrait, but the details on the face are vague. I did it over a year ago. It was only hung in the gallery to fill a gap in the admissions. When I got the email to say it had been sold, I was shocked but pleased at the same time. It's nice to know someone's enjoying your work. It's even nicer to find it on the wall of a man you have feelings for.

"And you didn't ask who wanted your work? I'd have to know. I love knowing who's ordered the bouquets of flowers, what vase they're putting them in, and the reason behind it." Layla frowns, not understanding why I don't ask where my painting was going to be housed.

"That's because you love to be nosey and chat like it's going out of fashion. I think they give you the answers just to shut you up." She shrugs her shoulders, not denying it. "I do like knowing that he loved the painting before he met me though. There's something..."

"Romantic about it?" she questions, her eyes sparkling because she's happy that I've met someone. "Also, they can never shut me up. I was born to talk." I laugh and wince as my ribs shake from the movement.

"Or born talking," I jibe. She gives me the 'You're right' shrug and continues the tour of the *fancy* living room.

"Yeah, romantic," I say, getting back to talking about Ethan buying the painting, before we met. And finally getting the cushion right where I need it.

"Will you tell him?" I'm confused for a second, but then I realise she's still talking about my painting hanging on Ethan's wall. I'm not nervous that he has my painting on the wall. I feel honoured that, he bought it because he liked it. That's all I ever want from a buyer. I am apprehensive about how he will react, to it being mine.

"Tell me what?" he says from the doorway, drinks in hand. Layla's eyes widen. She can't lie for shit. She clamps her mouth shut and turns to look at the pictures on the fireplace, blanking him.

"Where did you get that painting?" I ask, pointing to the wall, where my painting of the ballerina hangs. I want the full story before I say anything. It's not the first time I've been in this room, but it's the first time I've noticed my artwork on the wall. Raff must have hung it while I was bed-bound.

"Stunning, isn't it?" He smiles, but it's shadowed by something unfamiliar. "I brought it from the gallery on the beach." I stifle my smile. *Yep, I know.*

"What do you think of it?" I'm intrigued.

"It's not my normal style." He has no idea how true that statement is. It's a self-portrait after all, and I'm far from his normal style of woman. "But it captivated me from the moment I saw it. I bought it the following week when I couldn't stop thinking about it. I don't know what it is about it, but it still captures my attention every time I walk into the room." I'm just staring at him; I have no words. That's so...

"Beautiful," Layla says, wiping her eyes. Is she crying? She's right, it is. There's something I'm not getting, though; his voice and eyes say one thing, but there's a tension in his body I can't miss. With Layla's encouraging smile, I pluck up the courage to tell him.

"I'm glad you like it; it was a self-portrait I did over a year ago." There's nothing, no reaction for a second. Like he's frozen, not knowing what to say.

"What did you say?" he demands placing the drinks on the small table to the side of me. My heart dips, dripping cold at his reaction.

"It's mine, I painted it." His eyes widen.

"You painted it?" I look to Layla, who's looking at me with equal interest.

"Yeah," I say, biting my bottom lip. "The name I signed it with, I thought it was something I made up. Turns out it's my mum's name, or so says the email off that woman. Luna. It's beautiful, isn't it?"

"You painted it?" he repeats, looking more like the stern man I first met. The man who told my ex to back off, or he'd have him arrested.

"Ethan, what is it?" I reach for him, and he snaps out of whatever that was.

"No wonder I loved it so much," he murmurs, like he can't believe what he's heard. It's not the reaction I was expecting. Far from it. "I need to head out," he grumbles, his tone low and threatening almost. "I'll see you later."

And just like that, he turns and leaves.

Chapter Thirty-Two

A Word

Ethan

I'm in my truck, parked outside the Cerberus building, only I can't get out, can't get my head around what's happening. I don't know what the fuck to do.

I do know what the right thing to do would be, but I can't bring myself to do it.

It's her. Aggie.

The girl from my gran's story *is* Aggie.

It can't be. The story my gran told me, the car crash, finding the little girl, the woman—*Luna*—being killed, hiding the child.

Maybe it's a big fat fucking coincidence? The name Luna has to be popular, right? I know, even as I say it, I'm talking out of my arse. I need to fact check before I fly off the handle.

Fuck.

Resting back against the headrest, guilt almost swallows me whole as my chest tightens. *God-damn.* I just walked out on her. She probably thinks I'm a prick for not reacting the way she expected. I should have been jumping all over her, praising her.

Idiot.

I've loved that painting from the moment I laid eyes on it, just like I have her.

I'm in love with Aggie.

The realisation floods over me like a tsunami, pulling me under. I struggle for breath. It's not really great timing to confess my love when I'm about to tell her I know why she was placed in foster care. That her mother died protecting her, for what reason, I have no idea. It'll have to wait.

When's the right time to tell someone you're in love with them?

I can't answer that, but I know it's not now, when I'm keeping things from her.

I *love* her, and I walked out on her while she's recovering from being attacked, after she told me the painting was hers. I walked out, too in my own head to be able to say anything meaningful.

The initial wave of happiness I felt, knowing I'd bought her painting, was quickly and painfully pissed on when I realised what she was truly saying. Her eyes sparkled at telling me her mum's name. How can I tell her she's dead, that she died after supposedly being chased, and crashing the car with both of them in it? I don't know how she actually died. But I can guess.

My Aggie is Luna's daughter. The girl my gran hid from the world, to keep her safe. I can't focus, as my skin tingles with discomfort at knowing something she doesn't. The more I think about it, the more my chest tightens.

How can this happen? Of all the planes she could get on, she got on mine? The grandson of the woman who saw her mother die. Were we meant to find each other? Am I meant to help her though this? Are we destined for each other?

Does she know? She can't know, can she? Is she hiding this from me too?

I'm desperately trying to think of everything she's ever said to me.

Alone all her life.

Can look after herself.

Placed into foster care.

Yet she tensed up when I said I'd help her find her parents. '*There's nothing to find.*'

You can't miss what you've never had.

The drawing of the woods in her sketchbook. The bad dream.

I slam my hands on the wheel of my truck; this can't be happening. What if she really has no idea about it? How old was she when it happened? Is it possible she can't remember?

She can't remember. Her words hit me like a brick.

She didn't know her own story.

I should take her to see my gran, tell her everything I know. Something's stopping me. I don't know what. Maybe it's me. I don't want to see Aggie hurting any more than she is right now. Maybe if I give her time to heal. Find the fucker that attacked her. I'll be able to bring her some closure on one thing before I destroy her with the other.

I need to get to work and find this man. I've been home for four days, doing nothing while she's been suffering.

Something in the back of my mind whips at me, sparking a thought that maybe there's something…

The man in her studio.

The man who attacked her, searching for something on her.

Why was her mother running?

Why did she want to hide her daughter?

I roar into the empty truck. What are they looking for?

She said he called her Sophie. I need to speak to Gran. Tell her about what's been happening. Not the full details, but enough so she'll share the things she said would die with her.

> **Me**: I'm sorry I ran out, butterfly. Work emergency. Ask Layla to stay the night with you. Raff will be there, I'll be back in the morning.

Butterfly: Sure. Be safe, Joker.

My house is as secure as they come; working in security has its perks. I know she'll be safe there. Plus, I have cameras inside and out of the house. I've asked one of the teams to watch the house, but they can't get there for another few hours.

I've hurt her feelings. I know I have. I'll be there to wake her up tomorrow morning, and I'll be moving Aggie's painting from the *fancy* lounge, and I'll be hanging it in pride of place over the fireplace in our cosy lounge. *Ours.* I like the sound of that.

Fuck, I want to tell her I love her. In the depth of all the shit she's going through, and has been through, I want her to know she has me forever.

Me: I'm yours, butterfly.

Butterfly: I know. Joker. Come back to me?

Me: Always.

I'm surrounded by so much information, I don't know what to do or look at first.

Three separate events, the studio, the attack, and the car crash, twenty-one years ago.

Owen and Cole have been hard at work trying to find the guy who put Aggie in the hospital. Unfortunately for us, there were no cameras on the beach or the path leading to it. Cole hacked the main street cameras, so we have the aftermath on camera. My heart tore in two as I watched Aggie being wheeled into the back of the ambulance. She looked so fucking scared, her hands trembling as she clung to the blanket that covered her, dried blood on her swollen, bruised face.

After seeing that, I doubled down on my efforts to find the guy. I'm not leaving until I have something to go on.

I'd like to say I'd kill him for what he did to her, but that's not our style. Whoever he is, he'll pay though.

Cole, our genius hacker, has taken images of everyone who was around the scene, and anyone who may have entered the time frame I gave him of two hours before and after. He's been sifting through them since it happened and is getting close to a reasonable list of suspects. I know the police are doing their own thing, but our resources are quicker and more efficient. The system Cole and Owen built is bordering on illegal. It's why we do other, more... unknown jobs. Things that make us the very best at what we do, all over the world.

I've looked into the guy at the studio. Max, Aggie's photographer friend, sent me the images of the man and the car he was driving. But whoever it is isn't stupid. The car was a dead end. And his face hasn't pinged on the facial recognition yet. And it's been days.

It's not unusual for it to take a while, but I'm growing frustrated. I want to give her answers, tell her she doesn't need to worry anymore, that we have him.

But I can't, and it's killing me.

"What if we retrace Aggie's footsteps and see if anyone was following her?" Owen asks as he runs his hand through his hair. "I don't know." It doesn't feel right invading her space like that.

"It could flag up faces we can cross-match against what we already have. Help me narrow the pool down a bit," Cole says coolly, not looking up from the laptop.

"Shit, I need to talk to her. I can't do that without asking her." Pushing from the table, I make the call as I head into my office and close the door. It rings and goes to voicemail. I dial again and this time she answers, a little out of breath.

"Sorry, I couldn't find it." She exhales down the phone when she answers.

"Hi," I say, sitting on the edge of my desk.

"Hi, I didn't think I'd hear from you today." I'm silent for a moment, thinking of the right words to say. "Ethan?"

"Sorry, baby." There's enough tension in my voice to make her breathing stutter.

"Is everything okay?" She sounds worried. I hate that I'm going to worry her further.

"I need to ask you something."

"What is it? Should I be worried?"

"We're working on finding the motherfucker that attacked you." She stays silent, but I can hear the unsaid questions. "I need to know if we can go back and follow your movements for the last few weeks." My hand fists at my side.

"I don't understand. Why would you need to do that?"

"I want to know if the studio guy and the attack are linked?" There's a sharp intake of air on the other end of the phone before she blows it back out.

"How do you know about that? I didn't... say anything."

"You should have called me the second it happened, Aggie. Even if I was with my family. I need to know if you ever feel threatened, you fucking call me." I'm pacing the office now, unable to contain the unease of holding back the truth from her.

"Max, god-damn, why can't he keep his mouth shut?" she almost shouts down the phone.

"Why didn't you tell me?" I ask.

With all the secrets I'm keeping from her I'm a hypocrite, I know.

"I didn't think anything of it. You were looking after your gran, and... I didn't want to worry you." There's something else, I know there is. What's she not saying?

"What else, Aggie? What aren't you telling me?" I stop pacing, waiting for her answer. Loosening my tie, I undo the top button on my shirt, hoping it will relieve the pressure in my chest. It doesn't. "Aggie," I warn.

"Okay, don't get your knickers in a twist." If I had them, they'd be twisted as fuck from the tone of her voice. I'm not going to like this. "When I was called to the hotel the day of the gala, I was in the hall making sure everything was okay."

She hesitates. "I felt like someone was watching me, then this guy walked into the hall, asked me if I worked there, but it wasn't like he was asking me, it was like he was accusing me, or questioning me working at a hotel. Like it confused him…" She stops. "He tried to…"

"Tried to what, Aggie?" Jesus, how many of these incidents has she been keeping to herself? "I'm seething on the inside, my stomach in knots as I grip my phone harder.

"He tried to take my arm, not angrily, but like he wanted to lead me away. Then Susan came in and he left."

"Baby, you can't keep this shit to yourself. I've told you, you're not on your own anymore. I need you to believe me."

"I know, I do, I just… find it hard sometimes," she says, her voice low.

"It's not just me, you have my team too. Cole, Owen, and Leon have been helping me find the guy who attacked you." She sniffles like she's crying.

"Is this why you're not coming home tonight?" Fuck yeah, she called my house her home. A grin splits my face.

"Yeah, I have something I need to clear up."

"Okay," she says, her voice weak. "You can do it." I sigh in relief. She's trusting me. "But Ethan," she says when I don't speak. "I need to talk to you when you get back."

"What about? I can come home now if you need me to?"

"No, no, tomorrow morning." She seems a little calmer now. "Layla's brought lunch. I need to go."

"Okay, baby. I'll speak with you later." *I love you.* I hang up the phone and take a moment to process everything. Then I walk out to the guys and tell them we can stalk the love of my life.

Chapter Thirty-Three

Chica

Aggie

"Why have you been hiding this from me, *Chica*?" Layla sat and held my hand when I told Ethan about the guy from the gala, comforting me when he couldn't.

"That's not all," I add, a sob bursting from my lips. "I'm so sorry." I break down again, unable to hold back anymore. "What do you mean that's not all?"

"I wasn't fostered," I blurt.

"Hang on. Back up. What?" She shakes her hands in front of me. "Start from the beginning." So, I do. I tell her everything I know. About my sort of foster parents, and the necklace I have, I reach for it on instinct, but it's not there. That's it's the only thing that's been with me since I went into care. I explain my self-diagnosed memory loss and the failed attempts to jumpstart it. How Ethan found me crying in the rage room, to the men who seem to be turning up, calling me Sophie. The creepy feeling I've been getting when I walk to work.

"Do you think Sophie is your real name?" she says after a few minutes of silence.

"I'm clueless, but it's a possibility." I never really thought about it, and there's no way to find out.

"And the necklace, you said it's a key?" I can see her mind working through her bright eyes, the cogs turning, trying to connect all the pieces.

"Yeah, it's old and beautiful. Do you want to see it?" Her eyes sparkle with excitement.

"I'd love to," she squeals, jumping up from the sofa. "I can't believe you kept all of this secret from me. I'm a little hurt, but I can understand why." She looks almost sad for a second. I open my mouth to apologise, but she doesn't let me. "We all have our secrets, Aggie." Easing myself from the sofa, I come to stand next to her, resting my head on her shoulder.

"I'm here when you're ready to share them," I murmur, hugging her arm.

"Some are just meant to be buried and forgotten." She sighs, and her whole body deflates.

"The necklace," I feel around my neck for it again, remembering it's not there. "I left it at Purple Passion."

"Let's eat, then we can go get it, if you feel up to it?" Although the aches in my body are still there, they are nothing like what they were four days ago. Maybe moving around will help ease them.

"Okay, yes," I say, excited to be going out of the house.

"There it is," I murmur as I pull out my wooden jewellery box from the bottom of the small closet space. Taking out the necklace I've always had and loved, it shines in the light of the room. "Here." I thrust my arm at Layla as she lies on the bed.

"*Precioso.*" Beautiful, she says, "just like you described it." Unhooking the long gold chain from my fingers, she examines it. I join her on the bed, sitting because it would take me days to get back up again if I tried to lie down.

"Do you think it opens something?" I blow out a breath, just thinking of the thousands of times I thought the same damn thing.

"I don't think so. It may have once upon a time, but it's too pretty to be of any use." She hands it back to me, and I place it around my neck where it belongs. "We should get back." I feel uneasy being here at the moment. "I don't want to worry Ethan any more than I know he already is."

"Okay, we can swing by mine and get my stuff for the night. We'll drive through the woods; it'll be quicker." An image of the dark woods flashes through my mind, and I shudder. It's the same feeling I got when I had that dream and drew the sketch afterwards. Passing it off as tiredness, because I am freaking tired.

Coming here may have been too much after so many days of nothing. I need to get back and chill, but it feels nice to be out of the house, even if I'm starting to ache all over.

With Layla driving along the winding roads, I'm reminded that I need to take some more painkillers. Each bump causing the aches to pinch into pain.

"Have you seen that?" Layla points to the woods, like I should be able to tell what she's thinking.

"Seen what, the trees?" She tuts at me, shaking her head.

"No, the big house behind it?" If I squint, I can just about make it out through the densely compacted trees that surround it. It's nice, but you can't see much from here. I get goosebumps as we take the scenic route, as she called it, back to hers. It's better than the view driving back through town, but I'm not a fan. It always feels too enclosed for me. "That's Ethan's Gran's estate." I open my mouth and gawk at her.

"Lady Celeste's?"

"Yes, have you met her yet?" She flicks her gaze to me before focusing back on the road ahead.

"No, but from what Ethan says about her, she seems fun."

"She's brilliant. The gala you ran the other week, she's the founder of the organisation that you were raising money for, she never goes to the galas anymore, she leaves that to her daughter and Ethan. She helps lost souls."

"Lost Souls?" I knew who we were raising money for, but I never got a chance to look into it.

"Yeah, kids or families who have lost someone. The money raised helps them get on their feet." She says it like she's proud of what they do. "She and her husband set it up over twenty years ago. But wh—" She's cut off by the screeching of brakes as a dark car barrels towards us.

"Layla," I scream, grabbing hold of the handle above the door as Layla jerks the steering wheel to get us out of its way, but the car turns with us.

Time slows down, and I hold my breath. There's nothing I can do but try and make sure my best friend is okay. My arm stretches across her in some frantic search to make sure she's safe and within arm's reach.

I'm not losing her.

I can't.

My heart stops as the other car's backend veers sideways.

This is it.

I wait for the crash, the noise.

My eyes close at the last second, and I'm plunged into darkness. A dream-like state. I can feel the car still moving. I can hear Layla shouting abuse in Spanish. But I see the thick woods capturing me, dark and unforgiving. My heart's racing. I can't breathe. I'm alone. It's holding me. I can't fight the fear as it rises, bubbling in my chest as I sink into the damp ground beneath me. I'm so scared, it's gut-wrenching. But it's not real. I'm not in the woods; I'm in a car. Layla's car.

"Aggie, hold on." My eyes shoot open at her scream.

I watch in horror as she spins the wheel in one last attempt to get away grabbing the handbrake, pulling it sharply. The car jolts and spins onto a verge and into the dirt, where it stops. The other car scrapes past us, metal against metal as it speeds away, not stopping, blowing its horn like it was our fault.

I grab her arm in my hand as she takes a deep, shaky breath, before she starts driving us away. Seeing her wide eyes, mirroring mine, from the side as she drives.

"Are you okay?" I cry. She's silent as she gulps down her cry. "Speak to me," I demand, needing to hear her voice.

"Yes, yes, I'm okay," she finally says, after a beat.

"Layla, how did you learn to drive like that?"

"My dad. I didn't think, I just..." She shakes, her voice trembling.

"Thank god you did."

Chapter Thirty-Four

In My Arms

Ethan

"Your girl was followed after the gala. The same car that was at the studio last time," Cole informs me. Aggie's not my girl, she's *my woman, all fucking mine.* Leon places food in the middle of the table we're all sitting at, handing us plates already full.

"Did we get a face?" I ask, not feeling hungry. Anything would be something at this point. "No, blacked out windows." He's annoyed about it just like the rest of us. "Still nothing on the car either. The rental's under a false name, all false documents. I'm working on getting an image from the rental company's security footage. See if I can get something there," Cole adds.

"I need to know if it's the same person or completely separate incidents. But all three, the studio, the gala, and the beach." Fuck. I shake my head. I have no idea what's happening. It's like I'm in a spinning vortex, I can't get out from; clinging to the side in desperation.

"We'll find out who it is, Ethan." Leon offers.

"From the street cameras we have, that car's been driving past Layla's place since the night at the studio. At different times, like they're checking the place out, maybe to see if Aggie's there still." Owen adds from the other side of the table. Leon stiffens, his muscles going rigid just like mine. "The car slows down, watches for a few minutes, then leaves."

"We need to warn her... Aggie and Layla," Leon corrects himself. He's not wrong. We do need to warn Aggie. Layla just needs to be told it's happening, I don't think we need to worry about her but I won't dismiss Leon's worry for her.

"They're at my house, safe," I tell him, but Leon's already taking his phone from his pocket. He hits a few buttons, bringing it to his ear. We all turn when we hear a phone ringing as the lift doors open.

"Layla?" Leon's deep tone reverberates around the room, obviously shocked when she appears looking ghostly white, even with her olive skin. She's closely followed by Aggie, who looks like she wants to be sick. The hairs rise at the back of my neck as my heart rate speeds into my throat.

I'm up and out of my chair before she can even blink, Leon meeting me step for step.

"I'm sorry," Aggie says, falling into my chest as I reach her. She's in my arms. She's safe.

I glance to the side. Leon stands in front of Layla, like he doesn't know what to do, other than stare at her. "We just drove here. I should have gone back to your place, but I..." I hold her tighter, before lifting her in my arms and carrying her over to an empty chair. I settle Aggie in my lap, caressing the soft skin on her hand.

"I'm glad you did, butterfly." I lift her face to mine. "I'm so fucking glad you did." I'm lost in Aggie for a moment until a throat clears. "Leon," I bark, and Leon snaps into action, bringing a shaky Layla to the table and sitting her next to him, while Cole and Owen share a worried look.

"What happened?" I ask, the torrent of blood rushing past my ears makes it hard to concentrate on anything but Aggie in my lap. My breathing and chest feel heavy as I push air through my nose, doing my best to calm the fear that I wasn't there to help yet again.

"It's okay, we're okay," Aggie reassures me, but it doesn't stop the dread I feel in my veins. "We're shaken up, but not hurt."

"What the fuck, Aggie?" I say as calmly as I can, but my tone betrays me.

"Someone almost crashed into us on the way back from my place." At this rate, I'm not going to see forty. I'll have a heart attack before the day's out.

"Crashed?" My jaw is so tight, the word comes out as a hiss. Aggie squeezes my hand, looking around at everyone.

"A car came careening around the corner, while we were driving past your gran's estate. It came straight for us." She sucks in a shaky breath. "Until Layla did this... manoeuvre, a sort of handbrake turn, but more." My eyebrows shoot up, and all eyes land on the girl from the flower shop. "I've never seen anything like it. We swerved, spun the car, and she landed us on the side of the road just as he clipped the side of her car." Layla stays silent. "He didn't hang around, most likely just some drunk arsehole, with no idea what he was doing."

"Thank you, Layla," I say. I'll give credit where it's due. "Are you okay?" I ask her. She relaxes a fraction, looking up at me.

"I'll be fine." Fiddling with her hands in her lap, she looks at Aggie. "Are you staying here? I want to head home." Aggie nods as Leon makes his feelings known to the whole room.

"No," he barks. "You can't."

"I think I can." She stands. "I'll see you later."

"No, please, fuck..." Leon stands too, fumbling with his stuff before he chases after her.

"What's that about?" Aggie asks, watching the whole thing with curious, tired eyes.

"We just found out that the car that was at the studio has also been surveilling Layla's house." Aggie gulps, her muscles tensing under my hold.

"Oh my god, I'll go after her." She goes to get up, but I hold her back.

"Leon's got her covered." I smirk, or he will have. At this rate, he'll be parked outside her house like Cole did with Ari, his now wife.

"But..."

"No, you're staying right here *on* me, where I can see and feel you," I say, pulling her back to me and kissing her temple.

"Ethan, you're being ridiculous." It's my turn to tense, and she must feel it as her hand wraps around my forearm tighter as I lean in, so only she can hear me.

"If you weren't still recovering, I'd take you into my office and spank your pretty arse pink for that comment, butterfly." A shiver runs down her spine as my warm breath coats the flushed skin on her cheek. And fuck, my dick throbs realising that she likes the idea. *Next time.* She needs to heal first. "God-damn-it," I mutter, and she giggles. The sound like a siren's call, drawing me closer, hooking me in, making my cock an iron bar. "What were you doing at your place?" I ask, needing the distraction before I fuck her where we're sitting. And where is it? I don't ask, still not having been there. I bought her everything she could need when she came out of the hospital, and I know Layla grabbed some basics to bring over too.

"Oh, I wanted to show Layla my necklace, and I'd left it there." She sinks her teeth into her bottom lip, and I pull it free with my thumb before I speak.

"Show me." She takes the chain from where it's hidden inside her jumper, dangling the key so it spins. I've seen her wear it before. "Is it important to you?" I ask because I need to know why she'd need to drive to get a necklace to show Layla when she's still in pain. The car ride must have been uncomfortable for her.

"It's just always been with me." She yawns.

"I'll take you home," I say.

"Can I stay here?" Her voice is tired.

"Of course you can, but I'll be working all night." Cole and Owen, who have wandered off somewhere, groan in the background. "I'll sleep on your sofa in the office."

"I'll get Raff to bring you some things."

"Leave Raff to enjoy his day off. I don't need anything," she says, wincing as she tries to pull herself from my lap.

I stand, carrying her into the office, grabbing everything I need to make her comfortable. I lay a pillow and thick blankets down on the couch for her as she tries to take off her jumper and shoes, but struggles. I ease the jumper over her head and pry her boots from her feet. While she settles back, I grab her some water from the kitchen and painkillers from my medical kit.

Sitting next to her, I watch her swallow the tablets I hand to her with fascination as a droplet of water runs over her lip, and she captures it with her tongue. I stand as she settles herself, groaning in discomfort, then sighing when she sees the crease in my brow. I'm already regretting not taking her home.

"I'm okay. Ethan. Just getting comfy."

"Did you still want to talk?" Crouching beside her, I move the hair from her face.

"I do, but can we do it in the morning?"

"Tomorrow," I murmur, leaving her to sleep.

Chapter Thirty-Five

Liar

Ethan

We pulled an all-nighter and still have nothing, other than we think it's two men. Some of the times of the incidents are too close to be one man in the same place at two different times.

It makes it worse.

I put off speaking with Gran until I could find something on the fuckers that are following Aggie, but there's nothing left for us to investigate.

Speaking to her is my only next step I have before I tell the guys everything. I need to speak with Gran and Aggie.

Aggie's been awake for a while. She and Jill went to grab some breakfast for us all. Cole followed on his bike.

Slipping my phone from the table, I walk to my office and call my Gran.

"Sweet boy, what do I owe this early call?" she says when she answers.

"Morning, and sorry. I need your help." I swallow, knowing what I need to say is not easy.

"You need my help? What a turn of events. What do you need?" I hate this.

"I found her," I say simply.

"Found who?"

"The woman who painted the picture," I affirm.

"Oh, Ethan, no." It sounds like she's covering her mouth.

"It's Aggie, Gran." She gasps and falls silent.

"What does that mean?"

"I think it's her daughter. Aggie, I think she's Luna's daughter."

"Oh my god, Ethan. I'm coming in to see you." I can hear her rushing around, no doubt getting dressed.

"No, you can't," I whisper shout down the phone.

"Ethan Henry James Ford," she yells. *Shit.* "If that girl is who you say she is, then she could be in some serious trouble. I need to know for sure."

"What trouble?"

"Bad people trouble, Ethan, some very bad people." *Fuck, I knew it.* "Does she know anything?"

"No, I don't think she does," I say honestly.

"She's been living in a curse, Ethan. The night I found her, she couldn't remember anything, not even her own name. I had to call her something, Ethan… I called her Agatha." She swallows.

"You named her after your mother?" It clicks into place. I feel numb. I've been so stupid.

"Agatha Rose Hope," she says softly. "The poor girl." Her voice is so unsteady, I know she's reliving the night again.

"Gran, I…" I've fucked up so badly. "I need to talk to her first. Fuck, she doesn't know I know." I panic, my hands trembling as I say it. It's gone beyond what's reasonable. She'll hate me. I don't like the idea of her seeing Gran, not before I get to tell Aggie what I know.

Fuck, I'm an idiot.

I'm going to lose her.

"Then that's your own stupid foolishness. That girl needs to know the truth. If this is really happening." I hear a door slam.

"What truth? Just how bad are we talking?" I'm staring at nothing in particular, bracing myself for her explanation.

"God-damn-it, don't make me tell you over the phone." She pauses.

"Gran, what the hell?" The hackles on my back rise. I need to know. I need to know what's coming, so I can keep her safe. So I can keep them all safe.

"The backpack I took from the car the night her mother was killed; it had all this stuff in it. Information on what and who she was running from." A chill pierces its way through me, leaving me breathless. What the fuck has my Gran got us into?

"Give me time," I plead.

"You have until I get there. See you soon."

She hangs up the phone, and I sit back in my chair. I know how badly this will go. My chest squeezes painfully. I know who she is and what happened to her all those years ago, and I'm the fool who never told her.

Gulping down my regret, I walk back into the central area where the guys are all hard at work. I've lied to them all. I can't tell them while Aggie knows nothing. But I have to warn them.

Chapter Thirty-Six

Cold

A shiver runs over my skin as we pull up to the kerb. It's warmer today, but I can't shake this feeling. Maybe I'm finally coming down with that cold. A stress cold more likely.

"We could have ordered this in, you know," Jill chimes from beside me as we gather the bags of food and drinks we bought from Bruno's café.

"I know, but I needed some air. Plus, they've been working on something for me all night, and I need to repay the favour. Food seems to be the best way." She gives me a kind smile. I don't know how much she knows about what's happened, but I'm grateful she doesn't say anything more.

"You're not kidding. You'd think they were never fed, the way those men shovel it down." I chuckle, feeling myself relax a little. Jill steps out of the car, hands full with fresh coffees, in the two trays. "I'll take these up and come back down to help with the rest." I lift my chin in agreement; there's no way I can carry all of this by myself.

Getting out of the car myself in the underground garage is a challenge in itself. I leave a few bags in there, while my arms are full of others.

I struggle towards the door, trying and failing to open it, as our driver steps up and holds it open for me. He tries to take some of the bags from me, but we're uncoordinated, and almost drop them as he takes two bags that have tangled together. I laugh as we get them straight, and he heads upstairs, leaving me behind. I know Cole's around somewhere. I have no doubt Ethan's watching the cameras, waiting for me to get back.

I hear the heavy thud of feet running down the steps in front of me, and then a faint cry from my side. Turning my head, I find Lady Celeste next to me, unshed tears in her eyes. I've never met her before, but I've seen pictures around Ethan's house.

"Sophie."

I gasp. The name tumbles from her lips, like she can't believe what she's seeing. I look around to make sure there's no one behind me, but there's no one else here. Only the sound of someone descending the stairs quickly. I swallow. She's talking to me. She's calling me Sophie. She's the third person to do so in over a week.

Is it my real name? I lose all feeling in my hands as the bags crash to the floor. She reaches for me, but I jerk back, taken aback by my own movements. I force myself to be more... me.

She stares at me like I'm a figment of her imagination. "Sophie? I can't believe it's you," she mutters. "You look just like your mother." My breaths become choppy. My shaky hand flies to my mouth to cover the sob that's falling from me.

"How?" I ask. I can't process this. "You knew her?" The lump in my throat is like razors. Hard to swallow and painful.

"No, sweetheart." She stops talking, and I have to blink away my confusion.

"Then how would you know?" My tone is demanding, angry almost.

"There's so much you need to know."

"Like what? I don't... I don't get it." I'm choking on my own words, my own breath. How does Ethan's Gran know who I am?

"Ethan and I will explain everything, I promise, sweetheart." I can't swallow the pit of despair that's crumbling beneath me.

"Ethan?" I whisper sob, the world dropping from below me. There's a loud intake of air behind me followed by a low growl, but I don't look. I can't because I know it's Ethan. He knows? *He knew.* My legs suddenly feel heavy. *He knew.*

He knew? I can't get past the question. All along, he knew who I was when I didn't. He knew, after everything we've become, after I fell for him, and he didn't say a word.

Stepping back, I hit a wall of solid muscle. And flinch.

Ethan tries to wrap his arm around me, but I push it away, my anger flaring to life like the spark of a rocket. I face him, my eyes on his.

His face says it all.

"You knew?" He looks so ashamed of himself, I can't look at him. I made a mistake. My heart says run, get away from them, have some time, just leave. But my head tells me to find out more. Find what I've been missing for the last twenty-one years.

Find out the truth.

Find out who I really am.

Ethan stays silent, his soulful eyes stormy. He looks lost, not knowing what to do. It's enough to see the pain he's in, to see the apology written all over his face, the way he tries to get my attention back on him when I look away by brushing my cheek with the back of his hand. The softness in his eyes when he looks at me.

But I can't talk to him right now. I can't handle his grief along with my own. I can't even look at him; this hurts too much. Does that make me as bad as he is? I'm a hypocrite. I never told him either.

I never told him what was holding me back, I never said a word when he held me in that rage room. I made him wait. Yet he already knew.

"How... long, how long have you known?" My heart pounds uncomfortably waiting for him to answer.

"Two days." I'm numb and exposed. Like a fragile flower in a deadly desert.

Forty-eight hours, and nothing. Relief and hurt colliding, relief it wasn't longer, but fuck, the hurt he still kept it from me is like a knife to my chest.

It's gutting me that he knows who I am when I don't. I have nothing in this fucking head of mine that can tell me how I came into this world. *I still don't.* And *he*, the man I have quietly given my heart to, knows, and didn't or couldn't tell me.

Then I see it. I know the moment he knew. "The painting?" It's barely a word. "Is that why you wanted to stay away from me last night?" I shout in disbelief.

He grits his teeth, but remains silent. That hurts so much more.

"Fuck you. You could have told me, Ethan. I was going to tell you everything today." The damn opens, and everything I've been holding on to all these years flows out; right here in the underground garage. "I was ready to tell you I have no memory of my childhood, or my parents. I have nothing before the day I walked into my so-called foster home." His nostrils flare as I speak.

His Gran winces in my peripheral vision, but he remains still. Just listening. "I've been alone all my life, left to my own devices. I had no one until I met... you, Ethan. You felt like home to me." My chest's caving in. I can't hold on to it any longer. "I was never fostered," I sob. "There are no records of me. I know I checked." My heart cracks, leaving an empty void behind. The emptiness forces me to take a breath, trying to fill my lungs with anything; something to feel like this is or isn't happening, because I can't tell which one I want.

His Gran takes my arm, turning me away from him. "That was me. You have to understand, there were reasons why." She's trying to reason with me, but I'm too far gone.

"There may have been reasons, but keeping me in the dark was never the right way to go about it. If you'll excuse me, I need to leave."

I shiver with cold as I step away. No one follows, and I think that upsets me more.

Chapter Thirty-Seven

It's Time

Ethan

"What the hell, Gran?" I spin to face her as I come to my senses. She levels me with an icy stare, and I know I'm in the wrong, but I can't stop my mouth. "How could you tell her like that?" I seethe, my pulse racing.

"Don't you dare pawn that off on me. You've known for two days, and you think it's my fault?" She's right, I know, but fuck, I've just watched Aggie walk away. She's hurting, and I did that to her.

I'm so sorry, butterfly.

"Fuck." I sink back to the wall, falling to my arse. "You just came right out and... Sophie? You called her Sophie?" I came straight down here when I saw Jill was back in the office and heard the whole conversation.

"That's her real name, Ethan. You seem to be a bit slow in catching on today," she chastises.

"Her real name?" I'm talking to myself, but she answers me anyway. *Sophie?*

"For such a highly educated man, Ethan, you're acting thick as shit."

"No, no, I'm just adding it all up. All the trouble she's been in, the guy that attacked her called her Sophie." My gran turns pale, bringing her hand to her chest as she inhales sharply.

"She's been attacked? Ethan, why didn't you tell me? You need to get that girl back and keep her by your side." She points her finger at me, the colour coming back to her cheeks.

"You need to tell me everything," I say as I stand back up and take her hand.

"Not until you bring her back," she adds, tugging her hand from mine.

"Just how bad?" I question. Gran looks me in the eye, a look of deep fear crossing her features.

"They killed her mother, Ethan. Do you think they'll hesitate to kill her?" I stumble back. She's right, I know she is. They've found and attacked her once; she might not be so lucky next time.

"She won't listen to me, not now," I say, running my hand over my hair and down my face.

"The very fact she walked away after you omitted the truth, rather than to stay and find out what she's been missing for the last twenty-odd years of her life, tells me you're more important to her than any of this. She'll fight you, but she'll listen."

"I hope you're right." If I have to kidnap the woman, I will.

"I normally am, sweetheart. It's what your grandfather hated most about me." She grins, walking to the lift and pressing the button as I race up the stairs.

Storming through the doors, I grab my keys from my desk and open my gun safe.

"Eth, fill us in," Owen says, watching me dart around, grabbing my gun and ammo before filling a bag with medical supplies, just in case. Owen's eyes go wide.

"Shit." Cole strides up to his side, watching when I slide my holster on over my shirt and drop my gun in, to sit snugly at my waist.

"She's in deep shit. I don't know what yet, but I'll find out. Gran's out there. She'll fill you in."

"Okay, switch your tracker on so I know where you are. I'll track Aggie's work phone for you." There's no question asked; they have my back.

I give him a chin lift on my way out, just as Gran exits the kitchen with an empty teacup in her hand.

Chapter Thirty-Eight

Lost

Aggie

I feel every ounce of the anger that's simmering beneath my skin, a volcano ready to blow; poked, prodded, and intensified by the ache of anguish and hurt that's flowing freely in my tears. Slamming the door to the boat behind me, I can't control the swell of emotions raging inside me.

He fucking knew, and didn't tell me. He kept it to himself.

The selfish arsehole.

I don't even care that I walked away from knowing who I am. All these years I've waited to find out, and it doesn't matter. Nothing hurt more than Ethan knowing who I was and not telling me.

My chest aches as I heave another wrenching cry. Every part of me feels the agony of his omission. My fists ball at my sides, and I throw the closest thing to me, only its soft thud against the wall that doesn't give me the release I need. I launch myself at my bed, punching the pillow, over and over again. Only it does nothing to release the tension building in my chest. I can feel it cracking.

How could he?

Two days.

I know it's not long, but I could feel the difference in him, like he was pushing me away. The truth too much after what we had. What we'd found in each other. After my own lies and omissions.

He never said a word. Just stood there. Silent.

Do I mean that little to him? Fuck, I punch the pillow again as I cry harder. *I love the bastard so much.*

Collapsing on the bed, I'm unable to stop the influx of tears. My whole body wrenching from the ferocity. I flip on to my back, trying to focus on anything but what's happening. How do we come back from this?

Maybe it's time for me to leave, go travelling again and never come back this time.

Can I live with never seeing him again?

No.

I cry at my own answer. I don't think it matters how much he's hurt me. I'd still love him even if there was nothing left.

There's a knock at my door, but I don't move. Instead, I place the pillow over my head and ignore whoever it is. *What if it's Ethan?* My hope flares, but then I remember him standing there in front of me, not fighting for me, and it pops like a pinned balloon.

It won't be him; he doesn't know where I live. The knock comes louder this time. There's a harshness to the next one when I don't answer.

"Go away," I shout, pulling the pillow from my face.

It's not Layla. She'd tell me it was her, and so would Ethan. My blood freezes. Did someone else follow me? Looking around, I make sure everything is as closed as it can be. The windows are all locked shut, and too small to climb in and out of.

There's only one way in and one way out.

I'm overreacting. It goes quiet, and I can't swallow my imploding fear. When I see a figure pass the window, I bolt up and move to the corner, so I can't be seen. The windows rattle, then the door shakes.

"Shit," I hiss, taking my phone from my pocket. I bring up Ethan's number, only I hesitate to call him. I don't know why, but I can't bring myself to press it. My thumb hovers over the call button. That's until the handle on the door starts to jiggle, followed by a loud bang. Someone's kicking the door.

I hit dial.

Ethan

"Butterfly?" I answer before it even rings.

"Are you outside my door?"

"No." I push my foot to floor to get me closer to her; we're only minutes apart.

"Ethan, someone's here," she whimpers. There's a shake to her voice. She's scared. I can't drive any faster; I'm already breaking the limits of our streets.

"Two minutes, baby. I'll be there. Stay on the phone. I'm coming." The engine groans as I force it forward. "I know where you are."

"They're trying to get in, what do I do?" I'm not close enough, but fuck am I going to let her down.

"Who is it? Can you see them?" I keep my tone calm, not wanting her to panic. There's a loud thud, something hitting wood.

"I can't see them. Ethan, I'm scared." I roar, unable to hold back, they're too close. I'm so fucking stupid.

"Hide, baby. Grab something that will hurt them if they get in. Anything," I rasp.

"Okay." I pull up the front of the dock, slamming the car door behind me as run, towards her *fucking* boat.

"One minute, baby. Do you have something?" I ask breathlessly, my feet pounding on the decking as I run.

"Yes," she replies, her voice quieter now.

"Now hide, I'm here." There's a massive crack that sounds like a door breaking. I push myself further, as the boat comes into view.

"Sophie," a deep voice echoes down the line, calling her. My stomach drops, knowing this stranger is inside. I listen intently for his next move, but all I get is silence and a small click, like something locking. My fear is palpable.

Footsteps thud through the silence, echoing around the wooden floor.

"I know you're hiding, but there's really no need." He's trying to coax her out of her hiding place. Fuck, he's too close. "I've come to collect, Sophie," he says as I jump off the railing of the small boat and onto the deck.

"You'll be okay, baby," I say as quietly as I can. I won't let her think she's alone.

"Stay quiet, baby." My voice is deep, low, and commanding. "I'm at the door." I can see him standing outside a door, no doubt where she's hidden. "Good girl," I say, "Stay where you are. I see him." I cut the call. I need both hands to give this arsehole what he deserves for trying to get to my woman.

He's bulky, but young, most likely out to prove himself. He reaches for the door handle, rattling it, making the sound of my entrance silent to his ears.

My eyes are trained on the door separating me from Aggie and the guy who stands between us. As I pass the debris of the door, I get as close as I can without being noticed. I'm more or less on him when I slam his head into the wall, he stumbles but doesn't fall, I add my brogue to his side, with as much force as I can, he falls into the side of the boat, grunting, as whatever was on the side falls and clatters to the floor with him.

His eyes snap to mine; seemingly unfazed, there's blood dripping down his face. He lurches forwards, his bulky frame hurtling towards me. I brace, crouching slightly, giving him my shoulder to his chest. I hear the air propel from his lungs, as he clutches and rips at my clothes. The small boat begins to rock from our movements, making him stumble backwards. I don't waste anytime, picking him up by his throat, my hand balled into a fist. I lay the first of many blows to his face, before I throw him across the small room. There's an almighty crack as the shelf he lands on snaps in two. He groans as his back hits the counter with a thud, the whole boat swinging dangerously to one side. "Bastard," he yells.

"That's my woman you hurt," I growl.

"She'll be dead come morning," he bristles. He swings a broken piece of wood at my face, catching me above the eye. Fuck, that stung. I move out of his reach, my knee lifting to his side, impaling into the soft tissue to his stomach. He grunts as I right myself.

"You'll have to get through me first." I give him everything, not giving him a chance to catch his breath, as I throw punch after punch at him. He grabs my jacket, ripping the material as he gives his best fight. It won't ever be enough to come between me and Aggie.

I force him to the floor, my leg taking him out. He crumbles, his body lying beneath mine. I snake my arm around his neck. His hands come to grip my arm, his silent plea to stop when I hear the click of a lock. I twist my head to see the handle of the door pull down.

Fuck, not yet. I don't want her to see this.

"Don't you fucking dare open that door, butterfly," I shout through gritted teeth. I stop what I'm doing, and hurl the guy to the door, trapping her inside.

He takes a chance to get up, but he's not quick enough. I kick out, my foot landing in his chest. He heaves a breath, crashing to the wall. Plates and bowls smash around him as he fumbles around trying to catch his breath.

I stalk towards him, two steps, my fist clenched. I land a hit in his face, and he goes out like a light. Falling to the floor face first like the dead weight he is.

I make quick work finding a rope to secure him, tying him up like a pig ready for slaughter. I'm just pulling the last cord tight around his wrists when the door opens. Aggie steps out, a paddle in her hand. As I step towards her, she swings it hard against my head.

My hand flies up.

"Baby," I call through a groan, my hand taking hold of the paddle before she can use it again. "Stop, it's me." This time she drops the paddle.

"*Ethan*," she says softly, like she can't believe I'm here. Relief overwhelms me before I get a sudden ache in my chest.

"Oh, fuck." Aggie grabs my face in her hands, her eyes wild while she kisses me anywhere she can. I hold her hips, looking at her. She's okay, I repeat to myself; not a new scratch on her.

"I'm sorry, I thought you were," she looks around, taking in the state of her little boat, "him," she adds, spotting the guy face down unconscious, hogtied on the floor. I smirk at my own handywork.

I clutch my head where she struck me. It's nothing, but still smarts.

"I've hurt you." She pulls my hand away, inspecting the damage. "You're bleeding." I gaze in wonder as she rips her jumper off and holds it to my head. "I'm so sorry," she mumbles. I'm covered in sweat, my suit torn and stained with... blood. I see the second she panics, her chest rising and falling, as her hands drift over my body, lifting my shirt in an endless search for where it's coming from.

"It's not mine," I state, trying my best to reassure her as I lean back against the door she came from. When she finally looks me in the eye, my lips tip up into a smile. She wobbles, and I don't think it's from what's gone on; the heat in her eyes says something else entirely. *Goddamn this woman.*

"Why are you smiling?" she asks.

"Why are you?" I ask right back, my hand sneaking around her waist, drawing her so close I can feel the ripple of her breath against my stomach and chest underneath my own as I breathe her in. I lift her face to mine, dropping the jumper to the floor before I feather my lips across hers. She shivers, clutching my forearms for support. "I got you, baby."

"I know."

"Let's go." Ethan moves towards the front of his black truck, everything seemingly forgotten about the events that have led us here. I'm conflicted, gulping down the heaviness in my chest. He just saved my life, but there's an undercurrent I can't grasp. I'm on a high from what's just happened. *Is that normal?*

I can't forget though, can I? I can't forget that he knew about my past and chose not to tell me. Worst of all, maybe not worst, but more inappropriately, my treacherous slapper of a body can't seem to feel anything other than a buzz, a buzz that's running rampant between my thighs.

Bitch.

It's unredeemable. I'm trying my best ignore it, but the seam of my jeans keeps rubbing against my clit, and I keep moving my hips because it feels so good.

I'm sitting in the passenger seat of his truck, after I watched Ethan haul the guy who tried to attack me—who was still out cold—into the back like he weighed nothing. His easy display of strength should not turn me on. I should *not* be turned on.

But, fuck me, it does, and I am.

Stifling a groan as the seam of my jeans grazes my clit, I bite the inside of my cheek. I don't know what's happening to me. There's never been a time I've been this horny. *Ever.* It's clouding my mind, like a fog, I can't and don't entirely want to come out of. I don't want to deal with... with the waterfall of emotions I'm hiding from.

"Aggie?" I'm staring at his hips as they shift when he settles himself in the seat. His dark grey trousers bunching around the top of his thick thighs, showing me the glorious outline of his cock.

Holy-hell, I'm done for.

"Yep," I answer a little too quickly, and he knows it.

"Baby, what's wrong?" *Oh god*, I can't tell him I'm horny. Not after the day we've had. Not when we have an unconscious man in the open boot. "Butterfly, I can see your mind whirling from here. What is it?" His hand settles on my leg, resting too close to where I'm getting desperate to feel his fingers. A small, needy whine leaves my lips. My hands grip the edge of the seat, trying to calm myself. I whimper, looking at him. How is he so perfect?

"Just drive," I say, turning my gaze to his hands instead of his crotch.

"I'm not going anywhere until you tell me." He moves to face me.

"Fine," I say, giving in. "I'm..." I groan. "Really turned on right now." Heat rises over my lower abdomen. "Seeing you like that, and like this," I wave my hand over the sweaty sexiness he is. "Has done something to me." His tongue darts out across his top lip, and a whoosh of air passes my lips before I can stop it. My cheeks heat at my own neediness.

"Do you need to come, butterfly?" His low, gravelly tone causes a shiver to run down my spine to my clit. *God-damn. Yes.*

"Obviously." I roll my eyes at him, and he taps the inside of my thigh, his fingers brushing over the seam of my jeans, adding to the pressure they are already creating. I whimper, almost losing my breath. My eyes focus on Ethan, his knowing smile, and dark, seductive eyes, igniting my need for him further. "Ethan," I whine.

"Shit." He glances back, running his free hand over the stubble on his tanned jaw. Then he puts the car into drive and starts crawling forward out of the parking lot. His fingers rub between my legs as we drive, pressing my clit. I moan. "Fuck, baby." He does it again, my hips bucking into his hand as he drives. I'm so close already, I'm panting. "Undo your jeans," he growls, his whole hand cupping me, before he lifts it to pinch my nipple. I gasp at the shot of lust I feel.

I don't even hesitate. I need this. I don't care that he's driving. I fumble, unzipping them and opening them wide.

"Pull them down. I want to see my fingers slide into you." *Yes. I want that too.* Without a word, I shimmy them down just below my knees. "Spread your legs as wide as you can." I do, and the low rumble he lets out spikes the heat between my thighs as arousal pools.

Keeping one hand on the wheel, his hand wastes no time in teasing me, taking my flesh in an almost bruising grip, he skims over my hot skin.

"Ethan." Parting me with his fingers, he circles my clit, and I groan my appreciation. "Fuck, I need this," I murmur. I need his touch. Without warning, he sinks two fingers into me. I gasp at the intrusion, but fuck, it's a welcome one. My hips push forward, needing more.

Keeping his eyes on the road, he drives to wherever we're going. I couldn't care less if he drove me to the bank to make a deposit, as long as he keeps going, "Oh, fuck." I moan as he pumps his fingers faster, my arousal making it slick as he goes deeper. *Oh-my-god*. I'm going to come.

"That's it, baby, take it," he says through gritted teeth, the palm of his hand rubbing my clit with the perfect amount of pressure as he curls his finger inside me, dancing it along my sensitive spot.

My arm lifts over my head to hold on to the back of the headrest, while the other holds on to the arm that's fucking me with his fingers. My nails dig into his skin as he slows his stroke, becoming too long and languid. When he glances at me, the rough smirk on his face does it; I feel him everywhere. My heart, my soul, my body, my heated skin, like a fever spiking, I let go; my release, an influx of sparks collecting as one as I come all over his hand. "Fuck, Ethan," I mewl.

"Squeeze my fingers, baby," he groans, "let me feel you come." I am, I do. I'm so fucking lost I feel it break, the current surging, riding out every last drop, until I'm motionless.

He slowly and carefully caresses me until I become too sensitive and wiggle my hips. "Beautiful, butterfly." His eyes flick over me before going back to the road, he pulls away from me, licking his fingers clean. I watch with fascination. Listening to him hum at the taste of me. There's that feeling again… the current, like it's about to crest and fall, teetering on the edge.

"I love it when you do that," I wheeze through my panted breaths, pushing the feeling away as best I can. But it squeezes right back.

"Lick your cum off my fingers?" He grins, side eyeing me as he licks his lips.

"Yes, but no, you make this noise, like it's the best thing you've ever tasted." My cheeks heat at my own words.

"You *are* the best thing I've ever tasted."

Pulling my jeans back up, I fasten them back into place, as his hand comes to rest back on my thigh and we fall into silence. "What are we going to do with him?" I ask, tipping my head towards the back of the truck. I may have momentarily forgotten he was there. *He knew, Aggie, or is it Sophie?* My mind lapses, and I swallow it back.

"I'm going to interrogate him, butterfly."

'I've come to collect, Sophie,' he said.

"Oh." I frown. I don't know what I was expecting. "Can I watch?" *Another distraction when you're so close to the truth?* My inner voice torments me, but I don't want to think about the truth just yet.

"No," he says flatly while I shake my head, trying to remove my intrusive thoughts. "I don't want you to see that side of me," he grumbles.

He knows who you are, Sophie.

"Why? Do you hurt them? Is it that sort of interrogation?" I add, blinking away the hurt that's seeping through the cracks. I have no idea why he wouldn't want me to watch.

"I don't hurt them, not if I don't have to, but they say some horrible shit while I have them, and I don't want you to hear anything that might upset you." I love the look of concern on his features, the way his one eyebrow dips, creating a small crease between them, his eyes cloud like they're waiting for the storm. Perfection.

But he didn't tell you.

The man you love kept the truth from you.

Just like everyone else in your life.

"Okay," I squeak, my chest compressing. I'm disappointed.

"I have some explaining to do before that anyway," Ethan adds, his tone almost sad. I can't take my eyes off him. My body shudders. Am I ready to know?

Twenty-one years of lies, of hiding, of not knowing.

I stay quiet, the current I was holding back trickling over the edge. I can't stop it; the hurt, the pain, the loss, it's all there, like a gaping wound, not just from Ethan, from everyone who's ever known me. My dam doesn't just rupture, it crumbles, and so do I as it all comes back to me.

"Let me out," I yell, panic striking me for the first time in my life. It's like a bomb goes off; I'm doused in the fire I've lived in all my life.

Chapter Thirty-Nine

Fuck Sake

Ethan

"Let me out," she yells. I hear the pain in her voice as her hands fly to the door. I'm surprised it took so long to surface. Nevertheless, I'm caught so off guard by her outburst that the truck swerves, and I veer us to the side of the road. Slowing down, I look over to Aggie as she grabs the handle of the door, trying to escape. I slam on the brakes, trying to press the locks on my side, so she can't do anything reckless while we're moving.

I hear it click as she pulls the handle. The door she's leaning against pops open. My arm comes out to hold her in place, but she wiggles free. I'm too late.

She leaps from the car. "Aggie, fuck," I yell, rushing to park. Shoving my door open, I leap from car, ready to chase her down.

She's running away from the me, the car, everything, she's stumbling on the wet grass, trying to gain speed.

"I can't, Ethan…" She pants. I sprint behind her, I look her over, as best I can from here, she doesn't look hurt, her steps getting quicker as she runs faster, like she can't escape everything she's feeling. "It hurts too much," she shouts over her shoulder, her voice strained.

"I'm sorry, baby, so fucking sorry," I yell, as she runs away from me. For such a small person, she sure is fast. "Please listen to me. I can explain everything," I bellow as I move, trying to catch her.

"I can't. It's too much. You had a chance to tell me." Anger laces her every word, "and you didn't..." My heart splits in two that I did this. I caused the woman I love this agony. "That hurts more than all of this, Ethan." She stops running, her arms spread wide. "Even more than not knowing who I am, *you* hurt me more." I race towards her at full pelt. Until we collide.

She drops her weight on me, my arms wrapping around her trembling frame, as we crash on the grassy floor. I cradle her to me as she tries to fight me, but I'm not letting her be alone in this.

"Sorry will never be enough, butterfly. I have no excuses. All I hope is that you forgive me in time. Please, baby, don't..." I can't get the words out. I pin her beneath me. I need to hold her face in my hands. I need to see that she's still mine.

"I love you, butterfly," I say, kissing her lips again and again. "I love you." I don't care if she never says it back, I need her to know that I'm here. Even in my own stupidity, I'm here for her. I always will be.

"Fuck you," she whimpers, kissing me back with a small smile. "Ethan."

"No, baby, I'm here. I'm not going anywhere, ever. Like it or not, I'm yours, and I always fucking will be." I close my eyes, resting my forehead on hers. I can't deal with losing her.

"I've never had anyone." When I open my eyes, she looks so lost. There's a darkness in her I've never seen before. One that needs to be banished for her light to shine.

"I know, but you have me. I promise. You have me." Her eyes flick to mine, holding my gaze as she considers something, her breathing ragged.

"Tell me everything you know?"

"Everything, every fucking detail, no secrets," I promise. My voice is tight with emotion.

"No secrets," she murmurs. She sighs, her body relaxing beneath mine, tilting her head back to look at the greying sky above us. "I love the rain," she adds, a smile creeping onto her lips, one that reaches her glistening eyes, "but not as much as I love you." My heart beats wildly in my chest as I register those three little life-changing words.

"Say it again," I groan, nipping her bottom lip.

"I love you, Ethan." Her hand cups my face like mine is hers.

"I love you too, Butterfly."

Chapter Forty

Bag of Tricks

Aggie

I have to face this. I'm scared that my parents lived a full life without me. I hoped in my heart that I'd get to see the faces who brought me into the world.

I guess I'm hoping against all odds that I can see something in myself that will anchor me to a family. *My family*, something that will make me belong.

Because I've never belonged.

The loss I know I feel, but can't grasp, or place a memory to.

Ethan's reassuring hand has been in mine since he opened my door of the truck. Soothing me even when I have no idea why I'm being targeted by these people.

"What's happening?" I turn to ask Ethan as the lift starts to move up. Realising the guards are new.

"Why all the new security?" I ask as we get back to the Cerberus offices. My heart going a mile a minute.

"They're here to protect you," he says like it's obvious.

"Why?"

"I don't know the full story, only what Gran's told me. Let's get upstairs. I'll tell you everything I know, and she can fill in the blanks." I close my eyes. I can't believe this is happening. I'm terrified to find out, but so happy that someone knows who I am, and maybe my parents.

"How does your Gran know about all this?"

"She was there when it happened." My head snaps up to him, my eyes scrunching in confusion.

"When what happened?"

"She was the one who found you in the woods," he breathes out slowly. "She was the one who helped hide you." He swallows, letting the words sink in.

I stumble back, letting go of Ethan's hand, our fingers losing grip of each other.

Fuck me.

My whole body vibrates as nausea swirls in my stomach.

They hid me.

My unreasonable fear of…

"The woods." I'm talking to myself, answering one of the questions I've held for years. "Why was I in the woods?" My voice is shaky as I ask.

"Let's do this when we get upstairs?" It's a question, and I shake my head, no.

"Tell me," I say, and his expression pains further. "Oh god, it's bad, isn't it?" He cups my face.

"Yeah, baby. It was." I can tell by the tone of his already husky voice that this is not a happy ending.

My shoulders sag, but I need more. I want answers.

"Tell me, Ethan," I plead. "Just rip the band-aid off. I can deal with it." I'm not sure I can, but I'll give it my best shot.

What choice do I have?

Tilting his head to the side, he looks at me like I'm the most precious thing in the world. I think this is hurting him, seeing me like this. My already crumbling façade falls further.

"I'm sorry, baby," he says on an exhale. "It was on my Gran's property, the lane that runs through the woods." *The same lane where I almost had the accident the other day.* His hands brush up my arms, holding me steady, his thumb stroking back and forth. I focus on the movement and the way my skin feels beneath his touch. "She was out walking, and she found you first, alone in the undergrowth. Smelt smoke, and told you to stay there while she went to check it out."

"A car?" My mind flashes to the heat, the smoke that surrounded me. "Was it on fire?" He nods. I don't say any more. I only know what flashed through my mind the other day, after the near miss with Layla.

A flashback?

"It had crashed," he says as the lift door pings open to signal we're at the office level. I don't move, I stay rooted to the spot. "There was a woman trapped inside. She was in a really bad way." Ethan's eyes mirror my own, clouded with emotion.

"Her name was Luna, honey. We think she was your mum." I look past Ethan to see Lady Celeste standing in the lobby, waiting for us. Her hand outstretched, waiting for mine. "Come, let's talk in his office." I look to Ethan, his hands still on me, grounding me.

"I'll be by your side the entire time," he says, doing his best to reassure me as I step forward and take his Gran's hand. When we enter the office, I don't sit; I can't. It feels like a standing moment.

"I tried to help her, but she made me promise to hide you," she says softly. "She gave me this." She hands me a backpack from behind Ethan's desk. It's pink with a butterfly attached to the zipper. "Your mum told me to leave her before they came."

"Why? Why would she want to hide me? Before who came?" My voice is trembling uncontrollably.

"Darling, I had no idea at the time." Celeste pulls a tissue from her sleeve and dabs her eyes. "After I left her, I found you again and took you back to my house. I hid you when they came on the property, I pretended I was out, turned all the lights off. I think the dogs scared them away eventually."

"What happened to her?" I ask, already knowing deep in the pit of my stomach, she never made it out of that car.

"On our way back to the house," she takes a deep breath and I ready myself for the blow, "there were shots fired then nothing. We ran in silence, even the dogs." I sink into the seat behind me.

"She was murdered?" I...

Ethan crouches in front of me again. "We don't know for sure," he says, giving me a sad smile. "There was nothing in the police report other than she died on impact from the crash, but we know that's not true."

"Who was after her? And me? Was I mentioned in the report?" The questions round my mind quicker than I can say them.

"No. I'll show you everything. It's all in the file I've been working on."

"Who was after us?"

"That's where this," Celeste holds out the backpack, "comes in. In all the commotion to get you away from the house and safely hidden away, I left it behind. I didn't find it until I got back that night. I knew where you were, Aggie." She brushes her thumb over the dulled sparkle of the butterfly before nodding for me to open it.

"You looked?" She nods.

"Yes, I never intended for you to see it again. It was safer that way. I'm sorry, for all it's worth. After I saw what was inside, I had the best intentions; the less you knew, the better. It has everything you need to know." She pats my knee, placing the bag to my side before she heads out the door. "I'll be outside when you're ready."

"Okay." I sigh, feeling the weight of what I'm about to learn on my shoulders.

"Do you want me to leave?" Ethan asks. I shake my head. I'm not brave enough to do this on my own.

I lift the bag to my lap and pull the delicate butterfly keyring to open the zip.

"I see you've always had a thing for butterflies." I smile for the first time since walking through that door.

"I guess I have." My fingers shake as I peek inside the open bag. It smells musty, like it's been locked away and forgotten about for years. Ethan sits at my side, his arm resting around my back.

Reaching in, I take the contents out one by one, my fingers brushing over them as I do. I place everything on the coffee table in front of us, another hope lost that I'd remember something as I touched, felt, smelt, and saw my past with my own eyes.

A sketch pad. *Nothing.*

A passport. *Nothing.*

A teddy. My heart squeezes. But still, *nothing.*

Digging my hand back in, I feel a thick piece of paper. A photo.

My heart thumps a heavy but steady beat.

Three people: a man and a woman, with a small child.

My breath catches, and Ethan's grip tightens around me.

I guess that's me... me and my parents.

I stare at the picture of a family I don't remember. One I feel nothing for. I run my finger over the woman who's the mirror image of me. With her hair messy and button nose. She has the same warm blonde honey tones warming her features against her pale peach-tinted skin. *Just like me.*

Wetness covers my cheeks as Ethan caresses my side. He's trying to hold me together. He takes the picture, turning it over, like he needs me to see something.

Sophie, our sweet baby girl.
Love doesn't cover how we feel for you.
You're the brightest butterfly amongst a swarm of grey.
Mum & Dad

Placing the picture of my family against my chest, I wish for just a glimpse of a memory of them. Of how we were together before the world split us apart. I cry. I let it out, while the man I've fallen so deeply for holds me.

"May I?" Ethan asks, shifting us slightly so he can reach the table. I nod, too overwhelmed to do anything but breathe in his calming scent. He lifts the sketchbook.

I close my eyes.

I listen as he flicks through, hearing the pages turn. I sneak a peek. The book's resting in his lap, open, ready for me to see. "You need to read this, baby," Ethan offers, handing it to me.

"I can't." I breathe. "Will you?"

"Okay. If you're sure?"

"I'm sure." Giving this burden to him feels right, I need him by my side through this, or I'll continue to break.

"I'll read it out loud."

"My dearest Sophie, if you're reading this, my heart breaks for you. I'm sorry things have ended like this, but there was no other way. Mum."

Each note is short and scribbled like she knew her time was limited. I tune into Ethan's words, every single one hitting me like a knife. I swallow the pain they bring.

"We're running because they," he pauses, "shit." It's pained, like he doesn't want to say it, but he does. *"They killed your dad."* Ethan hangs his head as I gasp.

"I'm so sorry, baby." He holds me tighter as he continues, *"For something I did. Something I'm not willing to apologise for, and neither would your dad. I just hope one day you can forgive me enough to understand. Mum."*

Ethan carries on, and I'm grateful, because I feel numb, listening to how my mother was coaxed into a life she had no idea about until it was too late. About how she hid something from these men to secure our future. Telling me everything about how she was working for the police, that we were all going into witness protection after she handed them one final thing they needed to put them behind bars. That it was all for the right reasons. Or so she thought at the time.

"I can't see what's more important than living," I breathe as he turns the page.

"Nothing is, baby," Ethan confirms.

The rest of the book is covered with drawings, every single page hand drawn designs litter the pages, bringing to life sketches painted over with watercolours. We sit and flip through them silently. The drawings are beautiful; every single one reminding me of something, I can't quite put my finger on, and I put it down to my own failed memory.

How can I not remember any of this?

Being chased, hiding, scared for my life. My own mum and dad dying.

I sit back, closing the book as I close my eyes, the images playing in my mind over and over again.

It's like I'm watching my own life story; my heart is pounding, my breathing choppy, but there's nothing behind it. No real emotion, no connection, nothing that links me to the people in the photo other than we look alike.

It's an odd sense of loss and longing when you know who you belong to, and can't feel anything for them.

Ethan has been quiet, his kind soul is giving me the space I need. "When you offered before," I say, my palms sweaty with nerves, "That I could use your system to find out about them, does the offer still stand?" I dip my chin to my chest. "I need to see things rather than read about it. Can you help me?"

"Anything you need." He kisses me softly; it's caring, loving and reassuringly grounding all at the same time. "It's yours." My lips meet his again, in a sincere thank you.

"Where do we start?" I ask, having no idea what all this means.

"We?" He grins at me, kissing me chastely. "I like that." Just as I go to close the sketch pad, scribbled writing catches my eye on the back page, just under a drawing of a faded monster.

"What's this?" I murmur. It's faded and smudged, but as I look closer, I can see a name.

"Jonathan Isaac." I read and Ethan goes rigid beside me.

Chapter Forty-One

Bollocks

Ethan

Her eyes snap to mine when I react to the name. Not *them.* My grip on her is almost fearful. I know it; the name. I know of his organisation. I've heard whispers and rumours, but he's been quiet for a long time. But there it is written in the sketch book, the image that sits above it, a true representation of who he is.

A monster.

This is bigger than we could have ever imagined.

"You know him?" Aggie says, her hands coming to cover mine, comforting me as I fight the realisation of who's been after her.

Jonathan Isaac.

"No, butterfly, but I know the name." Dread seeps into every pore.

"He killed my parents?" And if reports are true, he's killed many, innocent or not.

"From his reputation, I'm going to guess yes." She shudders in my hold as she worries her lip again.

"The attacks on me?" she asks too cautiously, like she doesn't want to say it. There's a subtle jolt to my breathing, one I need to regain control of before I lose it. "The people that have been following me, you think it's him?" My mind's working overtime, trying to process what this is, what this means for us, what I've missed, and what I can do.

I need to keep her safe.

I need to keep her by my side.

I need to find a place to hide her. Until then, we stay here. We're going to need help. Lots of it. They already know where she lives, where Layla lives, and more than likely that she works for me and we're involved.

"If it is him... shit. Baby." I gulp it down because I know how he found her. "It's all my fault they found you." I rub my chest, the pain edging its way in, slicing me like I'm nothing. I did this.

"It was only a matter of time, Ethan; it's not your fault." My entire nervous system is alight in anguish. I should have paid more attention. I should have done something sooner.

I bury my head into her shoulder, deciding there's only one way to deal with this, with him, and to keep my butterfly safe. *Alive.*

He needs to disappear.

"I should have done more to keep you out of the papers." There's so much tension in my voice, it comes out cracked and rough. I see when she realises what I mean. Her eyes lower to our clasped hands as she steadies her breathing. When she looks at me, there's no doubt in her eyes that she means whatever she's about to say, and I'm not sure I deserve any of it.

But I'm a selfish man, because I'm never letting her go.

"It may be happening now, but it was only a matter of time before someone saw me, Ethan, before someone recognised me as her daughter. I'm the spitting image of her. Sooner or later, they would have found me." I know she's right, but it doesn't hurt any less that I'm the reason they found her. I don't say anything, I can't, the fury running through my bones prevents it. She exhales softly, and I fill my lungs with her sweetness.

"We need to find what she hid, Ethan. If he's coming, he's coming for me because he thinks I have it. Whatever it is."

"Bollocks." She laughs, and I tilt my head to frown at her. Why the fuck is she laughing?

"I can think of better curse words than that, given the situation. I think it calls for something stronger." She taps my nose, like my world isn't imploding.

"You really are the brightness in a storm of grey, butterfly."

I've sent Aggie to have a shower while I quickly changed and filled everyone in on what we found. I'm as filthy as she is, even with a change of clothes, but I'm not going to miss a beat of this. I psych myself up; this is what we do best. We find the bastards and take the arseholes down. For good.

I'll start with the guy who was in the back of my truck. Leon and Cole dragged him into the basement after we arrived back. I need to know what they know. How close they are and what they're after from Aggie. But I need eyes on Aggie first. I need to know she's with the people I trust the most before I head downstairs. I've given them orders to not take their eyes off her while I'm gone. I don't want her alone in this.

She must know she has us now.

I'm looking forward to this interrogation.

My fists clench again. This guy, Jonathan Isaac, is almost as good as Owen at hiding. Always has been. No one's ever seen his face, never gets his hands dirty, but loves to watch. There have been rumours about the jobs he's pulled, the firm he's built, and the people that work for him. Speculation on the white collar shit he's involved in, among other things. Nothing has ever been proven, and I need to change that. I need to link him to those crimes and the attacks on Aggie, and I need them to stick. For good.

If not, we can go for option two. I'll make him disappear.

Sitting around the table, I watch my Gran as she talks about the night she hid Aggie. The guys are captivated by what she's saying and what she did to protect such a little girl. We all knew she had an enormous heart, but this is next level.

"I saw the name Jonathan Isaac and did my own research on him. It's nothing compared to what you boys have found. I caught snippets of rumours, things he's done or would do to people. All of it horrifying for anyone, let alone a little girl." She looks wounded.

"You did the right thing, Gran. We don't know what he would have done to Aggie if he'd have found her in the woods instead of you," I say, my throat constricting. I try not to let it cross my mind, but I can't stop the feeling that Aggie wouldn't be here right now if it weren't for my Gran. "Thank you," I say, feeling the weight of it all sitting right over my chest. Gran smiles, reaching over to give my hand a squeeze like she can read my mind.

"I hid the bag as soon as I knew who he was. There was never a doubt in my mind that hiding it was a bad idea. I knew I had to get her away, but I never realised it would be for so long. I'd never send it to her, not when I knew what would happen if they traced it back to that beautiful girl in there." Cole's listening, but deep in the search for details on her parents. He's already pulled her father's information. Seems he may have been an innocent party in all this. He was an engineer, specialised in historic building reconstructions. I turn as Aggie steps out from my office and groan when I see what she's wearing: hair wet, in a pair of too big joggers, rolled at her hips and ankles, and one of my gym shirts. Fuck, she looks hot.

"You need to shower," she says, looking me over as she takes the seat next to me. She yelps when I grab the leg of the chair, hurling her and it towards me, so we're touching. I need her close. She's the calm in my storm. Just laying a hand on her warmth helps me focus.

"I will, but I have something I need to do first. I need you to stay here with the guys." My tone's low and unyielding, so she knows how serious I am.

"Okay." That's all she says, and the tip of my lips hitch in a smile. She trusts me. And fuck, it makes me crazy for her. "You are coming back?"

"Always." But first, I need answers, and I need them now.

Aggie

"The fuck, did he just smile?" Cole's shocked tone makes me jump as I take my gaze away from Ethan's retreating form. "I've never seen anything like it." I laugh at his reaction.

"It's good to see him smile," his Gran then admits. "I don't see it often enough."

"What can I do?" I ask, turning the conversation. "And don't say nothing. I need to keep busy." Laying my hands on the table, I tap my fingers on the wood.

"Okay, can you get the things from the bag, take another look. See if you can find anything that may help us find what your parents hid," Owen says, his fingers flying across the keyboard.

"Has Ethan... um, filled you in on everything?" I ask, trying to keep my emotions in check.

"Yes, and Gran has too," Cole says, giving me a kind look.

"Do they all call you Gran?" I look over to her.

"I insisted after they came back from the army together. I expect it from you too."

"What?"

"I expect you to call me Gran, no arguments," she states, putting her teacup on the table. I had no idea we even had them here. "I'm off, boys. Keep me updated." She pushes from the chair.

"Gran, Ethan would want you to stay here," Owen says, leaning back in his chair.

"Tell that overgrown boy I'll be at home." Cole quickly stands, grabbing something from the middle of the table.

"Take this then. Just so we know where you are." He holds out his hand as he rounds the table towards her.

"A tracker?" *How does she know what it is?*

"Yes." He's sheepish when he says it, but she takes it from his hand anyway and places it in her bag.

"Keep me updated," she says again and turns towards the door.

I watch her leave as Cole takes his seat again. "Won't Ethan be annoyed that you let her go?"

He chuckles as I worry about the guy out there trying to get to me, and maybe Gran if he needs to. Does this Jonathan know she's involved?

"No. Ethan knows well enough that she does what she wants. We have eyes on her though." I guess that's something. If they're not worried, then maybe I shouldn't be.

After retrieving the things from the backpack from Ethan's office, I place them in front of me, taking care with them, and getting a better look this time, now there are slightly less tears clouding my vision.

I look over everything, but there's something niggling at me about the sketches, something familiar about them. The way they were drawn, pieces fitting together like a story, or like pieces of a puzzle.

Puzzle...

Shit, could it be a puzzle?

The bag was mine, all the other things looks like kids' stuff, apart from this sketchbook. Why was it in my bag?

Did she put it there after we crashed? Picking it up, I turn it over in my hand a few times before I open it, questioning myself. What would it mean if it were a puzzle?

Am I being... I don't know, ridiculous? Childish?

There's only one way to find out.

I flick back through the pages, looking closer at the drawings I presume my mum made. They suddenly come to life.

The whole book's filled with them. All different. Letters cover the drawings and the corners of the pages, but each image has one thing in common: the familiar key that's been placed around my neck for the last twenty-one years lies in each one.

I would have missed it if it wasn't for its consistency around my neck. Every image, intertwined with so many other images, like a mini collage in each one. It's almost invisible, leaves, butterflies, portraits, a name, a church, a headstone, numbers, letters randomly intertwined with each other. It's a beautiful work of art on its own.

"It's a puzzle," I state. Cole's head pops up, looking at me with sympathy.

"I know, but we will figure it out." I roll my eyes at him as he's misunderstood.

"No," I clarify, "I mean this..." I point to the book. "The drawings. I think they're puzzles. The key on my necklace is in all of them." I spin the book around so they can see it. "Look." I jab my finger into the first picture.

"A puzzle?" Cole looks, scrunching his nose in confusion.

"This key," I say, pulling it from around my neck, "it's the only thing I've always had with me. All my life," I pause, the words trailing off, because there's no way I can know that. "Ever since I can remember," seems a better fit. "And it's been drawn into all of these sketches." I show him the pages. "Each one of these drawings is different, but they all have this."

"The common factor," Owen adds, starting to take note of my ramblings.

"Yes." A common factor, a *key*.

"What's the key for?" Cole asks, my shoulders slump as I let out an exasperated breath.

"I don't know," I say in honesty, twiddling the key between my fingers, feeling the disappointment creep into my fading smile.

"May I look?" Cole says. I hand the book over and watch as he assesses them all. Then he starts to take pictures of each one, and they appear on the large touch screen on the wall to the side of us.

"Your necklace. You said you've had it as far back as you can remember?" Owen asks.

"Yeah, I was eight when… when I lost my memory." Saying it out loud feels freeing, almost. "I have no idea if I had it before then." I unclasp the chain from around my neck and lay it on the table closer to Owen.

"Have you ever looked into it? It looks old?" Owen says, picking it up and admiring the key's intricate design.

"No, I've never really given it much thought. Other than what it was used for in a previous life. What it could open, what could be inside or where it came from." Owen smirks at my sarcasm.

"I'll scan it into the computer, see if it picks anything up," he says excitedly.

"Do you think you'll be able to find what it's from?"

"Most keys have a serial number or some sort of identification on them," he says from behind his computer, using the camera on his phone to scan the key. My heart thuds at the idea of finding what it's for.

Another question I could get an answer to.

"There's no numbers on this one," I add, remembering what he said, and the times I've tried to see anything on it.

"You may not be able to see them. Age and wear have a factor, but we can strip the image on the system and take a closer look."

"Huh, clever."

"Thanks," he chirps, and I roll my eyes again, then Cole calls my attention.

"I know you've used the screen before," he says, pointing to the touch screen, "but this is now linked to the system." *System?* He must see the question in my face because he adds, "It's what we use to find what we want, information, people, things."

"Right," I say, confused, not really sure what he's getting at. I'm an artist, dancer, and PA. This is way out of my league.

"You can split the images down into individual sections, picture by picture and page by page."

"Okay."

"See if you can find another common link between the images on each page, other than the key." Now I feel stupid that I didn't get it before.

"Easy, I can do that." I can, can't I?

Half an hour later, with no sign of Ethan coming back yet, I've done what Cole's asked. "I think I've found something."

"Show me," Cole says, at the same time Owen says, "Really?"

"Yes, really. Look." They both look up at the screen where I've separated all the images from each sheet. "Each page has this," I stand and point to a name, "tangled into the drawings, but each name is different." I show them the list on the other side. "Then this, two letters at the bottom of each page. If you place them together, you get, "*Seek and you shall find*. LS."

"Shit, they really do," Cole says.

"What about the pictures?" Owen asks.

"Each page had six drawings, three relate to a painting and artist, two are referring to the same location here in the UK, and the other one, they look like random buildings, headstones, etc. I've placed all of those together." I show them a page. "Like this one, the section of the painting refers to a Picasso, and the locations here in the UK. The odd one out is the headstone."

"What does that mean?" Cole asks. "She's trying to tell me something. All of the paintings in these drawings are spread out across the world, so why place the location here in the UK?

"Could it mean something else?" I don't answer because I have no idea.

"It's odd that they are all wrong," Owen cuts in.

"Yeah, I... why hide the painting amongst all of this and have the wrong location?"

"Could it be a map?" Owen must come to the same conclusion because he does something with all the images of the locations, his brow furrowing as he does.

"The site they refer to is an old mine, up north," he says. "Owned by a construction company, but I can't find a name. That might take me some time to find. It's buried deep in red tape."

"Cole, look into all the paintings and check out any activity that could have happened to each one between twenty-one and thirty years ago."

"Sure," he says.

"These images all point to a small village about an hour away from here; there's not much there anymore. Most of it was left to rot over thirty years ago," Owen announces after a few minutes.

He pulls up images as he speaks, matching the drawn images from the sketchbook to the old photos he's found.

"They match." He side eyes me. "I wasn't doubting you. I'm just surprised at how quick you found it." I get a sharp inhale for that one, and I hold my hands up in apology.

"Where does the key come into all of this?" I ask, staring at the run-down village on the screen.

"No idea. I'm sure we'll find a link though." I feel deflated, like someone popped my balloon. "We'll send a guy to check out the locations." "I'm going to go and do some work in Ethan's office." I don't want to wait around, feeling useless. I'd rather catch up on some emails and maybe do a few sketches of my own.

"Let me know if you find anything?"

"Will do." They let me go, even when Ethan asked me to stay around them, but I know I'm safe.

Chapter Forty-Two

Tremor

Ethan's been gone for over an hour and a half, and I can feel my composure slipping. I don't know where he is. I assume he's still in the building, but I have no idea, and I'm starting to worry.

I tried to draw, but I'm too distracted. I've paced, lounged, and now I'm at Ethan's desk, and it feels a little naughty, like I'm in the boss's seat. *You are in your boss's seat.* I tut to myself, then chuckle. I swing in his massive leather chair, and my arm catches the side of his laptop, making it come to life.

Fuck, what the hell is that? I gasp as I see what's on the screen.

Is that the guy from the boat?

My hands tremor slightly as I watch him, thinking of what could have happened if Ethan hadn't been there. He's banged up. He doesn't move, he can't. When I lean in closer, I can see his hands and feet cuffed to the chair.

You're not going anywhere.

It never even crossed my mind as to where he went when we came in. My heart thuds against my ribs when I hear the low barrel of Ethan's voice through the small speakers of the laptop.

"There is no good ending where you're concerned," Ethan says. He's not angry; there's nothing in his tone but ice. Pressing his hand to the wound on the guy's face, Ethan leans close, crowding his space, his broad frame almost filling the screen. The guy clutches his jaw, trying not to make a noise, only you can see the pain in his eyes. My heart races.

"You tried to lay a finger on my woman," he states. *His woman.* Me. Fuck that does something to me. I shouldn't like this. But he's in there… for me?

Is this where he's been all this time?

This is what he does for them, isn't it? Other than being a medic, this was his field job. He's an interrogation expert.

I watch as Ethan wraps his hand around the man's throat, pressing against his windpipe. My breath catches. I can't take my eyes off the screen as the guy turns purple, spluttering. "No-one will get near her again," Ethan seethes as the guy's eyes bulge, "You'll tell me everything." His tone is deadly, and I grip the table for support as his words have a damning effect on the man in the chair. The guy shakes when Ethan speaks in his ear. Letting go of his neck, he gasps, his eyes wild as he regains his breath.

I can't help but watch, enthralled. I know Ethan doesn't want me to see this side of him. This is why he wouldn't let me watch. This is why he snuck off.

I'm watching now.

I sit back in the leather reclining chair, absorbed in what he's doing, the way he takes him to the edge of something lethal, only to bring him back. Using his injuries to cause further pain, a knee pressed to his ribs, the scream the guy lets out is guttural. It's gruesome, but… again, I'm weirdly okay with it. I'm fascinated to see the side of Ethan that he keeps from me. Relishing in the way he moves, the way he eviscerates him with his words. Words I can hear loud and clear, words defending me.

Turning me on when I know it's wrong on some level, but I don't care. It makes me love him more.

I see the moment the guy breaks, telling Ethan they need the key I have, and how desperate Jonathan is to get his hands on it. That my mother stole and hid some sort of ledger.

What do the images in the scrapbook have to do with all this? Maybe one of the locations I found in the book was for the ledger. So, what's the other one?

She was trying to right a wrong. And my parents paid the ultimate price for it.

And that's where my story ended and began on that one night.

I tune out the details the man in the seat spews as Ethan waits for him to crumble further. I sit and wait for him; I don't dwell on my past when all I see is my future. My future with a man who would follow me to the ends of the earth; a man who will protect me, any way he can.

Chapter Forty-Three

Fear

Ethan

I stalk into the office already pissed that it's come to this, that I let it get this far. Then I find Aggie's not with the guys, and I almost lose it. My pace quickens, needing to see that she's okay. I need to feel her against me, feel her warmth, after listening to what that prick had to say.

He was hard to break. Took me over an hour before he even shook.

He kept resisting, like he wasn't listening. I switched up a gear when I remembered everything they had put my Aggie through, I let rip. I could feel him shaking with every word I said. I guess adding to his injuries helped. I don't care who the fuck he is. All I care about is making sure she's safe, and while this prick is out roaming free in the world, I can't do that.

As I shove the door into the wall, I find Aggie at my desk, feet propped up. She flinches at the door slamming, then settles back down, like she hasn't got a care in the world. All the anger I felt a few seconds ago dissipates.

She's okay.

But when her eyes focus in on me, then travel the length of my body, I know something has happened. Her tongue darts out over her lip, and her eyes hover on my cock, and fuck, if my dick doesn't start to swell at the attention. She is fucking me with her hooded eyes, dark with… then I see it, the way she's looking at me, it's different. I know something's changed.

I ignore my cock as I walk slowly past her desk to mine. I round it, coming to where she's sitting, but she's quick to stand and get out of my way as her eyes flick to the computer, a guilty look crossing her face. Taking the laptop in my hand, I spin it to face me.

Fuck.

My entire body rolls with unease, shit. She's seen it, she's seen me. *Like that.* I never wanted that to happen.

"What the fuck, Aggie?" I panic. I don't want to scare her any more than she already most likely is. "What did you see?" I groan, panic clawing at my chest, closing the screen, having seen enough of that piece of shit still sobbing in the chair. He'll be held there until this is over.

I start pacing back and forth, my hand rubbing over my short hair. I close my eyes, dreading the worst but needing to know. "Do you hate me?"

"No," she says calmly. I stop pacing. "Lock the door, Ethan." She wants me to leave?

"Aggie."

"I said, lock the damn door." I move towards it, ready to leave. But look at her one last time.

"What happens when I lock the door, butterfly?" I don't want to leave her in here, but I will if that's what she needs. I need an answer first.

I walk back to her, holding her gaze steady with mine. I'm met with her laboured breathing, her eyes flickering over me as she shifts towards me.

"Tell me, Aggie." I tuck a silky stray strand of hair behind her ear, needing her more than she knows.

"You get to desecrate me with your words, Ethan." My hand stills. Fuck, she's turned on.

"Aggie…" Cupping my face, she rises to her toes, bringing her lips to mine. "I don't understand." Her kiss deepens, expressing everything she's feeling, and

I take it all; every emotion she's pouring out. Her hand tugs at the front of my shirt, balling it into her fist, pulling me into her. My arm wraps around the small of her back as her back arches, thrusting her chest into mine.

"Ethan." She pants, her lips leaving mine briefly.

"What do you need, butterfly?"

"I want your words. I want you, all of you. Don't hold back."

"You saw everything?"

"Yes." My head lowers. "Don't you dare look away from me, Ethan." She tips my chin up with her fingers. "Jesus, Ethan, what you did in there, what you said, how you broke him..." Her soft, tender lips brush mine. "I loved it."

"I did it for you, baby," I murmur, breathing her in. I'd do anything for her.

"It did something to me, Ethan. Seeing you like that, it made me..." I see it: her skin flushes as her perfect body shudders in a sexy little wave against mine. I gulp down my need to feel her. "... Realise just how much you're willing to protect me."

"I am, baby." I don't want to move in case this is a dream, and she's not real.

Aggie leans into me, her eyes sparkling, trusting me. Our lips join, almost punishing this time, in a kiss so frenzied as we show each other how we feel.

"I want all of you. Every single inch." Her hips press into mine, my cock jumping to life. "Lock the door." She's already breathless when she tries to pull away, but I don't let her. Instead I lift her, listening to her groan, bringing my dick from hard to steel in seconds.

I stride us to the door, slamming it shut using my back, keeping Aggie wrapped around my waist where she belongs. My hand darts out to lock it. Heat burns over my skin, alive with the need to touch her. I need to consume her, like she consumes me.

"Take me, Ethan." My rough fingers inch across the underside of her arse, the loose material of my joggers she's wearing, unable to hide the heat that's radiating from her core.

"Fuck, baby, I'm not going to hold back." I can't. Her fingers work to undo my belt, and trousers. I slide my hands in the elastic waistband of the joggers, gripping her arse firmly, sinking my fingers into her soft skin. I growl loudly, and fuck, if she doesn't suck in a breath as her eyes flutter at my reaction. She's not wearing any underwear, and my hands part her arse cheeks finding her *fucking wet already.*

"I need you to... dominate me." Fucking-sweet-Jesus. *Yes.* My hips roll, and she whimpers. Fuck, I want that too. "I need it, Ethan. I need you." Pre-cum leaks from the tip of my dick. I want to tie her up and use her for days. She's mine, just for me.

"Love me, like I love you." She moans when my finger finds her clit, rolling it. She makes the sweetest sound, and my chest seizes. Trailing my one hand to the back of her head, I grip her hair and tug. She cries out as her head pulls back, mouth open, her cheeks that beautiful peach colour, eyes flaring at me, full of lust.

"*Never* question how much I love you." I tug a little harder.

"Fuck." She moans, and my lips smash against hers before she can finish. My tongue finds hers, invading like a Viking seeking a new land. I pull us apart, her silky strands gliding through my fingers as I let go.

My cock strains against my boxers, my trousers hanging open. She slides down me, feet landing quietly on the floor.

"On your knees, butterfly," I demand. I need to feel her sweet mouth around my dick. Her eyes go wide, but instead of doing what she's told, she steps back. Biting her lips, my nostrils flare at her defiance as my hand flexes at my side, itching to spank her arse for it. She proceeds to slowly strip off her clothes, exposing her naked body that flushes the more I stare at her.

"Beautiful," I murmur as I take my cock out, sliding my hand up and down my length. Fuck, I could come just like this. She sinks to her knees, gripping my thighs, her nails digging into my skin, I hiss, the feeling igniting me. Just like she does.

"Suck my cock like a good girl." My voice is like gravel, and our eyes remain locked as she opens her mouth and sticks out her tongue. She looks heavenly, perfect, ready to be made a mess of.

She moans as I pump my cock, placing it on her tongue. Her lips seal around me as her cheeks hollow. Wasting no time, she sucks me down as I grip the back of her head. I don't move; I don't want to push her too far. Fuck, she feels good; the warmth of her mouth overwhelming me. My head falls back as my woman cups my balls, my spine lighting up as she takes me deeper. I close my eyes, feeling her luscious mouth leave me with a pop.

"Don't hold back, I can take it, Ethan." I look down into her bright green eyes.

"Squeeze my thigh if it gets too much." My hand tightens in her hair as I pump forward, my cock pushing against her tight throat.

"Ahh, fuck."

Aggie

His hand grips my hair tighter and moves his granite-like cock in my mouth, only it's hot and silky. Fuck, I can't get enough. This is what I needed after seeing my Ethan fight for me. Defend me. I need to give him everything. And I will.

Breathing through my nose, I take more of him. He's so fucking big, I have to hold the rest of his thickness in my hand, working him more as he slides down my throat. My eyes flick up, my vision blurring as he pushes deeper, tears rolling down my cheeks. I moan around him. When I focus on him, I almost come just from the look of wonderment in his bright grey eyes; mouth open, his tongue licking his teeth as he hisses.

"Play with yourself, baby. Make yourself come with my cock in your mouth." I slip him free to take a breath, my lungs filling deeply, ready for more.

I lay my tongue flat as I take him in, then swirling it around his already leaking tip. Loving the taste of him, I take him deeper as I snake my hand in between my legs, finding my core drenched. I flick my clit and groan around him. He jerks forward, his hand moving me back and forward just how he likes it.

I love giving him this power over me. It's heady how my body hums from the sight of him. The taste of him. I groan again, feeling his cock twitch against my tongue.

His movements become frantic, his grip tighter as he starts to really move. Using me. *Fuck.* My hand on his thigh keeps me steady, my other finds my entrance as I sink a finger inside myself.

"That's it, come for me, butterfly," he groans, his breathing heavy. My body convulses, a fire lighting my lower abs. His muscled thighs form a powerful stance, even as they bunch and shake beneath my hand. I can only see a glimpse of his stomach, but I see the muscles flex and strain as he forces himself deeper into my throat, my eyes watering from the intrusion. My own orgasm fires like a gun as I pump my finger faster inside myself. My walls clench as it hits me so powerfully, and I struggle to breathe with his cock in my mouth. "Fuck, you love my cock deep in your throat." He pulls my head back, but doesn't pull all the way out, allowing me to breathe, before he pushes back down my throat. His cock jerks, and he lets out a feral groan. My mouth is so full, all I can do is hum my response. Because I do love it. My breasts feel heavy as my orgasm continues, or starts to take root, I have no idea which one, but fuck, it's consuming. My whole body is wired with sensations. He pistons his hips, rutting into me, his entire sculpted body taut as he suddenly stills, edging that bit further down my throat. I swallow around him, my lungs burning from the lack of air as he releases a growled fuck and comes down my throat. I pinch my clit, my vision blurring, as my orgasm peaks. I swallow his warm salty taste down, licking around his cock as I swallow, some of his mess spilling from my lips. His hand leaves my hair, but holds himself inside my mouth. I relish in the way his cock pulses on my tongue. Hot and heavy. Fuck it's such a turn on.

I groan around his cock, as my own release, surges through me, my fingers moving faster, circling my clit as I crest the wave and come over my own hand, my hips jerking as I become too sensitive, I crash, but need more at the same time. I look up to see him, Ethan, looking right back at me, chest heaving as he strokes the back of his hand down my cheek. Pulling his softening cock from my mouth, trembling and breathless, he kneels for me, eyes stormy greys level with mine. His hand holds my face firmly, kissing my puffy lips as he slides his free hand between my legs, feeling my wetness, he groans, slipping his fingers free.

I love that I can bring a man like Ethan to his knees.

Trailing his finger from my lips, Ethan wraps me in his suit-clad arms his body flush with mine and kisses me like his life depends on mine.

He's not wrong. I don't know if I can live without him. Happy tears blur my vision, as I stare back at him.

I've finally found my family.

Here with Ethan.

"Just for me. Always." His voice rumbles into my soul, settling there like I'm home.

"Just for you." I whisper. As he wipes away a tear that falls. "Forever." I agree. I feel his smile on my lips, as we seal our lips together one more time.

Chapter Forty-Four

Trap

Ethan

Fear took me over for the briefest of seconds when I felt her tears beneath my fingers, but she smiled. Her eyes shining, like she finally realised I was hers, and laughed as we kissed, kneeling on the floor in my office. It stuns me that I have her.

The way she laughed felt lighter, like an invisible weight has been lifted from her soul. I greedily ate them up, like I needed them to survive. Swallowing down her sunshine, and she let me. Fuck she lights me up from the inside out. It's one of the best moments of my life.

'Just for me, forever,' she said. I held her tighter.

Until there is a knock on the door, and some dickhead named Cole, who I'm no longer friends with, tells us to get our naked arses out there.

Heaving a sigh, I help her stand, leading us to the bathroom so I can clean her up. Her small hand in mine.

She's the most stunning woman I've ever seen. My heart aches that she's chosen me, and even when she's going through so much.

"Stand there, don't move?" I ask, finally dropping her hand, and forcing myself to pull away from her, as I move to the cupboards to retrieve a washcloth.

"Yes, boss." She teases, biting that damn lip of hers.

"Owen's found what the key used to be used for," Cole says as we settle back in the chairs around the central table. Aggie's hand tightens around mine as she sucks in a shocked breath, readying herself for what's to come next.

"Your parents were clever Aggie. Your dad had a fascination with old banks. One of his last jobs was at the location you found in the book."

"A location?" I missed almost three hours getting information out of the prick downstairs. "I need a recap," I tell the table.

Aggie tells me everything.

They left a trail for her to find.

"The village was abandoned, so why would he have been working there?" Her voice sounds a little higher than normal.

"The records show he was there six months before your parents died." This is hard for anyone to hear. I'm not taking my eyes off her until I know she's okay. When she looks down at her lap, I know she's struggling. Squeezing her thigh, I let her know I'm here. "He was there to see if the site could be restored, but he labelled the place too expensive to rebuild," Cole says, flagging the document on the screen.

"He lied," Owen adds, building my confusion. "The site was good enough, but your parents had other ideas." His smile gives him away that it's better news.

"It took a while, but it seems they bought it," Cole says, taking a sip of coffee.

"They owned a village?" Aggie asks, sitting forward slightly.

"No, you do," Cole and Owen say together, both turning to look at my woman.

"I own a *village*?" She looks at me like she's hearing things.

"Sort of. You own the land, and since you do, no one has been able to build or claim it. So, it's been left," Cole chimes in.

"The key that's been sitting around your neck is from an old post office lock box," Owen tells her. "A lock box that was registered to this building—"

"Right there," Cole finishes for him, and Owen punches him in the arm for stealing his thunder. Cole points to the photo on the screen. The building in it is small, like it used to be a shop and someone's house at some point in time. It has a tree growing out of the roof, and most of the rear wall has tumbled.

"What do you mean?" Aggie says, looking between them.

"We think whatever they hid is in there, in that lock box, is what Isaac is after, and you, my organised Aggie, have the key."

"Shit. The dip shit downstairs told me that they are after a ledger and that Aggie has something they need."

"While you were getting jiggy in the office, we took it upon ourselves to get things started." Owen smirks.

She giggles, completely unashamed that they knew what we were doing.

The look I give Owen makes him carry on.

"We have a team collecting any lockboxes and checking out the other location. As much as I wanted to go on a treasure hunt, I have a good feeling we're being watched right now." I tense. I know he's right. If we leave, they'll follow and get what they're looking for.

"Good call," I murmur, unable to shift the tension in my chest. "What's next?"

"We set a trap." I already don't like the idea, but I know it's what we need to do.

"Don't leave me out, I'm part of this, and it's all on me," Aggie adds, her voice determined.

Chapter Forty-Five

Payback

Jonathan

"Eyes on the target?" I hear Jasper, my son, question the ground team through my earpiece. I've been personally watching Sophie since we attacked her at the beach. We got close, but she didn't have the key on her. Reluctantly, we backed off, needing to know where it was before we could kill the bitch. I enjoyed watching her suffer. She shared the same look as her mum did all those years ago. Those green eyes widening in disbelief as my second in command tore her hair from her pretty head.

My son's been watching longer. The sick bastard even managed to get his dick wet with her. He loved the way it would fuck with her head when she finds out. His job was to grab the necklace and go, but he wanted to play with the bitch first. I smirk; he'll make sure she finds out.

She had nothing to do with what her parents did; she's a means to an end, I've been waiting a lifetime for. She'll pay just like they did.

I can't wait to watch her scream.

The one they took from her boat was a new recruit, trying to prove himself to me. He was only supposed to trash the boat, find what I needed and bring it back. When he never called it in, we went looking. My guys have trackers; we followed it to this building. Cerberus Security. We've had eyes on it for weeks.

Let's just hope for his sake, he kept his mouth shut. I'll have some fun if he didn't.

How the fuck cute little Sophie Solace got herself involved with these guys is beyond me. It doesn't work in my favour that she's with him, not with his connections and his company. I've managed to stay off their radar for a long time—that was up until now. They'll expose me if I let them. I know they know who I am and what I do. If they don't know it's me behind this, they'll soon realise when I walk through that door; then they'll find out just how capable I am at making people disappear.

"In the building, no visual," Jasper says, from my side. We've surrounded the place, avoiding the cameras we know are there. My son's the head of this operation now. He fucked up, losing her like he did on the plane, but he's more than made it up to me. He sent me a photo of the necklace and her pretty face sleeping, from their time together in New Zealand. He's been tracking her ever since, watching her with Ethan-fucking-Ford.

He's a sick fuck, my son. I'm proud of the man he's become. Gets a little dark even for my taste. He's going to enjoy destroying her. And he'll do it all in front of her new boyfriend.

It's time to end this. I need my ledger back, for no other reason than to burn the thing.

"Move in."

Chapter Forty-Six

Fear

Aggie

"You ready?" Ethan asks, coming to my side. He changed out of his suit while they devised the plan to get Jonathan. They're going to take me to Ethan's yacht. Yes, my beautiful, complicated man, has his own big-ass boat. Unfortunately, it doesn't have the name of a giant dildo like mine.

When he walked out of the bathroom, my jaw hit the floor, and my core lit up like a fucking firework. He strode out in dark blue tactical gear. My suit daddy, dressed down for the first time, and my knickers fell off in the process.

Black combat boots laced around his ankles, trousers that looked like they've been tailor made to fit his skin, even his thighs are bulging, his tight arse there for me to drool at. A button up shirt open at the collar, showing just the right amount of skin, above a bullet proof vest, his sleeves rolled up, showing his powerful arms that hold me so tight. I lost my breath; the whole damn thing should be illegal; he carries the look so well, I don't know which one I like best.

It seems to be some sort of uniform. As Owen and Cole step out of their offices wearing the same, but in black.

God-damn, these men are something else.

"Yes." It's weak, but I mean it, unable to take my eyes off him.

I'm worried beyond belief. The plan's not complicated, it's just that, all this... what the guys are doing for me, what Ethan's doing for me, it's bone-shakingly overwhelming. I can't focus on anything but what I need to.

Get out, drive with Ethan to his boat. Stay there while the others do something else. There are so many people involved, teams scattered everywhere.

"You don't sound it, butterfly. I need you to be in a safe place away from anything that might happen."

"I know." Because I know how much he's looking forward to taking a shot at Jonathan. "I'm fine, just... the whole day's been a lot, you know?" Ethan kisses the top of my head while we move to the lift.

"I like you in combat gear," he murmurs into my hair. I roll my eyes at him, not the time or the place, but given what we did earlier today, I'll let it slide. I got changed too. Owen lent me some of his wife, Charlie's, things. Apparently, she likes to do this shit too, and he can't stop her. I quite like it, as it makes me feel like a badass. Along with the matching vest to Ethan's. And there are so many pockets. "I'll get you some dark blue ones." His possessiveness shining through, and I chuckle.

I look down at my black outfit. "What don't you like that I match Owen?" I vex.

"No." His low, damming tone shoots a thrill through me as his nostrils flare. *Holy-shit.*

The lights around us dim, flicker, then hum to nothing as blackness surrounds us. Ethan grips my arm, moving me behind him like there's a threat. Eerie silence follows for a beat before it's broken by Ethan.

"Cole?" Ethan bellows, holding me to his back, moving me between him and the wall next to the lift. There's a rumble of noise from downstairs. My heart's going like a fucking clanger as I hold Ethan's arm in a deadly grip.

"On it. Back-up should click in any moment." I close my eyes, waiting for them to adjust to the light, listening to Ethan's unsteady breathing. I calm my senses, hearing feet shuffling. There's a click, but nothing happens.

"Ethan," I panic as the noise from downstairs gets louder.

"Not yet, Aggie, wait." He's so calm. I open my eyes, but I jolt back when I see what's in his hand. A gun. In his hand, aimed at the floor.

"What's happening?" I whisper.

"I—" He's interrupted by Owen's low growl.

"We have company," Owen grunts as he passes us. I don't need to guess. I know already, and so does Ethan. "All powers down, lifts out, cameras. The sensors tripped, sending it to my phone. From what I saw before it cut, we're outnumbered."

"Outnumbered," I whimper, fear striking my chest, making it hard to breathe. "What do we do?"

"*You* do nothing," Ethan says, forcing me back into a room. "Stay here," he demands and my stomach sinks.

"What, no, not by myself. Please, Ethan," I plead desperately.

"No, butterfly. I need to be out there. You're safer in here. Lock the door behind me. Only we can get in. Cole's working on the power, and as soon as that lift comes back to life, I'll get you down there and in a car." I don't want to be alone, but what choice do I have? I can't let Ethan sit here with me while his brothers fight.

"Okay," I swallow, holding back my tears. This is no time to cry. I'll get myself away if I have to. They are after me after all.

"Good girl. Promise me you won't open that door for anyone but us?"

"Promise." Lifting my shaky hands, I grab his shirt and pull him to me. "You best walk back in through this door, Ethan. Or I'll kill you myself." He laughs, fucking laughs at my threat.

"I will. Promise."

"Good boy."

Chapter Forty-Seven

Down

Ethan

As the door clicks shut behind me, they come in strong. They're forcing their way in downstairs. Setting my breathing, I need to focus. With my gun at my side, I flick the safety off. I won't use it unless I must, or they shoot first. We don't know this guy's men. We don't know what we're up against. We need to be as cautious as we do fierce.

Stepping away from the door, leaving my heart behind, as quiet as I can, I run to the opposite side of the office, giving me a full visual of the only entrance point. My mind and heart race in unison, despite my attempts to settle them.

"Jill's on comms," Cole whispers into my earpiece. *Fuck.* "She's safe downstairs." Cole tells her to switch to our channel, to keep us updated on what she can see, and I hear her familiar voice.

"Too many, heavily armed, vests," she mutters. "Heading up now." Jill's not just our office manager, she was a communications and information specialist in the Navy for years before she retired and joined us. "SOS sent. Bear's ETA seven minutes."

Pressing my small device in my ear, I reply. "Tell him to head to the basement. I'm sending her down as soon as I can."

"Copy." I hope we can get this done before the others arrive. I don't want to drag anyone else into this, if I can help it.

Keeping quiet and low, I wait in the dim lights of the emergency lighting.

They have another thing coming if they think they can come into our space and take what's mine. We have the advantage; we are the fucking advantage.

I slink back, waiting for them. Listening to their feet pounding on the steps as they rise to our floor. Closer, I think, getting closer. I slow my breathing, readying myself for the onslaught. I'll give them hell for daring to touch my woman.

Three. Muffled voices fill the stairwell.

Two. They're not even trying to be quiet.

One. Bring it on.

Sucking in a steadying breath, I raise my gun. The door to the stairs opens with a bang, and they fall in, filling the space quickly. They cover the main area, guns raised, looking for any sign of movement. My pulse races as they pass Owen's office window. My eyes flick to the room. *Don't move, baby.*

Even in the dark, the backup cameras are running; we'll get every shred of evidence we can to put these pricks away.

"Stairwell's blocked," Jill's voice comes through. Now they can't escape. Even if they wanted to.

As they begin to spread out, I watch as they try and open the doors as they pass, searching for any sign of Aggie.

The first bullet fired sends bolts of light exploding across the room, glass shatters, and one of the screens on the wall comes loose and falls with a crash.

More shots are fired as they lose patience, tearing through the central area, flipping chairs, and desks. Shooting anything they see. My chest heaves at the stark reality of our situation.

Aggie's only a few metres away.

They're waiting for us to react, three against eight, I count so far, with more coming in as I watch from the shadows.

Aggie's safe, I remind myself, but it does nothing to steady my fear as my heart tries to bore its way out of my chest to get to her. *Stay hidden. Don't move, baby,* I silently plead with her.

A tall guy dressed in black, knives strapped to his chest, strides up to Owen's office window. My pulse hammers—they've already tried the door. Sweat drips down my spine as he taps the barrel of his gun against the glass. A shiver follows as he laughs. He drags it up the glass before he steps back and nods to another guy, who shoots the glass repeatedly. It's like someone stamped on my chest; I can't breathe.

Did he see her?

There's no way. He couldn't have. The toughened glass fractures, just as my heart does. Fear splinters my skin as a single bullet pierces through and enters the office, leaving a small hole behind. I raise my gun, aimed at his chest. I fire and watch as he hits the floor with a satisfying thud.

Bullets rain in my direction. Ducking, I quickly move out of their sight. I take out another, and another as I go. They fall like flies as my brothers join me, and I try not to imagine how scared Aggie is right now.

She'll be okay. I'm getting her out of this.

Rushing through the room, I run for the kitchen, slamming my fist into one of their heads as he rounds the corner. Knocking him out cold.

Stay still, butterfly, it'll be over soon.

I've been in many situations, all with dire consequences, but this one has my heart racing for what I could lose. I lower my shoulders, my focus steady, when a guy talks.

"Give up the bitch," he yells over the eruption of gunfire and chaos, "and you can all walk free." *Fucking liar.* My lips curl, and I bare my teeth, my anger reaching out of this world. *He called my woman a bitch.* I'll tear his fucking head off. It must be Jonathan.

They've fucked with the wrong woman.

Unflinching, I watch as one of his men falls to the floor, then vanishes into the stairwell. The only giveaway, the light from the exit sign illuminating them.

Owen, the sneaky fuck. He'll have him hog-tied in a locked room within seconds. Not before he throws him down the stairs.

Just as the door closes behind them, another man offloads a full round into the room. I duck, sinking low to the floor, eyes remaining on them from my position behind the partition. Bullets scatter, plunging into walls and windows, sending debris flying into the air. I need to get closer. Ducking low behind a desk, grateful I went for metal, I turn it over; the noise covered by the gunfire.

"Cover me," I grunt, knowing they will.

The dickhead from earlier steps forwards as the room goes still. "Tell me where she is." His anger bursting through, he sounds almost desperate. "Or I'll shoot the lot of you."

"Power in one," Cole whispers through the comms.

Cole steps out of his corner, the butt of his gun swiftly rising behind the prick next to him, striking the guy in the back of the head. He wavers before he spins around. Cole's clenched fist connects with his face, and he goes down like a sack of spuds. Then Cole slips away again out of sight before the others even notice what's happened.

We have to focus on drawing them away from Aggie's position. And right now, they are too close.

"Fuckers," That's Jonathan, it must be. I can see from his profile that he's the oldest guy in here. He came himself.

I smile; it may not be the kind smile I give Aggie; no, this one is reserved for men like him. Knowing they will get what's coming to them. And I'll enjoy every second. Our men have the ledger, or the box it's in, and are currently making their way to Owen's safe house, or Lodge as he likes to call it. We don't need the key to get into it. Whatever they find will be scanned and uploaded to the system before we give it to Xander, a contact of ours. He'll do what needs to be done. Keeping us out of the limelight, like he always does.

"I'm done being patient," Jonathan yells. I take a chance. Squeezing the trigger, I shoot two men in the chest and another one in the side. I hit another as I slide into position by another upturned desk. His body rocks back as the force of the bullet lands in his bulletproof vest. He lets out a grunt as he falls back, smashing onto the littered floor. I race forward, my knee connecting with someone's back, bringing him down awkwardly onto his knees, before my elbow strikes at his masked face, making a satisfying thud as he lands on the ground. I edge closer. Jonathan raises his flashy gun, an evil smirk as he pulls the trigger at the spot where I was standing, emptying his chamber into the wall. He sniggers.

"Jasper," Jonathan seethes as he looks around at his men littering the floor as one of his remaining few guys fires as Jonathan reloads. *Jasper?*

The whiz of a bullet passes my ear, and I turn and aim. Taking another man down, piercing him in the shoulder. He drops the gun, crumpling to the floor. His cussing bring a wicked smile to my face. There is a deafening sound of a crash. My head snaps to the side I watch the glass falls from the window of Owen's office, crumbling from the pressure. Exposing everything in sight. *Fuck.* I need their attention on me, so I stand, take aim, and fire at the fucker, Jonathan's feet. He doesn't flinch, but he does send his remaining men my way.

"Get her out," I yell into my earpiece.

"Ethan, together," Owen shouts. I hear him, but I'm too focused on what I need to do. Nausea racks my stomach as I see her move in my peripheral. *No.* I can't stop to help, because they see me, just like I wanted. Her eyes go wide as Jonathan's men run for me. Using everything I have, I dodge, fight, and shoot back as Owen and Cole take down as many men as they can, A perfect mix of muscle, skill and guns. *Together.* Fists and bullets fly as they gain on us, leaving Owen's office free.

The lights flicker back on, illuminating the havoc they've brought to us. Aggie stands there, exposed, and vulnerable hands by her side, eyes bright and red rimmed in the flare of light. The lift door opens. Like slow motion, her head turns to watch it.

I can see it in her eyes; she's going for the lift. There's nothing I can do to stop her, so I help.

"On the move," I bark into the comms as I take a shot to my chest. The blunt pain takes my breath away, but my vest keeps the bullet from piercing my skin; the force reverberates in my lungs. I stumble back as his men come towards me. Two men surround me, guns raised and ready to shoot. I blink, finally getting the air I need, when they're both tackled to the floor by Leon as he pushes his way through the door. Pummelling them into the ground, fists raised, guns scattering away from them. They don't stand a chance. He's giving me a chance to move.

I roar as I move, my body obeying its command to get going. My limbs are heaving and heavy, but I move fast, away from her as they focus on me, and 'Bear', Leon, who's just joined our fight.

Chapter Forty-Eight
Move

Aggie

The noise around me gets louder, and I tremble harder with every passing second. Pop, then a thud. I freeze, my mouth open as the window to the office I'm hiding in cracks but doesn't shatter. It's enough for the sound of fighting to filter through. I'd cry, but I'm not sure I can. My muscles flinch with each shot fired. It happens over and over again as the guy in front of the window stands and shoots it, like he knows I'm in here.

The window stays put, but the glass fractures. Like ice on a frozen lake.

Pop.

The sound jolts me from staring at Ethan.

No. Shit. The glass splinters, a spider web effect spreads, before the floor to ceiling window shatters and falls to the floor. Covering my head with my hands.

I can't move.

Frozen crouched where I am, I watch what's happening because of *me.* Because of something I have.

Living is more important than anything.

What if these men lose their lives because I have a key?

A stupid fucking key.

I'm trying to rationalise what's happening, but I can't.

All of this for a key to find a ledger.

"They know I'm in here," I say to no one. Clutching the key in my hand stupidly, I stand. I know it's a brainless thing to do, but I can't stop myself.

A life is worth so much more than this.

They won't stop unless someone stops them. Or leads them away. I can't see the guys. It's too dark, but what if... they're already dead... what if it's just me?

I swallow hard as the tremor in my fingers grows almost uncontrollable.

I can't think like that... I won't let that happen.

I move in the darkness. Flashes illuminate the space, and I blink rapidly at the brightness. I try to focus, only seeing fractions of what's happening. The ear-splitting noise from out there reaches my heart. Each shot fired like a splinter entering my soul. Breaking me.

I need to know they're okay. Another pop, as a bullet skims my arm. But I don't flinch. I can't let them get hurt because of me, because of a key.

I need to stop this.

A bullet embeds itself into the chair near where I was. It snaps me from my thoughts, as my arms fly up to cover my head. Shouting erupts outside; I know that voice.

Why? A name penetrates through the space, but I can't be sure.

The lights flicker on, and I see him, *Ethan.* He's okay. My heart lurches as his eyes meet mine as a soft ping gains my attention. From the corner of my eye, I see the lift doors slip open. *This is my chance.* This is what Ethan told me to do. I watch his body jerk back, his eyes wide as he slumps. *Oh god. No.* My heart aches as my limbs lay heavy at my sides, motionless with what I'm seeing.

He's been shot. He's still moving. Relief and fear spin together like a twisted thorn in my chest. How? His vest, it will have saved his life. I don't know how to feel. My skin prickles, tormenting me with confused thoughts. The lights flicker. I want to run to him, check he's okay, but it will only make this worse. I can't see much, other than his tall bulk of a shadow leaving me.

Moving away from me.

Move, Aggie. Go.

A shudder crawls over me, leaving a chill over my skin, my heart in my mouth, as the room behind the broken window lights up. Flashes of light and loud, deafening pops of gunfire vibrate across my flesh. I cover my ears, but it's not enough to drown out the noise.

I'll take my chance. If I leave, Jonathan's men will leave with me.

Ethan and his friends deserve more than this. I move, crouching low, as Leon hauls himself through the door, flying towards the man who shot at Ethan.

I run.

I leap over the small partition separating me from them and through the broken window, holding my breath, tripping over a man on the floor, his face covered in a mask. I swallow down the lump in my throat at the thought of leaving Ethan and his friends behind. I have to believe this will work.

Hoping to hell that Jonathan's men follow me.

Slipping on something, my feet lose balance, and I hit the floor with a thud, pain shooting over my side and hands as glass pierces my skin. I hold in a scream, biting my cheek, as I crawl on my hands and knees. I scramble, then stand, running for the lift. I grip the doors, swinging myself inside and hitting the button to make my escape. My hands leave a bloody fingerprint as I press the basement button.

I can't lose anyone else.

Not like this.

I stand central, watching the love of my life fight, my body trembling with fear and guilt and watch me with equal measures fear and regret in his eyes. I cry, as they lead the fight away from me.

Knowing I need to get their attention, I close my eyes, and shout as loud as I can.

"Looking for this?" A man I know well turns to face me, smirk on his lips as he runs for me. *Jasper.*

My ex-boyfriend Jasper.

What the fuck? I gasp. Stunned.

Lifting his gun, he aims it at my face, the door closing just as he presses the trigger, the bullet thudding as it embeds in the door.

I crumble to the floor as the lift descends to the basement.

Jasper?

I don't understand, but I don't have time to think.

When the door opens, I run, my hand fumbling to open the key safe for a car. I drop them twice as I run towards it.

I don't have long before they know where I've gone. Before they come after me. I climb in the car and I start the engine, backing out of my space, to see three men running through the door of the stairs, only to be taken down by Ethan.

He's okay.

Relief floods my body as I tear out of the underground car park as fast as I can. Ethan will kill me for leaving him behind, but... but what? I don't want him to follow me.

But I know he will. Even if I knew how to take the tracker out of the car, he'd find a way to get to me.

I drive as fast as I can, my foot firmly on the accelerator. I don't know where I'm going. I just drive.

My hands sting as I grip the steering wheel. I'm barely able to see through my tears and the street lighting blinding me in the dark. My heart and body beat collectively as it leaps with every sound, bump, and set of lights that follow me as I drive deeper into the woods. Darkness soon encases me, the sky-high trees concave around me. My chest becomes tight, and I have to fight the urge to lose myself in a panic-filled nightmare.

Jasper. He was there. He tried to shoot me.

Why was my ex there? Why did he try to shoot me? Is he part of all this?

Stupid question. Why else would he be there?

Bright lights flash as screeching tires fill my ears. My head snaps to the side too late to do anything but hold tight to the wheel. My breath catches in my throat as a car's headlights blind me. I blink. The rev of their engine roars as they ram into the side of my car, my head hitting the side window, searing pain bursting through my temple. My hand leaves the wheel as the sound of the metal crumpling and groaning under the force of the impact splits my ears. I cover my head. My body jerks, taking the brunt of the hit. I don't breathe. The window next to me smashes, glass showering me.

The airbag explodes, suffocating me and shoving me harshly back against the headrest. I'm thrust sideways, my body screaming in agony as the car rolls. I'm thrown from my seat. Weightless, tossed around, like a ragdoll. Until I land, wedged between the seats, my arms hanging over my head, as the car comes to a stop on its roof. I need to move.

If I stay. I'll end up like my mum.

Warmth trickles down my face, my eyes feeling heavy. I claw myself free from between the car seats, but there's no relief that follows. Far from it. I crawl through the wreckage of my car, my body demanding rest, screaming in agony, protesting with every movement.

Get out of the car, Aggie, move.

My clothes snagging on a chunk of metal. I yank them free, tearing them, as smoke fills my lungs as I try to open the door. Tugging on the handle as hard as I can, it doesn't move. The soft drop of fuel catches my attention as the flames of my car grow brighter, hotter, scorching my legs the closer they get. I yank at the door again.

Smoke everywhere.

My body is lagging, my vision blurring.

A sob breaks free as I realise I can't get free.

Chapter Forty-Nine

Thick

Ethan

I almost tore the guy's arm off as I laid him out when he tried to chase down Aggie. I took all three men down without a second thought.

Watching in agony as she drove away from me, unprotected, is akin to someone setting fire to my soul. I'm struggling to maintain any decorum; I'm losing my shit.

Why didn't she wait?

I wasn't fast enough to catch the man who took a shot at Aggie. He fled with Jonathan. The strong feeling in my gut tells me they followed her.

"Ethan." A yell comes from my side, pulling my attention away from Aggie's retreating car. The red taillights fading with my sanity. I boot the guy in the stomach for good measure.

He tried to hurt her.

Leon dives into his truck as our SOS team arrives, and head upstairs to help Owen and Cole fight and detain what remains of Jonathan's men.

My hard boots pound the concrete as I sprint towards Leon. I take the passenger side, immediately tracking her car through the GPS system. We follow at breakneck speed, already knowing they could have the lead on us.

After Aggie shouted from the lift, it was like watching my world collapsing around me, as a few of Jonathan's men ran after her.

She could have died. Why would she do that? "Why would she put herself in danger like that, Leon?" I ask, my voice broken. Rubbing my chest, it aches from where the bullet hit me just above my heart. The hole in my shirt, proof of how close I came to... not being here.

"You really want to know why she did it?" Leon grumbles, like I'm stupidly asking a question I should know the answer to.

"Yes," I say, my voice cool and pissed off. Because when I get my hands on her, her arse will be red raw by the time I'm finished for that little stunt she pulled.

"She saw you get shot, Ethan, and she didn't want to take another chance with your life."

"She made the wrong fucking choice," I yell, staring at the tracking for her car.

"I would have done the same. We all would have. Tell me I'm wrong. What she did was right, reckless." *Too close.* I gulp. She was almost shot. I almost lost her. "But we were able to finish that upstairs and take the few remaining men down because of what Aggie did." My chest heaves. I don't want to admit it, I can't.

"No. She put herself at risk, Leon. I can't make that right. It's never the right choice." My jaw clenches shut, knuckles turning white when I clench my fists as we speed down the road, heading out of town.

"Right or wrong, it helped, and we can thank her for it later." He grits, gaining speed and blowing through a red light.

"Fuck you," I don't mean it, and he knows it, huffing a deep laugh as we gain on her.

"What if we don't get to her first, Leon, what if we're too late." I can't take my eyes from the small green dot on the screen, she's still moving, Still about two minutes in front of us.

"We won't be. Whatever happens in those two minutes, we will be there when she needs you." His eyes flick to me.

Just as the fields turn to woods, the dot stops, and so do my lungs. That spot, the frozen green light, the woods. That's where her mum died.

Why has she stopped?

Something's happened. My stomach plummets through the floor of the truck as we round the corner and see her car.

Upside-fucking-down. Smashed up. On fire. My hand's already on the handle to open the door as another vehicle pulls back away from her in the other direction.

Leon slams on the brakes, the car screeching and slowing. My skin turns cold, my pulse dead, as fear grips me.

No. Butterfly. Fuck, I need to get to her, I pull on the handle.

Only I'm thrown backwards as the door slams on me as the car explodes, throwing out a combustion of flames and smoke, shaking everything around us, deafening.

Time stops. My world ends.

As I watch the flames tear through the car, ending anything that could have been.

Oh god, no! Aggie.

A thundering yell tears from my bones. It doesn't sound like me.

My Aggie, no.

My hands fall to my sides, as heat scorches my face, even through the glass of the truck. I sag in my seat, my breathing laboured as numbness sets in.

This can't be real.

I'm vaguely aware of Leon shouting, punching the steering wheel, his own distress evident. But I can't feel.

I can't feel anything without her.

This can't be over, not like this. I force myself to move, my eyes bulging as I take in the scene before me. Flames heating my skin, the smell of smoke choking me as I try to breathe. Grabbing the handle, I leap out, my limbs heavy, not giving two shits if it blows again. If she's gone, I can't live my life without her.

I need to know.

Leon throws something at me, and on instinct, I catch it, my med bag. He's followed me, a solemn look crosses his face. I run towards the burning car. Heat ignites my skin as I sink to my knees beside the wreckage, trying to see through the flames.

My voice rocks as I shout her name repeatedly.

"Aggie!" My head shaking in denial, smoke clawing at my throat.

Check the car, I repeat, check the seat, check it all, leave nothing untouched.

Find her, find her.

If she's here I need to find her. I can't touch the car. I can't get near it. All I can do is watch as it burns.

"Aggie," I scream, but the roar of the flames drowns out any noise I make. I can only hear my heart shattering. I can't lose her; she's the light and soul of my life.

I reach for the car, but Leon pulls me away, holding me back as I fight him. I sink into grass, staring at the flames as they flicker bigger and brighter, just like Aggie.

My soul's on fire, along with the woman I love.

Crumbling, my whole life shatters before my eyes. *She can't be gone.* Not my butterfly.

No, no. No.

Chapter Fifty

For Her

Ethan

Search for her.

Look for her.

Find her.

It's not in you to give up so easily, Ethan.

Move, Ethan. Move.

If she survived this, she needs you.

She needs you. Fucking run.

Run.

The smoke is clouding everything. My vison, my mind, my thoughts.

Don't give up. Jumping to my feet, Leon steps back. Eyes filled with tears, I refuse for this to be the end.

"I'm not giving up," I yell at him. Searching the car again. *There.* A small break in the flames allows me to see the seat Aggie would have been in. *Fuck,* I mouth as I catch another glimpse of her empty seat. "There's nothing there," I murmur as my skin soothes with relief, even in the intense heat. *She's not there. She's not in there.* "There's nothing there," I yell at Leon this time, getting to my feet. I rub, my eyes clear from smoke to get another look, cementing what I see.

My chest vibrates as I breathe unsteadily again, while I frantically search for her in and out of the car.

"The back windows smashed. Maybe she got out," Leon yells, adding hope to my tortured heart.

"Call everyone," I sort of whimper shout. Leon nods, bringing the phone to his ear. "There, look." I point, spotting two figures cloaked in darkness, enter the woods further up the road from us. "Why would anyone be entering the woods at this time of night, let alone in this exact spot. It has to be Jonathan and his men. Why would they need to be here if she was dead?" Something switches in me.

I'm not leaving you, Aggie.

My muscles pump as I race into the woods, focused on the two men ahead of us. The trees give us enough cover to remain unseen; Leon running next to me, we spread out, running through the undergrowth, my feet forcing me forward, my arms propelling me to move faster.

I know the injuries she could have sustained from that crash; she can't have gone far.

I'll find you, Aggie. Even if you stay hidden, I'll find you.

With my dying breath, I'll be there for you.

Is she panicking? Disorientated? I hope not, but I can't discount it.

I want to bellow her name, tell her I'm here. Did she hear me at the car? I want to scream at her to run to me. But I know I can't. I can't give away that we're here.

Fuck, I want her in my arms.

"You prick." Loud and clear. Cracked and broken, but I'd know it anywhere.

Aggie. I almost crumble to the floor with relief. She's *alive.* My fire comes back to me at the sweet sound of her voice.

She's alive. I'm coming, baby, hold on. I'm so close.

My head snaps in the direction of her voice. I push through, feet hitting the ground, wading through the thick woodland growth. I spot Leon heading to the opposite side.

We nod to each other, silently planning. We've done this too many times not to know what we're doing.

"You can take the key; we already have the ledger." She laughs; it's choked, emotion-laden. But it's a laugh, nevertheless.

Aggie

"Bitch, I should have ended you in New Zealand. I'm going to enjoy killing you." Jasper says. *My ex-boyfriend.* I don't know how he fits into all this. My hands shake on the ground as I move back, wincing. My body convulsing from the horror it's been through. I'm on the edge of passing out, I know that, but I won't give him the satisfaction of ending my life without a fight.

I know it's coming; I know that Ethan's coming too, but... I'm running out of time. The gun in Jasper's hand is a reminder of what he tried to do when I was in the lift.

"Why are you a part of this, Jasper?" I ask, my voice wobbly. I lift my head, looking him in the eye. "You loved fucking with my head. Was this all part of it, for this key?"

"End it, son," the man next to him says. Oh, that's his dad. I guess it makes sense now. "I've had enough." *Jonathan.*

"Where's the ledger?" The man who killed my parents demands.

"I don't know." It's an honest answer. "Some safehouse somewhere. Being copied and sent to someone else, and someone else," I cough at the last word, my lungs squeezing in pain.

"Fuck," Jasper screams, aiming his gun at me once again. My heart slows to a thud as he clicks off the safety. His dad rolls his eyes, like he's bored.

Bored that his son's about to take my life.

How fucked up can people really get?

Jasper's fingers tighten on the trigger. Backed against the tree, I close my eyes, letting out my final breath, acceptance washing over me. Prying my tear-soaked lids open, I look into the eyes of the man who's going to kill me.

Then three things happen at once.

Jonathan falls to the floor with a grunt as Leon's bear-like form lands on top of him.

I see Ethan, and my heart starts to beat faster; he's here. Without warning, he lunges forward, his body twisting in the air, putting himself between me and the gun. And the bullet meant for me, releases from its chamber...

Straight into Ethan.

In a split second, Ethan has the gun and turns it on Jasper, sending a second bullet into Jasper's chest.

Both men hit the floor at the same time. The ground beneath me shakes. Or is it just me?

Motionless. They're both motionless.

My screams echo around me.

The ringing in my ears starts to slow, then begins to intensify. The pain I felt before is nothing compared to *this*. My world lies in front of me, not moving.

Each breath I take is painful. Like barbed wire cutting through my lungs and heart.

It's excruciating.

"Ethan," I scream.

I shove my hands into the ground, my muscles crying out as I crawl to Ethan. Stumbling, I try to stand, falling to my hands and knees, dizzy, my vision becoming hazy, edging with darkness as I push through the annoyance lacing my system at my feeble attempt to get to him.

"Baby, no," I shriek, my voice disbelieving. "Why would you do that?" My hands search his body for the entry point, as blood darkens his shirt. My fingers settle on the blood pouring from the wound by collarbone, millimetres above the vest. His eyes land on me, blinking slowly as his face turns pale. I place my hands on over the hole, his blood covering them as I press down, applying pressure as best I can.

"Ethan," I cry, kissing his face. "No." Why isn't he moving? His eyes are unfocused as I scream his name.

"Butterfly," he whispers. "Safe."

"I won't be if you leave me. You can't leave me, Ethan. Not like this. Please," I plead, beg, and cry into his neck, my body covering his. His breathing becomes slower. "No. Ethan, no." He's leaving me. *He can't. I won't let him.* "Hold on," I wail, clutching him as close to me as I can.

Things happen around me, more people come, but I stay here on the leaf-covered floor.

Blood pouring between my fingers.

His eyes growing heavy.

Leon pulls me away as the ambulance crew arrives and takes over. That's when his eyes close. Those stormy greys losing light.

I fight Leon's hold, ignoring the raging pain wrecking through my body. He won't let me go. I can't hear a word he's saying, blood rushing through my ears as pain starts to take me under, my breath stuttering as I lose hope. *Not like this, Ethan.* I slump in Leon's arms, my body giving out on me as he's carted away.

Don't leave me.

Chapter Fifty-One

Lifeless

Leon

I've never seen anything like it. Scrap that, I have. Three times in my life, I've witnessed a love so devastating and true, a person would give up their life for them.

First was Millie, when she tried to protect Jack's family from her ex.

Second was Owen, when he ran into a burning building to find Charlie.

And third was Cole when he took out Ari's abuser.

These are the closest people I have in my life. Watching Ethan take that bullet for Aggie wrecked me.

I couldn't do shit about it.

In the end, I knocked Jonathan out with my elbow to get to them. There was already a crew on the way. Five minutes; that's how long it took. Watching Aggie scream, shout, and cry. Looking at Ethan's fading eyes. I couldn't do shit but hold her away as the ambulance crew did what they needed to do.

I saw it though, the moment the light left his eyes, and then I pulled her away. With all her injuries, she still fought me to get to him until she passed out.

The second crew came in as I collapsed on the floor holding her to me, for Ethan, for me, for the friends we've lost, for my own need. I needed to hold on to her. To feel her breath, so I could tell Ethan that I was there, that she wasn't alone.

Knowing this was his worst fear has come to life.

I will tell him when he's out of surgery, when he can listen, I'll tell him.

Every one of us sits in silence, waiting for news on them both.

Aggie's injuries are bad; she was banged up and bruised from head to toe. She needed surgery on her hands and shoulder. She has a severe concussion, with small burns to her legs, but nothing life-threatening.

Unlike Ethan.

The bullet entered at an awkward angle from above and tore through the edge of the vest, hitting his chest, going down, rather than through. The bullet missed all the vital organs, but caused some serious damage.

I feel helpless. Layla's on the other side of the waiting room, sobbing, as Charlie holds her hand. All I can do is watch her. She refused my comfort, so I backed away. Now I'm having second thoughts.

My phone's been vibrating in my pocket for hours. I stashed it there after I called Ethan's parents, Gran, Cole, Owen, and our friend, Jack. There's still so much to deal with, but not until I know they will both be okay.

I'll right the wrongs of our military past. And Layla... I need her like Ethan needs Aggie. I'm tired of pussyfooting around. I'll make her see what we could have.

After what feels like hours, the door swings open as the doctor walks in, wearing scrubs, looking tired from hours of painstaking surgery. I stand.

"How are they?" The room falls silent as she speaks.

"They are both out of surgery and doing well." The atmosphere in the room washes with relief. "They've been placed in the same room as requested." She looks at me. It's what he would want. "They are sleeping now, and you can see them in the morning." I'm not leaving, I can't. I'll be here when they wake up.

Layla cries uncontrollably, and I hate that she won't let me hold her. "I'm staying until I can see her," Layla says to the group. "I'm all she has right now."

"I'll stay too," I add, leaving everyone to move through the doors, telling them, "I'll update you when I can."

"Can someone grab some clothes and stuff for them both and bring it in?" Layla asks as Charlie hugs her with a nod.

"Call Raff," I say to Owen. "He'll help, if he hasn't done it already."

I slip my phone from my pocket as soon as they all leave, checking over the messages and calls from the teams we had in place today. Layla makes an excuse about getting some fresh air, and I make a call.

"Xander," I say as my first call connects. "Do you have what you need?" He's our 'special' contact, the guy we know we can trust with sensitive information, and to hand it to the right people to get the verdict we need.

"The mighty bear, it's good to hear from you. I don't like it when you dodge my calls. I heard Ethan and Aggie will be fine." He's frustrating. Dodging my question like a pro.

"I don't know how you know, but yes, they will be fine. Sleeping off the anaesthetic as we speak."

"Good. Your boys did a good job cracking the safe. They've scanned and uploaded some very damaging information. Jonathan Isaac has been arrested, and will be serving a very long sentence in a cement box."

"What about his son?"

"Pronounced dead at the hospital. No one but his sick dad will miss that arsehole." He huffs a laugh.

"I'll let Ethan know when he wakes up."

"The other address you found up north?"

"Yeah, what about it?"

"Aggie's a great little detective. She hit the motherload. The place was heavily armed and secure, but..." He stops mid-sentence.

"But what? I don't have the patience for you today, Xander." I groan, dipping my head to my chest as I lean against the wall.

"Well, that's rude."

"Xander," I say, elongating his name with frustration.

"It was full of original works of art. Shit that's been missing, forged, and stolen for fucking years. All hiding down in that mine."

"Hell, really?" I'm shaking my head in disbelief.

"Really. I've never seen a detective look so fucking happy when I showed him the goods."

"Glad we could be of service, Xander." I smile for the first time in... days? He hangs up without another word.

It's about time I made a change in my own life.

Starting now.

Layla appears, wiping her eyes, forcing a sad smile my way.

"Layla." The tension between us is thick now it's just us. I take a seat next to her, turning to speak to her face to face.

"Leon." Fuck, my name on her lips, with her accent, makes me groan.

"Layla. I know you feel this thing between us," I say, it's been circling for months; a year almost.

"Leon, now's not the time."

"It's the perfect time. I'm not giving up. In fact, I'm more determined than ever to get you in my arms." Her breath hitches, her eyes heavy with sadness and maybe longing. But then I see her hand shake on her lap, like she's scared.

"Layla, please. Don't push me away."

"No, Leon. We can never happen."

Chapter Fifty-Two
So Still

Aggie

I've been awake for a while. I woke with a start, no slow groaning, like you see in the movies, to see the man I love gazing at me.

No.

I gasped for breath like someone was choking me. Thrashed on the bed and screamed when the pain in my shoulder hit me like a bullet.

A bullet.

The only name on my lips was his. *Ethan.*

I lost my breath all over again when I saw him lying next to me. I couldn't reach him. Couldn't touch, couldn't check for myself that he was alive and with me.

I'm not going to stop looking at him. I'm not moving.

There are wires, tubes, and machines attached to his chest and arms. I can see the bandage covering his chest and shoulder.

Where the bullet hit him.

I want to feel him beneath my fingers, feel his warm skin, feel his chest rise and fall under the palm of my hand. But I can't move.

Everything hurts, even with the medication I presume the doctors have given me. I feel the pain radiating through my body from the car crash.

He took a bullet for me.

He put himself in the way of Jasper's gun. My ex-boyfriend tried to kill me; *twice*. Every time I close my eyes, I see it, hear it, and relive it.

I don't remember what happened to Jasper, and I don't care. I just want Ethan's pale grey skin to come alive.

They told me he lost a lot of blood. I know I was there. I saw it, felt it, can still feel the thick, sticky blood on my hands, even though it's not there anymore.

It's just the bandages wrapping my hands.

I tried to turn on my side to watch him closer. I really fucking tried, but the machine I'm attached to went bonkers, nurses ran in, so did Layla and Leon, worried I was trying to do something I shouldn't.

They don't get it. I need to be next to him. My chest aches, hurts.

I'm raging inside. Burning for him to open his fucking eyes and tell me he's okay.

He's so still.

If all I can do is stare at him until he wakes up, then that's what I'll do.

I can see the rise and fall of his chest as he takes shallow breaths. Each one a relief. I cry harder, for him, for us, for what he did to protect me.

Tears are leaking down my face. I can't stop them. And I don't want to.

I want to feel it all. The love, the loss, the fear of nearly losing him, after I just found him. "Ethan, please wake up, baby. I love you so much," I whimper. Nothing happens, so I repeat my words over and over again, hoping he can hear me.

Ethan

I hear crying, someone whispering the same thing repeatedly; it doesn't sound real. I feel heavy, like there's a ton of weight on my chest.

"I love you, wake up. *Please.*" It sounds pained. My chest twists painfully as my head clears from its fog, focusing on the voice that's drawing me closer.

Aggie?

My Aggie. It's her, I know it is. She's okay. Some of the pressure lifts.

"Ethan, please wake up, baby. I love you so much," she says, her voice thick with emotion, as she sobs each word.

"I love..." My voice breaks like I've swallowed razors. "You too, butterfly," I croak, panting as they leave my mouth. "Aggie." I groan, turning my head to see her in the bed next to me, her face wet from tears. Eyes red, glossy, and focused on me.

"Ethan." It's the relief in her voice that chokes me. Like she's been waiting for me. We stare at each other in disbelief. Like we've lived through a nightmare, only now to see the dreams that lie in front of us.

"Fancy going sailing?" I ask, her smile a winning conformation that she's mine and I'm hers.

"I'll go anywhere with you, joker," she says, and it's music to my ears.

Chapter Fifty-Three
Epilogue

Aggie

"You do realise that sailing implies you use a sail, right?" I tease as we drift over waves of the Mediterranean Sea. I'm on my back, in the smallest bikini I could find, soaking up the sun like it's going to go behind the non-existent clouds any moment.

Ethan's fetching us both another drink from the built in bar just behind us; mine a virgin daiquiri, Ethan's a water.

"I know," Ethan says from where he stands at the bar, mixing my drink at the back of his big ass yacht. It's really put Purple Passion to shame; I mean, the bathroom in this place is almost twenty times bigger than the one in my old place. And that's not an exaggeration. I don't miss that little boat, not for the few times I *actually* stayed there, and not after it was trashed. I paid the woman who rented it to me for any damage and handed her back the keys. That was a few weeks after we came out of hospital. And before that, Ethan told me he would never let me live anywhere he wasn't.

And I could never see him living on a tiny boat made for one. To be honest, I never want to live anywhere without him either. I guess that makes me just as bad as him.

I love his possessiveness; it makes me weak at the knees, while my heart does all the fluttery things.

I'm happy.

He makes me happy. I know the stuff of my past now. It's not nice, but I know. Some memories have been coming back the more I've settled into this new life with Ethan, but they are still distant echoes of me.

The one big change I have in how I feel is that I don't mind not knowing now. It's in my past, and although it will always be a part of me, I have so many new memories to make and look forward to that it doesn't cross my mind to dwell on it anymore.

I've not stopped smiling, which means Ethan's not stopped staring.

Rubbing my hand over my stomach, I still can't believe that in seven months' time we will have our own little family. Which has only made Ethan's smile wider, which makes me feral for him. At the rate we're going, I'll be pregnant again before this one is a month old.

It's a vicious circle.

My smile deepens when I think of what my parents left me. Unbeknownst to them, what they bought as cheap land to hide a secret was actually... well, let's just say there's a nice little nest egg already waiting for our baby when he or she is born.

I sold it to an environmental development scheme. They plan to build a safe haven for kids; a retreat in wildlife they said. I can't wait to see it.

Perfect.

I've not kept all the money. I donated half of it to Celeste's Foundation, Lost Souls. She said that she started it because of what she did for me. How could I not help her?

I help there as much as I can, but my new painting collection is almost ready. My first show is set for three months' time. A whole gallery just for my work. I still can't get my head around it.

Me and Ethan have spent many hours in my studio, him reading, or working while I paint, it's become our happy space to be together. I think that's where we created our own little life.

I'm still his PA, and I don't ever see me giving that up. I love working with him, but we have hired a new PA for his parents. He's brilliant, which means we have a lot less to worry about now.

I've seen a more casual side of Ethan since the crash and shooting. Like today, and the last week we've been yachting. *Is that a word?* He's in just a pair of swim shorts, his tanned body on show just for me.

I've not stopped staring. The clinking of the glass pulls my attention back to the man in question.

"So, when you asked me in the hospital three months ago, to go sailing with you, you lied?" I tease, "Knowing this was what we would be doing." I turn to see him adding the ice, and he smiles, big, bright, and beautiful. Causing the corners of his eyes to crinkle ever so slightly. God I love this man, and my core lights up like a firework.

My eyes wander over his chest. His scar is still pink, but fading slowly, just like the silver scars on my own hands and legs.

"Yes," he admits. Huh, I'm trying to get a raise out of him, and it's not working. I feel a little devilish today. I want a reaction, and he's not giving it to me. I need my dominant Ethan. *Need* being the optimum word.

In the weeks after the accident, we were not alone for more than a few hours. Leon and Layla took it upon themselves to become our full-time carers. Even his parents helped. His gran soon shooed them away when his mum asked if he was going to marry me. I didn't mind the question, but it was the look of disgust on her face more than anything, that sent Celeste into a spiral. She and Raff kicked her out, while his dad stayed and made us all dinner.

It's been a whirlwind, one of love and my newfound family.

Lying back on the lounger, I close my eyes. Leon and Layla have been acting weird, and that's putting it lightly. He's where she is most of the time, which she complains about endlessly, but when, on the odd occasion, he's not around, she looks for him. And you can see the disappointment in her eyes.

Something is going on between them. I don't know what, but it's one of the reasons we've come away, that and it's our honeymoon.

Yeah, we got married last week at The Manor Hotel in Livington. It was small and beautiful, and I have a whole new set of friends in the wives of Ethan's army brothers. I couldn't ask for a better fresh start; women supporting women is one of the finest things you could have in your life. I'll treasure it and keep it close to my heart always.

I still get butterflies when I say my new married name. I'm now, Aggie Rose Hope-Ford. A married woman. Looking at the rings on my finger as they sparkle in the sunlight, I get the feeling I always do when I gaze at them. Love. It circles my chest, wraps around my heart, and keeps me smiling like a mad woman.

"I want to go skinny dipping?" I yell, loud enough for the entire crew to hear. I bite my lip in anticipation of Ethan's gruff response. Or for him to attempt to fire the crew just so we can. Because he'd join me if I wanted to dive into that sea with nothing on, he wants to be part of everything I do.

But nothing comes. No gruff noise, no scurrying of feet, no throwing me over his shoulder. My shoulders sink. So, when I look over to where he was standing, and I don't see him, I sit up.

Our drinks are still on the bar, but the entire deck is empty.

Pushing myself up from the lounger, I go in search of my husband. I don't think I'll ever get used to that, *my husband*. Where the hell has he gone? My feet pad over the smooth wooden decking as I walk through the hallways and massive lounge area, searching each room as I go.

When I open our bedroom door, I step inside. The suite is vast, with sofas, office space, en-suite and the biggest, comfiest bed you have ever seen.

My breath catches when I feel the strength of his warm arms circle my waist. His heat immediately soaking into my skin.

"Wife," he grumbles seductively into my ear, and I melt into his embrace as he holds me tighter against his chest. His hands already slipping beneath the top of the soft fabric of my bright green bikini.

"Husband." I mimic.

"Is there something you need, Mr Ford?" I groan as he rolls my nipples between the pads of his fingers as a shot of lust shoots straight to my core.

"I have everything I need right here, Mrs Hope-Ford. But what I want is to see your arse in the air with my handprint on it for almost making me fire the crew again just so we could go skinny dipping." The smile I give him runs deep.

"I knew you were listening." I grin, biting my lip, knowing how much it turns him on.

"I'm always listening, butterfly. And I know this is what you need." I groan as his hands skim my waist, causing my skin to flutter just like my heart.

"I do," I mutter, as the hand on my waist teases its way up and circles my neck in a soft but possessing grip.

"I've sent the crew to land for a few days." A small sliver of panic pinches in my chest. I know he would never let anything happen to me, to us. *But no crew.*

"What? Who's driving the boat?" I yell, and his gruff laugh tickles my ear, relaxing me a fraction as he presses his hardness into my arse through his swim shorts and my bikini bottoms.

"We're anchored and not going anywhere." His way of saying he's got this.

"Oh." The air in my throat constricts as he adds a little more pressure. "So, we're alone?"

"Just us." *Just us.* My head instantly fills with all the ways I will have him in the next few days while the crew is on land.

"You can be as loud as you want." He growls into my ear as the hand on my breast sneaks its way into the front of my bikini bottoms, cupping my core. My groan gets louder, just because it can. I love the pressure he's building within me and around my throat. The way he just holds me captive.

"Hands behind your back, baby," he demands. I do as he asks. I'm putty in his hands. Whatever he has planned, I'm willing and always will be. I move my hands behind my back, trying to grip his length, but he hisses and pulls away. Taking both of my hands in one of his, he ties them with something soft. Peaking over my shoulder, I raise my eyebrows at what I find. My new pink knickers.

"They've been in my pocket all day." He smirks. And fuck, it makes me wet seeing him like this: demanding, flirty, smiling, and devious.

"Husband," I murmur as he pulls the fabric tighter around my wrists so I can't move them. He yanks me softly back against his chest, causing my back to arch and my chest to stick out.

"Wife." He groans, spinning me around, taking a hard nipple into his mouth and rolling it between his teeth. The pleasure-pain, shooting through my breast sends me almost delirious.

It's torture not been able to touch him. And he knows it. His eyes fixed on me as he makes his way down my chest and stomach, kissing, licking and nipping as he goes. Hooking his thumbs into my bottoms, he slides them down my legs and pushes me back onto the bed, my arms trapped beneath me. Something between a whine and a moan leaves my lips as I land. But there's no time to think as he spreads my legs, holding them open. He licks my centre from entrance to my over-sensitive bundle of nerves.

"Ethan," I squeal as he does it again and again.

"Butterfly, you're so fucking wet for me." His grin is feral from between my legs, as he looks up at me.

"I am." It comes out needy as his tongue slides into my entrance, my back arching off the bed as my core begins to flutter around his tongue. Moaning when he stops and flips me over, my legs hanging off the bed, my face in the soft yellow bedding on full display for my husband.

The room goes still, the tension crackling. I know he's watching me. I want to see him, but stop myself. The anticipation so much sweeter when I can't see, my hair covering my eyes.

I shiver when he traces his rough finger down the centre of my back, stopping briefly at my puckered hole. I squirm as he adds the slightest bit of pressure.

"Fuck," I groan, my body pushing back for more.

"One day, butterfly, your arse will be mine." He keeps the pressure on my taint, slowly rubbing back and forth as the first strike of his hand thwacks my soft cheek. I gasp, sucking in air at the sting, as wetness floods my thighs.

"Count, baby," He grits through clenched teeth, like this is about to send him over the edge.

"One," I say, my body shivering from the aftermath of his touch as the next strike hits the same spot I jolt and my clit throbs to be touched. He pushes his fingers into my entrance. "Two," I groan. There's so much sensation, but not enough at the same time. My hips buck and push back, needing more, almost frantic.

"One more baby, then I'll fuck you." My core squeezes around his fingers at his words. God, I need him to fuck me, but I also need that feeling of his hot hand hitting my sensitive, heated skin. "You're dripping all over my hand. Will my wife drip all over my cock too?" His hand on my back entrance disappears, and I hear his shorts hit the ground, readying himself.

I grunt as the last *thwack* of his hand hits my arse; the sting and the pleasure swirl into one as Ethan thrusts his hard cock into me.

"Three." I gasp at the intrusion, the fullness of this thick, heavy cock, and the overwhelming sensations of everything he's giving me.

"*Fuck,* baby. Are you coming already?" He groans, pulling out and sliding back in so slowly, I whimper.

"Yes," I scream. My walls tighten as Ethan starts pounding into me relentlessly, my body moving with each powerful thrust of his hips against mine.

Ethan pulls at my tied hands until I'm up against his chest, his hand on my neck, as he kisses me so fiercely, I whimper into his mouth.

He undoes my hands with deft fingers, slipping out of me, and spinning me around to face him. We fall onto the bed. Kissing my lips, his tongue hot, claiming mine, Ethan's frame covers my body, heat passing between us. His hips roll as he pushes his length slowly back into me.

"Fuck, Ethan," I meowl as he sinks into me so deep, my eyes roll back, and I can't focus on anything other than the feel of him inside me.

"That's it, take my cock like the good girl you are." *Oh, my god.* I grip his shoulders for support as he fucks me slowly, pinning me to the bed, building my need for him again. A need so intense, I can barely breathe.

His forehead touches mine in a tender moment, solidifying our connection. Kissing me like he owns me, and he does fucking own me, mind, body, and soul.

I wrap my arms around him, and he holds me like he will never let me go. Our hearts beating together like they need the other to survive.

This man is my everything, the future I never knew existed. The life I never knew I could lead, and the love I was never able to dream about until Ethan Ford stepped into my life.

The End.

Also By Bekki

About the Author

Bekki Vowles writes romantic suspense filled with tension, emotion, and characters you can't help but root for. Her stories blend twists, danger, and heat with strong, complex leads who fight for the love and healing they deserve. She is the author of The Protected Series, an elite ex-military romance world packed with high stakes and heart.

Bekki lives in a small UK village with her husband, two energetic boys, and her beloved fur baby. When she's not writing, you can usually find her curled up with a spicy romance and a glass of wine.

Find Out More

www.ingramcontent.com/pod-product-compliance
Lightning Source LLC
Chambersburg PA
CBHW042031120726
47911CB00026B/539